"Sentimental and sweet, Wilson's tale proves her an empathetic storyteller whose plainspoken Yankee characters have strong appeal."   —*Publishers Weekly*

"Susan Wilson weaves two stories into one with the touch of a master magician. . . . The characters are all warm and their motives feel genuine."
    —*Midwest Book Review*

"Wilson's writing is like filigreed platinum; delicately spun and priceless. *Hawke's Cove* is a poignant, evocative love story."   —*BookPage*

"The lessons about choices and never-forgotten love are haunting."   —*Library Journal*

BEAUTY

"[W]ill leave tears in your eyes and hope in your heart."
    —*Women's Own*

"Lovable."   —*Entertainment Weekly*

"Wilson has recast the classic story with a modern setting. . . . *Beauty* sails along."   —*People*

Also by Susan Wilson

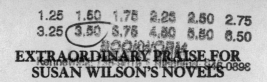

EXTRAORDINARY PRAISE FOR
SUSAN WILSON'S NOVELS

SUMMER HARBOR

"Hot off the presses: A summer beach read."
—*Wisconsin State Journal*

"[E]motionally inspiring. . . . The undercurrent of romance will draw readers into this dramatically written novel, as past misunderstandings threaten to destroy the chance for future happiness." —*Romantic Times*

"[An] engaging contemporary romance. . . . [R]eaders who appreciate a strong character study will want to visit *Summer Harbor,* a fine New England second chance tale." —*Midwest Book Review*

THE FORTUNE TELLER'S DAUGHTER

"A compelling blend of romance, intrigue, and passion . . . a rich story, filled with likable, interesting characters who leap off the page."
—*New York Times* bestselling author Kristin Hannah

"A beguiling bit of storytelling." —*Publishers Weekly*

"A poignant drama. Susan Wilson builds characters that are deeply layered and quite compelling."
—*Romantic Times*

CAMEO LAKE

"As in her previous work, *Hawke's Cove,* Wilson uses a clear grasp of family and marital dynamics to bring us a touching story of people dealing with real problems in a very human way." —*Library Journal*

"Wilson's tale is a sensitive scrutiny of one woman's struggle to discover what she wants in life." —*Booklist*

"A deep and compelling read." —*Romantic Times*

"This is a beautiful love story full of strong emotion; of tragic endings and beginnings; of healing and forgiveness. It touches something deep inside of us all. A great novel, Ms. Wilson." —*Old Book Barn Gazette*

"*Cameo Lake* is a moving, unforgettable tale of the many facets of love. Delving deeply into the complexities of the heart, this powerful story of endings and beginnings, healing and forgiveness will strike a chord for all readers and resonate in their hearts. Susan Wilson is a superb storyteller, deftly weaving all the story's elements into a vibrant, richly patterned tapestry."

—AOL's Romance Fiction Forum

HAWKE'S COVE

"[A] gem of a story that can't fail to touch all who read it. . . . Wilson writes with compassion. . . . Romantic and tender, *Hawke's Cove* will appeal to a wide variety of readers [who] will cry, be joyful, and be surprised at this story that proves love is timeless."

—*Under the Covers Reviews*

SUSAN
WILSON

SUMMER
HARBOR

A Novel

POCKET BOOKS
New York   London   Toronto   Sydney

This book is a work of fiction. Names, characters, places and incidents are products of the author's imagination or are used fictitiously. Any resemblance to actual events or locales or persons, living or dead, is entirely coincidental.

 POCKET BOOKS, a division of Simon & Schuster, Inc.
1230 Avenue of the Americas, New York, NY 10020

Copyright © 2003 by Susan Wilson

Originally published in hardcover in 2003 by Atria Books

ISBN: 0-7434-4233-4

First Pocket Books paperback printing August 2004

10 9 8 7 6 5 4 3 2 1

POCKET and colophon are registered trademarks of Simon & Schuster, Inc.

Cover design by Julienne Ha
Cover illustration by Robert Hunt

Manufactured in the United States of America

For information regarding special discounts for bulk purchases, please contact Simon & Schuster Special Sales at 1-800-456-6798 or business@simonandschuster.com

Dedicated to my parents

With gratitude

To my agent, Andrea Cirillo, and the wonderful team at JRA;

To Micki, I think this blind date is working out;

To Matthew Stackpole, who introduced me to Leeds Mitchell Jr.'s *Introduction to Sailing* and Jan Adkins's *The Craft of Sail* and taught me port from starboard;

To the captain and crew of the *When and If* for the ride;

and, as always, to my dear family for putting up with the crazed woman in the shed.

SUMMER HARBOR

Prologue

It was just past four o'clock, and the living room was winter dark as Will came through the front door. Before he even shrugged off his coat, Will plugged in the Christmas tree lights, then stood back to admire the big spruce cluttered with packages under its widely spread lower branches. On Christmas Eve there would be even more, when Nana and Pop got there and added their gifts to the pile. And, in a silly adherence to implausible belief, on Christmas morning there would be three or four for him signed by Santa.

In his left hand, Will carried the mail. Mixed in with the bills addressed to his mother and the Christmas cards addressed to them both was an envelope with just his name on it—one he'd been waiting for ever since finishing his last class of the semester. One that, in some sense, he'd been waiting for forever.

One

At the foot of the porch steps, the metal For Sale sign clattered in the breeze off the water. A discreet sign, with letters overarching a stylized lighthouse, all done in blue and white, advertising the local agency that handled important real estate: "Seacoast Properties, Ltd."

"Limited to what?" Will asked.

"Limited to the wealthy," his mother, Kiley, replied.

"Like Pop and Nana?"

"Only in the old days of yacht club cotillions and madras shorts. Today's wealthy, the ones who survived the downturn, put Pop's money in the chump change category."

"Chump enough to send me to Cornell."

"This house is sending you to Cornell." Kiley immediately regretted her involuntary sharpness. But the impact of seeing the house, so eerily unchanged from her memory of it, was like grit against polished wood.

She bent over to snag a piece of litter tangled in a *Rosa rugosa* bush. Nowadays, the owners of these shingle-style summerhouses had landscape architects swarming over the small yards to plant "native" plantings and develop cottage gardens. Her father had stuck in a hedge of old-fashioned privet, a couple of spiky yuccas, a scattering of lace-cap hydrangeas, *Rosa rugosa* bordering the cement path to the front door, and let the yellowish grass do as it pleased. "This is a summer place. If I wanted a fussy garden, I'd stay home in Southton." It would probably be a selling point—not much to tear up, and the *Rosa rugosas* were native.

It was frustrating, how every little action prompted a memory. Even the key in her hand prompted a vivid memory of it hanging on the hook by the back door, the seashell key chain exactly as memory served. In her eighteen-year moratorium from Hawke's Cove, the house had remained inviolate in her thoughts, pristine and untouchable, and being here verified those chosen memories.

Kiley had never forbidden herself memory. Sometimes, in the early morning hours when the infant Will suckled on her breast, refusing to go back to sleep, or when an old Don Henley song on the radio so clearly brought back the feel of sand beneath her feet, Kiley relished the companionship of her two friends, even though only in selective memory.

It was out of a great need to keep this place and the good memories in the vault of sanctity that she had refused to come back. Nothing remains the same once reality has overridden the imaginary. How could she keep the cherished youth of summers in Hawke's Cove separate from the tragic end to those days if she set foot again where it had all happened?

Her parents' decision to sell the Hawke's Cove house came as a mild shock. Her grandfather had purchased it for a song in 1933, and it had been the summer focal point of the Harris family ever since. Kiley had paid little heed to her parents' frequent conversations about the place's disposition, assuming that ultimately it would come to her. The idea of selling it out of the family hurt her in a place she had long kept apart from her adult self. Intellectually, she knew that maintaining the place was beyond her parents now, as her mother lost skirmish after skirmish with brittle bones and her father struggled against the emphysema slowly choking him. Childishly, she had hoped that her parents would neglect to really do anything about the house, despite all their talk, and that, at some magical and undefined point, she would find herself suddenly able to go back to it.

When her parents abruptly announced that they had decided to sell the house to fund Will's education, Kiley felt the irony acutely.

By his very existence, Will had cost her Hawke's Cove. Now Hawke's Cove would pay for *his* absence.

Until her parents offered to pay for Cornell, Kiley had expected that Will would go to a state college closer to home, where she could afford his tuition. The sheer distance between Southton, Massachusetts, and upstate New York made Kiley weak, knowing she'd see her son only rarely once he left for school in the fall. Always at the junction of feeling unbearably proud that he had been accepted at Cornell, and unbearably sad about letting him go, Kiley buried her feelings in busyness. She regularly went over Will's ever-growing list of items to take with him, focused on the minutiae of preparing for college, and mentally pushed away the distant day in September when he would leave her behind. Maybe it was easier for parents who had spouses and other children. But Will, he was her world.

Then her parents said they wanted her to go and

inventory the place, to ready it for sale. She had no intention of breaking her moratorium against being in Hawke's Cove with the task.

"Mother, why don't you just have the agency hire someone to pack it up, or, better yet, sell it with the contents?"

"Kiley, I will not have strangers stealing from me."

Lydia Bowman Harris, now in her seventies, was obsessive about theft. Their Southton home had all kinds of burglar deterrents, which, on average, were accidentally set off once a week by her father's slow motion in getting to the right buttons to disarm a device. It was kind of a family joke.

"I can't just up and take off for Hawke's Cove. I don't know when I can get free, and certainly not for long enough to get the job done."

"You have vacation time."

"Yes, and I was thinking about going to Cameo Lake with Will. It's our last—"

Her father stood up, then took a moment to pull in sufficient breath to add weight to his words. "Kiley, we buried the past, got on with our lives. There's nothing there which is going to change anything, or revive anything, or matter much anymore. We need you to do this for us. We don't ask much of you, but this, we're asking." Merriwell Harris walked with slow dignity out of the parlor.

"Don't mind him, Kiley." Lydia Harris waved a still-elegant hand in the air in dismissal of her husband's remarks. "He's not happy about having to give up the place. It was in his family for seventy years."

"Then don't."

"Why should we hang on to the place when there's no one to use it? You won't go."

"Mother, you know the memories would choke me."

"Kiley Anne Harris, for eighteen years you've done well, made a good life for you and the boy. I know we were uncompromising in the beginning, but what's done is done. I don't think that any of us would wish things had been different." Meaning that Will had not been born.

"No. Of course not. But, I can only keep focused on the good things if I can keep the past out of sight."

"It was your own doing. Until you face that, you'll never grow up."

Lydia's sharpness only served to keep Kiley's back up. No, she would not cross that little bridge over the wetlands that separated Hawke's Cove from Great Harbor. In some ways, she was the opposite of that old guy who took tickets at the theater when she and the boys were kids. Joe Green, it was said, could not leave Hawke's Cove, even to bring home his own boy's body for burial. They said it had cost him his wife.

She, on the other hand, couldn't return. As long as Kiley remained on this side of the bridge, she could choose idealized memories that were harmless.

At night sometimes, she would wake from dreams of water. Complicated dreams that left her sad. For a short while Kiley had gone to a counselor, a recommendation from a nursing school classmate. All the counselor could tell her was that she needed to get a hobby, that she was too concerned with serious matters. She hadn't told him anything of the past, only of her present: school, working full-time, raising a toddler single-handedly. The rift with her parents over Will's existence.

"You need a break, Kiley. Find some time for yourself. Go to the shore."

Kiley stopped seeing him after that.

The dreams were cyclical, and her journal noted that they most often appeared when, not she, but Will faced a life change. When he was being toilet trained, or trying out for youth soccer; when she went out with someone for more than two consecutive dates. Even as he entered high school. Periods when she worried more about him. About how she was raising him.

In her dreams Kiley never saw Mack or Grainger, but the constant of water in these dreams always made her feel that she'd been with them there. In Hawke's Cove, surrounded on three sides by the sea, providing years of summers together on the beach and in the water. The sailboat that they lovingly made seaworthy. And, of course, the insoluble association of water and the way things had ended between them.

Despite her parents' pressure, Kiley believed nothing could induce her to abandon her eighteen-year prohibition against going back to Hawke's Cove. It was her self-punishment. She would forever deny herself the thing she most wanted, in the belief that she deserved no less.

And that belief had held up, until Will and two of his pals got caught with marijuana.

The second-most-dreaded phone call in a parent's life. "Come down to the station." Kiley felt detached, as if she did this every day of her life. She brushed her teeth and combed her hair, then pulled on a clean sweatshirt over her pajama top and sweatpants over the bottoms, though normally she'd never go out in such an outfit this seemed all right under these circumstances. No one would know her. She found her car keys, and remembered to set the house alarm, then drove the few miles to the police station slowly, the radio off, as if music would be inappropriate. All the way there, she spoke aloud to herself, trying to anchor herself with the sound of her own voice.

"At least he's not dead." She couldn't pinpoint her emotions. Part relief it wasn't worse, part anger. Certainly shame would emerge, the hunt for a one-line acknowledgment of parental mortification to hand to those who would casually ask about the situation later, their curiosity masked as concern. *Déjà vu.* So clearly, Kiley remembered the raised eyebrows as she appeared in the market with her blooming belly. The "How are you feeling, dear?" code for "What a shame, the Harris girl knocked up, and no father."

In their moderately well-to-do town, there was a certain parental expectation that this might happen. Perhaps this was an initiation rite. "Come join those of us whose children have destroyed our credibility. You bring the coffee, and we can share our disappointments." A twelve-step program for failed parents.

Hadn't she played with him, taken him sledding and to miniature golf? Hadn't she made him sit at the table to do his homework even when he'd preferred to do it slouched across his bed? Hadn't she learned to cook and made him dinner every single night of his life? But she had left him in the care of baby-sitters while she pursued her certification as a physician's assistant. She had declined membership in the PTA because she didn't have time in the evening to go to meetings that weren't part of her education. Suddenly Kiley couldn't remember laughing with him.

The parking lot was empty of civilian cars, the station house door wide open in the late June night. Kiley rested her forehead on the steering wheel, her thoughts swirling. She took a deep breath and drew deeply on her professional reserve, the armor of unflappability she wore at work to assure everyone she was in charge.

Will was exceedingly lucky not to have had the stuff on his person, and that the arresting officer had chosen to charge only one of the three boys, but that was almost no consolation. Will's action—whether the first and only time, as he claimed, or one of many never discovered—meant that somewhere, somehow, she'd deluded herself into thinking she'd successfully raised this boy by herself. That all the long talks they'd had, all the rules she'd imposed, were laughable. In one night, he had proved that she was not the paragon of single motherhood she had occasionally thought herself, now that he was about to be launched into independent adulthood. His action had belied the thrill of watching him graduate sixth in his class, and served up a big portion of humility.

What had seemed, nineteen years ago, to be the hardest decision she would ever face had paled in comparison to the daily diet of hard decisions necessary to rear this child she had chosen to bear and keep. Even now, those interminable nights of wakeful debate while lying in her dorm room bed could startle her with a clarity of memory. As if those circling thoughts had been physical, as physical as Will's first kick in utero or the labor pains of his birth. Those pains she had forgotten—not so, the pain of struggling to tell her parents that she was, at eighteen and almost through her first semester of Smith College, pregnant. She deliberately told them after the sixteen-week mark; deliberately and resolutely never told them who had fathered the child.

The drive home from the police station with Will, deep in the predawn darkness, theirs the only car on the winding country route, was in a silence so extraordinary Kiley felt as if she could touch it. Will stared out the passenger window, as if unable to even look in the same direction as his mother. His form filled the small space with coltish length, accentuated by his baggy jeans. There was so much Kiley wanted to say. *You could lose your place at Cornell, you are risking your life, what in God's name were you thinking?* But she was afraid that she would be unable to stop once she got started, and the last thing she wanted was to become the shrieking banshee of his expectations. Often enough, he'd accused her of "screaming" at him when she had reprimanded him in a deliberately level voice. This time, the potential for her voice to rise into a penetrating howl was so strong she would not let herself even speak. Silence seemed the better alternative and, in the end, she simply told Will to go to bed. They'd talk in the morning.

In bed, Kiley watched the darkness with open eyes, unable to sleep. Eventually, finally, a trace of gray appeared beneath the edge of her shade. In that first notion of dawn, her bedroom door opened and Will stepped in.

"Are you awake, Mom?"

She heard his snuffling and sat up. At once, her big, bright, and independent boy was in her arms, crying out his shame and regret and pleading for her forgiveness. She rocked him, resting his head on her shoulder, and wondering how he could feel so much like the little boy who once cried with the same heartsick intensity when he'd broken her favorite antique vase.

The last few months had been a tug of war between them, as never before. His natural demand for independence and her equally natural desire to remain part of his life had warred mightily. Was she powerless to keep him from repeating his mistake? Despite his tears and apologies, how could she really trust him not to do the same thing if peer pressure and opportunity offered?

Kiley was shocked at how damaged her trust in him was. In her predawn imagination she'd seen him selling his blood to support his habit, then closed her eyes against the image. It was only pot, and only once. Or so he said. The fact she doubted him pained her, and Kiley knew that this loss of trust between them might only be healed by separating Will from the source of his temptation, in particular, those friends of his. They weren't kids she'd known since Will had been in grade school. These were kids from one of the other towns that made up the regional school district. She barely knew their names, much less who their parents were or how much supervision they got.

What Will needed was a safe place. They both needed an interim resting place where they could mend this rent in the fabric of their relationship, before he was launched on his final lap to adulthood.

Hawke's Cove had always been her place of refuge. When schoolwork or arguments with her parents or spats with girlfriends made Southton oppressive, she would think of Hawke's Cove, of the predictable routine of beach and reading on the porch, or the scent of damp air and hot sand. The peace that comes with being in the place you are the most happy. The fellowship of Mack and Grainger.

An early sparrow began to cheep outside the bedroom window, a distant reply.

More than any other place in the world, Hawke's Cove represented sanctuary. Her middle-of-the-night thoughts about Will tormented her; could time in

Hawke's Cove serve to repair the damage done to her trust? Just letting herself think about being there comforted Kiley. Not for any other reason could she imagine returning, not because her parents wanted her to, or even for herself, but for Will's sake.

"Will, I think maybe that we should go to Hawke's Cove."

Will sat up and pulled away from her, his eyes glittering with spent tears in the strengthening light of day. "I thought you wouldn't go."

"I don't want to, but I think that we need the distraction."

Will pulled away from her arms, a rapid, flat-palmed rub of his eyes wiping away the small boy who'd just been there. His jaw flexed. "You know I won't do it again; I promise. Swear to God."

Kiley took the corner of the sheet and wiped her own tears. "So you're promising to keep away from D.C. and Mike? All summer?"

There was exactly enough hesitation in Will's answer. "It wasn't their fault. I mean, it was my choice, I did it. No one put a gun to my head."

"You bought it?"

"No. I just smoked it."

"If I take the car away from you, you can't work. You're too old to ground, and I don't want to spend the last summer we're together worrying every night that, deliberately or not, you're in the wrong company."

"Don't you trust me?"

Kiley looked away from him to the yellowing light bordering the drawn shade as if she could read her answer written there. Over the years, parenting had taught her to temper her words. She knew that harsh words, even justifiably provoked, could be soul—breaking to young ears. Reprimands were always based on anger at behavior, not at him. Never *ad hominem,* always a little retractable. Until this minute, when there were no words for how betrayed she felt. He had done the one thing they had discussed and agreed on time and again. If he could fail her so easily in this, would mere words repair the damage? Talk, as her mother often said, is cheap.

"No, Will. Frankly, I don't."

Will stood up and gathered his dignity around him. "I really am sorry, Mom. I know that I screwed up. It was a mistake in judgment, but, whether you believe me or not, it won't happen again. It was stupid."

"So why did you do it?"

"I can't tell you."

Echoes of her own words nineteen years before. *I can't tell you.* She understood that there were times when it was enough to admit error, if not the reason.

"I understand why you might not believe me when I say I won't ever do it again, but taking me away won't give me the chance to show you that you can trust me." Will's voice had taken on his most reasonable tone, the voice he used to convince her to give him permission to do something against her better judgment. Like letting him attend that unchaperoned party at Lori's.

"Going away will give us both a little distance from this incident, Will. We need that." Kiley hoped he didn't see that she was convincing herself with her words.

"So, if we go, how long do we stay?" Will's tone verged on curious as he capitulated.

"I'm not sure. A couple of weeks, three maybe." Kiley threw back the bedclothes and sat on the edge of the bed. Sleep was out of the question. "I have a month coming to me, and July is a good time to go. The doctor is taking his vacation then, so things will be slow at the office." Kiley found her slippers and pulled on her housecoat. "Let's have breakfast."

Will shook his head. "Not for me. I'm going back to bed."

"We aren't done talking about this, you know."

Will stood in the doorway and shrugged a silent "Whatever" of youthful *sangfroid*. Instantly, Kiley knew that she'd made the right decision. He thought that his tears and apologies were enough. In that still childlike, solipsistic world Will inhabited, he believed that he had smoothed things over. That she was his mother, therefore, she must forgive him. Kiley remembered how that felt. If only tears and remorse could smooth away the mistakes of youth. This indiscretion would not affect the rest of his life in quite the way hers had, but neither would it go away.

"Tell me something." Will remained in the doorway, his hands pressed against the doorjamb.

Kiley pulled the belt of her housecoat around her waist. "What?"

"What is it about Hawke's Cove that scares you so much?"

"Stuff."

"Like my father?" A last arrow fired.

Kiley knotted the belt, not looking up at Will. "Your father was the love of my life."

That was all she would ever say. Will's father was someone who was kind, and handsome, and clever, whom she loved, and was now gone.

The truth was, she didn't know who his father was. Long ago she had loved two boys equally, only to find that that wasn't possible. In love, there can never be three. The uncanny part was that every now and then Will betrayed some characteristic of one, and then of the other, as if the two had joined together to create this child; as if her love had somehow caused the impossible to happen, and Will was part of all three of them.

The old summerhouse was so like she remembered it that for an instant, upon opening the double front door, Kiley half expected Mortie the cocker spaniel to greet her. Mortie had been her dog as a child, his fur a golden tan color that faded as he aged. He'd peacefully died in his sleep right there in the corner beside the hearth in the summer of her seventeenth year. Kiley glanced at the corner, half surprised that there was no dog bed still there. Stifling the temptation to tour the house as a memory museum, Kiley called to Will to start unloading the suitcases from the car.

Kiley's parents hadn't been back to the place since her mother's first fall. A shattered hip and the diagnosis of advanced osteoporosis had ended their summer pilgrimages to Hawke's Cove, despite the encouragement of Lydia's physical therapist to keep doing what she had always done. Any thought of going was further compromised as Merriwell's lungs began to lose their battle against his lifetime of smoking. So, the Harris house had stood empty last summer, for the first time in nearly seventy summers. No Harris had lounged on the front porch, morning coffee in hand, surveying the magnificent seascape that, no matter how often it was viewed, never failed to amaze. A three-generation continuum had been broken, in part by Kiley's refusal to come back.

Now there was Will, the fourth generation at Hawke's Cove, standing on the broad verandah . . .

staring across the short front yard and narrow road to the intense blue of the summer ocean below the bluff. His ball cap was twisted around backward, his baggy jeans exposed his boxers, and his face was glowing with that first view of the cove that lent its name to the town. Will hitched up his jeans and turned to face her. "No one ever said it was this beautiful."

"It's even more beautiful during storms. The sea becomes this gray green color, and the whitecaps are like cream. You can't see across to Great Harbor because the sky and the sea become the same color. When I was a girl, we'd sit out here to watch the storms come and go, like our own private show." She let Will imagine she meant herself and her parents. But it was Mack and Grainger with whom she'd sit, enraptured by the dramatic sky, jumping and grasping hands at each bolt of lightning spearing from the black clouds into the roiling sea, like Neptune's tridents.

"Do you think we'll get any thunderstorms while we're here?"

"This is New England seacoast, so anything's possible."

Kiley grasped the handle of her suitcase and climbed up the steep, narrow stairs to the second floor. She breathed in the slightly musty, salt-and-wood smell of a long-closed summerhouse. The scent acted like a door to the memories of other summer arrivals, made tangible by the same awkward weight of the overpacked suitcases, and the familiar sound of her sandals on wood floors. She half tasted the homemade chowder always left for them by the woman who used to open the house when she was a girl.

The wash of homesickness weakened her legs with its potency, and sharp tears came to her eyes.

"Mom, are you all right?" Will's voice betrayed his surprise at his mother's quiet weeping.

"I never realized how much I missed it." Kiley laughed at herself and brushed away the tears. "Oh, I feel so foolish." But was it the foolishness of sentimentality, or the foolishness of having stayed away for so long?

TWO

Will came upon the photographs when he pulled open the top drawer of the pine bureau in the tiny upstairs room that once had been his mother's. The pictures were loose, the pinpricks where thumbtacks had held them on the wall were tinged with rust. Will ran his fingers over the white beadboard wall above the bureau, and picked out the tiny holes. As he held up the photographs, Will could see that they matched the pinholes perfectly. Someone had come in and pulled these pictures down and stuffed them into this drawer in a random and thoughtless way. Some of the five snapshots were torn at the corners, where the culprit had yanked against the tacks.

Hearing his mother coming down the hall, Will instinctively slammed shut the drawer.

"Finding everything?" His mother stood in the doorway, her out-of-character crying jag no longer in evidence, her eyes dry, if bright, her smile fixed, if not genuine.

"Yeah. Fine. Just putting my stuff away."

Kiley seemed satisfied and went back downstairs to start dinner.

Will gently slid the drawer open again and removed the snapshots. Sitting on the soft mattress of the single bed, he studied the faces captured there. Two boys, and a girl who could only be his mother. He was taken by surprise at how much she looked like him when he was a kid; the shape of her face, the color of her hair, and the expression in her eyes reminded him of an old snapshot of himself that she kept on her desk at work.

Will flipped the first picture over, the one where they all looked about grade school age. "Grainger, Mack, and me, summer of 1976." The three were on the beach, a huge sand castle behind them. The colors had faded, but Will could still make out the red, white, and blue of his mother's one-piece bathing suit and the pale green of the warm summer sea. In the second photo, the same three sat on the flat wide porch rail of this house, legs dangling over the side, arms entwined. Kiley sat between the two boys, the three faces smiling into the camera. "Summer 1980." The handwriting and the color of the pen, a girlish lilac, made Will think that his mother had pinned these pictures up, not one at a time, but at the same time, as if she'd chosen these five as a sampling of her summers with these two boys. Could they be cousins? He rejected the theory that these two boys were relations; looking at how physically they touched in this picture, he understood that these three were friends, best friends. Teen girls were especially touchy-feely with each other; boys, more apt to loop an arm around a neck in a mock choke hold to demonstrate their affection. This gangly trio were tangled together with arms across each other's shoulders in every conceivable combination. Only best friends did that.

The next two snapshots were much the same. "Us at the beach, 1982." "Summer 1983." Each picture chronicled their physical changes. Grainger, darker haired and always photographed to Kiley's right; Mack, almost as blond as Kiley, positioned always to her left. In 1982, Mack was the tallest; in 1983, Grainger was a head above Mack and more than that over Kiley. Both boys were shirtless in this snapshot, and both had broadened, muscled up from thin puberty to robust young adulthood.

In the last photograph, marked simply in the same lilac-colored ink *"1984,"* the three friends leaned against the side of a small sailboat propped up on what looked like stilts. The boat's hull was freshly scraped and patched along the bottom with dabs of white. Hanging over the stern, the name of the boat was crudely hand-lettered on a piece of cardboard: *Blithe Spirit.*

Will spread the five pictures out on the bed and knelt down. By placing them in chronological order, he could see his mother grow up before his eyes like the images in one of those flip books. In 1976, she was a scrawny little girl with a Band-Aid on her knee. Her smile was glittery with braces, and her hair, nearly bleached white by the July sun, was cropped short. By 1980, the braces were gone, her knees were unmarred, and her body had begun to change toward womanhood. Yet there was a charming self-conscious gawkiness about her, as if she was caught in mid-transformation.

In the summer of 1983, Kiley had returned to Hawke's Cove a young woman. Her blond hair was long, a little brittle with the fashion of the time. Although they were again photographed on the porch, she wore a very minimal bikini. Her posture between the two young men was flirtatious, as if she had arrived that summer understanding her powers. Will studied the faces of the two young men with growing curiosity. Manhood had darkened Grainger's jawline with the shadow of a beard. Mack still looked boyish, yet his eyes, looking, not at the camera, but at Kiley, were mature.

Picking up the last picture, the one of the boat, Will thought he could see a change in the eyes of all three. A tension, a difference in their smiles. No longer open and laughing, these were smiles beckoned by the photographer. They were people with things on their minds. Their arms, at their sides, not touching. Will gathered up the photographs and put them back in the drawer. No one but his mother went through life not mentioning friends as close as these two obviously had been.

Maybe it was because she'd been so young when he was born, or maybe it was her natural liveliness, but Will had always enjoyed his mother's company, had enjoyed being the most important person in her life. She was still playful, still full of mischief and practical jokes. When he was ten, he'd worried that he'd be seen as a mama's boy and had tried hard to find fault with her. But his friends preferred playing ball in his yard, in large part due to his mother's easiness with them and her willingness to pitch; it helped that she didn't throw like a girl. Having to work full-time, she'd chosen to work in a medical office rather than a more exciting hospital job, so that she'd never work weekends or holidays. Every night after supper, before she started the dishes and he his homework, they'd talk and play a game. Effortlessly, she would pull from him his worries and triumphs, sharing with him stories of her own day. The only complaint he had about his mother was that she was so very closemouthed about the answers to the really important questions he had, like who his father was, and why she'd cut Hawke's Cove out of her life as if it didn't exist. The handsome photographs of scenery and boats hanging on Nana and Pop's walls belied what little she had told him about Hawke's Cove, always speaking of it as if it were a way station on the road to life, of no importance to her. She'd never wanted him to come here, always coming up with other vacation ideas. Even when he got old enough to want to go with his grandparents to their summerhouse, she'd never let him.

As he'd entered adolescence, she'd known when to ask questions and when to let him muddle on by himself. Until now, when he'd muddled himself into banishment, and he knew she was half-blaming herself. He'd screwed up royally and here he was. Maybe that was the hand of fate. Maybe his mistake that night would open the door on the great mystery of his life.

Will took the last picture out of the drawer and slipped it into his back pocket. He'd been born in May, 1985. It didn't take calculus to figure out that his mother had left here pregnant the August before. She might even have been carrying him as that picture was snapped. A bundle of cells about to throw her entire life into disarray. If neither one of these two boys was his father, maybe they'd know who was.

Will suddenly threw himself onto the bed with enough force to make the old-fashioned springs protest, flinging one arm across his eyes to block out the summer light streaming through the narrow window, and the visions which surfaced in his mind. He was no innocent; he'd had a steady girlfriend till she broke up with him. He knew what couples did. But this was his mother. She must have been in love with one of those two boys, or someone else. Maybe the someone who kept taking the pictures. Surely there had been a deep, Romeo-and-Juliet kind of love. Ill-starred. Star-crossed, whatever. There had to be a good reason that she had kept his father's identity a secret.

Unless she didn't know? No, that wasn't possible. His mother could never have been the type of girl to sleep around. Maybe she had been a victim. But how could she love him as completely as she did, if he was the product of rape? This scenario had crossed his mind before because of her avoidance of this place, as if it held memories so painful there was no purifying it. But she was a pro-choice advocate, a physician's assistant who campaigned for a woman's right to choose. But maybe he was the reason why. When *was Roe v. Wade?* Maybe she couldn't legally . . .

These horrific thoughts made Will press his arm harder across his eyes. Feeling a little nauseous, he rolled over and, with the implausible power of youth, promptly fell asleep, never hearing Kiley call him to eat.

Three

❧

Armed with her yellow pad and fluorescent-hued stickies, Kiley devoted herself to the inventory. She started before Will got up, marking down each item with its description, location, and whether it was to be saved or sold. Her mother had been told by the realtor that the house would sell for a lot more if it contained the cottage-style furniture that had been part of its decor since the beginning.

Part of the charm of their summer retreat was the simplicity of the furnishings. Painted pine tables, three-drawer chests, wicker and chintz, and lamps made from sea glass–filled jars. There had never been any question of replacing the chairs, or the marble-topped telephone table, or the four painted rockers on the porch. It would have been disloyal to unspoken tradition. Instead, her mother had tucked discarded pieces from their Southton home around the old cottage furniture, blending tastes and fashions with a skillful hand. Every year, they had traveled to Hawke's Cove with some chair or bureau on top of the station wagon. A new set of dinnerware at home meant the old would come to join the other cast-off plates and cups in the old cupboard. Kiley used to think that coming to the summerhouse each year was like seeing old friends. Once inviolate in the formal living room at home, the couch became a nest in Hawke's Cove, lounged on in sandy bathing suits, long bare legs draped over the arms as peanut butter sandwiches were consumed.

Every long-forgotten object now stood out so clearly in her mind; bursts of memory jolted her, distracting her from her task. There was the little jug in which her mother put her cereal milk so that she could get her own breakfast without waking her parents, the slight lines of crazing in the brown glaze intensely familiar. As a child, she had imagined that the erratic lines were tiny roads on which microscopic people traveled.

There was the white china dog that had belonged to her grandmother and which she was allowed only to look at, never to touch. Even picking it up now felt like the action of a disobedient child. Kiley laughed. No wonder they wouldn't let her play with it; it was Staffordshire. That would go home. Kiley wrote "keep" on a fluorescent orange stickie and stuck it under the sitting dog's behind.

The front sitting room was now festooned with yellow and orange tags. The framed navigational map was tagged yellow, for "stays with house," and the watercolor of a lighthouse, painted by a good friend from the yacht club, was flagged orange: "bring it home." Looking around the large sunny room, Kiley realized that more things were tagged orange than yellow, and she sighed. Maybe she'd have to come back to this room before they left and revisit her decisions.

Despite all the years of sending used things to Hawke's Cove, her parents' Southton house was chockablock full of stuff. Where would they put all of these formerly banished items? And what would happen in a few years, when they would inevitably have to give up the big house? Kiley saw herself going over all these same items again, and, ultimately, marking them for sale. Why not just do it now and be done with it? How much of this stuff did she want around, reminding her of how her life had moved so easily away from the life she'd expected? Could keeping that silly watercolor change what it stood for? Like people known in only one context, could its sentimental meaning withstand the change of venue? Or would it just fade from notice hanging in the hall in her house, powerless to remind her of playing endless games of hearts with Mack and Grainger on rainy afternoons?

They used to make up stories about the nonexistent lighthouse. Princesses trapped by evil knights, that's what she always wanted to tell. The boys liked to imagine spies lurking around, planning mayhem in the town. They'd get so detailed about their fantasies that they all half expected to see the lighthouse standing guard on the bluff, instead of the Coast Guard's beacon light at the end of the jetty at the harbor, its red light flashing every eight seconds to warn sailors of the entrance.

Sentiment was ineluctable. She was deluding herself in thinking she could hold it at bay with orange and yellow stickies; they only revealed how deep her attachment was.

Outside, the gulls complained. Kiley set down her pad and pencil and pushed open the double screen doors. It was July warm, just right for an afternoon at the beach; she should wake Will up before he slept this perfect day away. She looked at her watch: it wasn't yet noon, let him sleep, the beach could wait.

Kiley sat down in the rocker nearest the door and propped her ankles on the porch railing. The complaining gulls swooped at each other and moved out over the water. A group of cyclists passed along the bluff, then a clot of walkers. It was so easy to imagine it was Mack and Grainger she was waiting for.

She hadn't seen Grainger Egan yet. She knew he was in town, that he'd returned from a ten-year stint aboard ocean-going vessels. A couple of years ago, her father had mentioned conversationally that Grainger'd left the Merchant Marine before his twenty years would have guaranteed him a pension and now was devoting himself to boat repair. Merriwell had been oblivious to the pinking of her cheeks at the sound of Grainger's name.

It seemed that Grainger had come back to the life he had left, and Kiley wondered why. Where Mack had always said he'd come back to Hawke's Cove to settle down after he'd seen the world, Grainger had declared that nothing could persuade him to spend one minute longer in this place than he had to.

Of course, that was when his father was still alive.

Kiley set the rocker into slow motion, the thoughts of Grainger and Mack and of herself as a young girl a little disorienting. Here she was, where they had rocked so often, and so vigorously that her mother would yell at them; there was where Mack fell off the railing and skinned his arm. Over there, deep in the privet hedge, Grainger had found a bird's nest with eggs in it. Those moments felt dreamed, not real. Had the three of them ever been so easy and free? The balance of their friendship so perfect? If only it were possible to edit out the summer of 1984, to know only those better memories of other summers, then maybe they could recover the equilibrium of their friendship.

The motion of her rocker increased as her thoughts wandered. Maybe she should see Grainger. Just call him, say, "Hi, how are you. Yeah, it's been a long time, yeah, bygones are bygones."

Bullshit. Kiley put out a foot and stopped the motion of her chair. It didn't take a psychologist to figure out that she'd be the last person in the world he'd want to see. How could they make small talk when they'd never dealt with that awful night? They had never seen each other again, never talked, or even written. The image of Grainger's face filled with an admixture of pain and anger, and the contempt with which he'd last looked at her, had kept her from ever trying.

She'd lost them both that night. Mack and Grainger.

But she did have Will.

The first time she'd seen his face, wrinkled and squalling and more precious than any other sight, Kiley knew that she'd done the right thing. Though her world was irrevocably changed, and she was no longer the girl she'd been, the mysterious hand of God had rewarded her ignorance with this gift.

Over the years, aided by this funny, charming little boy, Kiley had regained much of the youthful *joie de vivre* lost during those lonely and terrible months before Will's birth. In reparation for her mistakes, she'd been charged with the responsibility of raising this boy to be a good man. And with one or two bumps in the road, she had. She'd made her peace with her fate.

Only now, sitting in this familiar and yet foreign place, only now did Kiley wonder if Grainger ever had found *his* peace.

Her thoughts were interrupted as Will flopped down on the other rocking chair.

"The living room looks like a confetti factory."

"It's going to be harder than I thought."

"Lots of memories?"

Kiley nodded, her eyes on the horizon. A pair of motorboats passed each other, one heading into Hawke's Cove, the other coursing for Great Harbor.

"I found this." Will held out the photograph from 1976.

She couldn't hide her smile at the sight of them. "Oh, my God, how cute we were! Just little kids, ten years old." Kiley pointed at her red, white, and blue bathing suit. "It was the Bicentennial summer."

"Who were they? The boys? Cousins?"

"We were pals. Playmates." Kiley felt the understatement redden her cheeks. She remembered the photo being taken. Her father had snapped them with his new Instamatic camera. Merriwell had liked the boys; it was her mother who didn't encourage the friendship. Kiley looked closely at the faces of the threesome caught on the beach. Could she see Will in either boy's face? Grainger was laughing in this picture, but he would soon turn into a solemn little boy. "Poor Grainger."

"What do you mean?"

"This was taken just before his mother disappeared."

"What do you mean, 'disappeared'?"

"She left. Ran away." Will was so hungry for details of her youth she knew he wouldn't be satisfied with a skimmed version. "Her husband was abusive. He was awful. Although he never admitted it, I think Grainger was afraid of Rollie Egan."

"And she left the kid with him?"

"Grainger pretty much lived with the MacKenzies. Mack's parents."

"Mack and Grainger then, they were good friends?"

"Best friends."

"Of yours, I mean."

Kiley handed Will back the photograph. One word, and it all would come out. All she had to say was yes. She fell back on her first description. "We were playmates. Pals."

He handed back the photograph. "I've got some postcards to mail. Okay if I go now?"

Kiley held the picture in her lap but did not look at it. "Sure. We'll go to the beach when you get back."

"Mom?" Will was standing now, hitching up his cargo-style shorts.

"Yeah?"

"What did he do? Grainger, after his mother left?"

"At first he just sort of hid from everyone."

"Did you go get him?"

"We tried."

"And?"

Kiley hadn't thought of that day in years, but now she remembered with astounding clarity that day when she and Mack hiked the four miles to the old Sunderland house the Egans rented. Grainger's family moved from place to place, and he was living that year on remote French's Cove.

The house lay below the slope of the weedy pasture they had reached by cutting through the woods, out of view except for the black-capped white chimney. It was so desperately poor. That their friend could live in this appalling squalor was something neither one could articulate. Looking down on the house from the top of the pasture, Mack and Kiley linked arms. In a coastal community, it wasn't unusual to see houses with cluttered yards: Boston Whaler hulls upside-down, lobster pots stacked like children's blocks, and their accompanying markers like bulbous lances beside them. That was to be expected of a working fisherman's yard. But here were the random leavings of an unsuccessful life. Rusted boat trailers and piles of tangled fishnet, empty cable reels and junk cars with open hoods, among which the house squatted like a derelict in a doorway. Bare earth surrounded the place; no garden or even pretty weeds grew near it. A crippled-looking television antenna canted off to one side of the chimney. The front door gaped open, no screen door to protect the house from flies. The screenless windows were also wide open, like blind eyes peering out over the ruin of the yard. A tattered curtain fluttered out of one of them. The house looked abandoned, not just by Mrs. Egan, but by humanity.

They both agreed that Grainger would die if he knew they had seen where he lived.

Without another word, the pair ducked back into the woods, between them a pledge never to speak of this. It was the first secret Kiley remembered ever having between them, their first secret excluding Grainger.

"We tried to find him, but we couldn't. He showed up on his own a day later."

"His mother never came back?"

"No."

Will hitched his shorts again and stared out at the seascape before them, at the utter peacefulness of the softly undulating water and the silent movement of sailboats on the horizon. "That sucks."

After Will had gone to mail his postcards, Kiley remained on the porch, rocking slowly, thinking back to their promising with linked pinkies to never let Grainger know they'd seen the squalor he lived in. Grainger was so proud. Mack so compassionate. Even at ten, Mack understood that Grainger would disappear from their lives if he knew they pitied him. But they loved him too, and never once thought of him as less equal. In fact, as his adversity provided him with a maturity beyond their years, they turned to him as their nominal leader.

Winter after winter, from the summer she first met the boys, Kiley marked time from September to June. Waiting for that day when school ended and the station wagon was packed, and Hawke's Cove was not six months away but only a couple of hundred miles, then just hours, finally, minutes.

The tempo of her rocking increased again as that old sense of anticipation arose. Kiley hadn't let it surface the whole time she and Will prepared to come back. She'd forbidden it heart-space on the long drive. But now, sitting on the front porch, the latent surge of excitement and expectation built up, part nostalgia, part hope.

Abruptly, Kiley stood up. This place could not be allowed to open that place in her heart where she had buried the past.

Any thought of seeing Grainger Egan was out of the question. She could not bear to see the man the boy had become.

Four

❧

Grainger Egan stood in line at the post office window, a month's worth of bills in his hand. He was standing behind a lanky boy digging in his capacious pockets for the right change for half a dozen postcard stamps. Dozens of youths cluttered the streets of Hawke's Cove in the summer, mostly indistinguishable one from another, camouflaged into anonymity by their baggy pants and backward baseball caps. Maybe it was the boy's intense study of one of the postcards in his hand, or the bend of his neck, but Grainger was certain that he knew this kid. As the boy turned away from the window, Grainger nodded to him, with a nominal I'm-sure-I-know-your-parents smile. Then Grainger's smile froze, but the boy turned away before the look on Grainger's face exposed how startled he was at the sight of those wide-spaced blue eyes. Grainger knew who he was, who he had to be. Without question.

He was the image of his mother. Masculine, to be sure, but the same honey blond hair, the same ocean blue eyes, so achingly familiar. The spontaneous dimpled smile as he responded to Grainger's half-smile.

The telltale arch of his eyebrows proved his heredity, perfect ram's horns, just like Kiley's. It might be believed that here was a creature of parthenogenesis, so deeply did he resemble his mother at this age.

Unable to avoid the thought before it was in his mind, Grainger wondered whether she still looked like that, like a gamine, a breath of fresh air, the blithe spirit he and Mack nicknamed Kiley, after being made to read Shelley's "To a Skylark" in ninth grade. "Hail to thee, Blithe Spirit," they mocked the writer. Kiley laughed it off, retorting, "Bird thou never wert." *Wert* became their code word that summer. "Hey Blithe, Grainger and I wert going to the movies tonight, you want to go?"

"You wert, wert you?" Oh, they thought themselves very funny. Or Mack very funny, because he was the one to use the word to the greatest amusement. He could always do that, defuse any situation with a joke or a funny gesture, or a non sequitur.

Until Kiley came into their lives, Mack and Grainger had been content as a duo. They had played the same games for so long they didn't have to discuss the details of the various missions planned as mock soldiers, or the complicated plots of their imaginary detective stories, or which superheroes they were, wearing towel capes and running along the beach. Mack was always clever Spider-Man; Grainger, the conflicted Superman. When Kiley came, they expanded their games to include her or happily played games of her devising, as long as Barbies weren't involved. On the rare occasions he let himself think back, Grainger remembered every childhood summer day as sunny and warm. Every day a beach day. He still saw the three of them as eight-year-olds, or ten-year-olds. When they were fifteen and life was golden. Beyond that, Grainger could not allow himself to reminisce. Dual abandonments, the bookends of his youth, inevitably subverted even the most innocent recollection.

Some cynics might say that adolescence changes everything; what could he expect? But Grainger knew that they had come very close to defying the odds in preserving a platonic friendship, devoid of jealousy, devoid of competition. Until one summer when it all came tumbling down and their lives were changed. Even then, they might have carried into adulthood only the sweet memories, if only . . .

Grainger slapped the fistful of bills against his leg. He had spent a lot of time keeping the "if onlies" at bay. One look at this boy's wide blue eyes, and his battlements were in danger of being breached.

"Grainger, you're next," Harvey Clark called to him from the service window.

The boy, poking his cards into the mail slot, turned and looked at Grainger, openly curious, as if trying to place the name, a little half-smile of his own on his face.

Grainger was certain of it then: this tall boy with Kiley's features must be Mack's son. Or his.

Grainger'd had some warning; he knew before they arrived that Kiley Harris and her son were coming to town to ready the old house for sale. Though Toby Reynolds had passed the word along only as casual gossip, to Grainger it was like storm-warning pennants being hoisted. Toby's business was to pass along stuff like that, stoking the furnace of commerce, so to speak, as a high-end real estate agent. Toby knew Grainger dealt with rich summer people in his boat business, and always let it drop when one of the premier properties in

Hawke's Cove was up for grabs. Toby, who moved comfortably among these people, had some skewed idea that Grainger's connection to them was likely to provide such a conversational turn. But Grainger merely repaired their boats, and launched or hauled them with the seasons. He didn't say much to them except what needed to be done, when it might be finished, and how much they should pay him. He didn't want to be their friend or move within their tight social circles, although he was often the recipient of invitations and occasionally attended a cocktail party or fund-raiser if the hosts were longtime summer people or good sailors, or if the benefit was one he supported.

Toby, a *washashore,* was only vaguely aware of the divide between the old Covers and the newcomers who had brought suburbia with them. His perspective was one of the immediate; unlike those who called themselves natives, he had only a minimalist's sense of history. And he employed it only when it suited his needs, as when a historic house came on the market. Then he would trot out his "local knowledge" to plump up its selling points against the condition of the roof or the limited view.

Toby's sense of Hawke's Cove history was building-centric. He had no concept of human history, the old grudges, griefs and secrets that lay behind the faces of those ordinary men he greeted every morning at Linda's Coffee Shop. And he could never have imagined the effect his words might have on Grainger when he casually mentioned that the woman whose actions forever altered Grainger's life was coming back.

"It's rare for these places to go up for sale, the shingle-style houses on the bluff. Almost never." Toby was on the verge of salivating. "But I guess they're not in good health. And the wife said the daughter, Kitty or Cathy or something, doesn't want it. So they want it sold. Pronto."

"Kiley."

"Beg pardon?"

"The daughter's name is Kiley."

"Right. Whatever. Anyway they're in a hurry."

As they walked out together, Grainger's dog, Pilot, waited patiently in the truck, his chin resting on the steering wheel. Toby's immaculate Lexus was parked next to the '99 Ford half ton. He was still going on about the Harris house, and Grainger felt an uncharacteristic urge to give him a good shove against his car and smack him into silence.

"Mrs. Harris said her father-in-law bought the place for five hundred dollars. Now it's valued at over a million. She said something about wanting to put her grandson through college. I told *her* even if they send the kid to Harvard, they'll still have loads of money left over."

The news of a grandson surprised Grainger. But it made sense then, this sudden desire to sell the place after all these years. Kiley had never come back to use it. If Grainger ever felt a twinge of something that might have been hurt, or anger, imagining that she'd successfully gotten on with her life, he'd stifled it pretty quickly. Just because he had been incapable of trusting anyone with his heart, certainly didn't mean that Kiley was similarly afflicted.

". . . and she says, no, he's been accepted to Cornell. As if Harvard had been an option . . ."

Not a little kid, but a college boy.

Grainger was very good at math. It was nineteen summers ago that they had last been together. He knew the last day they had ever seen each other: August 24, 1984.

As Toby nattered on, Grainger walked away from him without another word and climbed into his truck, pulling away from the curb a little too fast, ignoring the look on Toby's face as the loose sand dinged against his white car.

He drove in the opposite direction from his boat shed and up Seaview Avenue to Overlook Bluff Road. Pilot wiggled on the seat beside him, loving any departure from routine that might result in a walk.

The Harris's house, waiting for the arrival of its long absent daughter, sat behind its scraggly privet hedge. Still shuttered, as it had been for the last year, the house was unchanged from his boyhood memories of it. The porch looked in need of a new coat of deck paint, and the roof was a year or so away from needing replacement, but for all that, the place looked pretty good.

Although he had passed by a thousand times, he'd always kept his eyes on the view below the bluff. Now Grainger pulled off to the side of the road to stare at the house, trying to imagine that something besides the tragic implosion of their friendship might have taken place back then—but he could only think of the first time he'd set foot on that property.

By the time Kiley Harris entered their lives, the summer the boys turned eight, Mack MacKenzie and Grainger Egan had been buddies for what seemed like forever to two little boys, from about the time Mack and his family had moved year-round to Hawke's Cove. Mack's physician dad set up his general practice in the professional building, making the leap, as he called it, from big-city impersonal practice, to a small-town practice in the place he had summered all of his life. A move that meant that, although he certainly wasn't paid in chickens and eggs, he knew his patients very well. Hawke's Cove in the early seventies was still a small place, only just building into the summer resort it would become by the turn of the millennium.

Grainger was sitting in Dr. MacKenzie's waiting room, his nose running and his mother handing him tissues. Mack was cheerfully healthy, playing with a set of plastic trains on the floor of the well-child side of the room. Grainger was remanded to the sick-child side and sat despondent and rheumy, sure that he'd never have a chance to play with those marvelous trains. In his family, well-care wasn't an option. Without health insurance, only persistent coughs and fevers got medical attention. As long as Grainger's mother remained with them, at least he did see a doctor when really sick. After she left, his friendship with Mack provided care on several levels.

Seeing Grainger's obvious desire to touch those brightly colored cars, Mack began to push the train in his direction. One by one the cars passed across the invisible divide between them until Grainger was in full possession of the toy.

"I'm Mack."

"I'm Grainger."

"Is that your first name or your last name?"

"First. Egan is my last name."

"Grainger Egan. I'm not sick. I just have to play here when my mom's busy. My daddy is the doctor."

"My daddy is a fisherman."

"I wish my dad was."

"My dad can teach your dad."

"Okay. When you get better, do you want to play?"

Mack lived close by the Overlook Bluff Road neighborhood, in a neat, old, viewless Cape-style house that had two bathrooms and a den. Such a place was palatial to Grainger, who then lived above LaRiviere's Market in three rooms. Very soon Grainger became a fixture in the MacKenzie household, even having his own hook by the door to hang his coat on when they came home from school. As it grew dark, Mrs. MacKenzie would say, "Grainger honey, can you stay?" She knew dinner for him might be hot dogs or cereal, not pork chops or roast chicken.

If his father was out at sea, fishing on one of the big boats out of Great Harbor, he'd shake his head and say no thank you. His mother was home alone and would expect him. If Rollie Egan was home, either between trips or unemployed owing to the vagaries of the fishing industry, Grainger would nod yes. Please. Later he would run home in the dark, timing his arrival to occur just as his father fell asleep in front of the television, the three or four beers he'd consumed guaranteeing he wouldn't notice Grainger's coming in after supper. Occasionally Grainger would mistime his return, and Rollie would berate him about ingratitude and getting above himself. Depending on the degree of success his last fishing trip had brought, he might keep his abuse verbal. If the fishing had been poor, Grainger might expect the belt. His wide open eyes would fixate on the movement of his father's hairy hands to his belt buckle. Rollie knew that, and would tease the boy by touching it, just to see the fear Grainger tried so hard not to show.

Sometimes, though, he had already taken out his frustration on Grainger's mother. Regret and guilt are strange bedfellows, and that often made Rollie more dangerous. The less he brought home, the more he bullied. If Grainger could hear his mother's weeping through the thin walls of the building, he would sit in the hallway, waiting until his father's loud snores proclaimed it safe to go in. Sometimes Mrs. Katz in the other apartment would open her door and pull him inside. She'd never say a word, but give Grainger a slice of pound cake and a glass of milk, and *tsk tsk* her tongue as he ate.

As spring daylight increased playtime, one of his and Mack's favorite games after supper was "trespassing." They'd visit unoccupied summerhouses and scamper over porches, climb trellises, and dare each other to peek in windows. Once school let out, Grainger stayed at Mack's four nights out of five.

The long June sunset lingered until eight o'clock, giving the pair time to move through the neighborhood for new dares. The closer it got to true summer, and the arrival of summer people, the more exciting the game.

One evening they drifted into the Harris yard from the back, and moved around to the great wraparound porch with its tipped-over rocking chairs. In those days people didn't lock up their outdoor furniture, simply tipped the chairs forward to prevent rain and leaf mold from building up. In the evening half-light, the rockers looked like people bent over in prayer, foreheads touching the porch rail. The chairs beckoned to two small boys looking for mischief. They crept along the hedges, speaking in a code of their own devising as they scouted the territory. Mack dared Grainger, and he ran up across the porch to tip upright each of the four big chairs, then stepped on the rockers to get them to moving in a chaotic dance. The sudden appearance of headlights coming along Overlook Bluff Road made the boys quickly duck behind the wide, shingled balustrades. When the headlights didn't pass but instead pointed right at where they were hiding, Grainger could feel his pulse race with the same intensity as when he ran home those nights his father was there.

Mack stifled a nervous giggle and pushed Grainger from behind to crawl along to where the verandah turned against the side of the house. From there they were able to creep, on all fours, down the five wooden steps of the porch's rear access and dart across the darkened yard to the relative safety of the bushes, where they paused to watch the wonder of their mischief. It was full dark now, and they knew they'd be in trouble with Mack's mother if they didn't beat it home soon. But it was too much not to watch the puzzlement on the arriving owner's face, fleetingly illuminated by his lighter as he lit a cigarette. He put out a hand to stop the mysterious rocking of his porch chairs before unlocking the double front doors.

The slam of the car door pulled their attention away as a woman got out of the car and opened the back door of the white station wagon. Then a sleepy girl climbed out, one arm clutching a white stuffed bear, the other rubbing her eyes, for all the world like a child in a Disney movie. She stood alone for a few minutes as her parents busied themselves unpacking the massively loaded car; then she walked across the scraggly seacoast grass and right to where Mack and Grainger huddled, their hands over their mouths to keep the excited giggles suppressed.

"I'm Kiley. Are you playing hide-and-go-seek-in-the-dark? Can I play too?" At that moment her father called her in, and the little girl scampered off, letting the screen door slam behind her.

• • •

The morning that Toby Reynolds dropped the bomb of Kiley's return, Grainger sat for a long time in his truck, opposite the still-shuttered house. He heard her child's voice, still a little cloudy from sleep. *Can I play too?*

They should have told her no.

Now he'd seen Kiley's son. The young man whose future would be assured by the sale of his grandparents' home. Grainger left the post office in a hurry, afraid that his confusion showed on his face. He had a fleeting vision of grabbing the kid and holding him close in some stagy reunion. "My boy!" But he might as easily not have been his son. The only reliable truth was that he was Kiley's son. And she had kept him away from Hawke's Cove.

Grainger's mind raced with uncontrollable thoughts, even as he tried to recall his half-dozen Saturday morning errands. The drugstore. He forgot the aspirin he'd meant to buy and came out with a can of shaving cream he didn't need and a bag of M&M's. The hardware store. What was it he needed? Grainger wandered around, bumping into people he knew, remarking on the decent weather and the Red Sox. He stood in line with just a package of sandpaper and brushes, without remembering he needed to have a key copied or the piece of screening he needed to repair the screen door where Pilot had scratched a rip in it. All Grainger could think of was whether Kiley had been selfish in keeping this boy to herself, or selfless in not involving him. She could have contacted him anytime. The MacKenzies always knew his address, although they might only send a card at Christmas. Grainger had been a moving target for the ten years he'd piloted all manner of craft, from research vessels out of Woods

Hole to ferries in Puget Sound, but he'd always dropped them a note to say where he was. Even in those first couple of years, when he was in the Army, deeply regretting his mistake in not joining the Navy, he was accessible. Of course, if she hadn't wanted to contact him, perhaps she was also incapable of contacting the MacKenzies. With better reason.

Yet neither had *he* ever reached out to Kiley; he never could have. He'd once hated her for what she'd caused. Over time that had faded, but Grainger still blamed her for costing him everyone he had loved. Perhaps he'd evolved beyond hating her, but he knew he still hadn't forgiven her, or himself. It was what defined him.

When Grainger was a boy and his mother left, he had experienced the bitter desolation of loss. He had prayed every night that someday she'd come back, prayed until he outgrew the hope. In the opposite way, he'd prayed that he'd never set eyes on Kiley Harris again—a prayer that had seemed answered, until today.

Still, he would have wanted to know about the boy. Surely Kiley had known whose child he was, and chosen to keep Grainger away. As punishment? Or out of kindness? He was deeply curious about the boy, but didn't know how to satisfy that curiosity without encountering Kiley. Without starting a conversation that was nearly two decades too late.

Grainger stood in the checkout line of the hardware store, rubbing a thumb against the coarse sandpaper. *They say time is a great healer. That isn't quite true, but time does dull the pain.* No doubt they both were scarred, their lives etched with the disfigurement of their mistakes. His scars were no longer fresh; he had distracted himself with travel and work and even a couple of long-term relationships. If things had turned out differently back then, if their separation had simply been that of growing apart, maybe they could meet cheerfully now and again, as old friends with nothing left in common do. But it hadn't. They had acted on their desires, and self-destructed.

Yet, Grainger wondered, maybe they did have something left in common. The boy.

Whether he was Grainger's or not, he was *of them*. The three of them.

Coming out of the hardware store, Grainger saw the boy again, sitting in a dented blue Mazda. His sunglasses didn't disguise the fact that the kid was watching him. Something that almost felt like a suppressed laugh tickled his throat. At that moment, Emily Claridge Fitzgibbons called out Grainger's name. While she chattered about whatever it was she was talking about, Grainger kept thinking about the boy and sneaking looks at him out of the corner of his eye. How dangerous it would be to encourage him. The boy's look of startled curiosity in the post office convinced Grainger that, at the very least, he knew something. And if Kiley had told this boy about him, she must have told him about Mack.

With a sudden and absolute certainty, Grainger knew that he had to keep this kid at arm's length. If he was so interested in Grainger that he was following him around town, then they were both in danger of misplaced expectations.

Five

The black desk phone on the marble-topped table rang with old-fashioned shrillness. Kiley answered it, half expecting it to be Will explaining why he wasn't back yet from the post office.

"Kiley, it's Pop."

"Is everything all right?" Kiley's father never initiated phone calls.

"Fine. I want to talk to you about *Random*."

It took a moment for Kiley to draw her thoughts in line with her father's words. *Random*, his thirty-six-foot ketch. "Okay."

"I should sell her, too." It might have been his struggle for breath, or emotion, but his voice was faint. *Random* had always been his pride and joy, his ownership of the classic wooden boat defining him in the hierarchy of local sailors.

"Pop, you don't have to do that. Don't let go of everything all at once."

"I'm not able to sail her. What's the point of keeping her? She needs to be in the water, not stranded in a boatyard."

"Where is she now?"

"At Egan's Boat Works."

A knot began to form in Kiley's stomach. She knew what was next.

"Will you see to her?"

"I can't do that."

"Don't be so goddamned stubborn." Merriwell's voice strengthened in the face of his daughter's refusal.

"Can't you do it over the phone?" Kiley rubbed the aching place in her belly.

"No. Someone has to go and see her, get a surveyor over to get her worth. Sign whatever agreements need to be signed. Just like the house. It's no different."

"Yes, it is." Three words, distinct and sharp. Could her father really have no idea that Egan's Boat Works was owned by Grainger Egan? The same Grainger Egan who had featured prominently in any number of family arguments? Had her father forgotten that Grainger was high on the list of suspects her mother had assembled at the news of her pregnancy?

"Why are you making this so difficult?" Merriwell paused, gathering enough breath to finish the conversation. "Just go down there and see to it." There was another pause. "He won't bite."

Kiley settled the heavy handset into its cradle and sat down on the chair beside the phone stand. Her head dropped into her hands, and she tried to ignore the increasing ache in her stomach. Just like a little kid, with a stomachache on test day. Was her father testing her filial obedience, her maturity, her courage? No, this wasn't a test. This was an outrageous request. She wouldn't do it.

Kiley heard the screen door slam and the sound of

the car keys dropped on the wooden kitchen table. She pushed herself to her feet and went to greet Will.

He leaned into the half-empty refrigerator. "There's nothing to eat."

"There's ham and cheese. And, unless you drank it all at breakfast, there's milk. We'll go out tonight for dinner."

"Can I pick?"

"Sure. There's not much to choose from here in Hawke's Cove, so we might want to head over to Great Harbor."

"How about the Osprey's Nest? The place near the boat landing."

Kiley pulled a face. "That's kind of a dive."

"So?"

"I've never been there."

"Local color. Let's live dangerously." Will tossed the packet of ham onto the table. "Let's be anti-Harris tonight."

Kiley laughed. The Osprey's Nest really was about the last place her parents would frequent. Their dining experience in Hawke's Cove was exclusively at the Yacht Club, which served a mediocre dinner every second Thursday. Otherwise, they'd trek to Great Harbor to one of the better restaurants. They'd be horrified to know she'd brought Will to the Osprey's Nest.

Maybe it was a rebellion against her father's ridiculous demand. Maybe it was an attempt to rekindle the compromised closeness with Will. Or maybe it was because the Osprey's Nest was where the waterfront types went. People who made their living with boats and nets and lobster pots, like Grainger Egan.

"All right, we'll go. Now, eat lunch; then let's get to the beach."

"Aren't you eating?"

Kiley tested the knot in her stomach and shook her head. "No, I'm not hungry."

Will had been restless at the beach. After swimming, he'd been unable to focus on reading, tossing his *Sports Illustrated* carelessly on the sand. He'd lain down on his beach towel, but not fallen asleep. Kiley offered to walk up the beach with him, but he shook his head. "Do you mind if I take the car and do a little exploring?"

"I guess." Kiley hid her disappointment at being abandoned. She could stay here by herself and walk home, or have him drop her off at the house before he went rambling. She didn't quite feel like either. She, too, felt a restlessness that had nothing to do with boredom. "I guess I could stay here and wait for you to pick me up."

Will toed a line in the sand. "I might be gone awhile. Why don't I take you home? I'll meet you at the Osprey's Nest at, like, five?"

A little trigger of anxiety added weight to her stomachache. Was he up to something? Deliberately, Kiley pressed that thought out of her mind. Will just needed some time to himself. "If you'll put most of the stuff in the car, I'll walk home. I want another swim." Kiley stood up and folded her beach chair. "Don't go too far, okay?"

"Just to Great Harbor."

He gathered the umbrella and chairs, leaving Kiley with her book and a towel and her own restlessness.

Six

❧

Will stood in the doorway of Linda's Coffee Shop for a moment before spotting Grainger seated at the counter. Leaving the beach, he'd seen Grainger's truck pulling out of the gas station. Impulsively, Will followed, parking a few spaces down from where Grainger had left his truck. Will hadn't been very discreet this morning, and was pretty sure Grainger had seen him. This time he was certain that Grainger hadn't. He watched as the man got out of his truck, gave the gray dog in it a pat, and headed into the coffee shop.

There were two empty seats to Grainger's left, and Will chose the farther one, keeping an empty place between them. He picked up the laminated menu to feign activity as he stared at Grainger's reflection in the mirror behind the counter, his face framed between a cardboard ice cream cone and the chalked daily specials.

The face reflected there was a little bristly, with an unshaven Saturday look. His eyes were on his menu, never looking up. When Grainger removed his cap, setting it on the stool between them, Will saw that his hair was darker than the gray showing had suggested. Grainger kept his eyes down for so long that Will was startled to see him suddenly looking directly at Will's own reflection, a similar curiosity on his face. Will ducked his eyes, but couldn't keep a flush of guilty surprise from coloring his cheeks.

"Large coffee, Donna, and a piece of apple pie. To go." Grainger handed the girl the menu.

"And you?" Donna moved down to where Will sat.

"Umm, a chocolate cone. I guess." Will fished around in his pockets to see if he had enough money.

The waitress made Will's cone first, so he went out the door and positioned himself on a bench across the street from the coffee shop. In a few minutes Grainger came out. Anticipating that Grainger would go to his truck, Will stood up, still licking the rapidly melting homemade ice cream into a controllable ball. Instead, Grainger crossed the quiet main street and walked up to him, then sat down on the bench, throwing one arm casually over the back of it. "Do you want to tell me what you're doing?"

"I don't know what you mean." Will felt childish, standing there, six feet tall and licking an ice cream cone like a kid.

"You've been following me."

Will coughed, the ice cream suddenly too cold. "I'm not following you. Are you, like, paranoid or something?"

"A little. Sit down." Grainger's voice was firm but not frightening, something like his basketball coach's voice. A little gravelly and deep, the voice of a man who spoke only to say something useful. "What's your name?"

"Will. Will Harris."

"Harris." Grainger took a deep breath. "What do you want, Will Harris?"

Will stayed standing. The July sun, tempered only by the faithful southwesterly breeze, licked at Will's bare neck, and he twisted his Cornell baseball cap around to shield his neck with the bill. "I was, like, wondering if you can give me sailing lessons." Will stuffed the end of his cone into his mouth. He was pretty proud of himself, coming up with a plausible cover story so quickly, thanks to the "Egan's Boat Works, Repairs, Hauling, and Lessons" painted on the side of Grainger's truck.

Grainger said nothing, just stared out into some middle distance, which might have been the sliver of harbor visible between the facing buildings, or the street, or someplace behind his eyes. At the prolonged silence, Will finally sat beside Grainger on the green park bench.

"Why don't you ask your mother to give you lessons?" Grainger's voice cut through Will's nervous embarrassment at having been caught out. His tone was half contemptuous, half curious.

Will had tossed out the idea of sailing lessons only to save himself, but now he was annoyed that Grainger hadn't immediately said yes. In habitual contrariness, Will met the argument. "We don't have a boat."

"Yes, you do. It's in my boatyard."

"Oh. Well, Mom's busy." Will was nonplussed to have such easy confirmation this stranger knew his mother.

"I'm expensive."

"I have a little money. Enough for a couple of lessons, I'm sure."

"Why do you want to sail?"

"It's sort of in my blood. My grandfather's told me about how he sailed in races. I've just never had the opportunity to learn." Although he'd grown up listening to Pop talk about his glory days, detailing every race buoy by buoy, he'd never given sailing lessons a thought until this minute. Suddenly he could believe that this was a lifelong ambition, now that he'd spoken it.

"I don't know." Grainger shook his head, lifted his cap off, and ran a hand through his hair, then resettled the hat back on his head. "I'm pretty booked."

Will could have just said okay and gotten up to leave; but he found that he couldn't. Here was this man who held a clue to his own past, even if it was only in having known his mom as a girl. Will couldn't let go of the idea that Grainger would be able to tell him something important, something no one else would ever be able to, and he was determined that Grainger wouldn't just shrug him off. "Mr. Egan, maybe just one lesson?"

Grainger had been leaning with his elbows on his knees, and now he sat back and looked Will in the eye. For an uncomfortable minute he seemed to be assessing Will, holding him up against some measure.

"All right. Meet me at the boat works on Tuesday morning. Seven-thirty." He put out his hand for Will to shake. "One lesson. If you look like you can become a sailor, we'll see about a second."

"Okay. Great." Will felt the grip of Grainger's hand grow stronger, almost painful.

"One free lesson. To see what you're made of." Grainger let go of Will's hand, gathered his lunch bag, and started to walk away, then turned back. "How is she? Your mother?" Did Will imagine a fiber in that voice pulling it tight?

He wasn't sure how to answer that question. The truth was, she was still mad at him, and acting all weird about being here in Hawke's Cove. "Good, I guess."

Grainger nodded and turned to cross the street, moving with the broad, open step of a man who had spent a lifetime on the water.

Seven

At first Kiley was annoyed with Will for being late, then a little worried. As far as she knew he was only over in Great Harbor, poking around and looking for some new CDs. He'd promised to be on this side of the bridge by five, and to meet her here at the Osprey's Nest for an early dinner. Kiley assumed that Will would be a little late, and had taken her time walking into town from the house. It was now five-forty and she was fighting the sense of maternal panic that always overruled rational thought.

Will had been so remote since the pot-smoking incident—not so much sullen as distracted. Unfortunately, she'd been equally distracted with the house. No, being truthful, it was being in Hawke's Cove. Her initial hope, that bringing him here would open up the doorway of communication, was instantly put to the test when Will asked her about the photograph, and she'd failed. She wanted him to reveal his thoughts to her, yet she was unwilling to do the same. Well, maybe tonight she could get him to let her in a little. In her heart of hearts, Kiley knew that there had to have been some catalyst for Will's behavior that night, something that pushed him into doing it. Will reacted to things.

Kiley sighed. There was so much going on right now that this silence, whether it was a defense mechanism or simple weariness, must not be allowed to continue. All too soon he would be far away, only a disembodied voice on a phone. Living a life separate from hers.

The waitress came over a second time to try and take her order. "You ready?"

"No. I'm still waiting for my son. He really should be here any minute." Kiley resented her disagreeable need to explain to the waitress. "I'll just have a glass of water in the meantime."

"You bet." The waitress brought over a pint glass of ice-cold water, then moved away.

Kiley sipped the water, wondering if she hadn't asked for wine because she didn't want to look like some pathetic creature, making those around her speculate that she was only pretending a son was expected. After all, a lady never drinks alone.

The customers within her view disabused her quickly of the notion that anyone was even aware of her presence in the small tavern. Mostly men, mostly tucking into heavy dinners of meat loaf or fried chicken; even if they had made note of this lone woman in the place, it had made no mark on their communal consciousness. These were men tired from a long day of physical labor; the invisible Covers, surfacing only to mend a sail, repair an engine, or help move a boat out of storage. Men in oil-weathered jeans and rubber boots who belonged to a different Hawke's Cove from the one she knew. These were the men from whom Grainger had sprung.

Her parents hadn't approved of her friendship with

Grainger. "He's a townie. You should be nice, but you don't want to *encourage* him." The implication being, "he's not our kind." Even Grainger's accepted place with the MacKenzies failed to temper their opinion. The MacKenzies were "saints" for taking him in, but the boy was beneath regard.

Kiley wondered if Lydia's late-in-life fear of being robbed had actually been foreshadowed by her rejection of Grainger's annual offer to help unload the car. "Scurry along, we can manage." Kiley could still hear her mother's imperious rebuff; as if he would make off with the silver. And she'd been left to struggle with the over-heavy bags.

Then Grainger got the job teaching the young ones to sail the club's Dyer Dinks. Her mother's open disapproval changed into political correctness amongst her bridge partners, whose children "loved" him. But he still didn't attend the Friday night dances. Kiley wasn't able to avoid that enforced clubbiness, but as soon as she could, she always slipped out through the back hallway emergency exit, where Mack and Grainger would be standing under the lone streetlight in the club's dirt-and-crushed-clamshell parking lot, waiting for her to make her escape.

When Mack's parents finally joined the Yacht Club, both the MacKenzie boys, and Grainger as their guest, began to come to the dances. It was so hard to get either Mack or Grainger to dance with her. The pair preferred leaning against the wall with cans of soda in hand. Sometimes Mack's older brother, Conor, fresh from college, would take her out on the floor in a deliberate tease to his brother and Grainger. Then he'd pay her a courtly bow and rejoin his own social circle, leaving Kiley to catch her hammering breath.

Grainger always wore tan chinos and the same blue polo shirt with the collar turned up, as current fashion dictated. Kiley suspected that Mrs. MacKenzie had given him those clothes, probably castoffs from Conor, since Grainger owned only faded jeans and unremarkable T-shirts.

Once Kiley gave up the struggle to get the boys to dance, the trio would duck out through the back hallway and down to the empty beach. They'd scamper down to the club's private beach and shed their clothes, swimsuits underneath. Laughing, they'd plunge into the warm evening water. In the darkness that surrounded them, they'd tread water and stare at the Yacht Club lights reflected in the water in runny streaks of yellow, and think themselves rebellious. The music blared from the speakers—Pointer Sisters, Don Henley, or Donna Summer. Phosphorescence glittered greenish on the edges of the gently rolling waves tonguing the sand. Under cover of darkness, their intimacy was pure, eternal. They would always be friends.

Blind to each other in the darkness, their hands, gently stroking the surface of the water, would sometimes bump. Once a hand touched her breast and in the embarrassed silence, she assumed that whoever had touched her was as shocked as she had been. Her nipples had been prominent as the slight breeze over the water chilled her skin.

It was the first time that Kiley considered that their triangular friendship would be endangered if any one of them tampered with it. She dived beneath the dark water. Impossible. Nothing between them could ever change.

• • •

Kiley slowly became aware that she was looking at each nearby face, as if looking for one familiar to her. She dropped her eyes to the table's slightly sticky oilcloth cover. What were the chances that she'd recognize him anyway? The last time she'd set eyes on Grainger Egan was nineteen summers ago—a lifetime. Will's whole lifetime. Then she was equally afraid that he might be here and she *wouldn't* know him. Men changed more than women. Her fifteenth high school reunion had proven that. The handsome boys had run to fat and most were balding. Their necks had thickened and their voices were too loud.

What would she do if she saw him? What if he was here and she *did* recognize him? Could she withstand the possibility that he would look at her with the same hatred he'd looked at her that last time? There had been no healing between them. And what would he do if he knew about Will? How was she ever going to deal with Grainger about her father's boat, when she was so afraid to encounter him at all?

Kiley shivered in the faint air-conditioning. *Someone walked over your grave.* That's what they said when you got inexplicable goose bumps.

The bell over the door clanged, and Will came in. Kiley shivered again, relieved to see him, happy to see his smile.

Eight

❧

Will knew he was late; his mother's worried face was a pure indicator. He hadn't meant to be so late, although a little late would have been typical. He knew he was getting too old to use the "lost track of time" excuse, especially with the new watch his grandparents had given him for graduation. Maybe this would be a good time to suggest again that if he had a cell phone, she'd never need to worry about him. He flopped down in the seat to the left of his mother, breathless with his rush to park the car and get to the restaurant.

"Where have you been?"

"Ummm, I got lost. There's that other road before you get to the bridge. I went right instead of left at the fork."

"Will, you can read signs. Don't play with me."

"Well, maybe I did spend a little more time at the mall than I should have. It's pretty small, but they've got a great music store." Will opened his backpack and pulled out five new CDs. "I sort of got carried away."

Will's eclectic tastes were fanned out on the square table: Alicia Keys, No Doubt, Coldplay, and India.Arie, mixed in with a bargain-bin copy of the early Beatles.

The waitress returned to take their order. Kiley ordered her glass of wine.

"I hope you bought batteries. There's no CD player in the house."

"I know. I did."

Will was glad that his mom forbore to mention the amount of money he had spent on the five CDs, even though he had every right to spend his money the way he saw fit. When he actually took off for Cornell, then he'd bow to economy. Right now he was still warm from his grandparents' largesse. They'd been so happy Kiley had agreed to go to Hawke's Cove that they'd handed Will a nice "allowance" to make up for his losing a month's work at the burger place.

If Grainger agreed to keep teaching him after his first lesson, he'd use the rest of that money for that. Maybe there was something to heredity. His grandfather had been a competitive sailor. The waitress placed their dinners in front of them. An idea niggled at the back of his mind, prompted by the photo of his mother and the two boys leaning against the little boat, now tucked into his back pocket.

"Mom, who taught you how to sail?"

The question seemed to surprise his mother; she studied her plate for a moment. "Pop did. Although I was never that good at it, and he never let me race with him."

"Did you sail with anyone else? Or did you only sail with him?"

"The Yacht Club sponsored races for kids." She

pushed her meat loaf around on her plate, then looked up at Will. "Why?"

"I was thinking about taking sailing lessons." If she would just smile and say, *I have a friend who could teach you,* he could avoid pretending. "I mean, while I'm here and all."

"If you're serious, we can look into lessons at the club. And maybe we could charter a day sailer from the Yacht Club. I'll check tomorrow if you want, though we'll have to do it after I get the house . . ." For a moment she looked excited, just like she always did when they planned some fun outing.

"What about Pop's boat?" Will watched the tension build in his mother's face, supplanting the pleasure.

"It's in dry dock, and besides, it's way too big." She turned her face away from him.

Will took a big bite of his cheeseburger, wishing he had just shut up. It seemed like everything he did or said lately created this pained expression on his mother's face. "That's okay, I was just toying with the idea. Call it a whim."

Kiley reached across the table and touched his hand. "I wish I did have the time to teach you. It would be fun, although I'm not sure I could still tell a halyard from a turnbuckle, or port from starboard. Which reminds me of a joke."

"What?"

"Did you hear the one about the captain who had a wooden box in his cabin?"

Will shook his head.

"Well, the crew was mystified. Every single night the old captain would go to his cabin, open this locked box, and look inside. Finally, the old guy dies and the crew can't keep back their curiosity anymore. The first mate runs to the locked wooden box and pries it open. Inside lies a single slip of paper." Kiley paused for dramatic effect. " 'Port is left, starboard is right.' "

Will laughed with the sound of a person not quite getting the joke, more pleased to see the tension begin to fade away from his mother's face.

"I suppose you have to be a sailor to really appreciate that one."

Will felt a flicker of inspiration. "So who told you that joke?"

His mother was smiling, but kept her eyes on her plate. "I don't remember. A friend, I suppose."

The bell above the door jangled again, and Kiley's eyes went to it, as if she were expecting someone. Will finished his cheeseburger, hesitating to ask anything else of her.

He'd put the photo in his back pocket, hoping he'd have an opportunity to bring it out and get a flow of conversation going, like he'd done with the picture of when they were ten. In hesitating, he'd missed his best opportunity tonight. He should have pulled the picture out and, pointing to the faces in the snapshot, asked, "Is this the friend who told you that lame joke? Or this one?" But he didn't. He couldn't. In the end, it wasn't about jokes.

Will knew instinctively that his mother wouldn't like the idea of him taking lessons from a man she had so clearly excised from her life, and, by extension, his. If—Will's train of thought lurched onto a dead-end branch line—if Grainger was his father, surely the circumstances of his conception had been traumatic. Why else had Grainger been eliminated from his life so effectively? Will shoved the last of his french fries in his mouth. He'd known for years that his mother's reluctance to tell him the truth was not a sign of true and absent love, but of adversity. The french fries were suddenly tasteless in his mouth as his gut contracted. What if he was trying to befriend a man who had done harm to his mother? Will swallowed the fries. There was only one way to find out: he needed to keep at this quest and not balk at the first obstacle, no matter how scary. He'd started this undertaking to find out what Grainger knew, and he would, by God, get some satisfaction. If this guy had abused his mother, he'd pay for it.

Which brought to mind a slight problem. His lesson was at seven-thirty, and he'd have to come up with some reason he was up so early on Tuesday morning. No way his mother wouldn't suspect something if he was up three hours early for no reason, and then took off for the morning.

She worried about his movements so much since that stupid night when he and D.C. and Mike got caught with the weed. It wasn't like he was a habitual user, a slacker who thought only about getting high. And it really wasn't like him to keep things from her. But that night, the pot was available, and he needed to be a little wild.

They'd all been to Lori Amandie's party. Lori was his girlfriend all senior year, and when she brought him outside to the back porch that night, he expected she just wanted a little private time. Instead, she said, "We need to back off a little, Will. We're heading in two different directions, and I don't want to hold you to a commitment you might regret."

"You mean that *you* might regret." He was hurt. He felt like he really loved this bright, pretty girl. From the first time she'd appeared in his government class, breathlessly explaining her lateness by some silly excuse the teacher had happily swallowed, Will had had no doubt that he wanted to be with her. Now he felt as if he'd just been some sort of practice boy, someone to sit with at lunch, an assurance of a busy weekend, protection against the overtures of less desirable boys. A guarantee of a worthy escort to the Senior Ball, but not worth restricting her social life at Purdue.

Will had stared off into the darkness. "Fine. Whatever." He'd left Lori on the back steps, her face charmingly puzzled, as if surprised that he was unhappy with her. Apparently in her deluded view, he should have been glad for the parole. For the first time, Will understood what the poet said about there being in every relationship the lover and the beloved. He'd smacked his open palm against the porch post and gone to find D.C.

He meant to go home, to get into bed before his mother could notice the beer on his breath. He wanted nothing more than to bury his head in his pillow and let the unmanly tears make their silent way out, to burst this suppurating blister of feeling. Instead D.C. winked at him, oblivious to the anger on Will's face, and put his hand in the deep pocket of his baggy green pants, showing Will just the edge of the plastic zipper bag. It seemed the perfect retaliation. Lori was madly anti-drug, president of the high school's chapter of Teens Against Drugs. Screw her.

Will nodded and the three of them got into Mike's car to find a secluded place to enjoy the dope. All year long his friends had made fun of him because of his loyal prohibition against smoking, calling him "wuss" and "whipped." Though his pals kidded him, they'd respected him for his acceding to Lori's wishes. Even now, the invitation to smoke had been made out of politeness rather than any expectation that Will would say yes. The surprise on D.C.'s face made Will scowl and refuse any explanation for his about-face. Soon enough, they'd figure it out. Figure out that he'd been dumped.

But he still couldn't tell his mother that, even though he knew in some way it might comfort her and make her less worried. Kiley hadn't cared for Lori, which made Lori's rejection all the harder. For some stupid reason, Will dreaded his mother would bad-mouth his ex-girlfriend. He wasn't ready to hear, "You're probably better off without her," which is exactly what he'd been trying to tell himself. But it wasn't Lori's fault he'd smoked the dope; it was his own misguided rebellion.

He kept his eyes on his empty plate, afraid to make eye contact with his mother, because she would see that he had something on his mind. She almost always knew. It was like his brain was visible to her. A tightness to his smile or hollowness in his voice, and she'd jump on him. "What's the matter, honey?" It was a miracle that, distracted as she had been with the legal ramifications of his smoking the dope, she'd evidently chalked up his glumness to that too. Not to a breakup with his girlfriend. She didn't mention Lori, even in passing. Will supposed she thought, out of sight, out of mind.

Kiley put down her knife and fork. "Pop asked me to see about selling the boat."

His mother's voice yanked him out of his reverie and Will glanced up. The same degree of tension edged her jaw as when Nana and Pop had asked her to take care of the house, as it had when he'd asked about the boat just now.

Will shrugged. "Just tell him, 'one overwhelming project at a time.'"

"That's what I said."

"Good for you."

At his mother's laugh, Will was suddenly glad that he'd asked to come to this hole-in-the-wall tavern for dinner. She was still smiling, although now she seemed distracted, looking up at every face that came through the door. If he felt a little devious, not telling her that he knew where the boat was and with whom, Will stifled it.

Tuesday he would be able to observe close at hand this man who had once been a part of his mother's life. He would watch closely to see if any answers would be revealed; look for some mannerism or movement or preference or dislike that would bond them together not in coincidence, but by blood. Will wiped a film of prickly sweat from his neck. Despite the air-conditioning, he felt feverish with excitement. Something like how he imagined the Olympic snowboarders he'd watched last year must have felt as they stood at the top of the half-pipe. He could only imagine what they were thinking: *Am I good enough?* Knowing that the next minute would be life altering, whatever the answer might be to that single burning question.

Emotionally, Will felt as if he, too, stood at the top of an icy drop, board waxed, training completed. Only his burning question wasn't whether he was good enough, but more deeply primal.

Who am I?

Nine

☙

From across the dimly lit room, Grainger Egan had seen Kiley Harris come into the tavern, already murky as the hard cores came in after work and filled it with the sour smell of spilt beer and cigar smoke. He was in his usual corner, behind the fake timbers that looked like they held the place up. Grainger liked the little two-person table because he could sit there alone and be invisible. Too many of his customers believed he wanted nothing more than to talk shop with them, when all he wanted was Mattie Lou Silva's meat loaf and a beer. The Nest was a good place for a man smelling of creosote and oakum, too tired to go home and shower before eating. Pilot was welcome and waited underneath Grainger's table for the accidental spill that might make his day. Grainger could feel the dog's chin resting on his boots, a weight that some days he thought kept him held to the earth.

Kiley Harris made the bells on the tavern door ring with an arrhythmic chaos, matched by the beating of Grainger's heart as his eyes adjusted to the recognition his brain had already made. She looked uncertain as to

whether she should stay or bolt. She scanned the room
quickly right to left, looking for someone. For one shocked
moment, Grainger thought she was looking for him.

From his vantage point behind the timber, he could
see that she didn't look a lot different. No taller, no
thicker, no thinner. She wore a sleeveless black top,
nicely showing off her square shoulders; her hair, once
very long, just touched them. In the dim light of the
tavern, it looked as blond as ever. The same dimness
betrayed no hardening around her mouth, or lines of
undue wear. She was as recognizable to him as if the
time between them had been a month, not a lifetime.

No, there was a difference. As she walked to a table,
he could see that her way of moving had slowed. She
was deliberate in picking up the menu, didn't slap it
down as she used to as a girl. She sipped her water,
didn't gulp it as once she did, as though every glass of
water was sweet and her thirst was desperate. Kiley
moved without the girlish blitheness that had informed
their concept of her.

She said something to Mattie Lou, and he realized
she was expecting someone; no doubt the boy. In a moment, Will would come in and see him sitting there.
The boy clearly knew something or had guessed that
there was some connection between them, and had
made up the ploy of wanting a sailing lesson from him
to cover his curiosity. Would Will, either with calcula-
tion or innocence, introduce his mother to his sailing
instructor? What sort of awkward hell would that be?

Kiley sat at the middle table in the center of the
room with her profile to Grainger, and he thought he
might just be able to slip out of the tavern unnoticed
when Will clanged open the door and came in with
that lope of tall young men. He threw himself into the

chair next to his mother, his back to Grainger; facing the door and closing off escape. Instinctively Grainger leaned back against the wall so that the timber was even more obscuring: He didn't want to face Kiley Harris here, in a reunion neither one of them was prepared for. Not yet.

So he was trapped, then. Trapped by circumstance and by stubbornness. Pilot sighed at his feet, and when Mattie Lou came to clear his plate, Grainer ordered another beer.

Sitting in the Osprey's Nest, drinking a lukewarm beer, he couldn't keep his eyes off the woman sitting twenty feet away, sipping a glass of wine in a place where no one drank wine. Kiley and Will spoke to each other in between long pauses, short bursts of conversation spiced with a little laughter. Now that she had her son beside her, Kiley was more animated, her gestures and mannerisms striking him hard with their familiarity. He couldn't keep his eyes off her.

There was no intensive dialogue as he imagined might take place between mother and son. Despite his own rough upbringing, he knew that parents and children did speak to one another. Mack's parents spoke to him and sometimes their voices were the only kind adult words he heard in a week. Mrs. MacKenzie would scold, then joke. Even with him, her half-fostered son, she'd tease and then ask about homework.

Grainger bought her Mother's Day cards. The first time he did that, she wept, so sorry for the boy with the absent mother, never believing that he had wanted to do it for *her,* rather than out of some misplaced wish he could give it to his own mother. Grainger was never able to successfully express that, in her dependable kindness, Mrs. MacKenzie was more important to him than his deserting parent. He found those Hallmark cards addressed to "someone who has been like a mother to me." Saccharine, perhaps, but genuine. Grainger wished she'd invite him to call her Mom, but some delicacy prevented her from making that suggestion. Grainger couldn't remember ever calling her by name.

His mother's desertion had corrupted his love for her, and he never sentimentalized his memories of her. Where he had previously seen her as his father's victim, afterward he saw his mother as free. She had abandoned her son to Rollie Egan, freed herself and left Grainger as hostage. Once Grainger had given up childish hope, he'd never deluded himself that she had some plan to come to his rescue. He never expected an apology or an excuse. She had saved herself and that was clear, even to a boy of ten. Later Grainger told himself that if he'd had the wherewithal, he would have done the same thing. So he shut her away, forbidding her betrayal to hurt. Grainger did not fault her, neither did he defend her.

In the same way, Grainger had come to look at Kiley with different eyes. There could be no return to their old friendship. She had cost him the only happiness he had ever known as a boy, his safe haven. She had trampled on his feelings, and Mack's. Even now, a lifetime away from all that happened, the sight of Kiley Harris pained Grainger to the point of physical hurt. His chest felt tight and he realized he was breathing very shallowly as he hid from this woman who had wrecked his life, the same way wreckers had once lured ships onto the rocks to plunder them.

As Grainger nursed his unwanted second beer, he recalled the last summer Kiley had come to Hawke's

Cove. He and Mack had walked to her house to greet her return, excited that their pal was back. On this sweet-smelling late June night, walking along the bluff with a gibbous moon glimmering a path on the calm ocean, Grainger had an odd, almost physical, sense of knowing peace. He was perfectly happy in that moment, and grateful to have recognized it, however transient it might be. Life would never be better. In the fall, Mack and Kiley would head to college and he would be in the Army. But right now he had his best friend by his side, and his other best friend a few moments away.

Sometimes he was glad he'd had that one pure moment of clarity, that he'd recognized it for what it was: an incipient nostalgia that graced every movement that night. This was the last summer of their youth and they knew it. Sometimes he wished it had never happened, that he had never known what such peace felt like; and therefore, would never have longed after it.

Grainger and Mack had paused before going up the steps to the front door of Kiley's house. They looked up at the light coming from Kiley's bedroom window. Music spilled out, too faint to identify more than its relentless disco beat. A shadow crossed the window, and that shadow quickly transformed itself into Kiley, golden in the soft bedroom light, dancing to that barely audible music. Silently, they watched Kiley's private dance. Her arms rose over her head and then fell in graceful arcs as she turned, her dance half ballet and half *Flashdance*. As she passed in front of the lamp, its light shone through her thin nightdress and her silhouette betrayed the marvelous changes the winter had brought to her.

Grainger was grateful for the darkness, which hid the amazement in his eyes. He heard Mack's breath released in a soft whistle. And just like that, everything changed.

• • •

Pilot was getting restless at Grainger's feet. He stood up and shook, then came out from under the table—a forbidden maneuver until beckoned—and looked up at his master as if to say, "Time's up buddy, it's walk time." When Grainger didn't react, he returned to his former position with his chin on Grainger's boots, but not without first heaving a great sigh of disappointment.

Mattie Lou kept coming over and offering Grainger more to drink, a little more dessert? Normally Grainger ate, paid, and left, thirty minutes top to bottom. By now, an hour and a half had gone by. Grainger knew his out-of-character behavior was driving Mattie Lou nuts. She'd had a crush on him since high school. Even though she'd been married twice and had three or four kids, she still loved nothing better than to make flirty remarks that she seemed to reserve just for him.

"Another beer, or are you waiting for something else?" Mattie twitched an eyebrow at him.

"No, thanks. I'm okay." He kept his voice low.

Grainger was waiting out his opponents. It was like a game Mack and he had played as kids: who can stay underwater longest? He felt a little underwater now, watching Kiley and Will. He knew he could go over to their table, perhaps even should. But a simple, "Hi, how've you been in the last eighteen years, and whose kid is this?" wasn't possible. There was too much that would be forever unsaid if they reduced their reunion to a chance encounter in the Osprey's Nest. Any conversation Kiley and he might have would be operatic in proportion.

Ten

The waitress coyly asked if they wanted change of the two twenties Kiley laid down on a thirty-two-dollar tab.

"No, we're fine."

"That's a twenty percent tip, Mom."

"I'm feeling generous."

"Great, can I buy a car?"

"Not that generous. Besides, you won't need one at school."

"I could drive to school, save you having to take me."

"In your dreams, pal." Kiley shuddered at the idea of her child driving alone along the interstate. Falling prey to nut cases lurking in the rest stops who would steal his car, or do worse. She was going to have to get past wanting to protect him. On the other hand, Kiley refused to give in prematurely to the empty-nest syndrome which threatened. She would not think of the inevitable conclusion to this summer, imagine that very soon she'd be coming home to an empty house that would not fill as night drew in, and soccer or baseball or basketball practice was over. She would not give over to the thought that she would end up wandering from room to room in their small home in Southton, wondering where eighteen years had gone. No sports equipment carelessly tossed on the floor in the hallway, no dirty socks hanging improbably from the bedposts. No clutter of abandoned homework.

It was all so temporary—something a young girl couldn't know. Young, unmarried, completely at sea, Kiley had thought that she would always be tired, always be wiping noses and diapering bottoms. What once seemed to take forever was now speeding to its conclusion; one minute Will was a baby, the next standing tall over her and chiding her for leaving too large a tip.

Kiley waited for Will to shrug on his backpack. The tavern door clanged open and a stout man came in, nodding greetings right and left.

"Mattie Lou, my love, how's it goin'?" He dropped into a seat and scanned the room. "Hey, Grainger, you got a boat yet for the August Races?"

Did she imagine that the whole tavern grew quiet, or had the sound of her own breathing suddenly become deafening? Kiley looked to where the stout man's question had been flung. Looking back at her, a stunned and somewhat guilty look on his face, was Grainger Egan. She knew immediately that he'd known all along that she and Will had been in the Osprey's Nest.

"No, Pete. I don't have a boat."

"You'll find one. No problem."

"Doesn't matter." His eyes remained on Kiley, glancing to Will, then back to her. He stood up suddenly, stepping on the dog at his feet. He bent in apology, then straightened.

Kiley felt Will's touch on her bare arm. "Mom?"

"Will, I'd like to introduce someone to you." As if Will were a little boy, Kiley took his hand and strode over to where Grainger remained motionless, one hand on his dog's collar.

"Will, this is Grainger Egan. We knew each other as children." Kiley gripped Will's fingers as if afraid he'd bolt. "Grainger, this is Will Harris. My son."

Will shook Grainger's hand, but didn't speak.

Grainger held Will's hand longer than Kiley thought necessary. "Pleased to meet you, Will."

Did she imagine Grainger's voice was vaguely stagy, or was he as emotionally flummoxed as she was at this unexpected meeting? She swallowed hard, absolutely no words coming to mind that she could speak to this man who had lived forever in her mind as a boy. Then, she remembered. *"Random* is in your yard. My father wants to sell her."

"The house and the boat. I'm sorry to hear that." Grainger smiled a little, as if surprised he could speak so easily. "Call me, we'll talk about it."

Kiley took a little comfort with finding a safe topic. "All right. I will. Good night, then." Kiley turned away from Grainger, Will on her heels, loping to catch up with her.

There had been long stretches when Kiley hadn't given her past much thought. There was Will to nurture, school, then work. Friends, new memories of Christmases and vacations. She had packed her life full, wanting never to succumb to living in the past.

She'd even almost gotten married. A nice man, Ronald, who'd been smitten with her. He was quite a bit older, divorced with two teenagers, while she had a toddler, yet more than willing to be a father to Will.

Ultimately she'd gently turned him down, for she just hadn't loved him.

Maybe if Ronald had come into her life in her thirties instead of her twenties, she might have accepted him. She had been young enough still to want passion. She needed to believe that she had refused Ronald against his own merits, not because of some adolescent belief that marriage needed to be built on passion; not because of some ill-founded hope that someday she would be able to resolve the anger and grief of her past. Not once had she ever hoped that she and Grainger would meet and forgive.

Tonight she had seen the man Grainger had become, and, just for a moment, tasted of that impossible hope.

Their walk along the waterfront to the car was in complete silence. Will behaved as if the chance meeting was of no consequence, barely of interest. Kiley's breath was still hollow in her ears, her heart still beating its excited tattoo. *What else could she have said? What else should she have said?* Her circling thoughts taunted her, and Kiley was glad Will had said nothing, except to ask if Grainger was the boy in the photo.

"Yeah, he is."

Will hadn't said another word, just slipped the earphones up over his ears and listened to one of his new CDs. Kiley was grateful for the reprieve, at the same time wondering why he was so little interested.

The warm evening air felt good after the air-conditioning, and the fresh breeze off the water helped clean the scent of cigarette smoke off their clothes and out of their hair. The fading sky was starless as yet, the air damp. Kiley could hear the raspy sound of music leaking from Will's earphones. Music filling his head, sometimes with words and opinions she was uncomfortable with. Her music had offended her parents too, especially Michael Jackson, with his crotch-palming dancing. Every Saturday afternoon she'd watched a disco contest television show, later attempting the choreographed gymnastics in her bedroom. For years she'd taken ballet, but disco had seduced her for a time. All artfully ripped sweatshirts and leg warmers.

Walking down the street with her son plugged into a hip-hop CD, Kiley wondered if anything ever really changed. Every generation had its style: jive, swing, acid rock, disco, break dancing, hip-hop. Generations of parents appalled, crying out, *What will become of these kids!*

Of course, the boys had mocked her passion for disco. Mack would strike the famous John Travolta pose from *Saturday Night Fever*. "How's this, Kiley?"

"You're an idiot." She'd laugh, and do a few moves she'd learned from that television show. *Flashdance* remained her favorite movie, and she secretly imagined herself leaping effortlessly through the air into a roll, and then spinning, just to show the boys up. Just to amaze them.

Then Grainger or Mack would go after her carefully arranged hair. Boy, how they hated that stiff fringe look. They'd take every opportunity to get her wet, either by tossing her into the harbor, or spraying her with a hose. By the end of the first week, she'd given it up, letting her hair relax into its natural straight curtain, held back by a barrette or french braided.

Little flashes of memory like that had sustained her for years, forever young, forever happy. Kiley shivered in the fresh breeze redolent of low water. Why was it that every memory came with a shadow memory? Like overlays on an overhead projector, every slide adding more to the whole picture. The sea air against her chilled skin felt exactly as it had long ago. In the harbor, boats bobbed at their moorings, halyards chiming against aluminum masts. Offshore, the running lights of a sailboat drew closer to the harbor, and the picture that began to build was that of their last summer. The summer of the boat, of *Blithe Spirit*. The summer they were eighteen.

Mack bought the boat. A thirteen-foot Beetle Cat, mastless, missing her centerboard, coated in barnacles and algae, and, most disheartening of all, with a six-inch round hole punched in her starboard side. The hole was above the waterline, but was still a complicated addition to the list of tasks to get her seaworthy.

"Okay, so she's a project. No big deal, we have all summer." Mack was mildly defensive as Grainger and Kiley stood speechless, looking at the "surprise" he had promised them. The small sailboat was on blocks in Mack's backyard. "I want to get her in the water in time for the August Races."

"You'll be lucky to get her in in time for Labor Day." Kiley shoved her hands into the pockets of her shorts. "Not to rain on your parade or anything."

Grainger walked all around the boat, touching the rough surface of her barnacle-encrusted hull, sticking his fingers into the hole. "No, I think we can do it. It won't be easy, but it'll be fun."

"Good thing it's going to be fun, because this is going to cost a fortune to rehab." Mack leaned against the hull. "Lucky I got her for almost nothing."

"Oh, I thought the guy paid you to take her." Kiley poked a teasing finger into Mack's side.

"Funny, Blithe." Mack took her poking finger and made her poke herself.

"Well, it's worth a try. After all, there are money prizes for the August Races." Kiley saw the look of delight on Mack's face as his best friends validated his dream. "She might pay for herself."

"Hey, we'll scrounge. I know people at the boatyard." Grainger's job as youth sailing instructor often involved errand running for the Yacht Club members.

"Yeah, and my dad has lots of stuff. I'll bet he has a hundred gallons of leftover marine paint in the cellar." Released from Mack's grip, Kiley did a backflip on the spikey grass of Mack's backyard. "So, what are you going to name her?"

Mack reached over and plucked a blade of grass out of Kiley's hair. "I'm naming her for you."

"Me?"

"Blithe Spirit."

Kiley blushed with pleasure at the odd compliment. She laughed, then landed another perfect flip. Could life get any sweeter?

She had never heard the adage it was bad luck to change a boat's name.

Eleven

꙰

Will was awake before his alarm went off. Crows were making a ruckus in the big oak trees that bordered the backyard. The thin sound of light rain sizzled on the roof, plainly audible in the second-floor bedroom. Nothing lay between Will and the sky but a plank wood ceiling and asphalt roof shingles. He rolled back over, feeling something like relief that matters had been taken out of his hands. His mother still didn't know about the sailing lessons. When neither he nor Grainger said anything about having met before, it seemed too weird to suddenly confess that they had. He'd made up some story about wanting to begin running before school started, hinting at maybe joining the cross-country team, to cover his out-of-character early rising.

Lying there, resuming the troubling thoughts from his hours of sleeplessness, Will felt a mocking cowardice. Did he have the *cojones* to confront his origins? Once known, the facts of his conception might end up plaguing him more than his ignorance of them. Maybe he should just trust his mother's judgment in keeping these facts from him. Maybe he really was better off *not* knowing anything about how he had come to be.

With this weather, he could roll over and go back to sleep, and leave the sleeping dogs to lie. He opened his eyes again. Grainger hadn't said if these lessons were weather dependent. He'd better plan to go. He really didn't want to piss Grainger off first thing, asssuming the lessons continued. What was a little rain to a sailor? Anyway, it would probably quit in an hour.

He heard his mother's alarm go off and waited for her knock on his door. When nothing happened, Will assumed that she must have heard the rain too, and decided he'd abandon his running till later. He swung his feet to the floor and yanked open a drawer to pull out his bathing suit and a clean T-shirt. He was surprised to find that he was shaking a little with a blend of excitement and dread. Sort of like the first day of school.

Tiptoeing down the back stairs to the kitchen, he hoped that his mother would stay in bed. She seemed so tired lately. She wouldn't talk about it, but Will knew that readying the house for sale was emotionally hard on her. Little objects kept showing up on the kitchen table as if she had been sitting there examining them, weighing their significance, debating whether to keep them or let them go with the house. Did they have enough weight to be added to the growing collection of the Museum-in-the-Making? Or were they unimportant and destined to remain in the house for the new owners? This morning, a blue glass jar sat dead center on the small drop-leaf kitchen table. An ordinary, if authentically antique, jar that once held some salve or ointment. Why his mother had left it here, Will couldn't imagine. It was too wide in the mouth to make a successful vase, and the big chip on the lip spoiled it for antique value. He slid the object to the other side of the table and poured a bowl of cereal.

Will still hadn't told his mother about breaking up with Lori. With her, you just had to find the right time. Last night, she'd suddenly remembered that she'd picked up a letter from Lori for him. She had always been respectful of his privacy, requisite parental advice about protection and/or abstinence notwithstanding, and didn't ask him about the letter. He had taken it from her hand without looking at her. One glance in his mother's eyes and he'd have been pinned to the wall like a butterfly on cork, while she elicited the whole sorry story out of him. He'd stuffed it into one of the capacious pockets of his cargo pants and muttered something about reading it later.

The truth was, he just wasn't ready to tell her about Lori. Even though he was still hurting from Lori's dismissal, a residual defensiveness came up when he imagined his mother's satisfied statement: "Well, I never liked her anyway . . ." He just didn't want to hear it. He'd dropped Lori's letter onto his bureau without reading it.

Will did a few stretches on the front porch. The rain was like a beaded curtain sluicing off the porch roof, each drop a fat individual. Maybe he should just call Grainger and cancel.

"Rain before seven, clear by eleven. It'll probably stop by noon. Why don't you wait till then?" Kiley opened the screen door and came out, her arms crossed against the damp air. "I'll make French toast."

"It won't kill me, and if I don't do it now, I won't do it." Will wished suddenly that he could admit to what he was really doing. He needed confirmation that Grainger had once been a good friend. No, he needed evidence that Grainger was *more* than a friend. He hadn't been blind to the tension between the two of them in the tavern, like adversaries on neutral ground. Will bent to retie his running shoe. "Maybe I can outrun the rain."

"I'll have the water hot for tea when you get back."

"Thanks, but you should go back to bed."

"Can't. The real estate agent is coming by early."

Will stood up and impulsively bent to peck her cheek. "It'll be all right."

"I know." His mother turned away as she sighed. "I know."

Will leapt off the porch without touching the steps and set off at a mild jog.

The rain thickened as Will jogged down the hill toward the village. Still early, only minimal traffic moved past him, twice dousing him with tire splatter. As he jogged along the beach road, Will contemplated a quick dip to clean off the dirt, but it was taking him much longer to get to Egan's Boat Works than he had expected. Despite all the wind sprints and miles run for sports training, Will had never been an effective runner. He knew he pumped too hard and breathed too deeply, failed to pace himself adequately. Never once had he found the magic high so many of the track team members had told him about. He'd rather feel the hard smack of a baseball against the sweet spot of his bat than get a runner's high. Finally his lungs demanded he ease up, and Will settled into a jog barely better than a walk. No point in arriving on Grainger's doorstep and collapsing. Will smiled at the image of himself falling into Grainger's arms, with his last breath asking the unaskable question: *Dad?* The smile ran from his face. A photograph was hardly proof of paternity, a stilted introduction, no evidence. With sudden clarity, Will realized that it was only his mother he could ask that question, pointing to the last photograph: *Is this guy my father, or this one?* He should just turn around and go back and . . . what? Forget this whole stupid idea?

It was too late, he was nearly there. The peninsula of Hawke's Cove, its shape likened to Jimmy Durante's nose by some, was scalloped by inlets and smaller coves, some edged by houses, others like this one, mostly private. Grainger's boatyard was on the inside of Maiden Cove, a good-sized deepwater cove with easy access to the main road. A sign declaring "Egan's Boat Works" pointed down a gravel driveway, and Will walked the remaining distance to the boathouse.

Unaccountably, he walked a little ways past it toward the beach, looking at the cove beyond. A pier jutted out, with a wooden rowboat tied to it. A small sailboat swung at anchor a few yards offshore, and three or four larger craft were moored farther out. In the rain and wind, they all pointed southwest, the same as the weathervane atop the boathouse. A rubber dinghy was bottom up on the sand, a line running from under it to a granite block high on the beach with an iron ring hammered into it like a hitching post. Three big boats in varying stages of repair loomed in the yard. At a distance, Will could see a fourth boat, its small hull shrouded by yards of blue plastic sheeting, the cords tying it down green with age.

Visibility across the cove was nil, the opposite shore obscured, the narrow enfolding arms of the cove rendered invisible, the only sound that of the surf booming on the ocean side of the barrier beach. Will heard the

chime of a clock and glanced at his watch. Seven-thirty.
He went back to the side door and knocked.

It was nearly a minute before Grainger pulled open
the heavy door. He looked at Will with a vague surprise on his face, as if he'd doubted Will would show
up. Or maybe he hoped he wouldn't. "You've come."

"Yes."

"Well, come in, get out of the rain." Grainger disappeared for a moment and came back into the room
with a heavy cotton towel. "Dry yourself."

Will rubbed the white towel over his head, then
down the length of his dripping body. He wrapped it
around his waist and stepped out of his soaked sneakers. Most of the room was taken up with a large vessel,
its bowsprit almost touching the plank sliding door, its
stern close by the open sliding door of the opposite end
of the building.

Overhead was a loft, from the bottom of which
hung ropes on hooks neatly coiled in figure eights. Half
a dozen pairs of oars of varying lengths stood sentinel
against the walls between timbers and wooden blocks
and pulleys; mooring flags and glass floats made up the
remainder of the artwork on the walls.

In one corner was a woodstove, in front of it a soft
easy chair, a small coffee table stacked with magazines
featuring boats on their covers, and a thirteen-inch television set on a painted bureau. In the opposite corner, a
stove and refrigerator were separated from the rest of
the room by an island counter.

Will smelled a tantalizing mixture of pungent oil,
fresh sawdust, and coffee. A faintly fumy undertone
lingered like a taste behind the more pleasant odors of
the boatbuilder's trade. He saw the protective goggles
and masks hanging over a workbench, the hand and

power tools neatly stowed on hooks or in cubbies along the length of the massive workbench. A vise attached to one corner was gripping together two pieces of wood.

"You live here?"

"Yeah, I do."

Grainger's wirey haired dog eased himself out from under the workbench.

"What's his name?" Will bent to pet the dog sniffing him with deliberateness.

"Pilot."

"What is he?"

"A dog of uncertain parentage. His mother was a purebred springer spaniel, his father a complete mystery."

Will looked at Grainger to see if he was taunting him. He rubbed the towel over his hair once more, then handed it back to Grainger. Pilot left off his sniffing and wandered to his water bowl, where he lapped with sloppy abandon.

"Why didn't you drive here?" Grainger tossed the wet towel across a wooden dowel. "Or just call and cancel?"

"I want to start running, maybe do cross-country in college." If he repeated it often enough, it would be the truth. "And I didn't want to cancel either. I wasn't sure how you'd take that. I mean, given . . ."

"The circumstance of our meeting?"

"I thought you wouldn't think I was serious if I canceled just because it was raining. Besides, it'll stop."

"Not today." Grainger walked over to a bookshelf tucked beneath the wide ship's ladder leading to the loft. "Hands-on work doesn't make sense, so, here." Grainger handed Will two books; one an illustrated book on sailboats, the other a brief guide to learning how to sail. "Read those and come back and we'll apply what you've learned." Grainger pointed to the small sailboat framed by the wide-open rear doors of the boathouse. "That will be your craft."

"What kind of boat is it?"

"Beetle Cat."

"Is it a good boat to learn in?"

Grainger shrugged. "It's a good one for beginners." He grasped the handle of the big door and drew it closed, blocking Will's view of the cove.

Will bent to put his sneakers back on, the books on the floor beside him. The insides of his running shoes were sodden and unpleasant. He'd only brought the one pair of shoes with him, and he'd have to spend the day in flip-flops.

Grainger handed Will a plastic grocery bag to put the two books in. "Why don't I drive you home?" He pulled on a yellow slicker. Pilot met them at the door, his front feet pumping up and down with anticipation of an outing.

"You don't have to. I'll be fine."

"I'm worried about my books."

"Oh. Okay." Will stood up and patted Pilot's head. "He's happy."

"Yeah, he's always happy."

They ran out to Grainger's truck, Pilot leading the way.

"I live on the other side of the town. Almost to . . ."

"I know where your house is." Grainger slammed the truck door and twisted the ignition.

"So, where's my grandfather's boat?"

"That one." Grainger pointed through the foggy window to a wooden hull, lifted high in a cradle.

"Wow. She's a lot bigger than I thought."

"They always look bigger out of water." Grainger

backed out of the parking space and turned up the driveway. Then he put the truck back in park. "Why didn't your mother ever come back?" Grainger's voice was nearly a sliver, as if he'd spoken the question out loud accidentally.

Will shrugged, shifting away from the weight of the dog that leaned against him as if he were an old friend. "I really don't know. It has something to do with . . ." *With who my father was. Who you might be to me.* ". . . a family thing."

Grainger made a sound like a humph, or stifled pain, then put the truck in drive. They continued the journey in silence, with only the sound of the beating windshield wipers and Pilot's occasional whine as they passed other dogs.

As Grainger turned left onto Seaview Avenue, Will wondered if maybe this was one of those windows of opportunity, and he pushed the words out of his mouth. "You and my mother were friends, right?" One hand was on the armrest of the truck's door, clutching it as if they were careening around.

"Yeah."

If Will had hoped for elaboration, he was disappointed. "How come you didn't say anything to her that night, about our having met?"

"Don't know. Probably for the same reason you didn't."

"It was just awkward."

"So you haven't told her about your lessons?"

"Not yet."

Grainger kept silent the remainder of the drive, and Will could think of nothing else to say.

When they got as far as the Yacht Club, Grainger

pulled into the parking lot. "You can manage the rest of the way, I'm sure."

Will climbed down from the truck, tucked the plastic bag under his arm, and came around to stand beside the driver's side. "Thanks for the ride, Mr. Egan."

"Come back Friday. The weather's due to clear out late tonight, and it's predicted to be clear with light wind. We'll put what you learn between now and then into practice." Grainger put the truck into reverse. "And, Will . . ."

"Yes?"

"Tell your mother."

"Tell her what?" For a moment, Will thought Grainger meant to give him a message to take to his mother.

"Tell her about the lessons." Grainger backed away and then pulled onto the main road with a crunch of gravel.

Will stood gripping the bag of books, staring after the truck, Pilot's muzzle poking out of the open rear window. Somehow, this laconic man didn't seem like the sort of guy his mother would have had as a boyfriend. Her dates were almost always pale, balding, slightly rumpled businessmen, medical salesmen mostly. She called them "nice chaps." They talked a lot, about work, or sports, or politics. His mother said she liked them because she didn't have to work hard at these dates. "Just wind them up and off they go, yapping away about themselves, and I don't have to do a thing. They go away thinking they've had a great time, and I get a nice meal and a little adult companionship." She'd laughed when she said this to a friend over coffee, unaware of Will's eavesdropping. "It's a good thing

I'm not interested in a long-term relationship; I don't have the energy to work hard at these things." Will had been too young to understand that he was the reason she had little desire to pursue a relationship.

Now he was older and ready to leave, and he wondered what she would do without him. Would she, finally, have the energy?

Will walked along the bluff road. The rain came down in a steady drizzle, but the air had warmed enough to make it almost pleasant and the visibility had improved. Below the bluff, a motorboat ground its way toward the harbor. On the horizon he could pick out two boats heading out to the fishing grounds. It wouldn't become a beach day, but that was all right. He'd spend the rest of the day on the porch reading these books. He'd go back on Friday and surprise Grainger with his studiousness. After all, he'd had plenty of practice pleasing teachers. And, above all, Will wanted to please Grainger Egan.

Twelve

🐌

After Will had gone out on his soggy run, Kiley lingered on the porch, her arms folded against the damp morning air. She couldn't shake the image of Will jumping off the top step, exactly as Grainger and Mack had time and again. The rain began to sheet down hard, and Kiley went back into the house. Gray morning light softened the bright primary colors of the kitchen; the yellow walls and the wooden floor, painted long ago in big blue and red squares, faded to muted tones in the dim light. Kiley flicked on the overhead light and poured water into the coffeemaker.

The little blue jar had been pushed to one side of the oval table, and she pulled it back into the center. Imagine that jar still sitting on the shelf in the pantry all these years. With its deeply chipped lip and general uselessness, why hadn't anyone tossed it? It must have been saved simply out of the inertia of a familiar sight. No one could possibly know its significance to her.

"These are for you." Mack held a little blue jar with a bunch of field daisies crammed into its wide mouth.

The stems had been clipped very short and the effect was of a bursting white-and-yellow corsage.

She'd been sitting on the porch rail, waiting for the boys. Mack arrived first, handing her the improvised bouquet as he might have handed her a book or a half of his sandwich. *These are for you.* Slightly gruff, self-conscious. Kiley took the jar and sniffed the daisies for scent, as if the bouquet had been long-stemmed roses. "Thanks." Had he meant this as a joke? Should she take this seriously? She went for the slightly amused. "So, what's up with this?"

"Nothing. Just the field on Bailey's Farm Road was filled with them. I thought that you might like them." His voice was half muffled by a faked yawn. "You being a girl and all."

"Right." The comfort level righted itself like a gim-balled lantern on a boat.

They sat on the rail, the blue jar of flowers between them, waiting for Grainger to arrive from his morning at the Yacht Club.

"Don't say anything to Grainger. Okay? He'll bug me about it."

"Okay." The comfort level tilted a degree. Kiley was glad that the flowers were between them, acting as a nominal barrier. If she had moved it, and put out her hand, Kiley knew that everything would change. Neither spoke, feigning an interest in the horizon. Grainger came up behind them, startling them both.

One of them—Kiley was unsure if it was Mack or herself—knocked the little jar of daisies off the porch rail and onto the stones; a piece of the lip broke off and the water drained out onto the ground.

• • •

Kiley now ran a forefinger gently along the broken edge of the blue jar. As usual, her finger was ragged with hangnails and she self-consciously nibbled at the skin. Some women cherished their hands, coddling them with weekly manicures and rubber gloves. It seemed the height of vanity to Kiley; she preferred to clip her nails short and use whatever hand lotion was on sale.

She picked up the blue jar and carried it to the growing collection of sentimental items. Toby Reynolds was due to stop by early this morning to see how she was doing, probably to hurry the process along. All he saw was the fat commission this place would provide him. All he knew was the rarity of such a place being on the market. As if conjured by her thoughts, his Lexus crunched the oyster shells in the driveway, proclaiming his arrival.

She hadn't met Toby face-to-face yet, and unfairly imagined a powder blue leisure suit on an overweight, slightly sweaty man with a toupee. Of course, Toby was none of these things. Tall, slim, impeccably dressed in Hawke's Cove casual garb of pleated Dockers and a polo shirt, Toby extended a smooth, dry, manicured, and ringless hand to Kiley. Instantly, she felt underdressed in the cutoffs and yesterday's T-shirt she'd thrown on to send Will off.

"Ms. Harris, a pleasure to finally meet you."

"Kiley, please. Come in. What a miserable day." Was she speaking of the weather, which still pissed down with no sign of letting up, or the fact that Toby was here to relentlessly discuss this process of selling the house? "Where should we start?"

"Oh, I've already looked around. Your mother sent me a key."

Partially relieved not to have to take this stranger on a sentimental journey, at the same time, she was annoyed with her mother for having allowed the invasion. "Okay. Well then, let's go into the kitchen. I've got a pot of coffee on."

"None for me, thanks."

While Toby highlighted some of his concerns about the house, Kiley poured herself a cup, taking her time adding sugar and milk, glad to have her back to him for a minute.

"The roof might or might not be a problem. It's conceivable that, given the value of the house, buyers won't blink at having to reroof. In fact, it's possible that they'll pop the roof off and create a third floor with a widow's walk. Lots of buyers look at these places as footprints: they're ready, willing, and rich enough to renovate or even dismantle to create the perfect house with the perfect view."

"Dismantle? You mean tear it down?" As she set it down, a little coffee from Kiley's mug sloshed onto the bare wood table. She grabbed a paper towel. "What are you talking about?"

"Now, I'm not saying that anyone would do that; I'm just saying it's being done all over the place."

"And I'm saying that I will not sell to anyone with that idea in mind." Kiley sat down.

"You could be restricting a really good offer."

"Do you have such an offer on the table?"

Toby shook his head. "No. But it could happen. You should be aware of it."

"Then why the hell am I going through all this . . ." She flailed a hand around to catch the word. ". . . all this effort if, in the end, everything ends up hauled away to the landfill?"

"Look, Kiley, I'm only suggesting that someone might be more interested in the location than the building."

"Isn't this house in the historic district?"

Toby's ruddy skin deepened in color. "No. The historic district ends at Seaview Avenue. Incorporating the houses on the bluff is still in the planning stages; so far no one has gotten the paperwork together. Which is another good thing for you. Purchasers can, within reason, do whatever they want, without that layer of interference."

"Toby." Kiley reached out to touch Toby's lightly furred arm, to secure his full attention. "Promise me you won't sell to anyone with plans to change it."

"I can't do that. If that's what you want, you'll have to find another agent." Toby didn't move his arm from under Kiley's hand.

"Maybe I will." Kiley removed her hand, letting it drop to her lap.

Toby stood up; his chair scraped against the wood floor. "Tell me something, Kiley. If you haven't been in this house in umpteen years and have no interest in being here, why do you care what happens to it?"

Kiley got up and stepped to the back door, pressing her hand against it. "Because I love it." She held the door open as if letting out a cat.

"You're talking about sentiment, which isn't a practical consideration in these things. It only stands in the way of progress." Toby hesitated on the back steps. "Think of your son. The more money we can get for this place, the better off he'll be."

"What makes you say that?"

"Your mother told me why she's selling. That's a very fine use of the investment quality of real estate, good planning. Using the money to put your son through college."

"My mother had no business telling you that."

"I make it my business to know why people want to sell. It helps me help them."

"Altruistically, I'm sure."

"No. It's my living." Toby strode to his car and yanked open the door, then turned back to face Kiley. "Think about what we've talked about. Don't do anything yet. Call me."

If it hadn't been a light screen door, the slam would have been much more satisfying.

The phone ringing from the front room exacerbated Kiley's annoyance and she wished that she'd brought the answering machine from home. Maybe she'd just let the stupid thing ring. But the momentary irritation fell away as she realized that only her parents would call her here; and, right now, this minute, she had to convince them to change agents.

"Kiley? Kiley Harris? This is Emily Fitzgibbons, née Claridge. Do you remember me?"

Oh, yes, Kiley remembered Emily Claridge, and her twin sister, Missy. "Oh, Emily. Of course I do."

Kiley had stood on her porch, chewing her lips in grumpy disappointment. Mack and Grainger were heading over to Great Harbor to see about a mast, and she was stuck having lunch with the Claridge sisters. Missy and Emily. Mrs. Claridge was her mother's best friend in Hawke's Cove. The two families often did things together, but the girls had grown up without becoming friends. Her mother wouldn't hear of her bowing out of the planned luncheon.

In an allusion to their twindom, Missy and Emily,

always in that order, were referred to as the "Double-mints" behind their backs. When they were little, their mother always dressed them the same, a habit that had continued to their teens, as if they felt a certain safety in keeping the outside world confused as to their individual identities.

The Claridge twins never needed anyone else. They were each other's perfect companions, and anyone else was extraneous. The three girls were polite to one another, played nicely together when their parents played bridge, but they had never shared a meaningful conversation any more than they shared their toys.

For years Kiley had been forced into these little "girls" luncheons, her mother insistent that she have proper girlfriends in Hawke's Cove. Yet, in the same way that the Doublemints hadn't needed anyone else, Kiley hadn't needed them. She had her boys.

Today as they worked on *Blithe Spirit*'s hull, Kiley had complained to Mack and Grainger over the sound of the electic sanders. "I'm being forced to have lunch with the Doublemints."

"That's the price you have to pay, Blithe, for being so popular among your own kind."

"Shut up, Mack."

"Make me."

They were making such good progress on the boat that Kiley was loath to give up even an hour of work. They'd cleaned the barnacles and algae off the hull, and were nearly done with the sanding. After much debate, the boys had decided to patch the hole with fiberglass. The best way would be to replace the boards, but they didn't have the expertise to do that job. After that repair was made, they'd start painting and varnishing and polishing the brightwork.

The boys dropped her off at her home on their way to Great Harbor to look at the mast. Kiley waved good-bye, looking as if she were going to her own execution.

Lydia was standing in the doorway. "Do you want me to drive you?"

"No. I'll walk."

"You can clean up and put on something more re-spectable than those." Her mother's gesture toward her paint-dust covered cutoffs was eloquent in its disapproval.

Once changed into bermuda shorts and crisp white blouse, Kiley went out by the back door, avoiding her mother on the phone with her father back in Southton. This would be a quick visit; sandwiches, a glass of lemonade, two cookies, and off to snag another half hour with the sander before her tennis lesson at three.

The bluff road ran behind the Claridges' house, so the view from it was undistracted by traffic. Today the sky and the sea matched in faded blue. Like so many of the Hawke's Cove summerhouses, this one was named: *Sans Souci,* "without care." Missy and Emily were slouched on the white Adirondack chairs set up on the lawn, still in their tennis dresses, racquets propped against the sides of their chairs, reminding Kiley of Ralph Lauren's advertisements in the *New York Times Magazine.* Poster girls for the preppy look. Seeing Kiley come through the garden gate set in the carefully trimmed privet hedge, the pair waved her over.

Around egg salad sandwiches, the chat was gossipy and centered on their own interests. They'd had a great doubles game this morning, creaming the Eastlakes. Did you hear that our father was going to buy a new boat, a thirty-six-foot yawl this time? Custom-made. The old boat wasn't nearly as fast as this new one will be. Daddy was going to christen it, can you stand it,

Miss Emily, a pun on our names. Missy and Emily took turns speaking, like actors in a play. First one let it drop that they were both heading for Wellesley. Then the other described the difficulty in choosing between Wellesley and Vassar. Once they'd entertained each other with the tale of their heroic debate, one finally asked Kiley where she was going in the fall.

"Smith. A foregone conclusion in my family." Her mother was a Smithie, and her mother before her. But it suited Kiley, partly because of the family tradition, partly because she liked the college's emphasis on nurturing strong women. She might major in art, or maybe philosophy. Everyone she knew who went off to college inevitably changed majors, so she'd wait to see what was out there before declaring her intentions to the world.

"We were accepted there."

A vaguely dismissive gesture from the other. "We wanted to be closer to a major city."

"So, where are your two friends going?"

The question surprised Kiley. Generally Mack and Grainger were not a topic for this pair. Of course they knew them from a distance, Mack as a newcomer to the club, and Grainger a familiar face from the kiddies' sailing school; but until now they'd never shown any interest in them, any more than they took an interest in any of the other year-rounders of the Cove.

Kiley took a bite of sandwich before replying. "Mack's going to the University of Rhode Island." Her tone was light, pleased a little that they were interested. Still, she felt an unreasoning need to defend Mack's choice of a state university. "He's going to major in marine biology and that's the best school for it."

"What about the other one? Heathcliff."

Kiley set down her half-eaten sandwich. "You mean Grainger?" Her tone remained light, but her defenses were engaged. *Heathcliff?* Bitch. "He's going into the Army first. He'll be attending college while he's in."

"Hmmm. He's cute in a rough sort of way. Mack is cute in a more Andover sort of way."

"I guess. I hadn't thought about it."

"So, Kiley, which one do you date?"

"Neither. We're just friends." An unpleasant heat touched her cheeks. What a ludicrous idea.

"So if you don't care, then maybe you'd introduce us at the next Y.C. dance?"

"Sure. I guess." Kiley looked from one twin to the other, trying to see if, behind their matching Ray-Bans, they were winking at each other. A wave of suspicion washed through her, countered immediately by self-doubt. Why wouldn't Missy and Emily want to meet her friends? Like the twins said, they were cute. She had no romantic claim on them. Yet there was something out of kilter here. The Claridge twins were the products of prep schools and privilege. They consorted with her only because her family had been in the Yacht Club since 1935. *Their* parents allowed that *her* parents were acceptable because her father was a successful litigator in an affluent community, and her mother came from good stock, second-tier Boston Brahmin. Kiley herself had the right physical attributes of good skin, straight teeth, and a powerhouse backhand.

Slumming. Wasn't that the word for what the Claridge twins were suggesting? No, there was nothing wrong with Grainger, nothing rude or crude about him, or risky. In the strange social hierarchy of the clubbier summer folk, those who made Hawke's Cove their home year round were viewed as lesser souls.

Because of their own "summer people" origins, the MacKenzies were tolerated, particularly because of Dr. MacKenzie's professional status. But Grainger, as she well knew from her mother's remarks, was beneath regard. She'd known girls at school who liked to date the rough boys, to flout convention and strike fear in parental souls by running with the dangerous ones.

She was surprised to see avidity on their matching faces. Something just this side of it. Curiosity?

Kiley forced the wave of discomfort to settle. She was being an idiot. After all, the club was overrun with young women; boys were at a premium. It didn't mean anything, yet she had the overwhelming feeling that she didn't *want* to share her friends with the likes of the twins.

Of course, Mack and Grainger would be falling down with laughter at the idea that the Doublemints wanted to date them. They'd all have a good laugh.

"I'll give them your number." Kiley swallowed the last of her lemonade, then made a show of looking at her watch. "I've got a tennis lesson in a little while, so thanks for lunch. See you at the club."

"Will you be there Friday? The dance?" The Doublemints were standing up, twinning the same stance.

"Yeah. I guess so." Kiley felt horribly monosyllabic.

"Are they coming?"

Kiley could see the italicized word *they* as if printed in front of her.

"I don't know. Maybe. I'm not their keeper."

Deliberately, Kiley turned left at the gate and headed back to the MacKenzie house. She wanted to laugh: how could they assume that she was dating either of them? The idea should have been ridiculous, but like a mischievous imp licking at the back of her subconscious, it took on a life of its own. Kiley couldn't imagine what profound alterations her relationship with the boys would have to undergo to enable that to happen. Having no siblings, she believed that Mack and Grainger filled some of that lack in her life, as fond cousins might.

Kiley stumbled a little on a rough spot in the pavement. Catching herself, she thought suddenly of Mack's blue jar full of daisies and her sense that day of things being suddenly off balance. As if walking through cobwebs, Kiley rubbed her hands down her arms as though to brush away the unwelcome thought. Dating would change everything. The easy camaraderie would become overladen with the things a romantic relationship required, demands and expectations that their simple friendship avoided. Surely they never thought of her that way.

And how could she ever choose between them?

She pushed open the gate into Mack's backyard. The boys weren't back yet from Great Harbor. Not satisfied yet, the imp brought up the memory of that anonymous hand touching her bikini-clad breast that Friday night. Surely it was accidental. It was inconceivable that either one would want to "cop a feel" of her breasts. It just couldn't be that they might see her as a "girl." Nor would she ever look at them romantically. Kiley, mindless of her white blouse, picked up the palm sander.

Let the Doublemints have at it, then. Yet a swift surge of jealousy surprised her. She saw herself standing outside while the four of them held hands, a fifth wheel. How could she bear to share them this last summer together?

Emily Claridge's voice brought Kiley back to the moment. "I was calling to remind you about the Fourth of July Picnic. Can you believe it? Some things never change, and the picnic is still going on after all these years." Emily chatted away, mercifully giving Kiley time to gather her thoughts. "Anyway, we're hoping you'll bring the famous Harris potato salad."

"I hadn't planned on . . . well, sure. Of course I will. Enough for how many?"

"We're asking everyone to bring for twelve."

"Great. No problem."

"So, how've you been?"

Kiley had no idea how to answer that question. "Good, fine. You?"

"Oh, there's my call-waiting. I'll catch up with you at the picnic. Same place, same time. Maybe you'll come for cocktails beforehand?" Emily's voice disappeared, leaving a soft hum on the line.

Kiley raised her eyes heavenward in thanksgiving for call-waiting.

Almost as soon as she stepped away from the phone, it rang again. Surely this time it was Mother.

"Kiley, I'm so glad I caught you." Not her mother, but Sandy from the office.

"Sandy, what's the matter?"

"Oh, God, Kiley, it's the doctor." Sandy's voice was muffled as she blew her nose. "Doc John is dead."

Kiley sat down in the small chair beside the phone table. *"What?"* Disbelief thinned her voice. Dr. John Finnergan, Doc John to them all, was only in his early sixties, fit, healthy and vital; surely he couldn't have dropped dead. "What happened?"

"He was on his way home from the hospital last night. When . . ." Sandy paused again to gather herself. "When his car was hit by a guy running a red light."

"Dear God." Kiley struggled to speak against the lump in her throat. "I'll come right home."

"No, don't. There's no need to disrupt your plans. His wife says there won't be a funeral, just a memorial service later. But you should know . . ." Sandy began to cry in earnest. ". . . we're closing the office. For good."

"On whose say-so?"

"It was in his papers. That if anything happened to him, Dr. Ruiz was to take over his patients."

Elmer Ruiz, principal in the family practice located in their building. The practice was fully staffed, and would have no need for a receptionist or additional nurses. Or a nurse practitioner. Kiley bit back the thought. "Sandy, it'll be all right. Don't panic. I'll come home and talk to Dr. Ruiz."

"Don't, Kiley. Don't change all your plans. It won't do any good."

"I'll call him anyway." Certainly there was something she could do. A long time ago, someone had warned her about working for a single doc, instead of a partnership that would endure anyone's departure. It just didn't seem possible that Doc John hadn't included them in his contingency plans. She and Sandy had been with him for over ten years, and his nurse, Fiona, had been with him nearly as long. "Sandy, we'll talk tomorrow, okay? Just don't worry."

"Okay, Kiley. I'll call you tomorrow."

After the knee-weakening shock passed, it leveled into grief. John was a good man, a wonderfully compassionate doctor, and she would miss him. It was so unfair.

After a few minutes, Kiley dialed Mrs. Finnergan's number.

Thirteen

Grainger drove away from the Yacht Club and Will as fast as he could. He didn't want to know if Will was entertaining any notion that he might be his father. It was obvious that the boy had some inkling that his mother and Grainger knew each other a lot better than a curt "yeah" revealed. Will's open-eyed examination of Grainger's face unnerved him. Grainger found only Kiley's face in Will's—not his, not Mack's. And yet, he kept looking.

Pilot fidgeted on the seat, turning to look at Grainger, then pointing his blunt nose at the window, as if to tell him he was being cheated of a walk. The spaniel part of him relished the rain, but the unknown quantity in him made him smell pretty rank, once wet.

Back at the boat works, Grainger knew he had a million things to do. The July deadlines were approaching: promises to have the Murrays' boat rerigged, and the Worths' little fiberglass fourteen-footer repaired where one of the kids had banged it up against a dock. It was too damp to paint. He should go back and start bending the replacement planks for *Miss Emily*.

Mr. Claridge had been the "Admiral" of the club for a little while before some long-forgotten minor scandal deposed him. Now he returned every August, when his daughters and their princeling husbands came to stay in Hawke's Cove.

Mr. Claridge rarely sailed *Miss Emily* anymore; the two-masted yawl was too much for him alone, and the twins' husbands weren't good sailors, or even very interested. Still, he kept her in trim, throwing a lot of business Grainger's way. Grainger hoped that eventually he might get to broker *Miss Emily* to a new owner.

Grainger ran into one or the other of the twins every summer, but they spoke only of the boat, as if their common past was forgotten. He'd been working on this boat for the better part of two months without giving much thought to either Missy or Emily, but, oddly, today he remembered their nickname. The Doublemints. And he recalled so clearly Kiley telling him to call them.

"They want you to call them." Kiley held out a piece of scrap paper between two fingers, reaching across the kitchen table, where they had Scrabble set up. Mack was in the bathroom, and Grainger and Kiley sat alone.

Grainger stared at the scrap, unsure what this meant. Certainly he knew the twins, and well enough to know that he wasn't considered their kind. They weren't his type, either. Kiley sat across from him, her blue eyes challenging him with this bit of silliness, one hand casually flipping her blond hair over her shoulder.

"Should I?" He meant to be flip.

Kiley lay the scrap of paper down on his last word, S L O P E. He'd gotten a double-word score and was ahead by six points. "I don't care."

"Maybe I will." Grainger wanted her to laugh, to see the witty sarcasm.

"Maybe you should." She kept her eyes on her tiles. "Is grezix a word?"

"No."

"Look it up."

"It's not a word, Kiley." Grainger was annoyed, not at her insistence on imaginary words, but that she so cavalierly would have him date one or both of the twins. Didn't they stand together, all three of them, against the world? Hadn't they an unspoken pledge to remain a trio? Especially this last summer. Whatever leave he might get from the Army, two things were certain: It would be brief and it might not be during this halcyon time of summer. The long summer days of swimming and Scrabble and working on *Blithe Spirit* were dwindling, and every day he felt the pressure of imminent change, the way barometric pressure portends a change in the weather. It might be years before the three of them were together again, and by then, they would be different people.

And here was Kiley, treating their remaining time together as cheap, as if they had all the time in the world. Her flippancy brought to the forefront the strain they were all under that summer to keep up the pretense that everything was the same.

Maybe it was the long nights of physical frustration as he dreamed of Kiley, and the more frustrating days of pretending he cared for her only as a brother might, or a pal. Whatever it was, he was hurt. All summer long, Grainger had believed that their threesome was more valuable than his own happiness, and that the sanctity of it was reward enough.

Mack came back into the room and plopped down

in his chair, rocking the small kitchen table a little when he banged his knee against the table leg.

They fumbled around straightening the tiles, but their desire to play the game was gone, and Grainger stood to go home. As if in afterthought, he plucked the scrap of paper off the tiles and stuck it in his pocket.

Kiley glanced at Mack, and Grainger could see that she'd already mentioned this nonsense to him and he'd rejected the notion. For him, it wasn't a challenge. For him, as with so much, it was a joke. It was an example of the two sides to their natures. Mack saw lightness, Grainger saw dark. But Mack wasn't in love with Kiley.

Walking along the high bluff toward the village, Grainger knew he couldn't make himself go back to Mack's house, knowing that Mack would soon appear and wonder what had gotten into him. He'd pester and tease until Grainger found an excuse he'd accept. He just didn't have the energy to make up some believable reason for his stalking away. Grainger punched the air. Maybe he should just confess to both of them his feelings. As he had repeatedly done since his first glimpse of Kiley dancing blithely in her window, Grainger choked back the impulse to speak of his love. Not this summer, not this temporary and fragile summer. He couldn't bear to ruin their perfect friendship with his secret desire. Especially if Kiley didn't share his feelings.

Right then, Grainger decided to hitchhike into Great Harbor and see his father. No longer a sleepover guest, Grainger had lived with the MacKenzies ever since Mrs. MacKenzie handed Rollie Egan a paper giving her rights *in loco parentis* over Grainger. She had explained gently to him that it meant he was safe.

With any responsibility for his son effectively removed, Rollie had given up having a permanent address, and, when he wasn't out to sea, stayed at the Seasaw Motel in Great Harbor. It was there Grainger headed, needing suddenly to remind himself of who he was.

He was lucky and caught a ride with Joe Green. Mr. Green was always good about not asking stupid questions of kids. Their small talk centered on Grainger's baseball success, and it was easy to give answers or remarks without having to let go of the thoughts he was chewing on.

"So, where are you off to in the fall?" An innocent enough question.

"Army."

Joe Green sighed deeply. "I've got to tell you, I'm sorry to hear that."

Grainger remembered that Joe had lost a son in Vietnam, a boy who'd signed up against Joe's wishes.

"Can't afford college unless I do."

"Scholarships wouldn't help?"

"It's hard to explain." He needed to strike out on his own, and the Army provided a way.

Joe Green pulled his truck onto the side of the road at the one-lane bridge that connected Hawke's Cove to Great Harbor across the marshy wetlands. Everyone knew the former milkman never left Hawke's Cove.

"Thanks for the ride."

Joe leaned one elbow out the window. "Tell your father hello."

"I will."

Rollie had been in the Marines. In Vietnam, he'd been wounded and sent home with a Purple Heart and an honorable discharge. Grainger's mother had been visiting her brother in the VA hospital where Rollie had been recovering. That's all Grainger had ever known about their brief courtship, which resulted in his conception and her misguided insistence Rollie marry her. Grainger often wondered if she'd ever imagined that the passive patient lying on white hospital sheets, seducing her in his hospital bed, would turn out to be the bitter, mean-spirited man he did. Grainger never blamed her for leaving, only for not taking him with her. Maybe he represented her youthful mistakes, and that's why she left without him.

Failing to secure another ride on the other side of the short bridge, Grainger walked the rest of the way into Great Harbor. From across the parking lot of the Seasaw Motel, he saw his father just coming out of his room. As always, upon seeing his father, he felt this desire to spit. He couldn't grasp the logic behind wanting to visit him, except that he needed a reminder of who he was. Where he'd come from.

Three days' growth of beard, condor eyes staring at Grainger as if he was an unwelcome stranger, his father stood in worn jeans and rubber boots, and, despite the July warmth, a flannel shirt, tucked incompletely into his pants. A leather case dangled off his belt, his fishing knife. In one hand he held a gym bag, and Grainger knew he was off again.

"What brings you here? I sent money."

"Don't know. Some filial urge, I suppose."

"Filial, eh. Big words, kid. Looks like living with the doctor's smart-ass son and his beautiful-ass wife has rubbed off."

Grainger never touched anyone in anger, but the desire to now was powerful, and served to remind him of their connection. "I'm here to see how you are."

"Out again. Squidding." He walked toward his son.

Grainger squinted against the late July sun as he approached.

"When do you leave for boot camp?"

"September fifteenth."

Rollie was beside him now, and Grainger smelled the beer on his breath. It was as close as they had stood in a long time, and Grainger was surprised to find himself taller than his father. Rollie took a step back, as if he'd noticed the same thing. "It was a good choice, boy. The service. Make a man out of you. Shake out some of that la-di-da crap you got from the MacKenzies. *Filial.*" He said the word as if to taste it, then spat. "Filial, my ass. Got no proof of that. Who knew who your mother was fucking?"

Grainger remained standing in the shadeless parking lot as his father walked away; then he turned around and started walking back to Hawke's Cove. It would be a relief not to be his son, not to contain the genetic material for abuse. It made sense then, this mistreatment of his mother. Yet if it were true, why did she leave him with Rollie? Could his mother have loved him so little?

His thoughts churned in his brain and into his belly, until he bent over by the side of the road and vomited.

Grainger hadn't realized how close to the surface his memories were, how fragile the layer of years covering them was. Two years in the Army, then college at Maine Maritime; the nearly dozen years in the Merchant Marine. Traveling, months at sea, even two love affairs. All of this had only covered his past the way topsoil covers seeds. Since hearing of Kiley's return to Hawke's Cove, the seedlings of memory had begun to sprout, to work their way toward the sunlight. Forcing him to yank them out by the stems before they took full flower.

He pulled into an empty parking space in front of Linda's Coffee Shop. Toby Reynolds' Lexus was in its usual place, straddling the white line in an attempt to prevent dings. Some devil in Grainger always wanted to make him slide his truck up close to the driver's side door, but his truck wasn't so old that he really wanted to get into a silent battle of dings and dents. As soon as he got out of the truck, Pilot took up his vigil, chin on the steering wheel, eyes on his master's back as he went into the coffee shop.

Grainger sat next to Toby, nodding to the teenage waitress who set a mug of black coffee in front of him and dropped a handful of creamers beside it. Grainger reached for *The Boston Globe* lying on the counter. Red Sox were doing okay. His day might brighten, after all.

"Mornin'."

"Mornin', Toby."

Their usual morning conversation.

"Watch the game last night?" Toby slid the sports section over to Grainger.

"Yeah, good one." Grainger dumped the contents of two of the creamers into his mug. "Nice to see them win."

"That Kiley Harris is a piece of work." Toby, in his inimitable way, leapt right into whatever thought was at the forefront of his mind.

All Grainger wanted was to glance at the paper and have his third coffee of the day before going back to work on *Miss Emily*. He stirred his coffee with slow counterclockwise strokes; he would not rise to the bait. Who better than he knew just what a "piece of work" Kiley Harris was?

"She's sounding like she could be an obstacle to a sale. Doesn't want the place to change, but doesn't want to be there herself, either. Go figure."

"I couldn't say." Grainger kept stirring long after the two creamers had turned his coffee a light tan.

"I shouldn't talk about clients . . ." Toby held the front section of the paper in front of him.

"No, you shouldn't."

". . . but she has this crazy notion it's up to her. It's her parents' house; she's just getting it ready. She practically threatened to fire me. No one else will get them the best money. How much influence do you suppose she has on their decision?" Toby was off on one of his monologues. "At the same time, she can't want to jeopardize her kid's education."

Grainger tossed a couple of dollars down on the counter and stood up, leaving his coffee untouched.

Toby still had his eyes on the paper in front of him. "I heard you used to date her."

"No. We never dated." What they'd had could never be mistaken for dating.

Grainger left and climbed back into his truck, his throat painful as he held back the words he wanted to say. *Shut up Toby. Do not mention that woman's name to me again. What we had was not the normal boy-girl relationship, and I know nothing about the woman she's become.* Until Kiley left Hawke's Cove, or Toby sold the damned house, he wouldn't be having morning coffee at Linda's again.

If he didn't have so much work promised to his customers, he might have thrown his tent and backpack in the truck and gone camping until August.

And there was something else keeping him here. Grainger had promised Will sailing lessons, and he wouldn't renege on that. He'd been thinking about it, and decided he wouldn't deprive either of them of the chance to get to know one another. Even if he wasn't Will's father, at least he could do for him what a father should do. Make a sailor of him. And if he was his actual father . . . Well, it would be better if he wasn't, the way he felt about Will's mother. Grainger wanted to think of him as Mack's son. That's what he wanted.

Fourteen

Will banged through the front door and up the stairs to his room. Kiley heard the thump of dropped sneakers and the squeak of the old-fashioned shower faucets being turned on. She lit the fire under the kettle and went back to the phone.

Her conversation with Mrs. Finnergan had been wrenching. Just yesterday, they'd sent in a deposit for their fortieth-anniversary cruise. He told her he'd be back, go back to sleep, and kissed her gently. Worst of all, the patient he'd been called in to see was fine; it hadn't been necessary for John to go in at all. Kiley and Mrs. Finnergan had wept together. Before Kiley hung up, Mrs. Finnergan reiterated that there was no need for her to cut her vacation short. The memorial service wouldn't be for at least two weeks. No need to go home at all, Kiley thought; nothing to hurry back to.

Afterward, she'd tried twice to reach her mother. She had to tell her about Doc John, but also needed to talk her into finding another agent. Toby, with his skewed sense of value, was the wrong guy to represent this house. It was more than just selling the place; it was finding it a new family. You didn't just *sell* a three-generation—no, four-generation with Will—family summerhouse, a place filled with memories; you chose a new family for it, someone who would love it and fill it with their own memories, compatible with those already in residence.

The line was still busy.

Will was in the kitchen making his tea, and Kiley went to join him, needing a few minutes of easy conversation before she told him what had happened. "So, how was your run? You were gone longer than I would have given you credit for. Maybe you'll run in the Boston Marathon next year." She took out a mug and dropped an Earl Grey teabag into it.

"It was okay. I got a ride back."

"I wish you hadn't done that, Will; you know how I feel about hitchhiking. Even here, you can't be taking rides with strangers." So much for easy conversation.

"It wasn't a stranger. Not really." As Will turned to hunt for the box of lemon tea, she could see his damp hair swirling at the crown with the undefeatable cowlick that had always charmed her and annoyed him. "Grainger Egan brought me home."

Kiley handed him the box, then poured hot water into her mug, watching the teabag plump with air. "How did you bump into him?" She jabbed the floating teabag with her spoon, sinking it.

"I didn't. He's giving me sailing lessons."

Kiley sat down at the kitchen table. Her hands encircled the hot mug and she stared into it. "And how did that come about?"

"I guess I sort of asked him if he would teach me."

"When did you do that?"

"A couple of days ago." Will yanked open the silverware drawer, rattling the loose flatware. "Before I asked you about lessons."

Kiley kept her eyes on the tea. "Before I introduced you to him?"

Will didn't answer, just fiddled with making his tea.

Kiley slapped the table. "Will Harris, how many more secrets are you planning on keeping from me? First you're smoking dope; then you're taking sailing lessons behind my back. What else aren't you telling me?"

"Hey, I never lied to you. I told you I smoked; I never denied it. And I just told you I'm taking the lessons. I'm only doing what *you've* done all my life."

"What?"

"Keeping back the truth."

"How dare you." Kiley lay her palms flat on the tabletop to prevent their trembling; she tried to imagine how Will and Grainger might have met. Their equal silence that night was damning. Grainger must have initiated the contact and then asked Will to keep it secret. "How dare he?"

"What? Give me sailing lessons? That's what he does."

"No, how dare he have you keep it secret."

"Grainger told me to tell you. He didn't want me to keep it secret. Frankly, I think he's as uncomfortable as you are with the idea." Will sat down at the table with her. "Why are you both being so weird? Why won't you admit you were good friends? Maybe better than good friends? What happened?"

You can't come back to a place where memory is so powerful and survive. The anger thinned into resignation. She looked into Will's eyes. "A very long time ago, we were friends. That's all. Now drop it."

• • •

The afternoon that she jokingly gave Grainger the scrap of paper with the twins' telephone number on it, things began to change. Kiley had expected Grainger to react to the suggestion with the same derision Mack had. Instead he'd stalked off, looking hurt, even angry. Kiley scowled. It was just a joke. What made him so damned sensitive all of a sudden?

She scraped the tiles off the Scrabble board into the dark purple box, Grainger's last word unscored. "So what's the matter with Grainger?"

Mack shrugged, bending to pick up a couple of tiles that had fallen to the floor. "I don't know."

"Do you think he's been a little different this summer?"

Mack dropped the tiles into the box and took the cover out of Kiley's hands. "I think he has the same problem we all do this summer."

"What's that?"

"We know that after this summer, it will never be exactly the same."

Kiley wished that she could say, "That's not true," and it wouldn't be. But she, too, had been feeling this sense of finality at odd times, fighting the maudlin urge to think, "This is the last time we'll ever do this," whatever the moment or activity. She took a deep breath, afraid of voicing this thing, this death of their idyll. Of their childhoods. "Then we need to make this the best summer ever."

"I'm trying, Kiley, I'm trying."

"I know." She stood behind Mack's chair. As she had often done without a thought, Kiley reached her arms around his neck and hugged him. A quick squeeze of friendship, nothing more. Except that her hands touched his chest and she lay her soft cheek against his sun-roughened neck. Mack stood up and turned around, holding her in his arms as if afraid she'd run away. They didn't kiss, but the action of his pulling her to him was enough to weight the moment with significance. Maybe for an instant, maybe a little more, she let herself enjoy the full physical sensation of his arms around her. In the next instant they separated with a guilty pulling away, as if they expected Grainger to walk back through the door; instinctively knowing he'd be upset that they had crossed that unspoken boundary, committing a nearly incestuous act, creating a chink in the walls that safeguarded their friendship. Mack left soon after, neither saying another word, pretending that nothing had happened.

The heat of the July day was palpable in Kiley's uninsulated upstairs bedroom. Stashed under her bed was a shoe box full of photographs from over the years. A lot of them were silly shots of too distant landmarks, or birthday parties, or Mortie as a puppy. Kiley spread all of them out on her bed, then selected five. When placed end to end, the five pictures created a photographic record of her childhood, of her decade's worth of summers with Mack and Grainger.

It seemed terribly important she remember that not only were they *both* her best friends, they were also each other's. Her friendship with either of them could never be romantic. Buddies. Mates. Pals. Boy friends, not boyfriends. Besides, how could she ever choose? She loved Mack for his jokes and loyalty. She loved Grainger for his kindness and intellect. She didn't *want* to love them in any other way.

They were the two halves of her whole.

If she became attached to one more than the other, it would disconnect all three of them. As she scribbled names and dates on the backs of the pictures, it came to her that maybe it was only Mack, with his flowers and hug, who'd begun thinking of her in a romantic way.

Kiley hunted around her dresser drawer for some tacks. What if the two boys had discussed this, this girl-boy thing, and decided between them who should get her? Had Grainger left Mack here alone for just such a reason? Kiley rejected the idea out of hand. But was there something significant in Grainger's strange behavior today? Between them, was there the tension of competing males? What value did their threesome have if she jeopardized it by making them compete for her?

Kiley swiped the scattered pictures back into the shoe box. The truth was, the tension was within her. Anticipation. Temptation. Would it be a sweeter friendship to claim one of them as more than a friend? Kiley knocked the box of pictures off the bed with her knee. No! No. No. Nothing should change. Not now, not just when their whole lives were about to change.

Kiley scowled at the the pictures. They had to keep this friendship pure and simple, or risk everything they valued about it.

Kiley damned the Doublemints for ever putting this suggestion in her mind. But they had done nothing more than open the box; the thoughts had already been forming. They'd been forming ever since she'd arrived back in Hawke's Cove, awakening at the first sight of her two friends, suddenly more men than boys. Their early tans showed off a winter's worth of sports, tall, lean, and no longer the gangly colts they'd been the summer before. Even their voices had changed, no longer treacherous but solidly masculine. They smelled of salt and air and that pungent smell of spring earth.

Kiley began to pin the five chosen photographs to the wall. She was glad that she had no close girlfriend here, one who might ask: If you *had* to choose . . .

Kiley sipped at her cold tea. "I had some bad news this morning."

Will gulped his tea and stood to dump the dregs into the sink. "What bad news?"

She told him.

Will had known Doc John all his life. The pediatrician had recently performed Will's college physical, kidding him that he was old enough to go to a grown-up doctor now.

"Aww, Mom. That's rough. I'm so sorry." Will gave her a quick hug. "Are you okay?"

"Well, I'm very sad, and, truthfully, a little afraid. This means I'm out of a job."

"Boy, you've taken a few hits this summer." Will pulled at one ear. "Look on the bright side. Maybe you can work in a hospital—a change of pace. Something exciting, for once."

"Thank you, Will Harris, philosopher. I can't even think right now. Too much is going on."

"Does this mean we can stay in Hawke's Cove longer? I mean, if you don't have a job to go back to . . . why not?"

"Because I should probably go back right now to start looking for a new job. So, let's just stick to Plan A." Will was right, she had taken some hits this summer. First his arrest, then selling the house, then the doctor's death and her sudden unemployment. Layered on top of all that, Grainger Egan was back in her life, his presence shadowing her.

• • •

The August Races were only a couple of weeks away, and it seemed like *Blithe Spirit* was nowhere near ready for launching, when suddenly everything seemed to come together. The sparkling white marine paint above the waterline nearly disguised the layers of fiberglass sullying the otherwise perfect plane of her wooden sides. Below the waterline, they had painted her blue. *Blithe Spirit* was painted in black and gold on the white transom.

They launched her on the first day of August. Mack's father was friends with a fellow from the Great Harbor Shipyard, so they bartered the cost of trailering her to the boat launch there. Kiley promised three free nights of baby-sitting for the man's three kids, Mack had lawn-cutting duty, and Grainger would help him rerig a similar Beetle Cat. Flanked by her two best friends, Kiley watched with openmouthed excitement as *Blithe Spirit* was floated off the submerged trailer. The boat immediately began to take on water. Her planks were so dry from years of exposure that, even with caulking, she leaked like the oft-described sieve. They began bailing. It would take a couple of days before the planks swelled tight; in the meantime, they'd try to keep the water from sinking her entirely. Mack, Grainger, and Kiley sat on the slatted cockpit seats, using old bleach bottles cut into scoops to control the inflow. They sat as the wraparound wooden bench allowed, starboard, larboard, and stern. Three sets of bare feet touched, toe to toe.

They wet each other thoroughly with mistimed casts of the scoops, laughing with each drenching, laughing with the pure joy of having accomplished the impossible. Mack's constant grin was testimony to his happiness.

"This must be what it's like to give birth." Kiley stroked the tiller as if it were a pet. "All that work, and suddenly, here it is."

"A labor of love." Grainger looked at her with handshadowed eyes.

"Keep bailing, or she'll be love's labor lost." Mack stamped his feet, spraying them with salt water.

Kiley rowed them back to shore in her father's dinghy. Grainger had afternoon classes to teach and hurried away as soon as they touched shore. Mack helped Kiley tie the little rowboat up to the club's floating dock. "Want to go swimming?"

"Sure. Why don't we stay here?" Meaning they could see Grainger and maybe tease him from a distance. Kiley was unaccountably edgy.

"I was thinking more about Bailey's Cove."

They seldom went there; the public beach was very small and a little hard to get to. Kiley nearly voiced dissension, but didn't. It would be fun to go somewhere different, have a little adventure. "Sure, why not."

Mack gave Kiley a smile that acknowledged a complicity in something she was only partially aware of. Since her conversation with the Doublemints, there was a slight awkwardness in being alone with either one of the boys; it was only comfortable to be with them together. As a pair, they remained the familiar pals of childhood, but separated, Kiley could think of them only as boys. Deliberately, Kiley shook off the silly notion. "Bailey's it is."

Like so many of the old farm roads, Bailey's Farm Road ran off the main road and straight back to the shoreline. The public path led through woods and across a meadow, back into woods, and then onto the tops of carved-out dunes. On the windward side of the peninsula there were sometimes good waves, but this afternoon boasted none. The water over the sandbar was nearly turquoise in a pale, unthreatening ocean.

Kiley stripped off her white T-shirt and denim shorts, dropping them on the sand, and dashed to the water's edge, hesitating for only a moment before diving in. The water was sharply colder on this side of the peninsula, and she came up gasping, then struck out for the huge rocks that loomed at low tide. Reaching those massive remains of glacial progression down the East Coast a million years ago, Kiley let herself be swept into the eddying pools between them. The waves knocked her gently side to side until one big one doused her and she got a mouthful of salt water.

"Careful the tide doesn't carry you away." Mack was beside Kiley, the three menhirlike rocks surrounding them like petrified sentinels.

The water seemed marginally warmer where Kiley sat in the shallows, and like a great dog, it lapped at her. "Tide's on the turn. It could only carry me in at this point," she said.

Mack sat beside her as Kiley leaned against the rock. She felt his hip bumping against hers as the water carried them together and then apart. Then his hand was on hers, his fingers linking with hers. He would never be able to claim that this touch was thoughtless and ordinary.

"Kiley?"

"Mack?"

"Can I kiss you?" His voice was thick, as if he was afraid he'd ruined everything; knowing, as she knew, that these heartfelt words would change everything, but he was still willing to dare.

The water dragged them apart and then pushed them

together as Kiley examined her heart for the answer. If they did kiss, just kiss, then what could be the harm? They would know then and there if they were destined for each other. Or if the kiss fell flat, well then, they could just pretend it never happened, like the hug. Like little kids playing "doctor," curiosity would be satisfied. Better yet, this demon of uncertainty would be exorcised.

Kiley hesitated a fraction too long. Mack pushed away from the rock. "I'm sorry, it was a stupid thing to say."

"Mack. Yes." Kiley reached out for his hand. "I mean, I want you to."

Mack fought the incoming wave and rested his hands against the rock above her head. Gently, tentatively, he pressed his water-cold lips against hers. Instinctively Kiley's mouth softened in response, a little surprised that his mouth so perfectly suited hers. Mack's lips on hers erased all of the turmoil. Of course it was Mack whom she loved; loved as more than a friend. Their lips grew warm and they forgot the cold of the water.

A decisive wave broke them apart, and wordlessly, they struck out for shore, walking out of the water with hands held, their young bodies yearning to touch, to never break contact. It all made sense right then, and suddenly it was impossible to get enough physical closeness. They lay on Kiley's beach towel, hip to hip, legs threaded together; their mouths fed on each other, ravenous. No one else was on the beach to witness this transformation, no one to scrutinize their behavior.

Mack was the first to pull back. Kiley was glad. It was enough to have touched; it would have been too much to have done more. He sat up and looked at her with new eyes. "Wow."

Kiley sat up and wiped a few grains of sand from her shoulders. Then she asked the thing that had to be asked. "What does Grainger say about this?"

Mack, already flushed, flushed deeper. "He doesn't know."

"You didn't talk to him?"

"What could I tell him? I wasn't sure I had the . . . the nerve to finally act on, well, to act on what I've been thinking about since last summer. Grainger doesn't know about any of that. That I've wanted you. That I've hoped you've wanted me."

"We have to tell him."

Kiley saw Mack's anguish and knew that as she had feared, everything had changed. The balance of their friendship had shifted and now Mack and Kiley sat on one side. Grainger alone on the other.

Fifteen

❧

Ever since he'd come back to Hawke's Cove, the one day Grainger really looked forward to was the Fourth of July Picnic. This year was the town's centennial, and the preparations had been going on for days. Earlier in the week he had helped dig the pits in which steamers, corn, and lobsters would be layered in seaweed. In recent years the halved oil drum grills had given way to industrial gas grills, but the food was still good and well worth the ten-dollar contribution. Everyone brought salads or desserts. There'd be live music, games, good-natured competition in the toy boat race, a bonfire, and, as the July dusk gave way to full dark, fireworks over the water.

He didn't even mind that he had stockpiled memories of the three of them at this annual event: playing tag in the growing dark; eating watermelon and spitting the seeds at one another; teaming up on the same side for games. Those memories had no danger for him, surrounded by the activities of the day. Old friends, new friends, customers, neighbors; all gathered, celebrated too hard, and called it a success every year.

This year might be different. This year there was Kiley. And Will. Surely they'd be there.

"Come on, Pilot." Grainger held the truck door open for the dog. "Let's go have fun." Pilot cocked his head in a cartoonish puzzlement. His head-cocking was the reason Grainger had chosen this particular mutt from the litter. Pilot always looked as if he thought everything Grainger said was ironic.

The steamer pit was ready and the grills going by the time Grainger arrived. The smell of hamburgers and steaming salt water wafted his way as he walked over from the parking area. A game of pickup softball was already under way, and Charlie Worth hollered to him to get a move on and grab a glove. Pilot wandered off to sniff out the other dogs and tussle over scraps.

Standing at shortstop, Grainger pounded his fist into the middle of his glove. This was the best part for him; this game made up of players of all types, ages, and sizes, year-rounders and summer folk. Molly Frick, captain of the GHRHS girls softball league, was their pitcher. Catching was Fred Crockett, seventy if he was a day, and owner of the biggest yacht in the harbor. A casual survey of his teammates pleased him; they were well fielded and might whup some ass today. As the batter came up to the plate, Grainger smiled. It looked like the other team had some good players too. That was Will Harris, taking a few loosening-up swings. Just the way he moved up to the plate, toed in, and lifted the bat told Grainger that the kid had played some ball. In quick order, Will whacked the softball out of the ballfield and into the cooking area.

As Will trotted by, Grainger kidded him: "Not bad. Play much?"

"Not much. I was just the captain." Will jogged backward. "Of the championship team."

Grainger went back to his position. He'd been captain of a championship team too. He pounded his fist into his glove again. An insignificant coincidence.

The outs came quickly after that, and Grainger's team lined up to bat. He took a cup of beer handed to him by a teammate and sat on the bench to watch. Kiley was their pitcher. The beer must be too cold; his chest felt squeezed as he drank it. Kiley had a baseball cap pulled low over her eyes; bent from the waist, the ball behind her back, she took signals from their catcher, who happened to be Will. His own cap pulled low, Grainger studied the fluid way her back arched gracefully into her pitch. The batter whiffed. Will stood and tossed the ball into Kiley's glove. She caught it casually, as if she did this every day. Grainger sipped his beer. He'd taught her how to pitch, refusing to let her throw like a girl. *"You've got to use your whole arm, Kiley."* They'd been twelve or thirteen. He'd gripped her arm and shoulder and bent her into position. Obviously, she'd had practice along the way with Will. The way these two played, they were a two-person team.

Lost in thought, Grainger was startled when Harvey Clark shoved him. "You're up, Egan."

Grainger Egan hoisted his bat and faced Kiley Harris across the reach between the batter's box and pitcher's mound. She looked at him, then set the ball down and popped off her glove. She swept her cap off, tugged at her hair, twisting it up, and set the cap back on. Then she leaned toward him, shook her head at Will, and swooped a fastball at him. Grainger whacked it foul. He heard Will's chuckle, and smiled. Kiley smiled back, and fired another fastball at him. He tipped it. Grainger pulled the smile off his face.

Kiley shook off the sign again, and suddenly he remembered that Kiley was a good fastball pitcher, but she'd always end with a curveball—and she was a lousy curveball pitcher. As she threw the ball, Grainger stepped in. The sound of aluminum on horsehide rang in his ear and Grainger dashed to first base.

Once the clambake was declared ready, the unfinished game was called a draw at six to six and everyone made their way into the serving line. It seemed the easiest and most natural thing to fall in behind Kiley. "I see you've still got your arm."

"And you still whiff at fastballs." Kiley handed him a paper plate.

Grainger handed her a napkin-wrapped set of plastic utensils. "I take it Will played baseball in high school."

"Yes, he did. He's hoping to play in college."

"Using my name in vain?" Will cut in front of his mother.

"Just bragging."

Grainger handed Will his packet of utensils. "So I hear you're going to Cornell in the fall."

Will nodded, his mouth full of biscuit.

"Good for you."

"Will, grab a biscuit for me."

Before Will could, Grainger put a homemade biscuit on Kiley's plate. With that action, an elusive peace touched him in exactly the place his chest had felt squeezed an hour before. For half a moment, he could pretend there was nothing strained between them. Maybe what had happened could be left in the past, if they could just have a little time to warm up to each other.

"Is it okay if I go sit over there?" Will nodded to where a group of young people were arrayed in a loose circle.

Left without the buffer of Will's presence, Grainger looked to Kiley to see what she wanted. An empty table was close by.

"Kiley Harris, is that really you?" Conor MacKenzie came across the picnic grove with big strides. He scooped Kiley into a big bear hug. "It's so good to see you. You look great."

Their stiff reunion in the Osprey's Nest should have been as exuberant as the one being enacted in front of him. Grainger looked away. The feather-light hope that they might move ahead was blown adrift. Leaving Mack's brother and Kiley still embracing, Grainger went to sit at a crowded table. What a fool he was.

Twisting the claw from his lobster, he swore to himself that he would never again put his heart in harm's way.

Mack and Kiley had kept their romance secret for a little while, thinking that they could hide the change in their relationship from the one person who knew them both so well, but Grainger knew from the first moment. He looked at Kiley, and knew that a sea change had occurred in their lives. Maybe it was her uncontrollable grin, or the way she took every opportunity to be next to Mack. Maybe it was Mack's intensified teasing of Kiley.

They were in Great Harbor at the shipyard, watching as the friend of Mack's dad stepped the mast between the eyes of the sailboat. The three had walked the mast down to where she waited alongside the pier. Mack said something to Kiley and she giggled, almost losing her hold on the heavy wooden mast.

Grainger turned around to face them and, in their guilty expressions, got the proof of his suspicions. He knew he should be happy for them. But their splitting off would never be easy for him to accept, even as he told himself that, by any standard, Mack and Kiley were very well suited, very compatible. They came from similar backgrounds; they loved the same things. They both knew where they were going, and, more important, where they had come from. If they had been contestants on *The Dating Game,* Grainger knew that she would have picked Mack for those very reasons.

But what if he'd spoken of love to her first? The suppressed passion he tormented himself with every night was so deep, deeper than Mack's could ever be. Yet he knew without a doubt that, valuing their three-some above his own happiness, loving Mack as a brother, he would never have spoken, never have compromised what they had for what he wanted. Mack clearly had no such compunction.

Once the mast was in place, Grainger stayed behind to rig it. Mack had to work the afternoon shift at Linda's.

"Do you want me to stay and help?" Kiley was standing on the dock. It was low tide, so she stood above him, looking down.

He was on the boat, his bare toes clenching against the floorboards of the cockpit. Looking up into her eyes, Grainger could read the anguish in them; her fear that she was about to hurt him was so plainly written there. Her silent desire that, no matter what, they were still friends.

They were. He just needed to keep it platonic, to continue to pretend exactly as he had been all summer that his love was harmless.

For a moment he weighed the consequences of speaking his true feelings to her right then and there.

"Really, Grainger, I'll stay and help."

"No, Blithe. Catch a ride home with Mack. I'll see you at the club tonight." He turned away quickly so that she couldn't see the emotion threatening his reserve.

It was late by the time Kiley reached the gate of the Yacht Club. The boys were already there on the deck, cans of soda in hand, leaning against the wall, side by side but not speaking. Grainger had come alone, almost not going at all. He and Mack watched Kiley as she came along the asphalt path, her sandal heels making a little gritty sound against the sand that lay on the path like salt on a pretzel. Dressed in her white dress, her dark blue cardigan tied around her waist, Kiley looked beautiful, more beautiful than ever in Grainger's eyes. Mack pushed away from the wall to greet her, and Grainger walked away.

Inside, Don Henley was singing about summer. A few couples were already dancing; most were still arrayed along the edges of the room, no one sitting on the musty-cushioned fake bamboo furniture. Grainger wondered absently why the Yacht Club kept holding these "socials" for the kids. No one ever looked like they had a good time. Kids preferred their own dark fun, and he knew that several of the kids still in high school were dribbling stolen nips of bourbon or rum into their Coke cans. Others were making use of the empty dressing rooms. Every family had a locked cabana, and a determined teenager could always filch the key to it. The cabanas were only four by five and primarily taken up with a bench and hooks, but kids still managed to use them for privacy.

Grainger thumbed through the LPs as if desperately interested in them. He was acutely aware of Mack and Kiley as they went out onto the half-empty dance floor and began to move with the heavy beat. Then Kiley stopped dancing and leaned into Mack's ear. They both looked at him. Grainger kept to his feigned interest in the records.

"Let's go to the beach." Kiley was at Grainger's elbow.

Grainger shrugged. "You guys go. I'm not in the mood."

Mack stood on his other side. "Man, you have to go with us. We won't let you say no."

"Won't let me, huh? Since when are you—"

"Grainger, please. We have to talk." Kiley lay one hand on his sleeve. He wore one of Conor MacKenzie's cast-off button-down shirts, a tie from the lost and found knotted tightly against his throat. Gently Grainger removed her hand, holding on to it for a moment, then let go. "All right."

Ducking the less-than-eagle-eyed post–cocktail-hour chaperones, they went through the back hallway and out the unalarmed emergency door. This late in the season, full dark had already come on, with only a trickle of daylight left in the western sky. A sliver of moon hung over the sea, stars punctuating the black sky in a seemingly random arrangement. The breeze was lively and newly cool, jangling the halyards against the masts in the crowded summer harbor. In front of them, invisible but audible, were the constant waves rolling onto the beach.

It seemed suddenly important to pretend for a moment that they were only out here for the usual swim. Kiley dropped her sweater on the sand and stripped off the sleeveless dress, then shivered in the breeze. Neither boy moved to join her as she walked to the water's edge. They sat side by side on the damp sand and said nothing. Grainger had nothing to say that wouldn't sound like jealousy.

"Kiley." Mack called to her to come sit beside them. In the darkness they were visible only as two white shirts, Kiley's white dress on the damp, cold sand between them.

Kiley moved up the beach to stand in front of them, her arms folded against herself, either from nervousness or chill. "Grainger, Mack and I have to tell you something. Mack and I . . ."

"Save it, Blithe. It would take a blind man not to see what's going on here." Grainger stood up and yanked at the tie around his neck. "I wish you both the best." He tried hard to make his tone match his words.

"Grainger, are you sure you're all right with this?" Mack was standing up now, on the other side of him.

He put a hand on Mack's shoulder, then his other on Kiley's. "What's not to be all right about?" He pulled both of them close, but his face was inclined to Kiley. He breathed in deeply of her scent, a lively mixture of lemon and powder. As soon as he had drawn them close, Grainger let them go. Without another word, he turned around and went back into the building, hoping that they would be fooled by his act.

Inside, Grainger grabbed the hand of one of the Doublemints and pulled her out onto the dance floor. Over her head, he saw Mack and Kiley come in, arm in arm. After a moment, they took the dance floor. He was unable to prevent himself from watching Mack and Kiley dance. Mack bobbed up and down, but Kiley used the music, arching her back, raising her arms over her head in graceful motion. Then Conor MacKenzie broke off from his group and went over to them. He gave his brother a good-natured slug before bussing Kiley on the cheek. Grainger turned his partner so that he could no longer see them.

At the end of the song, Grainger walked out of the club and back to the beach. The breeze was stronger now, and the incessant din of halyards disturbed the silence. Grainger pounded across the sand, dropping his clothes before plunging into the cold water. He stayed under until his chest felt as if it would burst. That night he began to stay in his father's motel room.

The breeze the next morning was down to six knots, so they returned to the shipyard to sail *Blithe Spirit* to her permanent mooring in Hawke's Cove harbor. Grainger was waiting for them as Mack and Kiley walked side by side along the wooden pier to where the boat was tied up. In one hand he held Kiley's blue cardigan.

"Where'd you find that?"

"On the beach." He gave it to her, neatly folded. "It was almost in the water."

"I'm so glad you found it; it's my favorite." Kiley tied it around her waist. "Thanks for bringing it with you."

Grainger looked away from her, his gray-blue eyes on the boat. "You shouldn't be so careless with your favorite things."

They christened her with a rare glass bottle of Coke. "Hail to thee, Blithe Spirit!" they chorused, and Kiley swung the Coke bottle against her prow. Nothing happened. Grainger took the eight-ounce bottle out of her hand and, kneeling on the pier, swung it like a bat. The bottle shattered and they looked aghast at the sticky brown fluid running down her bow. Hastily, Mack grabbed a hose and sprayed the hull off with fresh water.

As if they were his students out for a lesson, Grainger handed Mack and Kiley each a life jacket. He was the last to board, casting off the ropes and then sitting in the stern to man the tiller as Mack raised her gaff-rigged sail.

As the most experienced sailor of the three, Grainger called the orders, keeping his hands on the tiller and the mainsheet. Mack, the least experienced, made fast the peak and throat halyards once the sail was in place. The wind gently pushed them away from the dock, and they easily threaded their way out between the other boats making for the opening of Great Harbor.

Grainger felt like they had the proverbial elephant in the living room. Mack and Kiley kept their boat shoes well apart, the sail effectively keeping them from each other's sight. Grainger kept his eyes on some point in the middle distance, but from his vantage point could see both of them. Once out of the harbor, they tacked. As her patched sail took the wind, Mack moved over to sit beside Kiley on the high side of *Blithe Spirit*. They let their knees bump, but kept their hands to themselves.

The three spoke only of the boat, proud of themselves for rescuing her, proud to have done so as quickly and as cheaply as they had. But it was a flat victory. All the joy of the moment was tarnished by the change in their friendship. If they had still been as before, this would have been a jolly expedition. Instead, they spoke of *Blithe Spirit* as if she were their child, their only source of conversation.

Maybe it would have been easier if he'd gotten mad and fought with them, Grainger thought. But he didn't. And this adherence to polite neutrality was maddening. He wanted to stand up and scream at them, but what words could he say that would describe half of what he was feeling?

"So, Grain, how was the Doublemint? Which one were you with?" They were halfway around the point before Kiley asked the question.

Grainger adjusted the tiller slightly. "Emily."

"Did you have a good time?"

"It was just a dance. She's okay."

"Are you going to take her out?"

"Why? Do you want to double-date?"

Kiley wiped spray from the varnished rail. "Maybe. Sure."

Mack stretched and casually dropped his hand to her bare knee. His fingers gently squeezed it.

Was this a newly possessive gesture? Hadn't they always leaned on one another? Grainger studied the horizon, trying not to look at Mack's easy familiarity, aware that he'd no longer have that harmless intimacy with Kiley.

"Prepare to jibe." Grainger stood up, one leg cocked against the tiller, his hands on the mainsheet.

"Let me do it, Grainger." Mack crept over Kiley's legs to stand beside Grainger.

Grainger shrugged and gave up the post to Mack.

Mack let go of the sheets too quickly, and the sail flapped and the boom swung. Kiley ducked, nearly banging heads with Grainger. Mack recovered the mainsheet, gripped the tiller with white-knuckle intensity, and began to bring things back under control.

"It's been a while." He looked sheepish, and Kiley smiled at him as if she thought him charming.

Grainger drummed his fingers on the side of the boat and said nothing. Fortunately, the wind was gentle. In rougher seas, Mack's carelessness might have been disastrous, and they all knew it.

Their maiden voyage went off with a minimum of fuss, and they rounded the tip of the peninsula within an hour. At that point they had to tack. Mack gave up the helm to Grainger without a word. Grainger made the maneuver easily, deftly handling tiller and sheet, ducking nonchalantly as the boom swung. He hoped Kiley would make a comparison.

Kiley crept out onto the bow to snag the mooring's pickup. Grainger luffed the mainsail at exactly the right moment to shoot the mooring, bringing them to a slow glide, and Kiley caught it on the first try. They took a long time putting things away, making sure all the lines were properly coiled, the sail lashed to the boom correctly so that it would raise easily next trip. They lovingly wiped down the salt from her varnish, slid the crutch under the boom, and made sure everything was Bristol fashion.

Kiley rowed the three of them to shore, facing the other two as they sat side by side on the stern seat of the small rowboat, Mack looking port and Grainger gazing starboard. He couldn't look at Kiley for fear she would see his anguish. Behind them *Blithe Spirit* swung into the wind, tethered by her lines. Suddenly Grainger knew that he had to separate from them, that this pretense that everything was fine would be impossible to maintain.

• • •

Even dipped lavishly with drawn butter, the lobster tasted flat. From where he sat, Grainger could see Will, laughing with some new friends, and Kiley, still next to Conor, deep in conversation. So be it. Just like Mack, Conor was more Kiley's type. Conor was a doctor like his father; Will had said Kiley was a nurse practitioner. Nice match. Nowadays, Conor only occasionally reminded Grainger of Mack. Surely, as she talked with Conor, she saw something of her true love in the face of his brother.

Pilot sagged by Grainger's feet, sated with scraps. The fireworks would begin in a few minutes, the bonfire was already blazing, but Grainger couldn't make himself stay any longer.

"Let's go home, boy."

Pilot cocked his head.

Sixteen

❧

"I hear that your parents are selling up." Conor grabbed the untaken table and set his plate down.

Kiley looked back at Grainger, but he was gone. She caught sight of him sitting with a crowd at a distant table. She set her plate beside Conor's. "It's too much for them."

"And you don't have any interest in keeping it?"

"No. I can't." Kiley wondered if everyone she ran into was going to keep asking her the same question. She needed some surefire response to keep the rest of the questions at bay. "The truth is, I can't afford it even if they gave it to me. I find myself unexpectedly unemployed." The word *unemployed* had so little to do with the sad fact of Doc John's death. "My boss was killed and his patients are being transferred to another doctor who has a full staff." There, it was out. It would take a little practice not to choke on the words, but they were said.

"Are you a nurse?"

"Nurse practitioner, pediatrics."

"Good for you." Conor was vaguely condescending, as so many of the docs were. Not quite one of us, a little better than a nurse.

"You're a doctor like your dad?"

"Not quite. I'm a gastroenterologist in a six-man practice. Six-person, rather." Conor expertly split open the thorax of the lobster. "I practice in Great Harbor."

She listened to Conor talk about his practice and the difficulties of being over half an hour from the nearest hospital, and how two of his partners were threatening to form their own group. Kiley began to relax, confident the conversation was safely away from her. As soon as Conor had come up to her, she'd been fighting panic. What if Will walked over just then? What would she do? How would she introduce him to Conor? Would Conor's face show sudden puzzlement, then mental calisthenics as he tried to fit Will into what he knew of Kiley, "doing the math," as the saying went? As she was certain Grainger had.

Conor took a breath. "So what are you going to do? About a job, I mean."

"I'm thinking I might apply to work in a PICU." Kiley took a mouthful of steamer.

"You might find it terribly stressful after so many years in an office."

"I could use the challenge."

"Do you want me to check it out at our hospital? We have a small unit; maybe there's a spot."

"I don't want to move, Conor, but thank you."

"Oh, come on. What's holding you?"

"My parents. My commitments."

"Husband?"

"No." Shields up. "What about you? I mean, are you married?"

"Once. It didn't last past medical school."

"Sorry."

"Don't be." Conor arranged his empty lobster shells neatly and picked up his corn. "My parents would love to see you. They're just over there. Finish up and I'll bring you over."

Kiley followed Conor's pointing finger to see a group of older Covers sitting in web-and-aluminum lawn chairs. She recognized Dr. MacKenzie only by his lifelong uniform of plaid shirt and khaki trousers. Mrs. MacKenzie had grown stout, and her once lush brown hair was steel gray and permed into a mass of tiny curls. Although Kiley hadn't seen them since that last summer, she remembered with awful clarity the last time she had. "That's okay, Conor. Maybe another time. I need to get home."

"Why? The fireworks haven't even started. You can't seriously think of going before they do."

Kiley picked up the biscuit off her plate. She looked over and saw that Grainger was no longer at the table with the crowd. Trying not to look like she was looking for someone special, she glanced around. It was full dark and she couldn't see Grainger, or Will, anywhere. Suddenly the first rocket went up, exploding into a chrysanthemum of purple and white. In the dazzle she saw Grainger walking to his truck, the wirehaired mutt on his heels.

"See, it's too late to leave now. Come on." Conor stood up, his paper plate in one hand, the other extended to her. "They'd love to see you."

The boom of a second firework split the air. Kiley jumped. In the flash she saw Will sitting on a blanket, surrounded by boys and girls. He gazed heavenward, his mouth open in delight, having a good time.

"Kiley, they'd love to see you." Did he think that if he repeated it enough, she'd capitulate?

She closed her eyes. "I'd love to, Mack, but I can't." A flush crept up her cheeks as she realized what she'd said. "Conor, I mean."

Conor smiled at her, his face illuminated by the next green-and-red burst. "I'm sorry, I didn't mean to press. Another time."

"I promise."

"Good. And I will make some inquiries about jobs."

"You don't have to."

Conor dumped his plate into a barrel. "Kiley, I want to."

"Who were the kids you were with?" The traffic leaving the beach was heavy and Kiley drove slowly.

"Just some of the kids that played softball with us. Molly, Andrew, and Catherine. Some others."

"Are they year-round or summer?"

"I guess year-round. They knew each other from school."

"What did you talk about?"

"I don't know. Nothing big." Will drummed a rhythm on the dashboard. "What did you talk about?"

"With whom?" After Conor, Kiley had moved through the crowd, speaking to several old acquaintances.

"That guy you were sitting with."

"Sex and drugs, of course." Kiley pulled into the driveway. "See, it's not so hard."

"Mom!" Will slapped his forehead in feigned exasperation. "Talk is talk. What do you say to people you just meet? Nothing heavy."

Heavy. She needed to talk to Will and the subject *was* heavy. If she didn't tell him herself, there was the very real danger that someone else would; a danger illustrated by Conor's wanting her to say hello to his parents. A danger looming every time someone who remembered her from the club saw her with Will. A danger made imminent with Will's upcoming sailing lesson. It wasn't that people didn't know about Will. It was just that he was the Harris's grandson in the abstract. At first her parents had declared that the child and his mother would not be welcome at Hawke's Cove. That was their initial reaction to Kiley's unwelcome news of her pregnancy and anonymous lover. But soon the baby Will had endeared himself to his grandparents, proving to be the most perfect grandchild. Once he was old enough to be away from his mother, they began to suggest he might come and stay with them while at the summerhouse. Maybe they'd been unable to refrain from speaking about their clever, charming, handsome grandson; but they never found it necessary to explain his existence, always letting Hawke's Cove friends assume a normal—acceptable—genesis. So, Kiley reasoned, the MacKenzies might *know* about Will, but not really know who he was. And she wasn't going to change that. But, it was clear that one change had to be made.

"Will, are you very tired?" They were on the porch steps.

"No, I'm still pumped up from the fireworks."

"I have to tell you something." Kiley sat down and patted the arm of the other rocking chair.

"I know you do." Will took the empty chair.

She took a deep breath. "Once, long ago, I loved two boys."

"Mack and Grainger"—a statement, not a question.

"Yes."

• • •

She rowed them away from *Blithe Spirit*, the boys not speaking to each other, or to her. An impasse had been reached.

The dinghy's bow ground onto the beach. The three jumped out and the two boys dragged the rowboat up onto shore. Suddenly, Grainger was gone.

Kiley ran to catch up to Grainger. At her touch on his bare back, he turned. "I have to go to work."

"I know. I just wanted to say . . ." What words were there?

Grainger gently stroked the length of Kiley's blond hair, touched her cheek as if in blessing, and smiled at her with kindness. She felt the pang of loss, of waste. "There's nothing to say, so don't try."

"Will you be home for dinner, Grainger?" Mack was close behind her.

Again Grainger smiled, suddenly much older than they. His leadership of their troupe and his authority had so far outstripped them that he was looking at them as already in his past. "No, Mack. I've told your mother I'm going to stay in Great Harbor until I report for duty."

"Why?"

Grainger turned away.

"What about the race?" Mack's voice was tense and a little throaty. "You've got to help us sail her."

He didn't turn around to answer. "No, I don't. She's yours, Mack. *Blithe* is yours." Grainger left them standing together, Mack's height over Kiley's, his chin on her head.

Suddenly bereft, she fought back tears. "Why can't he just accept us? Be happy for us?"

"Because he loves you too." Mack's tone was without surprise or jealousy, even matter-of-fact.

As if, she thought, he loved Grainger as a brother, but loved her in a stronger, deeper way. As a man loves a woman. He didn't begrudge Grainger his love; neither would he allow it.

It should have been easier, not having Grainger around to remind them of the fracture in their threesome. But this strange new partnership had no framework. It was as if she and Mack had to redefine themselves.

Every day Kiley found some pretext to call Grainger at the motel, ready to hang up if she got his father. When Grainger answered, she'd blurt out, "We're going to the movies, want to come?"

"No."

"Then, are you coming to the dance Friday?"

"No."

"Are you ever going to say yes to anything?"

"No. It's okay. You guys only have a few days left together. You don't need a third wheel."

"Grainger, you'll never be a third wheel."

After this last attempt, Kiley hung up the phone and leaned against Mack's chest. "He hates us."

"Can we not talk about Grainger? Let's have one day when we don't worry about him. He'll get over it. You've got to stop worrying about him."

Something primal had taken place. It wasn't that he didn't still want Grainger's friendship; it was more that he was willing to sacrifice it for her. Their boyhood friendship was less important to him than having Kiley. She should have been flattered; instead she was dismayed. She had come between best friends. In less than two weeks they were going in three different directions, and this thing between Mack and herself might not survive winter's separation. They had destroyed the best thing they had for a transitory pleasure.

Kiley wouldn't let Mack touch her. Angry at him for caving in to his desires, more angry at herself for letting him, she pushed him away and walked home. As she had feared, loving the one didn't mean she loved the other less.

When Mack came to collect her that evening, he carried a rose, presenting it to her like a courtier. "Forgive me?"

"Just what am I supposed to forgive?"

"My being a jerk about Grainger. Of course I'm worried about him too. But I think that we need to go on. I mean, we can keep trying to get him to accept us, but we also need to be together, to enjoy what we have before it's gone."

He was right; they needed to focus on themselves, on what they had chosen to be, together. This time was so brief, Kiley no longer wanted to waste any of it on argument. "I know. I just can't bear thinking that he's alone."

Mack began kissing her neck. "Promise me that you won't mention Grainger again tonight?" He moved to her lips. "It makes me think you feel that you've made a mistake, picked the wrong guy."

"No, Mack. That's not true." She heard how thin her words sounded and pressed her lips against his.

They were in his father's car, the stick shift between them. Mack had driven to Bailey's Beach, parking off to the side of the narrow road. They got out and walked under a pretty moon illuminating the shimmering sandy path leading through the woods and field to the beach. Mack carried an Indian-print spread and a basket. It looked like they were on a moonlight picnic, and his romantic gesture surprised Kiley a little.

Mack spread the blanket on the sand beneath the dune, and she stripped off her jeans and sweatshirt, running to the edge of the black water in her bikini. Kiley heard Mack's feet pound the sand behind her, and his hands caught her up to throw her in the cold water. Kiley screamed and he put a hand over her mouth. "Shh, Kiley, we don't want to alert anyone that we're here."

She giggled against the restraint of his hand. "Who?"

"Smugglers, wreckers, other lovers."

"Lovers?"

Mack kissed her, his kiss tasted like Chiclets. Kiley was still cradled in his arms, and it felt different from all the other times he had playfully scooped her up until he walked into the water, flinging her away with a great splash. She came up laughing and swam to him, wrapping her legs around his, letting the seawater float her. They kissed some more; then Kiley realized he wasn't wearing a suit. His fingers released the three simple strings that held her suit in place. His lips and tongue touched her where he held her up, the water floating her into and out of his reach. His erection touched her and suddenly it seemed like there was nothing more in her life she wanted than for him to enter her. Right there, in the water where the salt taste of the sea mingled with the salt of his body, the salt of her happy tears. That single word floated above her head, a name for what they were, what they were to each other. *Lovers.* Their act had sealed them together.

Race day dawned pinkish gray, a streak of mackerel sky foretelling tomorrow's storm. Kiley and Mack rowed out to *Blithe Spirit* in silence. When he'd tried to kiss her hello, she'd turned her mouth away from him, afraid suddenly that their new intimacy would be spelled out for all to see. No, not for all—for Grainger to see. Grainger was already aboard *Gemini,* crewing for the Doublemints. Kiley shipped the oars as Mack grasped the sailboat's grab rail and hauled the dinghy close to the Beetle Cat. She took his hand as she stepped from one craft to the other, but let go as soon as both feet were in the boat.

This morning, they were shy with each other. Tentative. Kiley had lain awake most of the night, wrestling with guilt. Not from having had sex, but the guilty aftertaste of knowing she may have made a mistake. As hard as she tried to convince herself that Mack was the one, that what they'd done was the natural outcome of a prolonged, if odd, courtship, it was Grainger who kept haunting her sleeplessness. She had begged Mack to say nothing.

"What kind of guy do you think I am? Kiss and tell?" he'd protested.

"I think you're his best friend, and best friends tend to tell each other everything. Yes. You have to promise me."

"I promise." Mack looked slightly disappointed.

Grainger was standing in the stern of *Gemini.* He waved and Kiley waved back, glad of the distance between them. Just as he knew they'd paired off, surely he would know that they had carried their relationship to this new plane.

Mack climbed into the cockpit, blocking her view of Grainger for moment. "Ready?"

"Yeah, sure." Kiley hauled on the mainsheet. The sail rose easily, the breeze filled it and they were off, heading for the start of the race. As they moved away from the other boats, Kiley turned to look again at *Gemini*. Grainger was seated, one arm casually around one of the twins. From the distance, Kiley couldn't see if Grainger was touching her, or simply resting his arm on the gunwale behind her.

Mack snickered. "Looks like he's doing all right with the Doublemints. He could get a twofer."

"That's gross." Kiley felt a knot of something begin to twist itself in her gut. Some foreign emotion she couldn't quite define.

Mack chucked her under the chin as if she was a sulky child. "Come on, cheer up. We'll beat 'em."

"No, we won't." Kiley knew she sounded snappish, though Mack didn't deserve it. "We just aren't the sailors they are."

Suddenly quiet, Mack guided the little boat along until they reached the area where other boats in their class were circling like wary opponents, waiting for the committee boat to signal the start.

"I think maybe you're sorry about what happened last night."

Kiley shook her head. "No, I'm not." She reached out and took Mack's hand. "I'm just a little tired."

Mack squeezed her hand, then brought it to his lips. "I love you."

"I love you, too." But she knew that she didn't mean it in the same way he did. Mack was good and kind and fun . . . but he wasn't Grainger. Kiley kept her face turned away so that Mack wouldn't read the truth so plainly written there.

The next day Kiley drove to the Seasaw Motel, a two-story concrete building with little affectations of the seaside in the electric blue fake shutters that framed each window and the pots of geraniums outside each door, cigarette butts poking out of them like pegs. She could hear screaming children and splashing coming from the pool behind the building. Cars with out-of-state licenses filled the parking lot, and it was hard to find a free space. Kiley didn't know which room was theirs and, even as she went into the small office reeking of cigarette smoke and damp rug, she worried that she might come face-to-face with Grainger's father.

Mrs. MacKenzie had asked her to deliver a letter to Grainger. Postmarked "Boston," it was hand-addressed. "I think he should have it right away. Will you take it to him? Mack won't get home from work until four."

It was as if the hand of God had come to guide her. After the race Saturday, Kiley had avoided Grainger except to congratulate him and the twins on their third place finish. But avoidance was no good, the wrong fix. She needed to see him, to speak to him, to explode this bubble of uncertainty lodged in her gut. She needed to know that she had made the right decision. There seemed no way to accomplish that until now, *deus ex machina,* she was being sent to Grainger. She was nervous. What if he got angry that she just showed up, when so clearly he, too, was distancing himself?

No. No matter what, he was still her friend. And she had been sent. Kiley shook off the nervousness.

She asked the desk clerk which room belonged to the Egans, steeling herself against meeting Mr. Egan, steeling herself to look Grainger in the eye.

The desk clerk was about Kiley's age, a little hard around the eyes, and she took a long drag on her cigarette as she flipped through the guest register. "One oh one. First on the left."

"Is Mr. Egan there, or is he out?"

She stamped her cigarette out, grinding it as if pondering the question. "Beats me."

"Thanks."

Kiley clutched the envelope in her hand. She had no idea what she'd say to Grainger, assuming he was there, assuming he would talk to her. She had never struggled for words with either of them, and maybe it was that they'd never said a serious thing to one another in all those years. Always teasing, jousting, gossiping. Never sitting down and explaining what they were really made of. Never telling each other that they loved one another. In those days, so distant to her now, it felt incomplete to be with only one of them. When waiting for one or the other of them to arrive, it was a temporary bifurcation, soon brought into balance. Now, nothing was in balance—as if her ballast had shifted and she was in danger of sinking. She should be dizzy with love, not weighted with guilt.

Kiley was standing on the cement walkway, the envelope in her hand, staring at the number on the motel door, when it opened. For a moment she thought that Grainger had been waiting for her, had known she was coming.

"What are you doing here?" Grainger's voice was sharp, surprised.

Kiley could only hand him the letter.

He accepted it without taking his eyes off her until she blushed, wondering if he could see in her face what she and Mack had done. "Come in."

"Your father . . ."

"Out. Fishing. I'm by myself."

The room was tidy, the television on, and Grainger shut it off. Take-out wrappers were scattered on the small round table under the window. He'd been eating and must have seen Kiley through the half-closed curtains. Grainger stuffed the papers and napkins into the trash and gestured for her to sit down. She took the only chair. He sat in front of her on one of the double beds. "Why did you come?"

"Mrs. MacKenzie thought you'd want that letter right away, and Mack is at work. So I brought it."

Grainger looked at the letter. An ordinary number ten envelope, plain white. He studied his name, handwritten on it, as if trying to decipher a code hidden in the neat letters. Kiley leaned a little closer, her curiosity aroused by his long contemplation of it. Where the return address should have been, there were only black lines, someone's deliberate crossing out of the business address.

"Open it."

"Later."

"Why not?"

"I'd just rather open it alone, okay?" His voice wasn't gruff or even annoyed, but his excluding words hurt.

"Okay. Read it in peace." Kiley had the door open before he called her back inside. This was a bad idea. She shouldn't have come.

"I'd ask you to stay, but that isn't fair to Mack. Or to you." He kept his gaze on the envelope still in his hand, but the longing in his voice called to her, the same longing she felt for their old friendship.

But no, it was different. There was something else in his voice. Her eyes were open now. "Grainger?"

"Everything is different now; you've chosen Mack. You're right for each other. I'm happy for you."

Kiley pressed the metal door closed, and the sound of the latch clicking shut felt like her heart clicking open. He loved her, and she had been too blind to see it. No, not too blind, too disbelieving. "Grainger, why didn't you speak first? Why didn't you say something?"

"What difference would it have made? I never stood a chance."

Kiley moved away from the door. "It would have made all the difference." She reached across the divide between them and touched his face. "All the difference."

He moved away from her hand as if he'd been burned. "Mack is my best friend."

"And you're his."

"You were ours."

"I wish Mack had never said anything to me. He changed everything."

"But he had to. You can't go on feeling like this and not say something. You can't suppress these feelings. If he'd only told me long ago, come clean to me first, then I would have . . ."

"What?"

"Let go of my own dream."

"For Mack's sake? What about your own?"

"You don't understand. His family saved me, gave me a new start in life. How could I repay them by taking away his dream? What kind of friend would I be?"

"What kind of friend are you to *me*? Where do my feelings come into this? You two decide who gets me?"

"We didn't decide; we never planned this."

"I never wanted to choose between either of you."

"Then why did you?"

"I didn't know how you felt. If I had . . ."

Grainger paced across the small room, then came back and took her hand. "If Mack had said nothing and I said nothing, which one of us would you have chosen?"

Grainger stood in front of her, the shadows of the room somehow enlarging him into a prototype of the man he would become. Kiley could smell him, his sweat from honest labor mingling with the pungent smell of arousal. They were standing close now, too close. It was so easy to have his arms around her, a snug harbor. Tears rolled from her eyes, and she made no move to stanch them.

It was all clear. What she felt for Mack was childish, insubstantial. A mere shadow of the feelings flooding her at the touch of Grainger's cheek against her hair, his breath against her forehead. Lifting her chin, she breathed in deeply to receive it, hoping to find his mouth coming to meet hers. "You, Grainger. You."

At his kiss, the taste of his tongue and the salt of her own tears, she felt as if she were falling away, as if the ocean had opened up and dragged her down—not in a frightening way, more like the comfort of safe waters, knowing she could breathe underwater. *I am drowning in him,* she thought, *and I will not struggle.*

Seventeen

❧

Will watched his mother's face as she talked. He had the oddest impression that, as she reached deep into her memory to pull out the story she needed him to hear, the girl she had once been began to surface. Her eyes, seeing what her words described, brightened; she smiled, and long forgotten dimples showed in the corners of her mouth. He began to see her as she once was, and from the shadow of the beautiful girl she'd been, Will saw that his mother was now a beautiful woman. He was proud that his mother looked good, and, at the same time, a little unnerved by recognizing it.

As her story went on his mother's pace slowed, her words mined from a treacherous vein. The dimples receded, she tucked her hair behind her ears and her eyes clouded with pain. Her voice dropped lower and lower as if in amazement at the pictures in her mind she was giving to him. Will realized she'd forgotten to whom she was telling this story. And he'd forgotten that it was *his* story.

It was such a complicated tale. The way she was telling it, at least he was cushioned, hearing it as a legend, as a tale outside of himself, outside of her, his mother. These things that had happened involved those three kids beside the boat, those strangers.

Will tried to sort out that phrase: *In every love affair, there is a beloved and a lover. One who loves more.* He knew where he stood in that equation with Lori; it was very obvious. He couldn't quite parse it in his mother's story. It seemed as though they were all the lovers and, at the same time, each one beloved. Kiley was beloved of both Mack and Grainger. She believed that it was in equal measure. In turn, she loved them both, almost equally. What had she said? They had been two halves of her whole.

Then there was the third factor in this increasingly weird equation: the love Grainger and Mack had for each other. Brotherly, best friends, like no friendship he'd ever had. The kind of bond that can be badly damaged by betrayal, and remain unhealed for years. Decades.

Only the thump of the porch rockers kept the moment from complete stillness.

Will waited for his mother to go on until he understood that she'd come to the end of her story. He spoke gently, as if waking her. "Mom?"

She roused herself enough to remember he was there. "What, hon?"

"How did it end? I mean, after you and Grainger hooked up? What happened with Mack? How did he take it?"

She dropped her eyes, but not before Will saw the tears in them. Her lips trembled slightly and she bit at them. "Not well."

"So what happened?"

She pushed herself out of the rocking chair, sending

it into a wild canter. "I can't tell you. I thought that I could, but I can't."

"I have to know. You can't not tell me." He was being cheated. He tried to control the petulance in his voice as he demanded again, "Come on, Mom. You've told me this much. How did it end?"

She put one hand out to stop the motion of the rocking chair. She looked down on her son, then looked to the sea beyond the bluff, the water a deeper dark than the sky above it, a visible line defining where one began and the other left off. "You see, Will, my mistake wasn't in choosing Mack or Grainger, but in choosing at all. That was the answer I should have given Grainger. I wouldn't have chosen."

"So you really don't know who my father is."

His mother looked down on him with a smile, her dimples showing. "Your father was the love of my life."

Like Alice's rabbit hole, the entry to his mother's past had disappeared.

After breakfast the next day, Will tried to concentrate on the books Grainger had loaned him. He lay on his narrow bed and thumbed through the illustrated manuals, rehearsing the lexicon under his breath. *Jib, jibe* or *gybe, mainsail, cleat, clew, shroud, running rigging, standing rigging, bitt, block,* blah blah blah.

Every word conjured the image of the three friends in their boat, the tension between them like a foul wind.

Every instruction teemed with minute details: move the tiller in that direction to go in the opposite. Even directions for moving a boat away from a dock seemed unnaturally complicated. Will chided himself. He was going to major in architecture; surely he could figure this out.

But it was no good. He couldn't concentrate with the story his mother had told him whirling around in his head. For although he told himself that at least she'd loved the two boys, that he was not a product of rape, he couldn't shake the fact that he was very angry.

Fickle. That was the word; his mother had been cruelly fickle. No wonder the two boys, now men, wanted nothing to do with her. And, by default, him.

Will dropped the books on the floor of his bedroom and went downstairs. His mother was nowhere in sight, but the car was in the driveway and he helped himself to the keys. He would go to Great Harbor and try to shake this cloudiness away. After scrawling a note on the back of an envelope to say he didn't know when he'd be back, Will left the house, letting the screen door slam in anger and frustration.

Will pulled away from the stop sign a little too fast. Sand spit out from under the tires, making him think of Grainger pulling away too quickly from him. Grainger would know how the story ended. Something had happened; Will was certain of it. If Mack had only gotten mad and said horrible things, she would have said so. The look in her eyes told him there was definitely more to the story.

Even only yesterday, he'd thought it would be enough to know how he came to be. But now, every answer was shadowed by another question.

Great Harbor had all the shops and game rooms and movie houses Hawke's Cove lacked, as well as a strip mall with Staples on one end and T.J.Maxx at the other. A real town. Not like Hawke's Cove with its old-fashioned, uncool dry-goods store, and plain old coffee shop instead of Starbucks. Will pulled into the strip mall parking lot and went into the coffee bar. Sitting in the window, drinking but not tasting his latte, Will noticed the electric blue shutters of the motel across the street. A shiver of recognition raised the hair on his arms. The motel where . . . the thought formulated itself before he could deflect it . . . where he might have been conceived. In the darkness, accompanied by the soft percussion of the rocking chairs, his mother's story had seemed about fictional people—but seeing those blue shutters brought the truth of it home like a sledge-hammer.

"Hey, look out." A girl's voice behind him spoke in warning.

Will glanced back and saw behind him one of the girls from last night, swiveling to avoid a large man who was completely unaware of her. He had nearly spilled his tray of coffees on her, and she banged into Will's table to avoid being stepped on. Will reached out and grabbed her tall paper cup before it tipped off of her tray.

"Good catch. Thanks."

Will set the cup back on her tray. She stood a moment longer, scouting for a place to sit down. "I'm almost done, sit here." Will pointed to one of the cushiony chairs alongside his small table.

The girl gave the room one more look and then sat down, her tray taking up most of the table. "Thanks. It gets crazy in here."

"So I see." Will didn't know whether to say more, or if, like him, she'd come in here to get away from something. To think about something.

She gave Will a look. "Don't I know you?"

"I sat next to you last night at the fireworks."

"Will, right?"

"Catherine?"

"Catherine Ames." The girl opened up her bagel and began spreading cream cheese on it so that both flat surfaces were covered with exactly the same amount. "I work at the T.J.Maxx. Summer job, although I get a few weekends in during the holidays."

"So you live here year-round?"

"Mmm." The girl sipped her tall coffee. "Hawke's Cove."

"Me, too. I mean, I'm there for a couple of weeks."

"Summer kid?"

"No. Well, sort of. It's my first time, although my family's been here since the thirties."

"Where?"

"Overlook Bluff Road."

"That's where the rich folks live. You rich?"

"No, we're not rich. My mother and I aren't, that is." Will took another sip of his cooling coffee and wondered if he should leave. He didn't relish having to talk about his family right now. At the same time, he was glad for this break from the tyranny of his private thoughts.

"Ours is a new house, in Cove terms. About fifteen years old. We moved in when I was three. It's on Bailey's Farm Road."

Will startled a little at the name of the road. "Near Bailey's Beach?"

"Yeah. Not a lot of people know that beach. Do you go there?"

Will frowned a little behind his cup. *No, but I might have been conceived there.* "I've heard of it." Dear God, his mother had slept with two guys. He felt a little sick and only caught up to this girl's sentence halfway through.

"It's the best. No crowds. I'll take you there sometime."

He'd thought last night that she was cute; now he took an unabashed look at her. Catherine's short dark hair was highlighted with a little red, her nose, which fit her small face perfectly, sported a tiny pink stone in one nostril. He'd never much cared for nose piercing, but this one looked nice. Her thick dark brows accented the dark of her eyes, eyes he realized were looking at him in a similar critical exercise. He wondered what she saw. "When do you go back to work?"

"I have to go back"—Catherine checked her watch—"in one minute."

"Are you seeing anyone?" Will felt an unaccustomed boldness rise in his chest.

"No. Why?" Catherine was standing, her tray in her hands.

"Maybe you'd like to go out?"

"When?"

"Tonight? Tomorrow?"

"I'm off tomorrow."

"I've got something in the morning." His sailing lesson.

"After lunch?"

"Let's say two o'clock."

"Maybe we could go to the beach, if it's good."

"Could we go to Bailey's Beach?"

Catherine smiled at him, an odd smile, as if she'd made a bet with herself that's what he'd say. As if she knew him already. "I live at number fifteen Bailey's Farm Road."

"Perfect."

Eighteen

❧

Kiley walked down the hill into the village. Maybe she'd go as far as the harbor, admire the boats calling in from distant places. Or pop into the small library and pick out a mystery.

She was still agitated from her talk with Will last night, suffering from a galloping sense that she'd whitewashed the story. The facts were told, but purified by time and distance. Her bed had been too soft last night and sleep would not come. Maybe it was better this way: chewing on the past had certainly prevented her from dwelling on her immediate future. Over and over, Kiley replayed the mental tapes of her last three meetings with Grainger. The terrible words said, the horrific ending that last August night of their childhoods. Then, the stiff surprised greeting in the Osprey's Nest. Finally, the fleeting easiness after the softball game, countered with his sudden walking away, as if he suddenly remembered he hated her. Just what did Grainger Egan want from her?

Almost to Main Street, Kiley decided to get some homemade ice cream at Linda's Coffee Shop. But as soon as she turned the corner, she stopped. The Egan's Boat Works truck was parked on Main Street, with Grainger's dog sitting in the driver's seat, its small brown eyes fixed on the door of the restaurant. The door opened and Grainger came out, greeted his dog with a pat, and handed it something from the take-out bag, then shoved it over with his hip and got in.

Kiley stood motionless on the sidewalk, invisible. He'd been so prominent in her relentless thoughts. Now, there he was, and for the first time, she noticed how much he had changed. The Grainger of her memory was a lanky youth, with ropy muscles and a narrow chest. This man was broad-shouldered, the tanned arms revealed by his paint-spattered T-shirt well-defined, his waist narrow, his torso big but lean. In the harsh July sunlight, she could see that his hair had darkened to true brown, touched at the temples with silvery gray. His face was etched with the lines of a man whose life was outdoors. He was a grown man.

A good-looking grown man with a life. All the imaginary conversations she'd had with him over the years had not prepared her for the reality of him. He'd existed only as the eighteen-year-old boy who'd made love to her and then rejected her. The one she had apologized to in her dreams over and over, the imaginary friend who had always accepted her apologies. It had been necessary to keep Grainger locked up in that magic box where he would always be that boy. But the reality of the man released that boy forever. This was the Grainger she needed to know.

Kiley turned on her heel and walked away. Her pulse was audible in her ears against the sound of traffic on the narrow street. Walking back the way she came, Kiley thought that she'd be walking away from him. But Grainger had turned in her direction, and was suddenly alongside of her. His eyes were on the double-parked car in front of him, then on the dog. Then, as if drawn by some instinct to look, he turned to see her. They were motionless, staring at each other. A car horn roused Grainger from his transfixion. He nodded a greeting, but did not smile. She raised a hand to wave, but he sped away.

She didn't want to keep meeting Grainger like this, accidentally. After all, they did have Will between them. Regardless of paternity, Will existed, and Grainger could make what he wanted of it. The biggest secret from those days was now out in the open. What did he think about it?

Kiley remembered her father's request to deal with the boat, and Grainger's words: "Call me." She would. No more pussyfooting around; she had a reason to see him. Maybe then they could begin to repair some of the damage.

Will was gone when Kiley got back home. The black phone sat quietly looming, waiting for her to pick it up and call Grainger. All the way back to the house, Kiley had rehearsed what she would say. She'd keep it all business.

He had a nice ad in the Yellow Pages, a silhouette of a schooner. Kiley stared at it as the phone on the other end rang and rang until an answering machine picked up. "Egan's Boat Works. Please leave a message." What can you tell about a man by his answering machine message?

"It's Kiley. I'm calling about the boat. About *Random*." She left her telephone number and hung up, painfully aware of the beating of her heart. The sudden shrill ring of the phone startled Kiley and she grabbed the receiver up, half expecting it to be Grainger.

"Kiley? Hey, it's Conor."

Kiley sat down on the little chair and ran a hand beneath her hair, lifting it up off her neck, where a trickle of perspiration bloomed. "Conor, hi."

"Look, I know this is a little short notice, but would you like to have dinner tomorrow night?" When she hesitated, he pressed on. "I mean, if you don't have anything going on. I'm thinking maybe Anthony's in Great Harbor. Have you ever been there?"

"No. But . . ."

"Kiley, it's all right. I know there's baggage here, and we should talk about it."

Why hadn't Grainger said that? Why hadn't she? Conor had always been on the periphery of her world, glimpsed as he led his glamorous, grown-up college life when they were still teens. He resided on Olympus, deigning only occasionally to notice them, and they all looked up to him. When she and Mack paired off, Conor had congratulated them, telling Mack he was very lucky. Telling her to confide in him should Mack behave badly. Conor had no idea the weight of the baggage she carried.

"Okay. But I'll meet you there. I have some things to do in Great Harbor." She wanted to tell Conor about Will before she brought them face-to-face; prep him, so to speak, before handing him a boy he might think was his nephew.

"I saw him today." Kiley didn't look up from her plate of spaghetti.

"Who?"

"Grainger." Why had she even mentioned it?

"Where?" Will reached for the Parmesan cheese.

"He drove by when I was on Main Street." It seemed a terribly difficult thing to spool the strands of spaghetti around her fork.

"Did he see you?"

"Yes."

"Did you speak?"

"I think you could say that we were both struck dumb."

"Are you guys grown-ups or not?" Will jabbed his fork into a piece of sausage. "Jesus. You could at least have waved."

"Don't swear. And I did wave."

"Why don't you invite him over for dinner or something?"

Kiley didn't answer for a moment. "I don't think that's a good idea."

"I guess I just don't get it. You are dwelling on ancient history." Will's voice had risen; instantly, he lowered it. "Could you, for my sake, at least try to understand why I might want the two of you in the same room?"

"No, *I* really don't get it. This isn't some fucking *Parent Trap,* some happy-ending movie. We hurt each other. End of story."

"Now who's swearing?"

Kiley put her fork down and patted Will's hand. "You're too young to understand the difficulty—"

Will pulled away. "Don't patronize me, Mom. It's a pretty simple wish. I can't get to know Grainger better if I think it's making you unhappy."

"Oh, Will. It won't make me unhappy. I encourage you to get to know him. He was a wonderful guy; I'm sure he's still wonderful. Just don't expect us to want some orchestrated reunion neither one of us is looking for." Grainger still hadn't returned her call, and she took it to mean he didn't want to; that his offer to help was simply the conditioned response of a man in the boat business. He was probably having second thoughts after seeing her at the picnic. "Don't mistake wishful thinking for reality."

Will shoved his plate away and opened one of his sailing books.

"Conor MacKenzie called me today. Mack's brother."

Will took his eyes off the page. "You didn't tell me that Mack's family is still here."

"He's the guy I was sitting with last night at the picnic."

"Why didn't you tell me that before?"

"He doesn't know about you. His parents don't know about you."

"You've managed to keep my existence secret from anyone who might have cared."

"That's a little harsh."

"What are you so afraid of? That they'll want custody?"

Kiley got up to scrape her plate into the compost container. "Sometimes it seems like a good idea to wait on something. Then, before you know it, it's too late. It's too late to tell the truth."

"That's not what you've told me before."

"Well, he'll know soon enough. I'm going out with him tomorrow night."

"Good. I think that the MacKenzies will be happy to know that maybe they have a grandson."

Kiley set her plate in the sink and squirted dishwashing detergent across it in a rough Z pattern. "You don't think that it would be unfair to make them hope that you are their grandson?"

"It would be simple enough to prove it." Will added

his plate to the dishes in the sink. He leaned back against the counter and ran a hand through his hair exactly the way Grainger used to when he was debating something, gripping the ends of it in a tug before letting go. "I'd like to have a DNA test done."

"You could only do that if one of the MacKenzies or Grainger goes along with it." Kiley struggled to keep her voice even.

Will closed his eyes and pinched the bridge of his nose. Mack had done that any time he was preparing a rebuttal to Grainger's argument. "At least let's ask them if they would."

The water was scalding, and Kiley slammed the hot water faucet off, and pulled on the cold water faucet. "Can't you just let it alone? What difference would it make in the end? I raised you. You're my son. I didn't need any of them before, and I certainly don't need any of them now."

Will pushed himself away from the counter and stalked toward the back door. "*You* might not, but I do."

Kiley slammed the dish in her hand down into the soapy water, causing a geyser to slap the countertop and drip onto the floor. "This is exactly why I never wanted to come back here. This is exactly what I feared would happen. Things would be opened up, people would get hurt. I never should have come here."

"You're wrong, Mom. It was exactly what we both needed. You're like a clam, holding on to that grain of sand. You're starting to open up; now let go of the pearl."

"Oyster. It's oysters who make pearls, and there are no pearls here."

"Let go, Mom. I deserve to have this one piece of the puzzle solved. I deserve to know who my father is."

"I can't talk about this anymore." Kiley turned her back and addressed the dishes, scrubbing hard at the sauce pot, her dish sponge going round and round with a hollow splooshing sound. "Don't I have enough to worry about, getting this house ready for sale, finding a new job, without having to—"

Will grabbed the car keys from the hook by the back door and walked out.

Nineteen

Having seen Kiley, Grainger was half expecting the knock on the door. He was in that twisted place of half hope, half dread. But it wasn't her; it was Will. Grainger was sure the surprise of it was on his face; he could feel his expression change from clenched-jaw anticipation to pleasure. Surely Will saw it too, and Grainger was glad that the ultimate look on his face showed welcome.

"Come in." Grainger held the door wide and left it open.

Will was trembling in a way that precluded simply being chilly. There was fear in his eyes, as if he was about to jump off the topmast yard of a schooner without being able to see the water below. Grainger had spent the summer between his two years at Maine Maritime crewing on a charter schooner. His mates were a rowdy bunch, always daring each other to greater and greater feats of bravado. As first mate, Grainger set the challenges. The very first day he climbed aloft, he felt a loosening up of the vise that had constricted his heart for five years. Most days he was almost unaware of it. Joy, happiness, laughter, were rare moments in his days. This one day, he climbed so high the crew and guests below him were pinpricks; and suddenly it was only him, his balance on the footropes, and the sky. Below him, the deck of the ship was inconsequential, the water surrounding it so great. Suddenly, literally, he was above it all. His view was southeasterly, and it was easy to imagine that he might see Hawke's Cove jutting out into the Atlantic. He hadn't been back since that night, and had no intention of ever going back. But that never stopped him from wishing it could have been different; from longing for another time.

He remained where he was until the sails below his feet began their descent, as the guests and crew folded the heavy canvas sails like a giant fan to rest on the boom. Without the view-blocking sails beneath him, Grainger felt even more above it all. He pulled his bare feet out from the footropes and grasped the very top of the mast, bringing himself slowly to a balanced upright position atop it, the soles of his feet against the pinnacle of the mast, his arms outstretched for balance. The crew and guests stopped what they were doing and looked up as Grainger launched himself, dropping with more speed than he had expected, into the deepwater cove. It hurt, but his hands had pierced the deceptively hard surface of the water first, and he came up uninjured. And feeling more alive than he had been in years.

Now Will Harris stood in front of him, a pale, choked expression on his face. Grainger shook off the memory of that long-ago plunge, aware that his heart was beating as hard as it had in that last second before he had dived.

"I should have called?" Will's inflection was the one

that teenagers affect, every statement potentially a question, leaving the door open to escape.

"No. It's fine." Grainger bent and ran his fingers through Pilot's coat to check for ticks, acting as if Will's dropping by unexpectedly was as normal as anyone else's.

"This is probably random, and you can say no . . ." Will joined Grainger in the tick hunt, both of them avoiding a direct look. "But I wondered if you'd let me work here. You don't have to pay me or anything. I just like the boats. I'd like you to teach me how to, like, do stuff with them."

"Stuff?"

"Yeah. You know, what you do here, paint or scrape, learn to rig."

"Is that the only reason?" The words were out of his mouth before Grainger could think them.

Will looked at Grainger with those black-encircled blue irises, his ram's horn eyebrows over fair lashes that were long and almost girlish. He looked at him with a nonverbal challenge. The way Kiley had looked at him this afternoon, as if challenging him to speak first.

"No."

Will didn't offer his ulterior reason for wanting to hang out with him, but Grainger thought he knew what it was, and was suddenly overwhelmed with rising joy. Could it be that Will wanted to spend time with him in the hope that he might prove to be his father?

Grainger kept his embarrassingly moist eyes on the dog. "Great. Sure. Go get the tick jar from the workbench and then I'll get you started." Grainger was back in control by the time Will had located the mayonnaise jar with the kerosene in it, and he dropped a couple of wood ticks into the jar. "Okay. There's still enough light out, so grab a mask and that sander under the bench. I'll get you started outside."

Grainger always claimed not to be a sentimentalist. He threw out everything no longer useful. He sold boats he'd labored on for months without a backward glance. He seldom got misty-eyed at movies. Without a tremble, he could say good-bye to people he knew he wouldn't see again. That was life. People come, people go.

Only Grainger knew he was a fake, that he spent part of every day remembering the past. It was easier years ago, when he was kept on the move by his profession. He was distracted by card games at sea, long hours monitoring radar and Loran, reviewing navigational charts and taking orders. There was nothing with him or around him to remind him of the past. Then he came home. Back to Hawke's Cove, where he'd sworn he'd never return, and every day since had been a war of maudlin sentimentality versus getting on with his life. What was past was unchangeable, and yet it infiltrated some moment of every day. The simple fact of being in this place, of seeing faces of people he'd gone to school with, walking the same streets, the overall unchangeability of his small town. The clock in the town hall tower that had never worked. The same surnames of the people who run the town. There had always been a Silva or a Fielding or a French as selectman or county commissioner or dog warden. Grainger choked back the memories and moved on.

Grainger knew that his mistake was in not creating new memories. He had nothing worth remembering with either joy or grief, besides those years of his youth. Even his two attempts at having a romantic relationship had faded away because he spent more time afloat than ashore. Natural, unremarkable, endings to tepid affairs. He had intended keeping this boy at arm's length, keep him from awakening suppressed memories, but Grainger knew that from the moment he was aware of Will Harris, his defenses had been breached.

He got Will started sanding a hull. *Miss Emily* was still taking up all the space in the boathouse, needing one last coat of marine paint. Using a paint sprayer, it didn't take Grainger long to finish while Will kept at his task outside. Stripping off his protective white jumpsuit, Grainger had a moment to look out the window. He might look out the window five hundred times a day, but now he looked with purpose. Will was squatting, the power sander held at shoulder height as he ran it along the hull beneath the waterline. His Cornell cap was twisted around so that the bill rested against his neck. Cornell. Nice choice. Grainger wondered what he was going to major in and almost went out to ask, then pulled himself back. *Leave him be.* They could talk about school when he came in; it would be too easy to lose the remaining light trying to get to know a boy who would very quickly be out of his life.

It hit Grainger, then, that it was incumbent on him to make sure Will *didn't* slip out of his life. Whether or not he was his biological son, Will was a part of him. It didn't really matter if Kiley wanted it or not; Grainger wanted it. And, if his suspicions were correct, it was something Will wanted too.

"Hey, Will. Do you drink coffee?"

Will stood up and pulled the mask from his face. Even at a distance, Grainger could see the dimples forming in his cheeks.

"Sure do."

Mack had never liked coffee.

"Come inside in about ten minutes."

Grainger turned away from the door. Mack and he had battled over Kiley, and now he would battle Mack's memory for her son. Grainger knew he was doomed to read every mannerism, every blush or phrase, as a genetic marker. He knew that some days he would see Mack so clearly that there would be no denying Will was his legacy. And, maybe, on other occasions, he might hope that Will was his. Grainger slammed the glass carafe under the faucet, almost hard enough to break it.

Pilot barked in greeting as Will came in, his baggy green shorts and loose T-shirt dusty with sanded paint.

"Go wash your hands." Grainger sounded paternal even to himself and turned away to hide a self-conscious smile.

When Will came back, he, too, was smiling. The smile of someone who'd uncovered something. "You have that picture too."

"What picture?" Although Grainger knew. On his bathroom wall, hidden from public sight, was a photograph in a cheap black frame of Mack, Kiley, and him in front of *Blithe Spirit* as she sat on her cradle in Mack's backyard. The only photograph Grainger had ever kept from those days.

"Of you guys. And the boat."

Grainger said nothing, although he was pleased in some way that Will had seen that snapshot, seen a tangible connection between his mother and himself. They all had copies of that picture. The MacKenzies still had theirs in a gold-toned frame on a mantel in their house. Once or twice a year they invited him for dinner. Always overly cheery affairs; they never spoke of what went on before, they only spoke of today. Grainger called Mrs. MacKenzie "Doro," and they all pretended nothing had ever happened. But Grainger didn't think she loved him as she once did. He was now only a connection to her lost child, not the lost child she once saved. For a while, he was certain that she must have blamed him. He had run away that night, hitchhiked away from Great Harbor, heading toward the postmark on the letter his mother had sent, the letter Kiley had brought to him. Later, he couldn't bring himself to return to them, to find out for sure what they felt.

Will added an enormous amount of half-and-half to his coffee. Sort of the way Grainger did.

"How does your mother feel about you being here? With me."

"She's okay with it. She told me it was all right for me to get to know you. She said you were a nice guy."

Grainger sipped his coffee very carefully. "Ummm. I used to be."

"Oh, come on." Will laughed, amused for some reason at Grainger's demurral.

Pilot, always good for distraction, sidled up to Will, looking for a rump scratch. Will obliged, and the dog got that ecstatic look of doggy pleasure as the boy's long fingers dug into the perpetually itchy spot at the base of his tail.

Grainger watched Will's face, noticing the way he didn't make eye contact. "Why did you really come?"

"I told you . . . I'm interested in boats."

"Will. If you and I are going to get along, we need to be honest."

"Why? No one has been honest with me."

The urge to ask, "And what has your mother told you, what has she said about me?" was physical, a burning on his tongue. "Ask me what you want to know."

"I want to know what happened to Mack."

Grainger scraped his fingers through his hair, now unable himself to make eye contact. "Have you asked your mother?"

"She told me that . . ." Will was flushed, his voice suddenly a low growl. "She told me what she did, that she slept with both of you, but she won't tell me what happened in the end."

"Life doesn't have tidy endings. People hurt each other, and sometimes they don't behave well."

"But *I* was the result of her not behaving. And I don't know if I'm the reason she's cut herself off from this place, like she's *ashamed* of me or something. Was it something else that made it impossible for her to come back? If she loved you both the way I think she did, then she could never have *not* told you about me." Will rubbed the back of his hand against his eyes and moved toward the door. "I have to go."

Grainger caught him by the elbow. "I can't imagine that she was ever ashamed of you."

Will stared at him, wavering, wanting to believe him.

"Come back tomorrow, like we planned."

"No. It was a stupid idea."

"Will, take the lesson." Will's eyes were still on him, looking at him with the same confused intensity as . . . no, no more. It was time to put the past to rest. "I'll tell you what you want to know tomorrow."

Will nodded.

Grainger waited until he was certain Will was gone before walking past Merriwell Harris's *Random* to the covered Beetle Cat that had been sitting solitary in the boatyard for as long as he'd owned the place. She would be a good one for Will to learn on. Once again, she needed TLC and antifouling paint. Once again, she needed scraping and painting, brightwork renewed. It wasn't a big job. Just one that had, like the story he would tell Will tomorrow, been waiting for him for a long time.

Twenty

꩜

The next morning, Kiley flattened *The Boston Globe* out on the kitchen table to look at the want ads. There were a fair number of nurse practitioner positions open, all in the greater Boston area; too far from Southton to commute to daily. Her local hospital was always on the brink of financial collapse, and she knew that the staffing was bare-bones. Maybe she could get a studio apartment in Boston and do three twelve-hour days. She could be home the rest of the time. Kiley leaned her elbows on the paper and rested her forehead on her clenched hands. *Come on, it's time to live large.* Will would be in Ithaca. What was holding her to Southton except her parents? And she'd be home four days out of seven. When Will came home for semester break, they could do Boston properly, without the mad rush to get home. Museums, the theater. Fine dining.

Kiley folded the paper and crammed it into the wastebasket. She had time, and so much else held her attention; she just couldn't focus on job hunting too. Sandy had called again this morning to tell her that everyone in the office had been given three months' pay—a short reprieve from having to make a hasty decision. Will was right; it was time to try something new. Maybe she'd even get out of the medical profession and do something completely different.

Kiley went out to the front porch and sat down in one of the rocking chairs. Out in the wide cove, sailboats glided across the water. Will might be in one of them. Kiley wasn't sure how she felt about it. On the one hand, she was quietly pleased that he wanted to learn how to sail; on the other, aware that he would probably badger Grainger for more of the story. What would Grainger tell him?

He still hadn't called her back. If he didn't want the business, he shouldn't have told her to call him. She wasn't going to try again. He'd backed off so quickly from her yesterday it was pretty clear he didn't want anything to do with her. She should just leave him alone.

Kiley thumped her hand against the rocking chair arm. She hadn't tagged the rockers yet. Wherever would she put them at home? They were too big for a living room, and her parents' sunporch, with its white wicker, was all wrong for the painted chairs. She stroked the flat arm of the rocker and picked at its chipped paint. They needed painting; where it wasn't chipped, the green paint was powdered.

Now that she had been here for a while, Kiley could see that everything wasn't exactly like she remembered: everything was old and worn, and the warmth of their familiarity had gone. These objects had entered her present, and the luster of their existence in her memory was dimmed. Now she looked at these objects dispassionately. Just as she should look at Grainger Egan.

Heaving a dramatic sigh, Kiley got up to call him again. She was only acting in her father's interest.

As she was looking up the boatyard's number, the phone rang.

"It's Dad. Have you made arrangements for the boat yet?"

"I was just about to leave another message for Grainger. He apparently doesn't return phone calls."

"Well, I've had a change of heart."

"I'm so glad. I think that selling both the house and the boat in the same summer is too much."

"No, no. I'm still going to sell her, but first I'm going to race her one more time in the August Races. It's a great way to draw attention to her. So I need you to find me a crew."

Kiley rubbed her forehead with tense fingers. "Dad, I don't think that's doable."

"Course it is. Just put up a notice at the club; you'll have half a dozen interested. *Random* is a winning boat; everyone wants a chance on her."

"How many do you need?"

"Well, you and I are two, if Will knew how to sail, I'd ask him . . ."

"He's taking lessons."

"Good for him. That's my boy. Great, if he's any good, we'll bring him aboard. Now, we need at least one more. I'm not likely to be any real help, to tell you the truth, so get someone who knows what they're doing."

"One problem, Dad."

"What's that?"

"Will and I won't be here in August."

"You're unemployed, so if you wanted to stay on, you could."

"I don't want to stay on. I'm almost done now with the inventory, and maybe we'll head home sooner."

"Don't gyp Will out of his vacation." Merriwell's voice had begun to feather away, as it often did when he conversed for more than a few minutes.

"I'm almost done, and I might even leave early if a job suddenly comes up. But I'll put a notice up on the board with your home number on it."

"Think about it, Kiley. This is the last time you'll ever be in Hawke's Cove."

The last time. Her father was right, but about something else besides simply being in Hawke's Cove. This was her last chance to make things right with Grainger. Kiley dialed his number again, but this time the phone rang and rang without the answering machine picking up. Either he had it off or the tape was full. Kiley went back out to the porch. Shielding her eyes against the morning sun, she gazed out at the sailboats, wondering which one might hold her son, and Grainger.

Twenty-one

Grainger saw the blinking red light on his answering machine as he plugged in the coffeemaker. He felt a slight guilt. He hadn't checked messages for several days, a bad habit born of an innate distaste for the phone, and the tape was full. Most of the calls would be from anxious clients hoping to convince him to put their work first. Every year after the holiday, owners got nudgie, as if they suddenly realized half the summer was gone. Despite all his efforts to get these folks to call him in March instead of June, they persisted in believing they could get their boats in the water by the Fourth.

Just as Grainger began to play the messages, Will pulled into the driveway. Grainger pressed the stop button. Time enough to catch up once they were back from Will's lesson. Will was a little early and waited on the doorstep, shivering in the early morning chill. Grainger let him in and handed him a cup of coffee. "Go get a life jacket out of the locker and meet me on the beach."

Ever since hearing that Kiley and her son were in town, a viselike grip in Grainger's chest had begun to tighten, its constriction more pronounced after his having seen them together in the Osprey's Nest, tighter as he watched Will play baseball and Kiley pitch the way he had taught her. Tightest of all when he saw her with Conor MacKenzie. Grainger wondered briefly if there was something physically wrong with him, but it was an all-too-familiar sensation. There was no cure. He was too old to be jumping off mainmasts, too old to be running away from unhappy memories. This kid, so like his mother, had him reliving a past he had successfully suppressed. Will's existence destroyed his former ability to keep his past in check simply by not thinking about it. How could he keep this kid out of his mind?

Grainger had promised to tell Will the story. The sorry tale of how three best friends could lose the very thing they held most dear, because of human nature.

He pushed the dinghy into the water and waited for Will to amble out of the boathouse. He had the life jacket on but not fastened, and Grainger gestured to him to get it done. "Safety first, Will." He took Will's mug of coffee and sat in the bow of the dinghy. "Do you know how to row?"

"Sure, I've rowed a dozen times on lakes."

"Row us out to the boat, then." Grainger sipped coffee out of his own travel mug as the boy rowed them out to the waiting sailboat.

In literature the protagonist is brought face-to-face with his bête noire; why else would the story be written? In the person of this boy, a boy exactly the age they had been, Grainger couldn't shake the sense that there was no escaping his demons.

They climbed aboard the little Beetle Cat and into

the cockpit, Will's bare knees as coltish as Mack's had been. It suddenly seemed exactly the right place to be. Where else could this story be told except on the water?

Will followed Grainger's orders with a minimum of questioning, and they were under way in a few minutes. Grainger handed Will his cool coffee and reviewed the lexicon with him, then helped him settle in at the tiller. Will was a quick study, and in fifteen minutes they were into the arms of the little private cove, and swept by the outgoing tide into the open waters surrounding Hawke's Cove. He jibed correctly if not gracefully at Grainger's orders, and they set off, keeping the length of the peninsula as their guide. Grainger and Will were half a mile offshore. The most private place on earth.

A fine sizzle marked their speed. There was nothing left to do but sit in silence or speak.

"Mr. Egan?"

"Yes, Will?"

"Will you tell me what happened now?"

"What are we going to tell Mack?" Kiley had gone into the small bathroom and taken a quick shower. Grainger remained on the bed, breathing in the scent of their lovemaking. She stepped out, fully dressed. "What are we going to do?"

Grainger pulled the bedsheet over his nakedness. "I don't know. Maybe we don't say anything."

"He'll know."

"How?"

"The same way you knew." She sat down on the bed.

Grainger watched her bend to tie her sneakers. "How I knew what?"

Her hair was loose and sheeted across her cheek,

hiding her face from his view. "That he and I had, I
don't know, paired off."

Grainger knew that he had robbed Mack of the
woman he loved. It was worse than the way that Mack
had deprived him of Kiley; Grainger had stolen her.
And Grainger had slept with her; they'd made love all
afternoon. That made her his, and bonded them together now in a way he could never have imagined a
day ago. Grainger lay back and pressed a pillow against
his face to hide the guilt. "What are we going to do? I
don't want to hurt him."

Kiley took the pillow away from Grainger's face.
Hers was a mask of sorrow. "No matter what happens,
someone is going to be hurt." She touched his cheek,
then touched his lips with the tips of her fingers, but
did not kiss him. "I have to go."

"Do we tell him together?"

Kiley paused in the doorway. "I think I should do it
alone."

Grainger trusted her. She would be gentle and explain to Mack that, although she loved him, with
Grainger it was more powerful. They'd slept together.
With that act, they had memorialized the sincerity of
their new relationship.

There was a break in Grainger's story as he instructed
Will on coming about. Tall but agile, Will ducked easily under the boom. They had gone halfway to the end
of the peninsula; now they had to come back. Not
much farther lay glacier-strewn boulders, often hidden
by water-shifted sands, making navigational charts and
Loran a necessity to avoid them. It wasn't enough to
have experience. Here and there Grainger could see

lobster buoys marking pots, and he knew that they were coming close to dangerous waters.

Grainger was grateful Will said nothing as he talked, because then he could tell this the way he remembered it, to better explain himself when he approached the conclusion of the story. Will never looked directly at Grainger, either, keeping his eyes like a sailor on the sail or the tiller or the horizon. Grainger let him sail on, confident he was listening, confident that he would let him finish the story his own way.

Grainger got up and headed back to Hawke's Cove. Only a coward would stay away. Despite Kiley's desire to be the one to tell Mack of their love, he knew he couldn't let her do it alone.

It was a moonless night, and the only light as he approached the Yacht Club came from the three post lamps that cast a weak light along the boardwalk. Storm pennants snapped from the flagpole. They should put chafing gear on *Blithe Spirit,* Grainger thought as he felt the northeast wind against his face. He took a small comfort from the momentary reprieve from his crowded and uncomfortable thoughts. How was Mack going to take this? Would he behave as badly as Grainger had, sulking and hurt? Or would Mack rise to it, and be happy for them?

Inside, the lights were bright. Music blared out through the open doors—the Village People's "Y.M.C.A." song, signaling the end of the dance, the end of the dances for the summer of 1984. Grainger could see the Doublemints through the lighted windows, smiling at each other like faces in a mirror. He knew that Kiley and Mack wouldn't be inside; they'd have gone to the privacy of the beach.

As Grainger's feet crunched the moist sand he strained to hear their voices, but could hear only the high whine of the wind through rigging. He was nearly to the Yacht Club pier with its dinghy platform tied alongside. Grainger stood still and listened again.

Then he heard their voices. They were on the end of the pier, looking out into the darkness, speaking so softly their voices might have been the lapping of the waves against the pilings. Kiley's white blouse caught his eye, a ghost of shape, a slight movement against a motionless black.

"I'm so sorry." Distinct words, thickened by regret.

They both turned toward Grainger as he stepped on the splintery planks of the pier.

Mack stood up, and Grainger could see the belligerence in his posture. "You fucking bastard!"

"Mack, we couldn't fight it." Grainger kept moving toward where they stood on the end of the pier, compelled to close the space. "It was too powerful. We love each other."

"Is this true, Kiley?"

Kiley stood between them. She placed a hand on each of their chests, as if holding them apart, and, at the same time, connecting herself to both of them. She didn't answer.

"After what we did, how can you say you love *him?*" Mack grasped the hand that was touching his chest.

Grainger took a step back, away from Kiley's hand. "What did you do?"

"Grainger, I thought you knew." Kiley reached out for him, but he moved back another step.

His heart was pounding; he felt submerged, afraid to gasp for air because he might drown. "You slept with Mack and then with me?"

Grainger never saw the blow coming. His head hit the plank decking and he was numbed with the fall. He heard Kiley scream, but it seemed distant. Mack stepped on his fingers as he ran down the length of the pier. The pier beneath him was spinning, and the starless night gave him no point of reference to climb back onto his feet.

Then Kiley was there, tugging at his hands to get upright. "He's taken the dinghy. Stop him, Grainger!"

Grainger slumped on the pier, his legs unable to hold him up. Mack had sucker punched him, and with his blow came the realization that Kiley Harris had come between them. She would go on with her life elsewhere, graduate from her prestigious school, marry a lawyer, and laugh about the summer she'd come between best friends. Slept with best friends. Grainger pushed her away from him and struggled to his feet. "Leave him alone. Leave me alone."

Kiley grabbed at his arm, pleading with him. "Stop him, Grainger."

"*You* stop him." Kiley Harris had cost him everything. Foolishly, he had believed that her love would be worth Mack's hurt and anger, worth losing the only stable home he'd ever had. He'd even believed Mack would accept it over time. But Mack's punch had cleared his head, and the magnitude of his mistake tightened the pressure in his chest. She had slept with both of them. What he'd believed had been only his was a sham, a joke, a lie. "I never want to see you again."

"Grainger, no. Please. Let me explain."

The sound of a two-cycle engine cut through the inharmonic chiming of halyards against aluminum masts.

It was more than he could bear. "Get the fuck out of my life, Kiley Harris."

• • •

"Mack went out that night in *Blithe Spirit*. It was a stupid thing to do—there were storm warnings up, and he didn't have a life jacket. He was hurt and angry, and when you're in that state of mind, you do stupid things. Lobstermen found *Blithe Spirit* the next morning, on the rocks." It was as far as he could go with the story.

"But what happened to Mack?" Will adjusted his tension on the mainsheet, still not looking at Grainger.

How could he not know what had happened? Or did he just need to hear it said?

Grainger reached over and covered Will's hand on the tiller with his own. "Mack is dead, Will. Lost at sea."

Will looked down at their hands, then up to meet Grainger's eyes at last. "So, which one of you is my father?"

Twenty-two

๑)

The dining room was finally done. As were the front bedroom, the two bedrooms on the north side of the house, and the tiny cubby room that in an earlier time had been the housemaid's room, but in Kiley's lifetime had always been a spare room for overflow guests. These rooms had been a little easier to deal with. Furnished primarily in the original cottage furniture, they weren't rooms with undue significance for her. Only her room, where Will slept, was left to inventory upstairs, and her parents had emptied it long ago of everything but the furniture.

Kiley stood in the doorway, smiling with fond resignation at Will's clutter. Clothing lay draped over the bed and bureau, wet towels grew sour on the painted wood floor. Will's backpack gaped open on the only chair, and she could see his CD player and compact discs mingling with a tangle of headphone wires. In her day, it would have been a portable tape player and tapes. Otherwise, the room could have been hers again. Jeans, T-shirts, sand, randomly chosen rocks and shells.

She pulled her stickie pad out of her pocket and

took the pen out of her ponytail. So far, everything in
the bedrooms would stay. Well, maybe not the hand-
made quilt on this bed. Kiley reprimanded herself: *Sell
the quilt.* She didn't have a bed at home it would fit.
But, the evil imp of sentiment whispered, Grandma
Harris made that quilt and someday Will would have a
home. "Everything—except the quilt—stays." She stuck
the Post-it on the doorjamb.

The house seemed very quiet without the white
noise of Will's CDs leaking out of his earphones. She
tried to substitute the elderly radio, which only pulled
in a slightly buzzy NPR. Still, with nothing else to distract her from thinking, wondering, worrying about
what the two of them might say, it was better than the
silence. Would Grainger tell Will how angry he had
been? Would he tell Will how badly she treated him?

The photograph of the three of them and *Blithe
Spirit* was propped against the blue jar on the kitchen
table. Kiley ignored it, eating her cereal standing up
and looking out the back window. The small yard desperately needed cutting; she'd have Will haul out the
old reel mower and do that this afternoon. Was it still
sharp enough? The jar hovered in the periphery of her
mind. She rinsed her bowl out and left the kitchen.
Then she walked back in, picked up the blue jar and
dropped it into the recycling, where it cracked against a
bottle.

With the house almost all inventoried, Kiley had little to do except collect the items earmarked for home.
They still had ten days left of their vacation, so that
task seemed easy enough to put off. Besides, what if she
decided to stay on? Without a job, there really wasn't
anything to go home to. She should go get a book
and relax on the beach or on the porch. Plan a simple

meal. Kiley went upstairs, made the beds, picked up the towels, and gathered the dirty clothes for a quick Laundromat trip. These ordinary actions were comforting, something to do to fill in the wide-open morning. At home, it seemed as though every minute was scheduled; as though days were metered by her fifteen-minute commute to the medical office, the half hour for lunch, forty-five minutes in the Stop & Shop, ten minutes to the field where Will might be playing baseball or soccer or whatever sport was in season. Any dinner that took more than forty minutes was a luxury. Weekends were worse; all the errands that couldn't be fit into her half-hour lunch breaks dictated those days. Cleaners, another visit to the grocery store, housecleaning, laundry, laundry, laundry. At least the planning had grown simpler as Will grew up. No longer did baby-sitters, day care, and transportation heap complication upon simple tasks. She should be glad to have this free time. Except that in a few short weeks, she would have all the time in the world, and these homely tasks would be cut in half. She'd have only herself to remind to take out the garbage or drive to the recycling center. The loneliness she was about to endure stretched before her.

"Snap out of it." Kiley squared her shoulders. What parent hadn't endured this? It was the whole goal of raising a child, after all. Catch and release. Except if you were lucky, you had someone to share the loneliness with, halving it.

Kiley thought of Grainger's face framed by the window of his truck, the clarity with which she saw him, even to the silver gray touching his temples. He seemed too young for so much gray. Had his life continued hard? She knew next to nothing about him. Only that he was here, that he owned the boat works, and that Will had rooted out his historical relationship with her. Seeing Conor MacKenzie, with his obvious resemblance to Mack as Mack would have matured, then seeing Grainger, had been surreal—not quite a nightmare, not quite a dream. They were at once recognizable, and yet completely different. As was she.

She needed to know what Grainger was telling Will this morning, what version of the story he thought the boy should know.

Kiley tied on her sneakers, her mind seeing only Grainger. She struggled to loop the laces, her hands trembling so much she kept missing. It wasn't fear that caused her to tremble, but excitement—which was odd. All morning long she'd tried not to imagine what Grainger would tell Will; it was too awful to consider. The facts about herself and her teenage inability to see farther than the end of her own nose were highly unflattering.

Kiley walked along the bluff, oblivious to the spangled sea below her. She walked toward the village, heedless of cars passing by, unaware of bicycles swerving around her. Her route took her past the Yacht Club, past the brick medical building where Doctor MacKenzie had practiced, past the library where they'd feasted on books on rainy days, past Linda's Coffee Shop and LaRiviere's Market, where Grainger once lived. Her destination was beyond all landmarks of her youth. Her destination was the old boathouse, now Egan's Boat Works. Her destination was Grainger.

Kiley paused at the sign with its pretty schooner silhouette. The driveway was no longer swaled, but neatly graveled and smooth. A bend in the driveway and the topography of the shoreline kept the boathouse out of sight until she was halfway down the long drive, when it hove into view. It was so different from the last time she'd seen it, a derelict building, smelling of wino piss, where kids would sometimes congregate to drink.

Kiley hadn't given rehearsal space to imaginary conversation. She'd let the words come as they would. Maybe they would use Will as a buffer, letting him guide the conversation.

The gravel driveway straightened out to end in a boat ramp. Three boats in various stages of renovation were arranged in a row on cradles of blocks and poppets. One was partially sanded; another still under a parachute cloth of orange, blue, and green; the third was *Random*.

Across the driveway was the boathouse: a tall shingled building, its gambrel roof providing extra interior height, small casement windows running along the side facing Kiley, each having a window box beneath the mullioned glass, all open to the warm July day. White and purple pansies and deep red begonias were surrounded by dusty miller, and variegated euonymus draped over the edges of the blue boxes. The end of the building facing her was taken up with a sliding plank door, high and wide enough to accommodate a good-sized vessel. The side entry of the boathouse was wide open.

Except for Grainger's truck, the driveway was empty. Will was already gone. She had a momentary hesitation, a swell of nerves that nearly caused her to turn around halfway down the drive. Then Grainger's odd-looking dog meandered out to greet her. As he sniffed at her feet, Kiley bent and patted his head. He wore a leather collar with an ornate brass name tag fixed to it. "Pilot. Hello, Pilot."

Pilot politely wagged his tail and nosed her hand for another pat.

"He likes you."

Grainger's voice startled Kiley.

"He's cute. What is he?" Did her voice reveal her nervousness? It sounded terribly thin to her ears.

"Anyone's guess."

Pilot left Kiley where she stood, a few yards from the door. Cocking his head, he looked at his master standing in the doorway, then went inside. Grainger and Kiley remained fixed in their places.

If it had only been the confluence of adolescent hormones and proximity, if nothing had happened that night, maybe they would have simply outgrown their triangular crush and moved on. If Will hadn't been conceived. But Will existed and this man could be his father. She would never ask anything of him, but it would be good to try and explain why she had never let him know about Will. But, how could one simply step over the chasm dug over nineteen years? Once upon a time, they had been friends; and, no matter who had fathered him, they did have Will between them. Kiley took a short step forward. "How was Will's lesson?"

"It went well."

"Good. My father's happy he's taking lessons." Her pulse began to slow back to normal. "You didn't call me back about *Random*."

Grainger pressed a hand on either side of the doorjamb. "I only just listened to my messages."

"My father's talking about racing her in the August Races before selling her."

"To showcase her qualities?"

"Something like that. But he's pretty infirm and needs a crew."

"Will's going to be a pretty good sailor."

Kiley smiled. "I should have taught him to sail years ago. The truth is, I haven't been in a boat, except on a lake in a motorboat or a canoe, since . . . since that summer. I just can't stomach the idea. I was on the Vineyard a couple of summers ago, and when everyone went out on a chartered catamaran, I begged off and spent the day reading."

"As I recall, you were always a better passenger than sailor."

"Oh, stop."

Their laughter released some of the tension between them.

"Dad wants to know if you would consider being the fourth crewman. He needs someone who knows what he's doing."

"I'll think about it." He remained in the doorway. "Will you still be in Hawke's Cove that late in the season? Will you be aboard?"

Her smile vanished. "It depends on certain circumstances. I'm job hunting."

"Will mentioned what happened. Tough break." Grainger let go of the doorjamb. "Did you come only to talk about *Random*?"

"No. We both know there are a few other things we should talk about."

Grainger nodded and stepped aside. "You're right. We do." His voice hadn't changed from the one in her memory, still husky, as if holding on to words, reluctant to say them. "I have coffee on; would you like some?"

"Yes. Please." Her voice still sounded indistinct to her, as if from a great distance.

As polite as a host to a stranger, Grainger stood aside and let Kiley pass into the boathouse.

As polite as a guest, Kiley complimented Grainger on the place, on its working nautical decor. She noted the mahogany boat ladder angled against the edge of the loft, the corner devoted to reading and television, the galley kitchen with its marine-sized stove and refrigerator. The center space was occupied by a boat she recognized.

"*Miss Emily* still looks good."

Grainger nodded. "Claridge sails her only about twice a season, but he likes to keep her in trim." Grainger pulled a clean mug out of the dish rack. "How are your parents?"

"Elderly. Which is why I'm here in Hawke's Cove—to get the house ready to sell." As she spoke, tears lurched up in one last drive for freedom, and her last two words were drowned in a sob. "Oh, I'm so sorry. I don't know what's come over me."

Grainger remained behind the cherry-wood island counter as she tried to regain control. He made no move to console her, watching as one might an unavoidable accident, knowing there was nothing that would stop it.

As suddenly as the crying jag began, it was over, and Kiley hunted through her shorts pocket for a tissue. Released from his stasis, Grainger handed her a box of Kleenex.

"I've only done that once, the first day we arrived. I've been really good about not letting it get to me." Kiley dabbed at her eyes with a twisted corner of tissue. She'd long since stopped weeping at the thought of the house being sold; these tears came from being here, with Grainger.

"You'd have to be pretty heartless not to be upset about selling the old place." Grainger set the Kleenex box back on the counter. "Toby told me you fired him."

Kiley bit her lip, half in shame and half in amusement. "Sort of. Except that my mother won't hear of changing real estate agents at this point. I got mad when he said something about tearing the place down."

"Toby is an okay guy; he's just an asshole sometimes. No one is going to tear down your house."

Kiley went over to the boat, running a hand along its smooth, newly painted white hull. "How long have you been back in Hawke's Cove?"

"About four years."

"Not long."

"Not by Cove standards, no. I had some money, so I invested in this place. I make a living doing what I enjoy. Can't complain."

"That's such a Yankee statement."

"I'm a Yankee."

"Why did you come back?" Kiley almost didn't ask the question, afraid to disturb the fragile balance between them. "I remember that you always said you wouldn't."

"I'd had enough of traveling, and I finally came to the conclusion that, for good or ill, Hawke's Cove was home. And my father was dead, so at least one of my demons had been exorcised." Grainger came to stand beside her, and it felt almost as if he was going to touch her, but he didn't. "What about you? Why have you never come back until now, when it's almost too late?"

"I lacked the guts. I believed that as long as I stayed away, I could preserve the happy memories."

"We all have our delusions. No, 'delusions' is a harsh word—we all have our coping mechanisms." Grainger went into the kitchenette and poured them coffee, then sat beside her on one of the two barstools in front of the short island counter.

It felt almost normal, almost as if, as long as they kept to the present, they could have a civil conversation, that the overwhelming truth of their past might be put on hold. Even if just for a little while.

"Toby told me that your parents are selling the house to pay for Will's tuition."

"Toby certainly has a big mouth."

"He has no idea that I know you. He thinks he's still living in a city, where no one knows anyone else."

"So he's a carpetbagger real estate parasite."

Grainger laughed and nodded. "That about describes him perfectly. Although, in his defense, he is a pretty upstanding member of the community. He's always willing to be the clown at the dunk-a-clown booth at the annual carnival."

"True to type, I'd say." Kiley added a teaspoon of sugar to the overly cooked coffee. She enjoyed the feeling that this conversation was one they might have had long ago, relishing the familiarity of its rhythms.

"Tell me about Will."

The feeling of comfort vanished. "He's off to Cornell in September. He graduated sixth in his class; he was captain of his high school baseball team, and the team went on to the state championships. He works at a burger place, and has saved enough money that I may let him get a car next year."

"That's not what I want to know. I want to know why you never told him about me. Or about Mack."

"Because I didn't know how." This time the tears were silent, steady, but did not take her breath away. "Will was a boy, who did boy things and got into boy scrapes and left dirty dishes in his room under clean clothes. He, like you and Mack, loves baseball and other sports. He, like you and Mack, is kindhearted and clever. He, like you and Mack, is good to me. He loves me. He's a good son."

"Why didn't you tell *me* about him?"

"Because if I kept him to myself, he would always belong to all three of us," she whispered.

There were still some things she couldn't speak aloud. As painful as Grainger's rage was that night, Kiley had hoped that they might eventually be able to shuck their mistakes—her mistakes—and rebuild their friendship. But Mack's death meant their friendship could never be fixed. How could Grainger ever forgive her? They'd spun out of each other's orbit that night. Catapulted by the velocity of their mistake.

In the middle of October that year, Kiley realized she carried a child, one who might have been Mack's or Grainger's. Had Mack survived and Grainger come back to Hawke's Cove, she would still have had to choose between them. She still couldn't have them both. But she did have Will.

"I just couldn't tell you. Don't forget that we were kids, his age, when all of this happened. I handled it the best way I knew."

"Didn't I deserve to know?"

"Do you remember the last words you said to me? After that, how could I believe that you would ever want anything to do with me?"

Grainger looked into his coffee cup. "You're right. We were kids, and we had no idea how to handle ourselves. But Kiley, we aren't kids anymore, and haven't been for a long time. I would have wanted to know."

Kiley got up from the barstool. She couldn't sit there any longer; the conversation was too painful. She moved toward the door, then stopped, remembering the original reason for her visit. "You and Will talked this morning?" She came back to stand beside Grainger.

"Yes." They were nearly eye to eye as he remained seated.

"Do you want to tell me what you told him?"

"That I behaved badly. That Mack died because of it."

Kiley reached out and touched Grainger's shoulder. "It wasn't your fault, Grainger. It was mine."

"It doesn't really matter. Mack is dead because of us." His words were harsh, but he didn't shake off her hand as she touched his cheek. He opened his arms, gathering her gently against his shoulder. He rested his cheek against her hair and rocked her slightly, as if they were on the deck of a boat. "I wish you'd told me about Will."

"I have so many regrets, I can't even begin to apologize."

"Do you regret having him?"

"Oh, no. I've never regretted that."

Grainger held her gently, as if holding her closer would break them both.

Kiley pulled away from him. "I should go."

"Tell your father I'll crew on *Random*." Grainger let go of her. "Tell him I'll get her in the water by the end of the month. If I can have Will's help."

Grainger walked her to the door. "Maybe you and Will could come back later and we can go over *Random* to see what needs to be done."

Kiley shook her head. "I can't, Grainger."

He had his hand on the doorknob and leaned his weight against it. "I understand."

"No, it's not . . . I'm having dinner with Conor MacKenzie." Instantly, Kiley knew she'd said it wrong, but any attempt to rephrase it wouldn't make it sound any less significant. Grainger held the door wide, and she stepped outside where the sunlight made her squint. "It's no big deal; I can put him off."

"No. Please don't. It was just an idea."

The fleeting comfort Kiley had enjoyed was gone, in its place a new tension.

There seemed little else to say. "Nice to see you," seemed an awesome understatement. They were standing on either side of a gateless fence; she had raised the central division between them by speaking Conor MacKenzie's name.

"Good-bye, Grainger."

"Good-bye, Kiley." His dog sat at his feet.

Kiley started up the drive.

"Kiley?"

She hated the involuntary squeeze of her heart at his call.

"Tell Will to come back tomorrow if he wants to help." Grainger didn't wait for her reply, but turned and shut the door.

When Kiley got home, Will was on the porch. He'd made sandwiches and iced tea. She didn't realize she was holding her breath until she mounted the steps. What would he say to her? She wouldn't tell Will she'd been with Grainger just yet. She wanted to hear what his reaction was to Grainger's story. Would he retreat into the grunts and shrugs of adolescence, or would he open up?

Will was flopped in a rocking chair, his feet up against the railing, and half of a ham-and-cheese sandwich already down. "Where were you?"

"Out for a walk." She sat down and picked up a sandwich. "How was it?"

Will set his big feet down on the floor and put out one hand. Kiley put hers in his, amazed once again how big his were, how manly. She felt the roughness of a new callus where he'd been holding on to lines all morning. She heard her own breath going in and out of her chest, and waited for him to say something.

"It was okay. Grainger was pretty open about stuff." Will took another bite of sandwich, chewing slowly, as if his first hunger was in abeyance. "He says I'll make a good sailor."

"What else did he say?" Was Will being deliberately maddening?

Her son squeezed her fingers and then let go. "Enough. Enough for now."

Will needed time to digest this story, so long in the keeping. She'd have to let him come to his own conclusions about how to handle what he'd heard. At least— at the very least—he was here, wolfing sandwiches and smiling. It would have to be enough.

"Are you okay with it?" She was allowed that one question.

"I think so. I mean, it is a pretty romantic story. Let's just say that it could have been a lot worse. I don't mean that losing Mack like that wasn't a tragedy; obviously it affected all of you forever. But I mean . . ." Will set his crust down on the platter and picked up half of a second sandwich. He didn't bite it, but held it in his hand, studying it. "For a long time I worried that I was the product of a rape, that you made up a fairy tale about the love of your life. Thankfully, I'm not. I'm the product of one of the *two* loves of your life. How bad is that?"

Kiley made no move to wipe the steadily rolling tears

away from her cheeks. How bad, indeed? Had she wept more in front of him this week than at any other time in his life?

He finished the second sandwich and gulped down a glass of tea. "Gotta go."

"Where?"

Kiley was surprised at the flush that reddened his already sun-reddened cheeks.

"I'm picking up a girl and going to the beach."

" 'A girl'? Do you have one in mind, or are you going to cruise the streets?" she teased.

"Yeah, I have one in mind. We met at the fireworks, and then I ran into her at Starbucks the other day. Catherine Ames. Lives on Bailey's Farm Road." Will was standing over her chair, slightly to one side, where he could see her face but she couldn't see his. "She's taking me to Bailey's Beach."

"Oh. Right." Bailey's Beach.

"I can have the car, can't I?"

"Sure." Kiley busied herself rearranging the remaining sandwich halves on the platter. "Be home by five. I need the car."

"Where are you going?"

"I'm going to meet with Dr. MacKenzie in Great Harbor. About finding a job."

Will hovered for a moment, half in and half out the door. "A job here?"

"No. Just about making some contacts for me."

Will bounded into the house, the screen door slamming behind him. In five minutes he was back, stuffing a beach blanket and towels into his backpack. "Hey, tell me one thing."

"What?"

"Why don't you want to see Grainger?"

Kiley fiddled with the remaining sandwiches. "Actually, I did."

"Good. What did you talk about?"

"None of your beeswax."

"About me?"

"A little. He wants you to help him get Pop's boat back in the water."

"Sweet."

"So, tell me about you and Lori." For days now, Kiley had been wanting to ask Will this question. It was obvious something was up, with Will's never calling the girl, and her unopened envelopes collecting on his bureau. Now he'd given her the opening.

Will slung the backpack over one shoulder and went down the porch steps. "We broke up."

"Why?"

"She broke it off."

"She's a fool."

"She was right. We do need to see other people, and if I don't go now, I'll be late for my other people."

"Will?" Kiley called just as he reached the Mazda.

"I know, be home by five."

"No. I just don't want you to get any idea that . . ." She paused, waiting until Will fixed his attention on her. "Don't get any ideas about Grainger and me. About some reconciliation. It's a détente."

Will raised his chin in that way he had when he'd been told something he didn't want to hear. "Suit yourself. But it's my life."

"No, it's not. It really doesn't have anything to do with you. All you need to worry about is if you want to work with Grainger tomorrow."

Twenty-three

It felt as if he'd known Catherine Ames all of his life. She was so easy to be around. They played in the water like little kids, splashing and doing handstands. After swimming, they stretched out on his beach blanket, half dozing in the fading July afternoon. Even the silences were natural. Will lay beside Catherine and studied the curve of her long neck beneath the short-chopped hair, the way it looked so delicate coming to the point between her thin shoulders where it joined her back in a V. He wanted to trace one finger down each of her vertebrae. Catherine lifted her face to look at him as if suddenly aware of his contemplation. She smiled. "So, how long are you here, college boy?"

Will lifted himself up to rest his cheek against his fist. "Not long enough. We're gone the end of the month, unless Mom has a change of heart."

"Then you're off to Cornell?"

"Labor Day weekend. What about you?"

Catherine smiled, a slightly enigmatic smile. A pleased smile. "Ithaca College."

Will let the bubble of surprised laughter out. "No way!"

Catherine laughed too. "Yep. We'll be neighbors." She handed him a tube of sunblock. "Did your mother ever tell you about Joe Green?"

"No. My mother never told me anything about Hawke's Cove." Will hoped he didn't sound petulant. But it was true. Until two days ago he knew absolutely nothing. He stroked the sunblock across her shoulders.

"During the war this guy crashed his fighter plane into the Cove, and then swam to shore right here on Bailey's Beach. Technically, he was a deserter. AWOL. The woman who owned Bailey's Farm took him in, and they fell in love. But at the end of the war, she went back to the city when her husband came home. Joe Green stayed here. Not once has he ever left Hawke's Cove. He kept both his past and their love affair secret until, can you believe it, the nineties, when their separate children found out about both secrets. Then his daughter and her son fell in love and married each other, and still spend summers in the farmhouse. Charlie and Maggie Worth, I used to baby-sit for them. I've even met them, Joe and Vangie. They're wicked old, but they still hold hands. They never forgot each other over all that time."

Will capped the tube and handed it back to Catherine. "Charlie Worth was in the game on the Fourth. Pretty good for an old guy."

Catherine rolled her eyes, then slapped Will. "That's not the point. Don't you think that it's romantic, carrying a torch for each other for fifty years?"

Will wrapped his long arms around his knees and stared out at the rumpled water. "Do you think that's really possible? Don't you think that if too much time goes by, you just move on?"

Catherine handed him a box of cheese crackers. "I believe if you're meant for someone, it doesn't matter how long it takes."

"How do you know if you're meant for someone?"

Catherine fished a Snapple out of the cooler and passed it to Will. "I don't think it's like in the movies, all instant recognition and all. But I do think that there are signs."

Will popped the cover off the Snapple bottle and took a long drink. "I'm just beginning to find out some stuff about my mother."

"Like what?"

"I grew up without a father, and now I may have two."

"Like having two mommies?"

"No. Not exactly. Most of my life, I've just ignored the fact that I didn't have a father. In our town, it's not unusual to have a single parent. Shit, half the kids in my fifth-grade class were children of single mothers. Or patched-together families of steps and step-steps."

"So what's the matter?"

"It's hard to explain."

"You don't have to tell me, but I'm supposedly a good listener." They were a few inches apart, as befitted casual aquaintances, a safe distance, one that might be crossed or respected without challenge.

"I might have been conceived here. On this very beach."

"How do you know that?"

"You wouldn't want to know."

"Try me." Catherine, whom he had met less than

three days ago, reached across the tiny divide and linked her fingers with his. "I promise you'll feel better."

It was that little touch that did him in, which pricked his reserve and let the words begin to flow out. Slowly at first, then, more rapidly, as thoughts he had yet to formulate were suddenly articulated. He told this girl, gently linking her fingers with his, everything. About how he'd grown up always wondering who his father was. Why they were in Hawke's Cove, his run-in with the law, and his breakup with Lori. Lori seemed so distant now. So insignificant. He tested the recent hurt to his pride that her pronouncement had caused, and found it gone. Too much else had reduced it to a mere memory. Memory. That's what his mother wanted all of this to remain. She didn't want him to pursue finding out the hard truth about his paternity.

"So now my mother is all weird about seeing Grainger. I mean, think about it. She slept with him and she slept with Mack, and here I am and Mack is dead and only . . ." Will stopped talking. His mouth felt dry and the Snapple was gone. Surely he'd put Catherine to sleep with his tale. Then he felt her fingers increase their pressure on his. With his other hand, Will outlined circles in the sand.

"I think you need to talk to Grainger. I think that he'd go along with having the DNA test."

"It's not just that. I don't understand why he and my mother seem so angry with each other. It's not like they were divorced and there's all this animosity. It's like . . . I don't know. Nothing I've ever experienced."

"Like two proud, stubborn Yankees."

"Yeah. Stubborn."

"So, trick 'em."

"My mother already told me this isn't, and I quote,

'the fucking *Parent Trap*.' She's never used that word in my hearing before, so I'm not too keen on playing childish tricks to get them in the same room."

"Wow. Okay, you should use not-so-childish tricks."

"Like what?"

"Hmmm. It would be handy if you were struck with some nearly fatal disease. You could get them to reconcile over your sickbed."

Will felt a giggle rise in his chest, an unfamiliar sensation lately. Ever since Lori, there had been little to laugh over. Then Catherine laughed out loud, and he joined her until the laughter became guffaws and he had to grip his belly against the welcome pain. "That might get all three of them together: Mom, Grainger, and the doctor who might or might not be my uncle. Wow. Brilliant. I feel a fever coming on."

Suddenly Catherine kissed him. A sweet, gentle, friendly kiss. Will took her face in his hands; he breathed in her Snapple-scented breath and lowered his lips to meet hers. "Thank God you're here. I'd be banging my head against a brick wall if you weren't."

"I told you I was a good listener."

"More than that, Catherine. Much more." For some reason, the name of the boat came to Will as he moved to kiss Catherine again. *Blithe Spirit*. Exactly how he would describe Catherine to anyone. Exactly how Mack and Grainger had viewed Kiley. No wonder it had been impossible for them to not fall in love with her. Will gently pulled away from Catherine. He didn't want history to repeat itself on this beach. "I have to be home in"—he looked at his watch—"one minute."

"Oops."

"Want to come over tonight?"

"Sure."

"Mom's going out." Will got to his feet and pulled Catherine to hers. "She's going out with Mack's brother."

"Oh, the handsome Dr. Conor MacKenzie?"

"Yeah. Supposedly she's meeting him to talk about a job."

"My aunt has a wicked crush on him. She keeps finding reasons to go see him. Every twinge and belly-ache, and off she goes to consult Doc Conor. Hoping he'll do more than prescribe." Catherine stuffed her towel in her beach bag.

"So, he's single?"

"Yeah, I guess so."

"Great." Will jammed his towel into his backpack. "Great."

"Will?"

Will looked at Catherine.

"Are you playing favorites?"

"Favorites how?"

"You wish your mother would be with Grainger Egan."

"I don't give a flying fuck who she dates. It's imma-terial to me." Will slung his backpack over one shoul-der and started up the path to the car.

Twenty-four

॥

Grainger couldn't bear to listen to the chatter on talk radio, so he slipped a Muddy Waters tape into the truck's player and turned up the volume. Blues was what he felt, blues was what he needed. Having Kiley so close was like being faced with a living specter. She sounded like Kiley, she mostly looked like Kiley, but she wore neither the fangs nor claws of the Kiley he had created in his imagination all these years. The girl to whom he had attributed a callous disregard of anyone's feelings—a cavalier notion that she wouldn't break hearts—the friendship splitter, the betrayer, had never existed and he knew it. Kiley was simply a good mother, a caring person who, like him, lived too much in the past. It was past time to come to terms with it. Because of his own stubborn notion of keeping ancient history in his heart, Grainger had denied himself the one thing that might have given his empty life ballast: Will. At least she wasn't denying him Will any longer.

They had come so close this morning. He still felt the light weight of her in his arms, how his heart raced at the possibility they might be able to mend this great tear in the fabric of their friendship. Grainger turned up the volume, trying to crowd out the voice in his head with the voice on the tape. Fool. In one sentence Kiley had reminded him, once again, that he was in second place. She probably thought that if he forgave her not telling him about Will, he'd forget he hadn't ever been her first choice.

He drove past the hardware store, although he needed more sandpaper, taking the road that led up the hill and out of town. One of the benefits, or drawbacks, of his profession was too much time for thinking; much of what he did required only muscle memory, and his thoughts ranged freely. He was in no frame of mind to touch power tools, so he kept driving, the blues accompanying his incomplete thoughts.

Spontaneously, Grainger slowed down and turned into the gate of the old burying ground at the top of the hill beside the brownstone Episcopal church. It was a pretty place. The oldest graves appeared to be randomly placed around trees and up and down the gentle hillocks. Surrounded by flowering quince, apple, and pear trees in the spring, from a distance, the graveyard looked like an orchard. Grainger got out of the truck, leaving a complaining Pilot in the cab. He didn't know where he was going, only that the quiet peacefulness called to him, as if he was being pulled toward a solace as yet unexplained. The peaceful realm of the dead. The sea breeze fluttered the little flags the VFW had placed on veterans' graves for the Fourth. Someday they would put one on his grave, although he only spent two miserable years in the service and never saw action anywhere.

Grainger drifted, thinking vaguely of going into the church, of seeing if the small nave might take up the large and uncomfortable feelings filling the space around his heart.

When his mother first left, the MacKenzies brought him with them to this church, the old priest there attempting consolation by getting him into Sunday school. As if he could find any consolation in stories like Joseph and his coat of many colors; a story that only verified the treacherous behavior of families.

Grainger walked past graves of people he knew: a teacher dead of cancer; Howie Randall, who ran the drugstore, a coronary; and several others who had given their lives to the sea. To a man who had made his living on or around the water, who grew up surrounded on three sides by it, drowning and death on the water were commonplace. By the time Grainger was twenty, he could count on both hands the names of people lost whom he knew. Accidents, all. A wave over the top of waders, an underestimated undertow, a capsized boat. Or like his father, a drunken entanglement in fishing net. Or like Mack, gone overboard.

He'd left Hawke's Cove that night. In the morning, *Blithe Spirit* was found caught between the rocks near Bailey's Beach. It isn't unusual for the sea to keep what it takes. Eventually the search for Mack was called off, and a headstone placed above an empty grave in the family plot—as close to a burial as the MacKenzies would have.

In all the time he'd been back in Hawke's Cove, Grainger had never visited the gravesite. Every time the anniversary of Mack's death came, he'd plan to go and put flowers on it, but somehow he never did.

He hadn't known that Mack was in danger. He'd been hitchhiking to Great Harbor, aware of the wind and rain only as they mirrored his black mood.

Anger and hurt had been the only feelings occupying him.

A woodpecker hammered now at a dying tree. On his own unhappy road to Damascus, Grainger paused in mid-step. For an instant he felt exactly as he had years before, standing atop the mainmast of the schooner before plunging into the dark water. For he knew suddenly what it was he was looking for: it wasn't forgiveness between only Kiley and himself.

He had betrayed Mack by trying to take Kiley away from him.

Then he had run away, aware only of his own wounded pride. If he had stayed, maybe Mack wouldn't have gone out. But even if he had, Grainger and Kiley might have been able to grieve together. Like diving again from the mainmast, a cleansing impact was what Grainger was looking for. It was Mack's forgiveness he wanted. Impossible, and forever too late.

There it was, tidy and tended—Mack's gravesite. *William "Mack" MacKenzie 1966–1984. Beloved son.*

Beloved son. William.

Seeing Mack's whole name carved in the soft white marble, Grainger knew that Mack had to be Will's biological father. And Kiley had to have somehow known. Grainger sat on the ground, in front of the polished headstone marking the forever empty grave.

Will couldn't know he was named after Mack. Otherwise he wouldn't have asked which of them was his father. Kiley must have some reason she wouldn't tell him the truth. A reason that was tangled up in her desire to keep the mythological threesome alive. She was letting them both believe there was no answer to that question. Given his behavior that night, Kiley had every right to keep him out of Will's life. If Will hadn't discovered him, would Kiley have continued to try to keep them unaware of each other?

Atonement. Grainger rolled the word around in his imagination. If Mack had lived, there was no doubt that Grainger would have come to him seeking to repair the damage to their friendship. And no doubt that Mack would have done the same. But there had been no chance, and he could never know under what circumstances their reconciliation might have taken place.

Until now. He'd do what Mack would have wanted done. He'd make a good sailor out of Will—and give him the boat, *Blithe Spirit*. She was Will's heritage. Even if Mack had died aboard her, she was still his beloved boat. She hadn't killed him, *he* had with his betrayal.

Grainger got up and touched the top of the headstone. "I'll teach your son how to sail, Mack."

Twenty-five

❧

Will was late getting home, as usual, but Kiley still had an hour before she was to meet Conor in Great Harbor.

"I'll make you a hamburger, if you want."

Will's hair was wet from his shower. "Sure. Cheeseburger, though, okay?"

"Sure. And I need you to cut the grass before dark. Toby's coming tomorrow with a client."

"I was going out with Catherine."

"Again?"

Will gave her that slightly askew smile he'd perfected to charm her. "Yeah. Can she have dinner with us tomorrow night?"

"Of course." Kiley opened the refrigerator and leaned in, mostly to hide her own slightly askew smile. "So now you have your own reason for getting that grass cut. The mower's in the garage."

Will's grumbling was halfhearted as he went out to assess the situation.

Kiley recognized Anthony's Restaurant as Marge's Place from her youth. Now it had gone upscale, serving small portions on large white plates at a price an entire family once spent to eat there. Conor was waiting for her, standing up as the hostess brought her over to his window seat with its view of Great Harbor, perimetered on three sides with slips filled with cabin cruisers. Conor was dressed in a coat and tie, and Kiley felt underdressed in black clam diggers and a yellow cotton sweater.

"I'm sorry I'm late."

"Not at all, I'm a little early." Conor motioned to the waiter. "I took the liberty of ordering a bottle of wine. I hope you don't mind."

"Of course not." Kiley knew then that, despite what she'd said to Grainger, this *was* a date date. Conor had tricked her. Kiley kept her eyes on the waiter as he performed his ritual with the wine bottle. Not an expensive wine; good. Maybe it was just cheaper to order by the bottle. Conor pronounced it fit for drinking and the waiter poured the white wine into her glass.

"I've been making some inquiries."

"Conor, I'm really not sure I want to relocate."

"Kiley, I have contacts all over New England." Conor raised his glass. "Shall we toast?"

Kiley raised her glass and waited.

Connor said, "To reunions."

"How about: To new jobs?"

"Let's have a reunion first, before we talk business. I want to know how you've been. What's kept you away from Hawke's Cove all these years?"

Kiley set her glass down on the white linen tablecloth but kept her fingers just touching the stem. "I have a son."

"So, you did get married."

"No. Not exactly."

"Kiley, that's no big deal these days. Did you want to be a single mother? That's very brave."

Brave. No, brave would be telling this near stranger that her son might be his brother's. "Not really."

"What's his name? How old is he?"

Simple, half-interested questions. Polite conversation-starting questions. "He's named for my father, Merriwell William Harris. But we call him Will."

"I suppose Merriwell would be a tough name to go around with these days." Conor had his menu open.

"Something like that." Kiley took a sip of her wine. "He's eighteen."

Conor closed his menu. "I have to recommend the salmon. Nobody does a better salmon than Anthony's."

Kiley took another sip of wine and tried not to choke. Was Conor playing with her, or was he being obtuse? "Sounds good."

The waiter reappeared to take their order, giving Kiley a moment to collect herself. Conor was looking out the window at a big yacht inching its way into the harbor. In profile he looked less like Mack, and more like any doctor she'd ever worked with. Tense about the mouth, preoccupied with what he'd left at his office or in the hospital. Self-aware, cognizant always of the power he held and the power he lacked.

"So, I take it you don't have any children?"

Conor pulled his gaze away from the window. "No. I keep thinking that I should remarry, find someone willing to have kids with me before it's too late. But"—and Conor hid his expression behind his glass—"that special someone hasn't yet appeared on the horizon. Someone willing to put up with the crazy hours and undependable plans; someone willing to shoulder the burden of child-rearing solo, for all intents and purposes. Lots of terribly young women in the medical profession think that's what they want, but I know from experience, it loses its novelty pretty quick."

"That's why your marriage ended up in divorce?"

"Something like that. We were young, and now a lot of time has passed, and I don't think that I'll get my second chance."

Kiley reached across the table and patted Conor's hand. "That's not true. You just have to look for it."

Conor covered her hand with his. "I hope you're right."

A shiver of intuition coursed through Kiley. This was not the first time he had used those lines; it was the old vulnerable-man trick. She removed her hand gently and excused herself to go to the ladies' room. The glass of wine on an empty stomach made her path a little interesting to negotiate, but she got there quick enough to hide the bubble of laughter teasing itself out of her throat.

The salmon arrived as she made her way back to the table. As promised, it was delicious, and they ate in near silence, savoring the flavors. Conor poured her a second glass of wine, and Kiley drank it very slowly. Halfway through dinner, she brought up the ostensible reason for their date. "Where have you made inquiries?"

"Children's in Boston and UMass Medical. They both have outstanding PICUs and openings."

"Thank you. Can I use your name?"

"I wish you would."

There was an excitement beginning to build with the thought of starting again. Maybe, in an odd way, this was her moment, her time to fly away. Ever since that October day when she realized she was pregnant, her life had been on a branch line, switched off from her plans and dreams. Then that branch line had become her main route, her life. She would always miss Doc John, miss the close-knit little office with its wall of children's artwork and the weekly pizza lunches. But maybe it had been time to change routes, before she spent the next twenty years marking time, waiting for her son to come and visit. Kiley shuddered back the thought. What had she said to Conor about second chances? *You have to look for it.*

Conor was talking, but Kiley had lost the thread of the conversation. "I should go," she told him. "The real estate agent is coming early tomorrow."

"Do you have to? I was thinking we might take a walk along the harbor."

"Another time, maybe. I really need to go."

"All right. I should call it a night too. I have an early surgery tomorrow."

Kiley opened her purse.

"No, no. This is my treat."

Kiley allowed Conor to pay the bill and walk her to her car. He opened her car door but then blocked her way, his face very close to hers. She thought he was trying to kiss her and turned her cheek.

"Kiley, I think it would be best if we say very little of this to my mother. She's never gotten over it, and she's fragile."

"Tell her whatever you think best, Conor. Nothing, if that's better."

"Kiley, I do realize that your son might be . . . is probably Mack's."

"Don't make assumptions, Conor." Kiley slid past him and into her car. She wondered what he'd make of that; would he even remember that Grainger had been a part of her world too? That, as easily as Will might be

Mack's, he might be Grainger's instead? Grainger had lived in his house; Conor's mother had fed him, washed his clothes, and guided him through his adolescence. Conor had been the big brother, the college man, miles away from them in maturity and experience. Kiley couldn't imagine what his opinion of Grainger might be.

Toby Reynolds called early to say that the couple he wanted to bring over were very interested in buying a big house on the bluff, and had no thoughts of changing anything. "They're perfect."

"They haven't seen it yet. Maybe they won't like it."

"Kiley, you have to be positive."

Toby clearly misunderstood her. She was being positive.

Hanging up, Kiley chided herself that it had to be done. Every moment she spent here in Hawke's Cove underscored her reason for having kept away. Early on, she knew that there was no way she could have returned to Hawke's Cove, baby in tow, to be judged by the Yacht Club types whose own "mistakes" were generally the catalysts to good marriages—good in name only, but acceptable. If she had come back a young married with an oversized "eight-month" preemie, all would have been forgotten long ago. The raised eyebrows would have been lowered as the child grew and joined other children around the club. But Kiley had chosen a different path, and it led away from Hawke's Cove. Soon there would be nothing left to call her back; no one to call her back.

She busied herself with packing the objects she'd chosen not to sell. Before she wrapped each memento in its protective layer of *Boston Globe,* she made one last effort to choose to leave it behind. Some objects, like

the blue tumblers etched with sailboats, were put back
in the kitchen. Others she wrapped carefully and
nested among the other memory-laden items.

Will was in Great Harbor waiting for Catherine to
get out of work, when they would go windsurfing. She
was to have dinner with them tonight. Kiley felt a little
twitch of maternal concern at his sudden dedication to
a girl he'd only just met. Maybe a barbecue was a good
idea, a nice informal opportunity for all three of them
to get acquainted. Kiley was glad Will had found a
friend, which is how he referred to her. Not yet *girlfriend*, which probably was a good thing. The brevity of
their time together seemed a natural barrier to more
than a friendship. But she also worried about his heart.
He'd been so closemouthed about Lori's breaking it off;
she hoped he wasn't using this other girl in rebound.
Or, worse, that she would break his heart too. Did Will
understand the finer points of a summer fling? Have
fun, break no hearts? She certainly hadn't understood.
But then, in no way could what she had with Mack or
Grainger be called a fling. They had invested years of
friendship before their adolescent hormones had
changed everything.

Kiley barely saw the objects in her hands as her
mind wandered over the oft-visited landscape of her
adolescence. Did other adults remember so clearly
being that young, being that confused? Did most people outgrow those days, leaving them behind for new
experiences? Grainger had, certainly. He'd managed to
come back to Hawke's Cove, make a life. Having seen
him, heard his voice, breathed in the scent of his boatyard life, she could not recall the face of the boy he'd
been. This mature, rugged face bore vestigial traces
of that boy, and the shock of seeing him as a man had

teased her with unbidden speculation about the physical adult Grainger. That long ago afternoon they spent together had been imperfect for both of them. Despite their love and tenderness, they were both so inexperienced they'd had physical relief but little understanding of the act. Older now, awakened to bolder gestures of lovemaking, Kiley found herself imagining Grainger's hands on her, touching her with love. Unlocking the hard nut of his anger and her hurt with his skillful . . .

She brought herself up short. Nothing like that could happen. They'd had a chance at reconciliation yesterday. Though how do you pile eighteen years' worth of explanation into the time it takes to drink a cup of coffee? Her mind was cluttered with the said and the unsaid. They were polite strangers, with no hope of returning to their former intimacy. Certainly not the physical intimacy of their one night, but neither the intimacy of old friends who need no explanations, whose history is closely linked. The intimacy she remembered best, and missed most. That wasn't going to happen; it was obvious by his sudden withdrawal at her thoughtless evocation of Mack by speaking of his brother. The look in his eyes, like a force field suddenly between them. She needed now to stop wishing and set her mind against any further hope of amends. What she'd said to Will was exactly right: it was a détente.

Kiley heard Toby's footsteps clump up the front steps, and his excited voice, no doubt drawing attention to the magnificent view, rhapsodized about how the intense blue of the sky was reflected in the shimmering blue water. He'd fill the clients' inaugural visit with all the high points and none of the low, such as the roof or the flaking paint; those things would be called to their attention only after they fell in love with the house.

Kiley hadn't meant to be in the house when Toby brought the couple, but time had gotten away from her. "Hi, Toby. Sorry I'm still here. I'll go take a walk." She wiped her hands on the seat of her jeans.

"Oh no, we wouldn't dream of putting you out of your house."

Kiley wasn't sure how to answer that rather ironic statement.

The speaker, a woman about her own age, right arm linked to a man who might have been her father or her much older husband, realized her gaffe. "I mean, don't mind us; we don't want to intrude."

Toby quickly recovered the momentum of the tour. "Ms. Harris, this is Mr. and Mrs. Carlton Fenster. They're up from New York and have to get back this afternoon, so, if you don't mind, we'll just go in." A little ring of white appeared beneath Toby's lower lip, held in a trained smile. Clearly he was irritated that she'd lingered too long and bumped into his prospects. Bad form.

"Not at all." Mind? Of course she minded. As long as the sale of the house was more or less abstract, she could imagine it wouldn't take place. If the interlopers had faces, she couldn't pretend it wouldn't happen. Childishness, Kiley knew, but her own brand of childishness. "The items marked with orange aren't included in the sale, and I haven't inventoried everything."

"We're just looking at the structure today." Toby held the double screen door wide for the couple, who seemed reluctant to break the linking of their arms. Kiley thought, rather unkindly, that Mrs. Fenster was holding Mr. Fenster up. Or else, preventing him from running away. She smiled to herself. *Fenster*—a name like that would make the first cut at the club.

She should have had her bathing suit on; it was a perfect beach day. Too late to turn around and go back to get it, so it seemed an aimless walk was the only option left to her. She could go visiting, except that there was no one she could just drop in on anymore. That wasn't quite true. She did know one person she could call on—probably should call on—Mrs. MacKenzie. Hadn't Conor said she should?

Kiley was halfway there. She could simply walk up on the MacKenzies' back porch and hallooo in the way she used to as a girl. Mrs. MacKenzie had always been nice to her, lingering with her in the kitchen as she waited for the boys to come home from their jobs, or change into their bathing suits. They'd sip lemonade and chat about girlie things, things her boys would never chat about. As much as she loved them, Kiley did sometimes complain a little, eliciting Mrs. MacKenzie's soft laughter and commiseration that neither one would go shopping or give a helpful opinion about clothes.

Kiley knew that she should just do it. Go knock on the door and explain that she had Will, and he might be their grandson. Could she muster that sort of courage? By now Conor might have told them about Will. Or had he kept that unproven information to himself? He'd suggested she greet his parents *before* he knew about Will. What was best for his parents, to know or not to know? At the intersection of Linden and Overlook, Kiley turned left, toward town and away from the MacKenzies' house.

It seemed the better choice, to keep going. Besides, as long as she was this close to the village, she might as well pick up the things she needed for dinner. That way she wouldn't have to go all the way into Great

Harbor later, even if she'd pay a premium price for it at LaRiviere's Market.

Main Street was cluttered with day-trippers, shopping bags swinging, filled with souvenirs of their visit to a pleasant place. Kiley had to dodge the ones who simply stopped in the middle of the sidewalk, as if alone in the world. She had to step off the sidewalk to avoid the side-by-side strollers, barricading the way with sheer American bulk. When they were kids, they used to make rude remarks to the day-trippers. In the hierarchy of year-rounders, day-trippers were on the lowest rung, followed by the one-week or two-week vacationers. Kiley was only just above that as a summer kid.

"Kiley Harris!" A woman's voice called out to her from the doorway of a shop.

Kiley stopped, already certain she knew who it was. "Emily?"

"I missed talking to you at the picnic."

Pleased that she'd guessed the correct twin, Kiley took in the sight of Emily Claridge, noting her rather middle-aged attire of yellow, green, and pink Lilly Pulitzer skirt and sleeveless blouse, the Nantucket basket handbag slung over one arm. Her blond hair, once free-swinging and rather pretty, was a solid helmet streaked by chemicals, not the sun. A huge emerald-cut diamond flashed in the sunlight as she reached out to grasp Kiley's arm.

". . . just thrilled to death to see you. You haven't changed a bit."

Rather than lie, Kiley shifted focus. "Are you still here all summer?"

"I wish. Ralph is too busy in his practice to take too much time off and I hate being separated from him, so we come for two weeks in July and two in August."

"Is Ralph a doctor?"

"No, no. Attorney. Has his own firm."

"And you? Career?" Kiley knew what the answer would be.

"I was in law school when I met Ralph." Emily twisted her diamond ring around as if trying to screw in her finger. *"C'est la vie."* She flapped her hands in a dismissive what-can-you-do gesture.

"Had to make a choice?" Kiley always tried not to resent women who had been free to choose work over motherhood. She loved her own job, but she would have loved it more if it had been an option, not a necessity.

"I worked in Ralph's office as a paralegal, but I gave it up when the twins were born. Now I chair a lot of charities in Greenwich."

Kiley yearned to head to the store, but it would have been rude to end the reunion so abruptly. She touched the only subject they might still have in common. "I saw your boat, *Miss Emily*. She looks wonderful. Will she be in the August Races?"

"Oh, yes. Dad wants to keep the tradition alive, although it's getting harder to find a crew. Ralph and Fred, Missy's husband, aren't very good sailors." Putting a confidential hand to her mouth she hissed, "Seasick."

"My father wants to sell *Random,* but not before the race." By bringing up the boats, both in his boatyard, she'd brought the shadow of Grainger into the conversation. Did Emily make note of it? In for a nickel, in for a dime. "Grainger Egan is going to crew for him."

Emily wore the same smirky curiosity on her face she'd worn the afternoon the twins had asked about Mack and Grainger. Kiley remembered one of them calling him Heathcliff, just this side of derogatory.

"Egan's very good. I was hoping to get him to crew with us."

Kiley's tense muscles relaxed. She was being an idiot. Emily wasn't going to bring up the past; she had moved on a long, long way. The twins' tepid foray into the wild side with local boys was long forgotten. Just because she'd spent the last eighteen years brooding over the past didn't mean the Claridge girls even remembered that summer and the way it ended.

Emily waved at a passing car. "But naturally, he'd want to sail with you. I remember that you were close friends."

"We were." There seemed little she could add. "How's Missy?"

"Missy? Fine. Married, two kids—not twins. Her husband, Fred, is a partner in Ralph's firm. She'll be here Friday. Say, your parents must still be members at the club. We're having a fund-raising cocktail party next Saturday, to support the youth sailing program. Auction and hors d'oeuvres. We'd love to see you there. I'll make sure you get an invitation."

"Oh, please, don't bother."

"Nonsense. You'll know half the people there. I know that your parents are selling up, but don't let that stop you. We'd love to see you and your husband."

"I'm not married."

"Oh, that's right." Emily twisted her diamond around. "I did know that you were single, what was I thinking? No matter, there'll be several unattached men. We can find an extra man, I'm sure. Conor MacKenzie, you remember him? He'll be there."

For a sick moment, Kiley thought Emily was going to wink.

"Emily, I really can't."

The foot traffic had managed to skirt around them as they stood in the middle of the sidewalk in front of the new gourmet kitchen shop. Even so, Emily had come closer to Kiley, nearly close enough to feel her breath. "Kiley. It's for charity. Surely you can afford the ticket. They're only fifty dollars. Most of it tax deductible."

"I'll think about it. Send me the invitation; at the very least, I'll send a contribution. My parents still have their box—ten-eleven. I've got to run, but it was nice seeing you. Give my best to Missy."

"Kiley." She was three steps away when she heard her name again.

Kiley paused and turned back to see Emily, her fingers working hard at twisting her massive ring around and around.

"Yes?"

"You can bring your son along, if you want. Several of the older teens will be there."

Slam dunk. For years, she had refused to come here. Refused to let her parents bring Will. She thought she could save him from being the object of curiosity, of social conjecture, if she never exposed him to Hawke's Cove. Emily's words emphasized how right Kiley had been in finally telling him everything, warding off his hearing some stranger's version.

"I'll mention it to him, if I decide to go." Kiley edged between a pair of tourists blocking her escape.

In LaRiviere's Market, she forced herself to think only about what she needed: hamburger, lettuce, tomatoes. Chips and something for dessert. A liter of cola for the kids. She'd come across a case of California white wine in the cellar; her parents wouldn't miss one bottle if they hadn't missed the whole case. She made herself focus on the process, a decision that ultimately she regretted as she struggled with three heavy plastic bags. Naturally, there wasn't a cab in town. Nearly to the end of Main Street, Kiley half considered returning to the market to ask them to hold on to the bags until she went home to get the car, then remembered she didn't have the car. Soon she was fairly scowling in annoyance with Will, even though he'd asked twice if she was sure he could have the car.

"Dumb, dumb, dumb." Kiley's under-the-breath muttering became a marching song. Just because he wanted his little friend to come have dinner. What was so important about meeting her that Will would make his mother jump through these hoops? *Catherine.* Not *Cathy,* or *Kate; Catherine.* At least it wasn't Muffy, or Buffy, or Toots, or Pug. Those were the nicknames of some of the girls who used to be at those Yacht Club dances. Girls who attended the good schools, who were tanned year-round from vacations in the "islands" and who lived in a rarefied atmosphere of privilege.

Will said her parents were teachers, and Catherine worked, not spending her summer in leisure. Besides, she was making Will happy, giving him something to do besides hang around the house watching his mother be miserable. Kiley hitched the bags up in her arms. She would be particularly nice to Catherine. After all, she should be grateful to the girl. Kiley squelched the sneaking suspicion she might be one of those mothers who disliked on sight any girl who might come into their son's life. She wouldn't be one of those. No way. Lori had been a different kettle of fish.

She wasn't aware of the sound of a motor slowing down to pass her.

"Do you need help?" Grainger leaned out of his truck window, calling to her from across the lane.

"No, I'm fine." Kiley shook her head in emphasis. She didn't want him to see how startled she was by his sudden appearance beside her.

Grainger kept pace with her determined stride. "Put your bags in the truck. There's no sense in struggling."

"Toby has people at the house. I don't want to get back too soon." She knew that Toby had to be gone by now; it wouldn't have taken this long to show the house even if they'd gone around twice. But it was too awkward to ride in the confines of the truck with Grainger.

"Just shove Pilot aside. He doesn't mind."

"Thanks anyway; I'm really all right."

"Suit yourself." Grainger looked at her with slightly offended disappointment and drove away.

Kiley watched Pilot's head duck back into the cab of the truck. It took her a minute to get her feet moving again. As she came around the bend in the road that led up to the Yacht Club, she spotted the truck idling in a popular scenic turnout. The great expanse of Atlantic Ocean glittered beyond the truck. Surely he'd seen this view a million times. Was he waiting for her?

Kiley wanted to turn around and go in another direction, but there *was* no other direction home. She would look childish and silly to turn around just to avoid him. "Be a grown-up." She straightened her shoulders as best she could under the weight of the cumbersome bags and marched on, thankful she was on the other side of the road and could go past him without having to look at him.

"Kiley. Get in the truck," he called as she drew even.

"It's a perfectly nice day for a walk."

"Your ice cream is melting, and I don't want to be held responsible."

An involuntary smile raised a corner of her mouth.

"Just get in. No other civility required."

He was right; the ice cream would be soup by the time she walked the next mile. Besides, the plastic handles were beginning to stretch to the point of breaking. Pilot gazed out at her, his bristly nose poking through the opening in the rear window. A car passed between them; then Kiley approached the truck. She set her bags down amidst coils of rope and a pair of oars, and went around to climb in the passenger's side.

Pilot moved about half of his hindquarters out of her way, then rested his body against hers. Through her window Kiley saw a huge blackback gull effortlessly kite along the edge of the bluff, enjoying the updraft, free from all concerns except eating and breeding.

"Shove him out of the way."

"No, he's fine. He likes to snuggle, I see."

"Check yourself for ticks when you get out, then."

They rode the rest of the way as if the scenery held their full attention. Kiley almost said something about her conversation with Conor, then held back. What point was there in telling him that she'd told Conor about Will? After her conversation with Emily, it appeared to her that it was hardly news to anyone.

Toby's Lexus was gone, the empty driveway confirming her solitary occupation of the house. Grainger pulled his truck in, and Kiley opened the door and jumped out. Grainger met her at the side of the truck, pulling the three bags of groceries out of the truck's deep bed. Kiley took them from him, trying not to touch his hands as he transferred the awkward plastic handles to her.

"Thanks for the ride." It was on the tip of her tongue to offer a glass of lemonade, but Grainger moved away from her like a man afraid that an invitation to stay might be extended if he didn't get back into his truck immediately.

The crunch of clamshells broke the awkward moment. Will drew up behind Grainger's truck, holding it captive in the driveway. "Hi, what's up?"

Kiley hadn't seen Grainger and Will side by side before, and the sight of them—both tall and rangy, baseball caps pulled to the same angle shading their brows, a similar *maleness* as they greeted each other with a handshake—punched her with its significance. If she hadn't been so overly proud—yes, that was the word, *proud*—this might have been reenacted time and time again: while Will was tiny, as he grew, as he developed into this handsome young man. Kiley searched for similarities beyond their height and manhood. As they talked about *Random,* she indulged herself in looking for living evidence of Will's paternity. Did they have the same jawline, angular and deep? Or did their hands match in long fingeredness and the light furring on knuckles? Grainger's hair had gone dark with age; would Will's fair hair darken, as well? Would Mack's have darkened with age? Conor's hadn't, though it had receded.

Eye color, every high school biology student's first exercise in Mendel's theories, was useless here. All three of them had blue eyes. Grainger's were grayer than hers, and Mack's had been more pale blue, like a summer sky. Hers were a deep, unequivocal ocean blue, just like Will's.

Kiley knew she was staring and drew her eyes up to catch Will's. "Can you please move the car so Grainger can leave?"

"Mom, why doesn't Grainger stay for the barbecue?"

"No, I couldn't, really, thanks . . ." Grainger opened his truck door. "Another time, perhaps. I'll see you tomorrow, Will."

Kiley held out her grocery bags to Will. "Take these inside, please, Will."

"Mom, Grainger, why not? I'm sure we have plenty, and you'd both get to meet Catherine."

"Bring her by the boathouse sometime. I'd love to meet her." Grainger was back in his truck, but Will's hand stayed on the door handle, preventing Grainger from shutting the door unless he jerked it away.

"Mom would love for you to stay. Wouldn't you, Mom?" Will looked hard at her, challenging her to deny it.

"Will." Kiley's voice was a warning. "It's rude to insist when someone has declined."

Will kept his hand on the door of the truck. "Grainger, come on." He was a half step away from whiny.

Kiley watched Grainger's tension-hardened jawline relax, a slow sad smile come to his lips. "I can't."

"Forget it." Will gave them his shrug of I-couldn't-care-less.

Grainger realized that the blue car was behind his truck. "Will, why don't you take those bags from your mother and let her move that car."

Will pulled his hand off the door handle. Disappointment had leveled his mouth into a thin, hard line, but he did as Grainger said, handing her the car keys.

Kiley slipped in behind the wheel, backing the car carefully out onto the bluff road. She waited, but Grainger's truck didn't immediately follow. Concerned that Will was trying one more time to change Grainger's mind, Kiley got out and walked around the hedge to see Grainger still sitting in his truck. In the side mirror, she could see he was staring straight ahead, his hands on the steering wheel, making no move to start the engine. Unaware of her observation, he'd let his guard down and Kiley saw something like disappointment on his face. As if he'd been hoping she would endorse Will's impulsive invitation.

"Grainger?"

Startled out of his reverie, Grainger twisted the key in the ignition.

"Grainger, wait."

He kept his profile to her as she walked up to the truck, his gaze still on the middle distance. Did he regret yesterday's small, sweet moment of touch? Or had it been meant as a cruel physical reminder of what they had lost? When speech couldn't begin to describe what was forever sullied between them, the feel of his breath on her neck did.

"Grainger, would you consider staying?"

Without looking at her, he nodded. "Only if you're sure, Kiley."

"I'm not sure, but I am certain that it would make Will happy." Even as she said those words, she substituted others in her mind: *I want you to be happy.*

"I should go change. No civilized person would want to eat with me this way." He looked down at himself.

"You're fine." When she'd sat with him in the truck, Kiley had noticed his warm, masculine scent, not unpleasant, and disturbingly familiar. It was true, then; the nose never forgets. "If you go, you won't come back."

Grainger threw her a sharp look of mistrust. Did he think she was referring even obliquely to his running away that day? Kiley quickly tried to recover her meaning. "I mean, we aren't dressing for dinner. It's a barbecue for heaven's sake."

"I should go. This is a stupid idea. Clearly we aren't in a place where we can successfully pretend every other sentence isn't a reference to the past. I'm overly sensitive, and so are you. Let's just stop here, before it gets out of hand."

"Grainger, no. I really didn't mean anything about . . . about that. I would have said the same . . ." Her voice trailed off. No, he was right. She did feel as though once off her property, he was a flight risk. "You're right. This is a stupid idea. I'm just indulging Will in a little hopeless fantasy. Like he said, forget about it."

"Fantasy? What fantasy? That I'm his father, when we both know that's not true?" Grainger threw the truck into reverse. "Why don't you tell him the truth? Why keep him, and me, in the dark?"

"What truth?" Kiley shouted over the engine as Grainger gunned it. The hedges were overgrown and the view up the road obscured. Kiley held her breath as he backed too fast out of the driveway and into the road. She only let it out as he slammed the vehicle into drive and sped away.

If Catherine hadn't pulled into the driveway at just that moment, Kiley would have given in to the shriek of frustration rising in her throat. Instead, with a second deep breath, she put on a cheerful face to greet Will's new friend.

Twenty-six

🐌

How long does it take to self-destruct? What are the odds of spontaneous combustion brought on by a bursting heart, Grainger wondered as he drove straight home, forgetting that his original errand, before he foolishly stopped to offer Kiley a ride, was to get gas. He probably wouldn't have enough to drive to the gas station tomorrow, but there was no way he could conduct even ordinary business right now. Anyone who saw his face would read grotesque mistakes written there. Even Pilot, attuned to his every mood, rode with his muzzle leaning through the sliding rear window's opening, as if looking back at his master's stupid behavior. A day ago he had hoped that Kiley and he would have an opportunity to get past their hurts, move ahead, to forgive. And today, like some sort of self-destructive asshole, he had thrust the opportunity away like shoving a life preserver out of reach. Evidently he preferred to drown in his own emotions.

If Grainger had been a drinking man, he'd have stopped at the liquor store and stocked up, putting out the burn of lost opportunity with the burn of scotch.

But he wasn't. He derided himself: If he was a smart man, he'd turn the truck around and go back. But, he wasn't. He was a stubborn man, so he went home, and picked up a sander.

Before going windsurfing with Catherine, Will had spent the morning working on *Blithe Spirit*. Grainger hadn't told him who she was, only that he'd had her since he'd had the boatyard. Along with the boathouse, the beachfront, six moorings, and all of the equipment, *Blithe Spirit* had come with the sale. The MacKenzies had hired the former owner to salvage the boat off Bailey's Beach, and never taken her back home.

It was years before he could make himself uncover her from the blue tarp. Then the first thing he did was to look at the fiberglass patch they'd made. He'd always believed that it had to have been the weak spot, the cause of the accident. But he was wrong; the patch had held.

The second thing he did was sand the name off her transom. So unless Grainger told him, Will would never know this was the same boat in which his father died.

Grainger had come back to Hawke's Cove because he had gotten a call from the sheriff's department in Great Harbor. An economically worded message left on his answering machine at his one-bedroom apartment in Galveston, where he lived during those rare weeks not afloat, stated that he should call back ASAP; it was urgent. He knew that Rollie Egan must be dead; there could be no other reason for them to call. He was a little surprised they'd been able to track him down.

When Grainger called the sheriff's office, the female voice on the line was businesslike, not unkind, or particularly sympathetic. Exactly right for the impassive way he received the news. She detailed the accident as he asked questions, giving him only as much detail as he wanted.

"The official report states that he was somehow caught in the nets and pulled overboard. Cause of death was drowning."

"Was he drunk?"

"Yes. Alcohol was a factor."

"I figured."

"The coroner needs to know what arrangements you wish to make. He needs you to claim the body."

Rollie had barely claimed him as a son, and now Grainger was responsible for seeing that he got a decent burial. He wanted to say, "Toss him back," but instead he said "I'll be there tomorrow," booked the first flight he could to Boston, and began to jot a list of things he'd need to do to give Rollie Egan a funeral. In twenty-four hours Grainger was right back where he'd started, staring at his father's bloated ugly face, wondering why he cared enough to bother with a service. By some carelessness, Rollie's eyes were half open, hooded, and the tips of his cigarette-yellowed front teeth were exposed in a kind of grimace.

If he felt no sorrow at his passing, drunk and dragged into the cold ocean, neither did Grainger feel relief or happiness. A calm neutrality settled on him. Once he was in Great Harbor to claim Rollie's body and arrange for his cremation, it took very little to drive across the bridge to Hawke's Cove. Grainger drove around, noting how little things had changed, wondering if he had changed as little.

Eventually he passed the boatyard with a For Sale sign dangling, its worn appearance indicating that the ravaged old place had been on the market for years.

And he knew that without Rollie and the painful associations with him, Hawke's Cove might be where he could make his land-based living.

The other pain from this place he carried with him, so it mattered very little where he was. He accepted that. Maybe even, deep in his heart, he hoped that being there might vitiate his contract with grief.

That last night, angry, hurt, and confused, and thinking that his father was still out squidding, Grainger had gone back to the motel room. He didn't know what he was going to do; he wanted only to hole up, lick his wounds, and regroup. But when Grainger opened the heavy motel door, there was Rollie, quietly drunk. The small space smelled of his sour body and cigarettes, with an overlay of fish. Grainger knew he should go back out, but he didn't, he walked in and shut the door.

Oblivious to Grainger's anguished face, Rollie had begun a tirade against him. "So, you come crawlin' back to your old man when the do-gooders don't want you? Eh? Better to stick with your own kind, boy. Course, with your mother tramping around, who knows what kind that is?" It was a favorite theme with him in recent months, an inexplicable obsession. He'd been put off the squidder for drunkenness, and he was happy to take out his frustration on Grainger, as he so often had on his wife. He was sitting down in a chair, his head lolling as if it were still on the boat while his body was on land. Rollie's eyes were half closed, studying Grainger standing there in front of him. Grainger knew that look, the look that preceded a beating.

No more. Never again. Grainger plucked some money out of his wallet to drop on the nightstand, keeping his eyes on Rollie as if on a cobra, and slung his backpack over his shoulder. Rollie looked at the money, forty dollars, his lips drawing into a thin, tight line. Grainger knew he had either impressed or infuriated him. He wasn't going to wait and find out. Grainger slammed the door behind him.

It had started to rain hard by the time Grainger found a working phone booth. It was almost dawn, but he didn't care. He dialed Mack's number, hoping that Mack would answer, and that he'd want to try and patch things up. They mustn't let Kiley come between them.

Mrs. MacKenzie's voice answered. "Grainger, thank God, we thought you were with him."

"No, Mack went to go cool off by himself."

"Grainger." Mrs. MacKenzie sounded hard, cold. As if knowing that he wasn't with Mack, that they hadn't shared the same fate, had now penetrated her with ice and she had no will to be gentle. "He took the boat."

"Mrs. MacKenzie, what happened?" But he knew. He heard the raging tears in her voice and he knew. Mack was lost and he hadn't prevented it. Grainger had always been the one to guide, to lead; the responsible one. He should never have let Mack go out alone to *Blithe Spirit*.

"Why didn't you stop him, Grainger?"

"I had no idea what he was going to do."

"What made him do this?"

"We had a big fight. I thought he'd just sit out there." The first thin light of dawn illuminated the rough gray water of the harbor.

"But he didn't."

Mrs. MacKenzie didn't ask where he was, or how he was. She hung up the phone. He was no longer her care.

The postmark on his mother's one letter to him, the letter Kiley had brought, was from Boston. By holding it up to a bright light, Grainger could make out McLean Hospital underneath the blacked-out return address. In it had been a ten dollar bill and a short note: "I thought you maybe have graduated high school by now. Congradulashions. From your mother." Nothing more, no explanation or apology, nor love. He reread the note, not seeing its limitations this time, but interpreting a shy kindness.

At the entrance to the highway, he stuck out his thumb. He had three weeks before reporting for duty. In that time maybe he could finally find his mother. She was all he had left in the world.

Losing Will would be as painful as any other loss he had endured. But as long as Will agreed, there was nothing preventing Grainger from keeping in touch, from having Will return to visit, even going to see him at school. Grainger wouldn't allow him to disappear into the ether like his mother; or, like Mack, into the sea.

Twenty-seven

Catherine had charmed his mother. Not in a phony, Eddie Haskell sort of way, like in the *Leave It to Beaver* reruns on Nick at Nite, but in a genuine and cheerful way—much as she'd charmed him, but without the physical attraction. Catherine's plan to go premed had given the pair a lot to talk about and he'd been able to relax.

If only Grainger had agreed to stay. Or his mother had been more gracious in inviting him. Will was certain that, once in the same room, they would begin to renew their relationship. He wasn't looking for miracles, just for the two of them to be comfortable enough that he could speak of one to the other. Was this what it was like for kids with divorced parents? Right now, his mother winced whenever he brought up Grainger's name—like today, telling her how much fun he was having working on the boats. Grainger had told him about crewing for Pop on *Random,* and had all but suggested that Will might be a part of that team. On hearing this, Mom had turned away from him, falling back on the usual "We'll see," as if he were a little kid. And Grainger—Christ, he changed the subject so fast any time he said anything about his mother.

He had spent a very productive morning with Grainger. He was beginning to really enjoy the work, the physicality of it, the sight and feel of a smooth board. This morning Grainger had uncovered the smallest of the boats in his yard.

"This one needs a lot of sanding, then caulking. She's been out of the water for a long time. I'll start varnishing *Random;* you get started on this one."

Will noticed a line along the starboard side of the bow, above the waterline. The morning light touched it in exactly the right way to reveal an outline. He looked around for Grainger, but he was inside on the phone. Will pressed with the palm of his hand. Sure enough, the tactile difference between the bent wood of the lapped boards and the fiberglass-over-canvas that repaired the hole was obvious. She had to be *Blithe Spirit.*

Grainger came back out into the yard. "You wouldn't believe that some people think they can buy time. They think they can hurry me up with money." He came around the side of the boat. Will had his hands back on the sander. Grainger's eyes were on Will, then the boat and the unsanded bow. "Let's go sailing."

Grainger had let him work his way out of the small cove, threading the boat around the three other craft moored on Grainger's private moorings. Grainger sat on the starboard side, hat pulled down against the mid-morning sun, saying little, letting Will figure out how much to let out the mainsheet, how little to move the tiller. As they came around the edge of the cove, Grainger nodded.

"Well done."

Will had often been commended, for pitching a good game, or writing a meaningful essay, or raising more money for the AIDS Alliance than any other student. But those two words, *Well done,* touched a deeper part of him than any others. He grinned into the wind.

"Tell me about Catherine." Grainger was watching the blue pennant at the top of the mast.

"She's great."

"You really like her." A statement of fact.

"Yeah. I've never met anyone it was so easy to be with. She doesn't play any games." Will moved the tiller a degree, straightening their course.

"What kind of games do girls play these days?"

"Lori, my old girlfriend, liked to yank my chain." Will glanced away from the horizon at Grainger's slight smile. "I mean, she'd say she didn't mind if I went out with my friends, then get all mad if I did. I never knew if she was testing me or just changing her mind." Will pulled a little too much on the mainsheet, then quickly corrected his error before Grainger had to say anything.

"Sounds like a bitch."

Will grinned. "She could be. Especially the way she broke it off."

"How was that?"

"Her parents were away, so she had a party. She asked me to go outside with her and I thought she meant for some, well, private time." Will took a better hold on the mainsheet. "Anyway, she told me that since we were going to two different colleges, we should break it off. No sense holding each other back."

"Pretty harsh."

"I thought so."

They sailed in silence for a few minutes; then Grainger

gave the order to jibe. The mainsheet slid between Will's fingers and he watched Grainger deftly shift to the port side of the boat as the boom swung. For an instant all motion was suspended; then Will gathered the sail back into control, catching the wind with ease.

"Very nice."

Again Will felt the unaccountable happiness those simple words stirred in his heart. As if, all of his life, despite unstinting maternal confirmation of his worthiness, he was finally getting the paternal approval he'd craved.

"Did you love her?"

"I thought I did. But now, knowing Catherine, I see that I was mistaken."

Grainger poured some coffee out of a thermos into his mug.

"Then I did something totally stupid." Will adjusted the tiller slightly.

"What was that?"

"I went with my buddies and got high. And got caught."

"Pot?"

"Yeah."

Grainger didn't say anything to that, and Will was a little afraid that Grainger's opinion of him was sullied. "I only did it that once. I'm an athlete. I just did it because . . ."

"Because it felt better to hurt yourself than let someone else do it."

Will nodded.

"We all do stupid things, Will. It's how we behave afterward that counts."

"Catherine says that it was actually a good thing that I did it. If I hadn't, Mom wouldn't have brought me here to get away from those friends of mine. The stupid thing is, I have so little in common with D.C. and Mike except that we're in the same homeroom, and we've always just hung out from habit. We're not that close. I really wouldn't have been hanging around with them this summer, at least not much, but I didn't say that. And she went ballistic on me and decided that I would become a pothead if I stayed home. I guess I really fucked up her trust in me. Sorry, didn't mean to use that word."

Grainger's burst of laughter surprised them both. "I spent ten years in the Merchant Marine; I don't think you can shock me. Anyway, maybe Catherine's right. Sometimes things do work out for the best."

Will adjusted his course gently, and the bow sliced through the green-gray water with an audible hiss. They were clipping along, his sail set to maximize the light airs. It had felt so right telling Grainger the truth about that night; why hadn't he been able to tell his mother yet?

As a little kid, Will would sometimes pick out some guy and imagine he was his father. Never one of the guys his mother dated; usually some clerk in an ice cream shop or hardware store. Once it was a school-bus driver who'd been solicitous to him one day when he'd tripped and fallen on the sidewalk and his lunch had spilled out all over the pavement. The guy had actually gotten up out of his seat and helped Will scoop up his rolling thermos and scattered Goldfish crackers. Mom had been there too, and it was the broad thank-you she'd expressed to the guy for helping, instead of driving away to keep on his schedule, that had filled Will's daydreams for most of second grade.

But this was different. It wasn't a daydream. He could prove that Grainger was his father.

• • •

Will sat quietly, a glass of cola slowly warming in his hand as he happily listened to Catherine and his mother chat with animation about the medical profession. Kiley was already into anecdotes from her years in school. He was pleased, and happy to let them keep the conversational ball to themselves. The two women lazed on the porch rockers, keeping an identical slow rhythm. Will sat on the porch rail with his back against the post. The late July sunset was earlier than it had been even a week ago, and they sat in near dark. A tin bucket of citronella burned at their feet, its tiny flame the same color as the waxing moon that peeked over the eastern horizon, casting a yellow swath of light against the darkening water.

"This is so beautiful, Ms. Harris. Thank you for inviting me to dinner."

"I'm glad you came. I hope you come again." Despite the farewell quality of the words, neither one moved to end the evening.

Will closed his eyes and listened to the soft rhythmic thump of the rockers. The dinner could only have been better if Grainger had stayed. But all in all, it had been great. He smiled. Catherine was right; his punishment had become his reward. Unfortunately, his reward had been hard on his mother. Selling this place was taking a toll on her, and his friendship with Grainger was stressing her out so much that she'd taken to sleepless wandering around. Will knew the difference in his mother's fretting. The house-fretting generally meant under-the-breath cussing about Toby, and slamming doors. The Grainger stress was sharper, deeper, and was revealed only in her sighs when she thought herself unobserved. Sighs born of nostalgia and pain and maybe a little jealousy of his ease with her former friend.

When he was little, sometimes he'd hear his mother sigh like that, generally only in the late spring when Nana and Pop were loading the car up for Hawke's Cove. Then he'd hear her slow intake of breath, with a rapid release, like someone getting ready to scream or cry. As a child, he'd distracted her by dropping a glass, or skinning his knee. Now, older, he let her wallow a little before pulling up some half-interesting anecdote about school or friends to entertain her out of her doldrums.

"Well, I should leave you two alone." His mother got up, stretched, and leaned her hands on the porch rail. "No, stay put, Catherine, I can manage the few dishes."

Will slid down from the rail. "We might go catch a movie."

"Great. Home right after, though, okay?"

"Okay."

Will kissed his mother's cheek, then grasped his new girlfriend's hand. They called again their thanks and good-nights. As they pulled away from the house, his mother was still standing there, gazing out at the rising moon. Even though she was shadowed by the cover of the porch roof, Will sensed she looked out with sadness. Toby had said that he was coming tomorrow with an offer from that couple who had looked at the house today. How many more nights did they have to sit and watch the moon rise over Hawke's Cove? A very finite number.

"I like your mother; she's really sweet." Catherine's voice broke through the building nostalgia, sending it scurrying. There would be plenty of time later to be sorry the house was gone. Right now he had this great girl sitting beside him, one who, with the right care, might remain a part of his autumn and beyond.

"Not all the time, but I guess she's all right." Will was pleased with the way Kiley and Catherine had gotten along, only a little embarrassed that his mother had drilled Catherine about whether she had done the same sorts of things that she herself had done a million years ago. Did she go to the Yacht Club dances? Catherine's family weren't members. Did kids still hang out at the harbor? Mostly kids were discouraged from hanging out in Hawke's Cove; they went to the mall in Great Harbor instead. Those sorts of questions got a little old after a while, but Catherine hadn't seemed to mind. Will had finally moved the interrogation off memory lane and into the present.

They drove slowly along the bluff road. "Thanks for putting up with her inquisition. She's reliving her past by being here."

"I didn't mind. I can't imagine not ever coming back here, and then, when I did, knowing it was for the last time."

Catherine's remark brought a fresh lurch of nostalgia to Will. He'd been denied any contact with this place until the last minute, and now it was too late. He hadn't planned on loving it, he did love this place, despite his intention to spend the time here sulking. It wasn't just meeting the man who might be his father, or even meeting a girl he so instantly cared about. It was this place.

"Do we have to go to the movies?" Will turned the car radio down, the insistent beat of a rap song suddenly too harsh for the quiet between them.

"I guess not. Why?"

"I'd like to just sit on the beach for a little while."

Catherine took her hand off the wheel and touched his hand. "I'd like that."

They went past Catherine's house to the small parking area at the head of the path to Bailey's Beach. They found damp towels in the backseat of her car and carried them down to the beach. There the waves lapped hungrily at the shoreline, arrhythmic, sensual.

Will snugged Catherine close to him on his towel. "It's still so warm out; we should have brought suits and gone swimming."

Catherine stroked his back with her hand. "We don't need suits."

Will didn't move. "That's how my mother got in trouble."

"I'm on the pill."

"Are we ready for that yet?"

"Probably not, but if we were, I can promise you, you won't find me in the same place as your mother."

"I'm not sure I can talk about sex and my mother in the same sentence. I think that a dip in the cold water will have the same effect."

"Shall we go see?" Catherine stood up and, keeping her back to Will, dropped her clothes onto the sand. "Come on, shy-boy. I won't look and I won't tease. I just want a swim." Catherine was clearly visible in the moonlight touching her skin into silver. He watched as she ran to the water's edge, toed it, shivered, and then plunged in. In a moment, he was beside her. The cold water did nothing to discourage his natural, eighteen-year-old's reaction to the sight of Catherine's bare bottom, exposed for a moment as she dived beneath the surface. He was amazed at the sense of freedom being suitless lent him, like sleeping nude, the silken water like silk sheets caressing his body. He made Catherine turn around when he bolted out of the water for the shore, hastily covering himself with a damp towel. He kept his back turned as Catherine came out of the sea, but in his imagination he saw her as a short-haired Venus rising out of the shell, hands gracefully covering critical areas. The image did nothing to alleviate his body's reaction to her nearby nakedness. He sat with his hands over his towel-wrapped lap.

The night-soft July air dried them as they sat, side by side, chaste fingers touching. Will was proud of his restraint, of his self-control in not reaching over to remove Catherine's towel, of his willingness to wait until they were in a stronger relationship than that of a few days' acquaintance. It was a struggle, though. Will spoke to distract himself. "You know what I just don't get?"

"What?"

"My mother and Grainger. He picked her up this afternoon, and yet wouldn't stay for dinner. And she didn't help. I mean, I know they hurt each other, but that was a long long time ago. You'd think they'd want to get along for my sake."

"It's obvious they have history; maybe you should just leave it alone."

"I can't. It's beginning to obsess me. They loved each other once."

"You used to love Lori."

Will pitched a rock ino the silver path of the moon in the water. "That was different."

"What if twenty years from now you met her like at a reunion—you don't think that wouldn't be awkward?"

"Lori and I won't have a child between us."

"You don't know that your mother and Grainger do."

Will flung another rock, the deep gulp of the water underlining his muddled thoughts. "That's what I want to know."

"Not to be harsh or anything, but if those two have such bad feelings toward each other, nothing you want is going to change it. You're just going to have to be satisfied that you know at least as much as you do."

"I just want to know that he is my father. Not to get anything from him, or to complicate his life, but just so that I finally know who my father is."

"But, Will, he might not be your father. Could you handle the disappointment?"

Will drew a line in the sand. "At least I'd still know who my father was."

He should demand to have a paternity test done. Grainger owed him that much, if he wouldn't try and make up with Mom. At least Will could leave here with some satisfaction. Catherine didn't understand; his curiosity was deeper than his fear of disappointment.

After a moment Catherine stood up and gathered her clothes, walking a little distance along the beach to a protective dune while Will slipped his clothes on. When she came back to him, Will took Catherine in his arms, holding her in the shelter of his embrace. Will's lips touched hers, and for a few minutes they simply kissed, all confusion forgotten.

"Will I see you tomorrow?" he asked.

"After your sailing lesson?"

"Okay."

"How're the lessons going?"

"Grainger says I'm doing really good. He just sits there and lets me do everything without telling me what to do."

"It would be fun if you could take me out."

"That'd be awesome. Before we leave, I'll take you out."

"I'm going to hold you to that."

Will caught Catherine's fingers and held them against his cheek. "Sure. I promise."

Will watched Catherine drive away, feeling vaguely that if he hadn't exactly lied to her, he had maybe exaggerated his skills a little. This morning he had asked about going out by himself, but Grainger had shaken his head.

"Absolutely not. Not yet. You've only been on the water a couple of times. It would be different if you'd had a whole summer to practice. You're coming along quickly, but not yet."

Grainger was being overcautious—or, maybe, he was afraid that he'd catch hell. His mother would certainly have choice words for Grainger if she thought he allowed Will to sail alone. Grainger was being unfair and his mother overprotective.

He would take Catherine out sailing. A quick sail around the cove; no big deal. Not as big a deal as smoking dope. He'd just have to work on them, wear his mother and Grainger down with pestering. Just like any kid with two parents.

Twenty-eight

꩜

Toby Reynolds sat in the right-hand rocker, the geranium pink of his Lacoste polo shirt clashing with the growing red of his cheeks. "I could understand your reasoning if they had offered less, but their offer is a good one. A really good one. You're making a mistake not to take it."

Kiley Harris rocked slowly in the left-hand chair, the one closest to the door. "Do you watch baseball?"

"Yeah, why?"

"Certain batters always let the first good pitch go by."

"Is that what you're doing?"

"Something like that." Kiley kept her chair in motion. "I can see why realtors don't much like it when sellers meet buyers at the showing; but I was here, inconvenient or not. So, I can tell you that in no way are they going to be happy here. They have no connection to Hawke's Cove except that they've been here twice and it's pretty. That's no reason to drop so much money on a place. When Miss Gold-digger finds out that it's not the Hamptons, they'll turn around and sell it in two years. That's not who I want to have this house."

Toby's flush crawled to his ears. "Kiley, you can't vet potential buyers on anything but their credit history. You can't take a dislike to someone and refuse their offer on the basis that they have no history here. If that was the case, no Cover would be able to sell anything except to other Covers."

Kiley could tell that Toby was royally pissed off at her. He was behaving, in her opinion, much less like her agent, and much more like a buyer's agent.

"I'm calling your father this afternoon. I have to let him know that you've refused the offer. Without cause."

"Of course. His signature is on the contract with your agency, not mine. I just won't be held responsible for putting this house in the wrong hands." Kiley stood up and put out a hand to stop the reactive rocking of the chair. "Are you bringing anyone else to see it?"

"I've got two or three others who want to see it, including a couple with children, from Great Harbor. He's a banker; she's a consultant of some sort. They are deeply—what's the word we want?" Toby's voice was bordering on sneering. *"Rooted.* Deeply rooted here. But I can tell you that if they like it, there's very little hope they can make an acceptable offer."

"When are you bringing them by?"

"Is one o'clock okay?"

"Yes. I'll stay away."

"Please."

Kiley was surprised when Toby didn't leave, but followed her into the house.

"So, are you going to the Yacht Club fund-raiser?" In an instant Toby the Real Estate Agent vanished, and a new, uncontentious Toby hung beside her in the doorway.

"I haven't decided. Emily Claridge made sure I got

an invitation, but it's not something I planned on attending. I didn't come back for the social circuit, just to get this house ready."

Toby was lost on the first part of her sentence. *"Claridge?"*

"Sans Souci."

"Oh, right. Emily Fitzgibbons."

"Anyway"—Kiley put her hand on the screen door in an effort to clue Toby in on his unwelcome continued presence—"I'll probably just send a contribution."

"I'm on the committee this year." Toby lingered, oblivious to her cue. "It would be wonderful to have a representative from your family there, with your dad being such a staunch supporter of the club's sailing program and all, and I know that everyone at the Yacht Club would be thrilled to see you. Besides"—Toby reached out and touched Kiley's arm—"it would be fun to see you in a nonadversarial role."

"Toby, are you hitting on me?" Kiley couldn't stop her grin.

"Maybe a little."

As soon as Toby left, Kiley called home to update her parents on the difficulties she was having with him, trying not to think of it as a preemptive strike. Lydia answered and, after describing the Fensters' offer as subpar, Kiley mentioned the fund-raising party to change the subject.

"Oh, that's lovely. You'll be sure to say hello to..." And Lydia rattled off a list of old friends who would surely be there. Their names conjured the old days for Kiley, names forgotten during her long hiatus. Murphy and Sonderbend. Kensy and Deveaux. French and Altman. Boat names came back to her: the Kensys' gaff-rigged

Alphonse and Marie, the Deveauxs' stunning yawl *Digger,* and the Altmans' charming little catboat, *Catbird.*

Blithe Spirit. Where was she now? Would Grainger know her whereabouts, or Conor? Did she dare ask, or would that open up a conversation she didn't want? Maybe *Blithe Spirit* was simply scuttled, drowned in the sea that took her master.

Kiley pushed aside the thin curtain from one of the front windows and gazed out at the cove beyond. "I doubt that I'll go. And, Mother, don't imagine for a minute that any of those folks are pleased to hear you're selling the place. It's been like announcing a death."

"It's none of their business." Her mother was immediately imperious, and Kiley pictured her, at this hour, cocktail in hand; Dad standing behind her, his oxygen tank not far away.

"They're going to miss you anyway."

"They'll all be selling someday. These places are too hard to keep."

Kiley didn't want to get into a discussion with her mother about the difficulties of maintaining a shingle-style summerhouse; the constant battle against the elements as trim paint peeled and porch decking needed replacement, the annual prayer the roof would hold another season. She knew well that if you loved it, you'd do it.

She changed the subject. "Will's found a girlfriend."

"I hope a suitable family."

"Probably not by your standards, but certainly by mine."

"What's her name?"

Kiley told her, and then half listened as Lydia tried to place the Ames family in her circle.

"Her mother might be a French. I think one of their daughters married an Ames." As Lydia nattered on, Kiley felt her attention drift.

"Mother, it hardly matters. We'll be gone soon."

"These things always matter. One is judged by the company one keeps." An oft-repeated adage of Kiley's youth as she persisted in being with Mack and Grainger. Fleetingly, Kiley wondered what her mother would think of Grainger now that he was a successful businessman, miles away from the poor boy who lived on the charity of the MacKenzies.

"I have to go. Toby's coming back with another client. Someone he says has Hawke's Cove roots."

"That's very good. Now, make sure that the house looks nice. No dishes in the sink, that sort of thing."

"That's all I've been doing, Mother." She turned away from the window.

"And I appreciate it. Let's hope these people make an offer."

"I'm not going to accept any offer if it isn't perfect."

"Kiley, please bear in mind that this is Will's future you're gambling with. Neither your father nor I can support Will's education with our other resources. This is it. Otherwise, you'll have to come up with some way to pay for it, and you mustn't forget your current situation."

Her mother's cold dismissal of the house she once called her sanctuary was inexplicable to Kiley, who had put the house and its memories into a bell jar. "Have you no sentimental attachment to this place? After all the wonderful years you spent here?"

"None. Sentiment has no bearing in life; it clutters up the mind. If you give the past too much attention, you end up spending wasted time trying to recover it."

"Can you put Dad on?" Enough was enough.

It took a moment for her father to make his way to the phone. "Have you spoken to Egan?"

"Yes. He'll do it." Kiley pictured Grainger's angry backing out of her driveway. "He'll crew for you."

"What about Will and you?"

"We won't be here, Dad. You know that."

"You can be. Even if we sell the house, we won't close until after Labor Day."

"That's not the reason."

"Then what is?" Her father's voice was just above a whisper. "Tell me."

"I should never have come back here."

"You're doing fine."

"I told Will everything."

For a moment, there was just the sound of her father's thready breathing. "How did he take it?"

"Pretty well, I think. Except that now he wants physical proof."

"From whom?"

Kiley flushed. Could her father really think Will's was a virgin birth? The old tag line from *The Graduate* came to mind: "Every father's daughter is a virgin."

"From Grainger or from Conor MacKenzie."

"Conor?"

"Mack's brother."

"I always liked Dr. MacKenzie. Treated your mother's indigestion."

"Oh, Dad." Kiley gripped the handset tighter. "I have to go now."

"Wait. About *Random*, tell Egan I'm coming the Thursday before the race."

"I don't know, Dad. I've been thinking that you really ought to reconsider the race. It's very strenuous, even just getting into the boat. Besides, the house is half packed."

"We'll just be sleeping there. Leave the beds made."

"But the other thing is, I don't think that you should drive this distance, Dad."

"Kiley, we've already booked a driver; unless you'd be willing to drive us there."

"Why are you being so stubborn about this?"

Kiley knew that her father was alone in the room as his voice strengthened above his whisper. "Your mother wants to go. We thought we could just give it up without going back, but darling, we can't. Don't mind what she says; she misses the place terribly. Even if it's beyond us, we still love it."

"If you love it so much, why give it up?"

"You loved it and you did."

"That was different." His blunt, painfully respirated words hurt. "Don't sell it. I'll manage Will's education. After all, now I'm an unemployed single mother. Surely that must have some benefit."

"You're saying you'll take it on?"

"We've had this discussion before. The answer hasn't changed. I can't."

"That was before you came clean with Will. You're there, and nothing bad has happened."

Kiley squeezed her eyes shut. "I'm not so sure about that."

Nothing bad had happened; but, equally true, nothing good had, either. The often fantasized reconciliation had been stunted. Stillborn. Grainger was right: how could they ever be friends when every sentence came out with a subtext, a shadow-meaning so deeply embedded, it was as if all her words came through some

source other than her brain? She was like a ventrilo-
quist's dummy for her subconscious. They had loved
each other once. Did that indicate that they should be
friends again, or did it mean that they couldn't be?
They knew each other too well.

In the garage was an old Raleigh three-speed bike.
The tires were flat but not rotten, and Kiley inflated
them with the old-fashioned hand pump. Every time
she pushed down on the handle, she squeezed air into a
new resolve.

Enough, indeed, was enough.

Helmetless, on oozing tires, and with brakes that
made the ride down the bluff hill more than thrilling,
Kiley headed to Egan's Boat Works. She needed
Grainger to help talk her father out of his dangerous
plan to be on *Random* for the race. He simply didn't
have breath enough to shift from side to side as the boat
changed course. Racing meant quick, precise movements. There'd be no time to make sure he'd be all
right. Kiley pictured the green oxygen tank rolling
around the deck like a loose cannon, the old man gasping for air in the fresh breeze. The very wind would
steal his breath. He wouldn't listen to her, but he might
listen to Grainger. Surely Grainger wouldn't turn her
aside. He'd always liked her father; after all, it was her
father who'd suggested him for the position of instructor for the youth sailing program.

There was barely enough air left in the bicycle tires
to pedal down Grainger's long gravel driveway. As the
boatyard came into view, Kiley spotted her own car beside Grainger's truck. Maybe this would be easier with
Will there. She leaned the bike against the Mazda. The
sudden growly hum of a compressor startled her. Men
at work. Grainger, dressed in white protective overalls,

was spray-painting *Random*'s hull, his back to her and the sound of the compressor masking her steps.

As she walked beyond the three big boats, she could see Will working on a little boat. He leaned over the upturned hull balanced on sawhorses, easing a soft white compound between seams where time had separated the boards. Resting on another pair of sawhorses was a mast, freshly varnished and glowing in the July sun.

Kiley stopped. It looked so small, a fraction of the size it had loomed in her memory.

Will straightened up, scraping seam compound off his fingers and back into the can. "Hi, Mom. What brings you here?"

"It's her, isn't it?"

Will ran a finger along a freshly caulked seam. "I think so." The compressor's roar started up again. "I haven't asked him." Will glanced in Grainger's direction, then touched the spot-primed place where the boards were fiberglass covered.

Kiley moved around to the stern. The name she had handlettered was gone, sanded off, the bare wood spotprimed. It didn't matter; *Blithe Spirit* was recognizable all the same.

"She's just like the boat I'm learning to sail in." Will pointed to the Beetle Cat bobbing on her mooring, the midmorning sun striking sparks off the water around her.

"Why are you working on her?"

"It's what Grainger told me to do."

Kiley touched the fiberglass patch. When she looked away from it, she saw Grainger coming toward them. His protective mask was still in place, but his eyes above it were visible. "Hello, Grainger."

He pulled the mask from his face, revealing a smile. "Hello, Kiley."

Kiley was exquisitely aware of him, of his closeness, as he came to stand beside her next to the boat. "I always thought *Blithe Spirit* was destroyed on the rocks."

"No. I always thought so too, but she wasn't even damaged. The patch held." Grainger ran a finger along the white seam-putty, checking Will's work.

"He simply went overboard?" Kiley moved away from Grainger to the other side of the boat.

"It would seem so, yes. He probably lost control in the wind."

"Poor Mack." She touched the keel gently.

For a moment all three stood in silence, ranged around the Beetle Cat as if the bottom-up hull was a coffin.

Kiley took her fingers off of the keel. "After all this time, why are you working on her now?"

Grainger leaned his weight on the hull, bringing his face close to hers, making her look at him. "I want Will to have her. As his legacy from Mack."

Kiley took a step back. "Absolutely not. What are you thinking?"

"I'm thinking . . . I've been thinking that he should have her."

"I should have her?"

She hushed Will with a wave of her hand. "Why do you say that, Grainger?"

"Mack would have wanted him to."

"Mack would?" Will looked at Grainger and then at his mother.

"Shut up, Will." Kiley shoved her fists into her sides. "You cannot know what Mack would have wanted, Grainger. Mack is dead and that boat is the reason."

"No, Kiley. We're the reason."

"Stop it!" Will kicked at the sawhorse "Stop it, both

of you!" He aimed another kick at the can of seam putty, sending it clattering under one of the other boats, then stalked off. They could hear the sound of tires squealing out as he pulled onto the paved road too fast.

Kiley and Grainger faced each other over the up-turned boat. This was not the reason she'd come here today. But it was one of the reasons she'd stayed away from Hawke's Cove for so long.

"Grainger, please don't give him this boat."

"I need to."

"Why? What makes you think you should?"

"Mack." Grainger abruptly walked away. Pilot joined him as he kept walking along the brief shoreline of Maiden Cove. Kiley went after him, her sneaker prints filling his larger boot prints as she followed his path. When she caught up to him, Grainger was sitting on a short jetty, his back to her. The midday sun was bright, making his white coverall shine against the backdrop of blue water. He pitched a stick into the water and the dog launched himself off the jetty after it. Kiley climbed over the rocks and sat on a flat rock beside him.

"Why do you think Mack would want Will to have *Blithe Spirit*?"

"Because Mack is his father."

"You don't know that."

"But you do."

"No, I don't. Why do you think I do? How could I?"

"You named him for Mack."

Kiley ducked to avoid Pilot's vigorous, watery shake. "He's named for my father. Merriwell William Harris the second."

Grainger stared out at the cove, his lips twitching in what looked like resistance to a smile. Then it released, and a self-effacing laugh erupted. "Oh. Shit. I am a fool."

"Is that what you thought? That I'd keep it secret if I knew for sure?"

"I don't know what to think." He tossed the stick back toward the water; it fell short, and Pilot scrambled down the rocks to fetch it. "But I still think that Will should have her. She belonged to Mack; now she belongs to me. I guess you could say she's from both of us. Whatever happened, she's a beautiful little boat and needs someone to love her."

"You speak of her like she was a woman."

"All boats are, they say. But, no, I speak of her like a living creature, like Pilot. A creature that thrives with use."

"He wouldn't get much use out of her." Kiley felt a crack in her resistance. "And I wouldn't allow him to take her out alone."

Grainger looked at Kiley, covering her hand as it rested on the sun-warmed rock. "I'd never let him go out alone. He's not ready."

"Promise me?"

Grainger lowered his face to hers and for a heartbeat she thought he was going to kiss her. "I promise," his words tickling her cheek.

"I came here today to ask you to talk my father out of his crazy idea about being aboard *Random* when you race her." Kiley handed Grainger the jar of mayonnaise. "He's in ill health and can barely get from one room to the other, much less port to starboard."

Grainger spread the mayonnaise on rye bread and settled slices of roast beef on them. "We could get him settled in the cockpit, lashed down if necessary, and let him go for the ride. It would mean so much to him to be there. How can you deny an old man his dream?"

"He talked to you, didn't he?" Kiley took the sandwich Grainger offered and went to sit.

"Yes. He told me you'd probably try to get me to persuade him to give up the idea."

"Cagey old man."

"Would you want to be denied the thing you loved best as your days were waning?"

"You must think I'm a terrible cramp. I don't want Will to sail alone, and I don't want my father to sail with a crew."

"No. Overprotective maybe, but not a cramp."

Kiley threw Grainger a bitter smile. "Not much like the Blithe of your youth?"

Grainger set his sandwich down and took her face in his hands. "None of us are who we once were. We grew up."

Again Kiley thought he was going to kiss her, but he didn't; he simply looked into her eyes.

"Grainger, can we ever recapture what we had?"

He shook his head, but smiled. "I think that we need to forget about the past. Not recapture it, but get to know each other as we are now. If we like each other, maybe then we can look to the future." He released her.

"We have so little time."

"I'm not asking you to stay."

"Then what are you asking me?"

"Help me with *Random*. Hang around with me a little."

Kiley knew that she was grinning, and made no effort to hide it. "Okay."

. . .

Every day, as soon as Will headed off to meet Catherine after work or to the beach after his sailing lesson, Kiley hopped on her bicycle with its new tires, and pedaled to meet Grainger. Will seemed oblivious to her subterfuge, never asking her where she'd been if he got home before her, only what was for dinner. If she wasn't exactly avoiding mentioning this tentative friendship, she wasn't going out of her way to bring it to his attention, either. She'd told Grainger that first afternoon there was no sense giving him false hope. It had come out more callous than she'd meant it, but Grainger hadn't flinched. It was such a delicate thing, breathing new life into a relationship nearly dead of anger and neglect. As they worked each afternoon on *Random,* their conversations were topical or gossipy, or Grainger told complimentary little stories about Will's progress. They took care not to speak of the past, as if it was of no consequence. Still, Kiley felt it lurking behind them as they laughed together at local politics or argued about the Red Sox's chances this year.

It just felt good to be with him, a familiar happiness she'd thought long gone. Yet there was a fragility to it, like holding fine china with slippery hands. A moment's carelessness and it was shattered.

They mustn't expect too much, or move too fast.

But time was forging relentlessly ahead. It was almost time to go back to Southton and pick up the threads of her real life. The time that had seemed so long as its beginning was speeding toward its conclusion, and there was nothing she could do to stop its impetus. Sandy had called to tell her the memorial service for Doc John was scheduled for Monday, the day she had originally been due back at work. Any idea that they might prolong their time in Hawke's Cove was gone.

• • •

"Kiley, hi, it's Grainger."

She hadn't expected to hear his voice on the phone, and felt a frisson of pleasure that he would call. "Good morning."

"Look, say no if it's a bad idea, but would you be willing to help me make a boat delivery?"

"I guess I could. Where?"

"I'm bringing *Miss Emily* around to Great Harbor. Just motoring, it'll take less than an hour."

"No problem." Good, she sounded casual, not as if his invitation meant anything. Nothing that could cause the pounding of her heart.

"If you'll drive to the marina, I'll pick you up there."

That made sense. She'd leave her car in Great Harbor, so they'd have a way back home. "What time?"

"Now."

It was only seven-thirty, a hot summer day just beginning. Kiley knew that Will would be in bed until noon unless he had plans. He'd scarcely notice she was gone. "I'll meet you there in half an hour."

"Thanks for doing this. It'll be fun."

Fun.

Kiley threw sunblock and a hat into her carryall, then hunted around for the keys. Will had had them last.

She tiptoed up the stairs to his room where he slept, the keys on his dresser. Backing out of the room, she looked at her son, one long arm thrown over his eyes. In sleep he returned to the little boy in cowboy pajamas, the one who would crawl into her lap and grasp a hank of her hair, stroking it between his fingers. She smiled and left.

• • •

Grainger was already in the parking lot of the marina when she pulled in. He leaned against his truck, playing tug of war with Pilot.

"Am I late?"

He smiled and shook his head. "No, I'm early." When he opened the passenger-side door, the dog immediately jumped in, settling himself in the passenger seat. "Get in the back, Pilot." After the dog did as he was told, Kiley got into the truck.

Grainger gestured to a styrofoam cup sitting in a cup holder. "That's yours."

Kiley sipped the hot black coffee. "Thanks. I was one cup short of my quota."

As they headed back to the boatyard, they chatted of inconsequentials: the changes in Great Harbor, the ugliness of some of the new boats, the lack of tradition in the new rich. It was as if they clung to conversation like a life ring, she thought, spinning around and around, but never really making progress toward shore.

Miss Emily was tied up against the pier. Back in the water, she looked graceful and glowing in the late July sunshine.

"She looks great. You certainly do nice work."

"Will helped. He seems to be really getting into it."

"He used to make models as a kid. I suppose that working on the boats is a lot like that—lots of tedious and painstaking work."

"Lots of elbow grease." Grainger stepped onto *Miss Emily,* then reached for Kiley's bag.

Kiley took his hand as she stepped from dock to boat, then cast off the lines as Grainger started the inboard engine. In a few minutes they were powering away from the pier and out into the small cove, the bow pointed toward open water.

"Go take a look below if you want." Grainger was at the wheel, his attention on the outlet. He exuded self-assurance. This was his natural place: behind the wheel of a big sailboat, eyes pointed to the horizon, capable and confident. Kiley felt an unexpected desire wash through her, and she quickly backed down the companionway into the tidy galley.

A tiny gas stove and miniature sink were built into one wall; there were narrow bunks port and starboard, and a wide sleeping space in the forepeak. The head was behind a narrow door and Kiley hoped she wouldn't have to use it, with its complicated pedal and pump flush. Shelves and storage were cleverly tucked in every conceivable place. Kiley let herself imagine sailing away on this boat, Grainger at the helm. She must be glad of this short voyage, of this golden time. Not so long ago, Grainger had hated her. *Be grateful for this.*

Kiley went back up to sit in front of Grainger, to pretend that her enjoyment was of the view and the feel of a boat on water, not simply being in his company again.

Twenty-nine

❧

Now that *Miss Emily* was done, they were moving very quickly on *Blithe Spirit*. Will gave unflagging, uncomplaining dedication to the effort. Much of what they did was repetitive, boring stuff. Going over and over the same area with a sander or tack cloth or paintbrush is tedious at best, numbing at worst. Yet Grainger believed there was something reverential to the process, that it was a noble thing to bring life back to a boat. From the barnacle-encrusted, flaking, worm-riddled, ugly look of an old hull, to the brilliant shine of a clean hull, freshly painted, the new lines pure white, the brass untinged with green, softly shining in the sunlight. The warm maple-syrup glow of perfectly dried marine varnish.

As they floated her off the trailer into the water, Grainger saw Will's delighted amazement at the transformation of the little boat as she ceased to be an inanimate object and became a sea creature. Free of the bonds of gravity, she bobbed happily in her element. The boy's face showed the same joy Grainger had felt at her first resurrection. The old girl had beauty yet.

He hadn't thought that he could ever look on this boat as benign. Had he finally moved so far away from the tragedy that the boat no longer represented anything other than herself? Or was it the slow rehabilitation of his relationship with Kiley that helped purify his associations with the boat?

Inviting Kiley to help him with the short cruise on *Miss Emily* had been an experiment of sorts. Now that he and Kiley had spent some neutral time together, Grainger had wanted to test himself. Would being on the water, alone for an uninterrupted hour, be comfortable or awkward? Would the absence of the incessant phone, and the distraction of Pilot, give them the courage to enjoy themselves?

They had. Kiley had sat at his feet as he pointed out familiar landmarks on the shore. They'd even kept comfortably silent. For a little while it was as he'd hoped, simply the present, not the past.

Kiley sat in the cockpit, her floppy-brimmed hat waving in the breeze until she removed it, her blond hair loose for a moment before she captured its thickness in a barrette. Grainger stared at the vulnerable nape of her neck, and wondered if there might yet be a future for them.

Grainger planned to take Will out in *Blithe Spirit* on Saturday, if the weather continued fair. The plan today was to step the mast, then Grainger would give Will a lesson in rigging. If time allowed, they'd bend on her sails. Years ago, when he was turning the old sail loft into a bedroom, Grainger had found the musty old sail bag with Kiley's hand-stenciled *Blithe Spirit* still readable. Until now, he had left the sail bag in the storeroom among half a dozen others. The sails were mildewed, so he'd left them out in the sun this past week. They weren't perfect, but serviceable. He'd find a better set for Will if he could persuade Kiley to come back for the August Races.

They were renewing their friendship, but it was like beating upwind. Their headway was slow, the seas choppy. Kiley had asked that he not say anything to Will about this, afraid that Will would want more of them than they were able to give.

"He wants so badly for us . . ."

"For us what?"

"I think he has some romantic vision of a fairy tale ending."

"And you don't?" It was like being in a beam sea, this being with her, yet not being with her.

"I gave up romanticism a long time ago." Kiley turned away from him, reaching for a can of Brasso on the workbench.

"Will he be satisfied that we're just friends?" Grainger took the can from her and twisted the cover off.

"I think so." She took the open can from him and went out to the boat.

Grainger remained behind for a moment. "I'm not satisfied," he said quietly.

Pilot cocked his head

All the time Will worked at his assigned tasks, Grainger looked hard for Mack in his movements, the angle of his arms, or the cocking of his head to examine his work. Will looked at him too. They were like two birds from the same species, looking at each other for flock recognition.

"I knew from the start she was *Blithe Spirit.*" Will said this casually.

"When did you figure it out?"

"I could tell by the fiberglass patch." Equally casual, as if it had just occurred to him, he asked, "Why didn't you tell me that before?"

"I wasn't sure how you'd feel about it. I was afraid you might not want to work on her, that you might think she had bad karma." Grainger secured the lines holding *Blithe Spirit* close to the pier so they could step the mast. "Sailors are terribly superstitious, you know."

Together they hefted the mast and eased it into place. With the mast between them, Will looked at Grainger with Kiley's eyes, full of hopeful expectation. "I want us to have a DNA test. Can we?"

Grainger was aware of his heart beating in a way that couldn't be healthy. Did thirty-six-year-old active men, albeit with a hankering for red meat, die from being asked such a question? It wasn't that he hadn't entertained the idea himself; it was the abruptness of Will's request. One minute they're talking about the boat, the next, paternity. Were all dealings with youth so vertiginous?

He didn't know how to respond. So much hinged on a simple test. The world as he knew it would no longer be the same. He believed Kiley when she said she had no idea which one of them was Will's father. If he was Will's father, that lent a whole new dimension to his understanding of himself. If he wasn't, could he live with that disappointment? Equally, could Will take the disappointment?

In self-defense, Grainger had chosen to treat Will like a beloved nephew. Mack had been, for all intents and purposes, his brother; if Will was Mack's blood, Mack lived on. Submitting to this test could deny Mack his only legacy.

Will kept his hands on the mast but his eyes on

Grainger, who read in them the self-surprise in asking that question outright—the hope, the fear, the confusion.

Grainger rubbed his hand down his face, aware of the day's bristles, his unkempt, solitary workingman appearance. Since his military and Merchant Marine days, he'd rarely thought of his appearance, shaving when he felt like it, letting his hair grow long until he couldn't stand it, wearing worn jeans and threadbare flannel shirts every day, his rubber boots his only footwear most of the time. He was no example of fatherhood to anyone. Most days only Pilot saw him, and his customers expected a boat mender to look as if he'd just come off a year's single-handed sail around the world. God only knew what Kiley saw when she looked at him, just an ordinary man.

"You're asking a lot of me, Will. You're asking for a life-altering swab of cells. Have you thought this through?"

Will's expectant look turned sullen, disappointed. "I don't want anything from you. I just want to satisfy my curiosity."

"I'm curious too, Will. But maybe I'm a little more afraid."

"Of what? I told you, I wouldn't want child support or anything. This would be just between you and me. Mom doesn't even have to know."

"I'm not worried about your motive. I'm worried about the emotional outcome of knowing."

Will nodded. "I've thought of that too."

The slight acquiesence relieved Grainger. "Let's give it some time. If you still want to do it in, say, December, call me and we'll get it done. We've only known each other for less than three weeks. I think we both need to step back."

"I don't think I'll change my mind."

"Fair enough, and I won't break my promise." Grainger handed Will coils of rope, then hefted the sail bag from the pier into the boat. He looked at the western sky, an orangey red, smudgy fair-weather clouds streaking it. "I think we can get the rigging and the sails on before dark. Then she'll be ready to sail."

Will was quiet, taking orders without comment. The tense look of disappointment began to fade, and he even smiled a little as they finally hoisted the sail in a smooth test.

"Are you really going to give *Blithe Spirit* to me?"

Grainger handed Will several lashings to tie the lowered sail to the boom. "If it's all right with your mother. Which I think it is."

"Cool. Awesome. When can I take her out?"

"We can go out Saturday if the weather holds."

"No, when can *I* take her out? I want to take Catherine for a sail."

"Will, I've already told you, you're not ready."

"That's so not true. I'm good at it; you've said so yourself."

"Being good and being experienced isn't the same thing, especially to take out a passenger. If you want, she can come with us. Okay?" Grainger tied off the last of the lashings and climbed onto the wooden pier. "Make sure that bowline isn't too short. There's a moon tide tonight; we don't want to hang her."

"Come on, Grainger. A little sail around this cove isn't dangerous. What do you say?" Will's voice, sweetly persuasive, made Grainger appreciate what Kiley had lived through. Debating a teenager was wearing.

"Will, the answer is no." He didn't have time to go

into all the dangers of inexperience on the water. "Maybe I should rethink this."

Will snorted a little exhalation of disgust. "You sound like a father—and guess what? I've never needed a father, and I certainly don't need you." He pulled himself onto the pier and past Grainger.

Grainger made no move to follow him. *Let him blow off steam.* He didn't blame the kid for being a little angry; he'd had a hell of a couple of weeks. He'd cool off.

Had he really sounded like a father? Had he sounded like Rollie, impatient and accusatory? Grainger called him back, but Will kept going.

Thirty

"He's just being a kid. They say terrible, hurtful things, then turn around and sweetly ask for the car," Kiley told him.

"So I shouldn't be worried?"

"No. You did the right thing, Grainger. The thing we both agreed on."

Grainger handed Kiley a new sheet of 120 grit sandpaper. With careful strokes, she gently went over the last foot of decking on *Random*'s bow, roughing it up for yet another coat of varnish.

Every day but this one had been sunny and warm as she pedaled along the bluff road, the sea at the edge of the horizon pure blue, no whitecaps disturbing its surface calm. Today the weather had changed, the brewing clouds providing a suitable background for her emotions. They were leaving tomorrow. The last week with Grainger, working on the boat or sharing a coffee break, hearing about his life here and telling about hers, had loosened a knot of tension that had formed so very long ago in her. There was a different tension now: once separated, would they lose touch, let go of each other again? Like returning to Hawke's Cove, was this her last time to be with him? This tension was flavored with a new awareness of him as a man. Kiley woke in the night, hot beneath the light blanket. Throwing off the covers, she thought of Grainger and reminded herself that, despite this reunion, they were really two strangers just getting to know each other.

Conor had made some phone calls, and Kiley had interviews lined up for Tuesday and Wednesday next week. Once she had a new job, there would be no possibility of going back to Hawke's Cove for the August Races. Kiley pressed the sandpaper too hard, leaving a gouge in the deck surface. She sat back and looked at it, then looked out at the disturbed water of Maiden Cove, its color ever-changing from gray to green.

"You know, the job I'm interviewing for calls for working a lot of weekends."

"No race for you." Grainger put on a Soup Nazi voice.

"No race for me."

"But if you could, you'd come back?"

"I'd come back."

"What about Will?"

"Do you really think he's ready for racing?"

"No, but if he could stay on, I could take him out on my big boat with a couple of guys for practice."

"I'm not leaving him, Grainger."

"I know that." Grainger folded his sandpaper into a neat square. "I'm not suggesting that you should. I know you've only got a little time left with him before he goes off to school, and I wouldn't deprive you of a minute of it."

"Would you have time to take him out before we go tomorrow?"

"There's a small-craft advisory out —just look at that chop. A storm system is coming up the coast, which is why I didn't take Will out today in *Blithe Spirit* like I promised. Another reason he's mad at me." Grainger turned back to the area he was working on.

"He'll get over it."

"Maybe we can do it another year?"

"Right, maybe another year."

Before she left the house, Toby had called to tell her another offer was on the table. If it wasn't this one, it would be another, until eventually, the house was gone.

Kiley pushed herself upright and glanced over at Grainger, on his hands and knees, his back to her. His shaggy hair hung over the collar of his blue work shirt, like a boy's. Kiley felt an advancing dismay, just like in her childhood when it neared time to say good-bye and return to Southton. Would being with Grainger always be temporary, seasonal?

A glimmering rush of desire ran through her, from heart to loins. Not just physical desire, but a stronger desire for connection. Kiley wanted to lay her body against his and absorb him into her, to take his essense back with her. Maybe there would be a next year, a wholly different next year.

"Grainger?"

Her voice betrayed her thoughts, and he came without speaking to kneel beside her, opening his arms to let her rest her head against his shoulder. For a few minutes they knelt quietly on her father's boat, feeling the dampness of the rising breeze touch their cheeks.

"Will I see you before you go?" His breath in her ear tickled.

"I hope so." It was so familiar, this lump in her throat, this need to keep her emotions under wraps. No girlie tears shed. "Would you come to breakfast tomorrow?" Breakfast was a neutral meal, fraught with nothing more meaningful than having to choose sausage over bacon.

"I'd love to. It'll be a good opportunity to ease Will into this." Grainger pointed to her, then himself.

"This?" Kiley's fingertip mimicked Grainger's gesture.

"Us." Grainger grasped her finger and held it. "If you think you can get rid of me by leaving Hawke's Cove, you're sadly mistaken."

The lump shrank a little, making it possible for Kiley to laugh without tears.

After a few minutes, Grainger let her go and went back to his work. Half an hour later, he looked at his watch. "Damn, I'm late for a Historic Commission meeting."

"I should be going, anyway." The bow was done, ready for its last coat of marine varnish. Kiley gathered the discarded squares of sandpaper into a trash bag.

Grainger slid, sailor-fashion, down the ladder set against the side of the boat, and waited for Kiley to climb down. As she reached the ground, Grainger scooped her close for a moment's hug. "Tomorrow, then. What time?"

"Eight?"

"Perfect. Look, I'm sorry to rush off . . ."

"Go." Kiley pushed him away. "Go, protect Hawke's Cove from people like Toby."

Grainger lightly kissed her forehead. "I'll see you tomorrow morning." He jogged to his truck, Pilot scampering behind him.

• • •

Toby was waiting for her on the porch as she pedaled into the yard. Her car was in the driveway, so she knew Will was home.

With a heraldic tootle, Toby flourished a signed P and S agreement, setting it in her hands. "It's better than we hoped for."

" 'We'?" Kiley's eyes widened at the amount typed in. "Whoa."

"Shall we celebrate?"

"I'm fresh out of champagne."

"Come with me tonight to the Yacht Club Auction. We'll spend some of your new money."

"I don't know, Toby."

Toby handed Kiley a pen. "Sign on the dotted line." He watched as she hesitated, then scrawled her name. "I'll pick you up at six-thirty."

"I didn't say . . ."

Toby was already down the steps and halfway to his car. "Six-thirty!"

"So what are your plans tonight?" Kiley came out of the bathroom with her head wrapped in a towel.

"Going out with Catherine."

Will was playing solitaire at the dining room table. Piled all around him were boxes loaded with the things she couldn't leave behind. She was certain they wouldn't be able to fit them all into her Mazda; she'd forgotten that they hadn't come in a beach wagon. That's what they'd always called the enormous Ford station wagon. Now she'd have to rent a van, or buy a roof rack. Well, that was tomorrow's issue. Just for tonight, she was going to try and forget that by noon tomorrow, she and Will would lock the house for the last time and head back to Southton.

Kiley looked at her watch. Toby would be here in a half hour to collect her. "Are you going to get something to eat with Catherine, or do you want me to heat up some soup?"

"We'll get a burger in Great Harbor."

Will had been a little truculent about her going to the auction with the real estate agent.

"What do you want to go out with him for?"

"I'm not"—Kiley hooked her fingers into air quotes—"going out with him. He's just taking me there, which is lucky for you: now you can have the car."

"Catherine can drive."

"Will, it's not a date."

"Then what is it?"

Good question. "A peace offering."

It certainly wasn't a celebration. He'd had her sign the agreement so fast she hadn't been able to imbue it with the weighty significance it deserved. Wham, bam, it was done. As soon as Toby was gone, she'd called her parents with the news.

"I signed the P and S agreement."

Her mother's voice betrayed no emotion, neither joy nor sorrow. "Good."

"Tell Dad, Grainger will put the boat in the water next week. He wants to know if he should keep her on one of his moorings or the club's." It seemed imperative that she say Grainger's name aloud, to counterbalance the feelings of loss. She hadn't lost Grainger; she'd found him. Or maybe he'd found her. Kiley smiled reflexively. Though she was going home tomorrow, he would never be farther away than a phone call. Never again.

Will moved a line of cards onto a newly revealed king.

"We have an early day tomorrow, so don't be out too late."

"Mom, it's our last night together. Don't make me stick to a kid's curfew."

"I'm only saying be realistic. I want to leave by noon, and if I have to fight to wake you up, we'll never get out of here." She didn't mention Grainger's coming to breakfast, because she wanted to see the pleased surprise on Will's face when he saw the two of them together.

Will's mouth twisted into a half smile. "All right by me."

Kiley rubbed her hair briskly with the towel. "The idyll has to end sometime. There's the memorial service, and then I have interviews this coming week. Vacation's over, kiddo."

Will sat back in the ladder-back chair and began to scoop the cards into a pile. A growing cloud of emotion tensed his mouth and jittered his fingers as he tried to gather the cards into a block.

"What is it, Will?"

"Do you really have to sell the place? I can go to the financial aid office and beg for more money. I can say you're not going to support me. They'll have to give me more money."

"Will, this isn't my decision. It's Nana and Pop's."

Will slammed the deck of cards down on the table, scattering them. "It is too your decision. You decided not to ever come back, and then you did, and now you're going to take it away from me." He slammed out of the room, leaving Kiley to wish for the millionth time that she had someone to back up her decisions, or talk her out of them. Someone to share the responsibility, someone else to occasionally be the bad guy.

It would be easier to think he was mad about having to leave Catherine, but Kiley knew that wasn't the root. He'd be able to keep the romance going through phone calls and e-mails until they got to school. Then they could hook up again in Ithaca.

Something else was frustrating him. Grainger Egan? Will had grown fond of him; that was obvious from his excited conversation about their every inch of scraped paint. Fond and aware of this man as someone that, blood or not, he was intimately connected to.

That made it doubly difficult to negotiate the hazards of a renewed relationship. It was so tempting to say to hell with it, and plunge headlong into what their bodies so obviously desired. But would it fortify their relationship to announce it boldly, or undermine it, like a waterfront house built on sand? They had to build their own trust, before earning Will's.

Having brought nothing from home to wear to an event like the benefit auction, Kiley had dashed into Great Harbor this afternoon, heading straight for T.J.Maxx and Catherine's advice. Her new persimmon red slip dress was hanging in the steam of the bathroom, to smooth out and remove the scent of the store. Catherine had talked her into buying new strappy sandals to wear with it and a choker of faux pearls. They'd forgotten earrings, so Kiley put in the plain gold hoops she wore every day.

She looked at herself in the mirror. What was she thinking? She looked like she was going on a date. It promised to be a long, awkward evening of explaining the sale of the house to the curious auction goers. Struggling to fasten the skinny straps of her new sandals, Kiley decided that as soon as she could, she'd beg off and head home. She should probably bring her sneakers with her so that she could walk. Capitulating to Toby's insistence he bring her meant she'd either have to ask him to leave early, or walk home.

"You look great, Mom." Will leaned against the doorway of his room. "I'm sorry I got mad."

"Thanks. And I still want you in by one."

Will was obviously disappointed that his apology hadn't won him any points, and he went back into his room to flop on the bed, making the bedsprings sing out in protest.

"Oh, and have everything you can packed tonight before you go out." Kiley leaned into the room.

Will made a grunt of acquiescence without looking at her.

"Have a nice time."

Another grunt.

"And be careful."

"You, too."

"Funny boy."

Kiley heard Toby's step on the front porch, and started down the stairs. Before she got to the end of them, Will caught up with her. In an uncharacteristic physical show of apology, he kissed her.

"I'm sorry, Mom. Go have fun. Don't worry about me."

"I'm sure some of it will be fun." There was something in Will's overture that eluded Kiley, some motive, but Toby had let himself in the front door like a friend instead of a date, drawing her attention away from Will.

"If I could whistle, I would. You look beautiful."

Toby was decked out in crisp white linen trousers and a blue blazer over a white shirt, his tie a tasteful pattern of tiny signal flags on a field of dark red.

Kiley complimented him, glad to have something nice to say to him for once.

"It's black tie optional. This is as close as I wanted to get. I figure you can't go wrong with a nautical tie."

He put out an elbow for Kiley to take. She felt a little silly, but the new sandals were already challenging her balance and she was glad of the support. They were halfway to the Yacht Club before she realized that she'd forgotten her sneakers.

Thirty-one

Will watched his mother leave the house balanced on the real estate agent's arm. He slumped in a rocker on the front porch, nursing his annoyance. He still had a little while before he could pick Catherine up from work; then he planned to take her to a nice restaurant with the last of the money from Pop. That was fine, but he and Catherine needed something to do this last evening together to solidify their relationship, some symbolic gesture they could refer to again and again as they brought their summer romance into the winter months.

Mom was pretty clear about being home on the early side, so the one obvious homage to their new relationship was probably out of the question. Besides, he wasn't entirely sure Catherine was ready for sex with him yet. The birth control was for her complexion, she'd said conversationally, in the middle of a make-out session. It had taken a month or so with Lori before they'd reached that decision, and Catherine was already too important to him to jeopardize their association by pressing her too soon.

It felt good, this new relationship. It felt true and in no danger of dissipating as soon as the wheels hit the road. This was a keeper; Will knew it in his soul. They had plenty of time.

What didn't feel good or resolved or satisfying was this thread of hope that he might, at last, solve the mystery of his birth. He had all the tools and even a blueprint, but he didn't have a place to build the house. It was almost as frustrating as knowing nothing at all. The "might be" of Grainger offset the "could be" of Mack. Everyone had attributed thoughts and motives to Mack, but only from their own points of view.

Like Grainger wanting him to have the boat because he thought Mack would have wanted him to have it, promising him to go out in the boat today and then using a lame-o excuse about it being too rough. Will didn't see any whitecaps; how rough could it be? On top of that, then refusing to have the DNA test done. Grainger acted like he didn't want to be his father. To hell with him and his leaky promises.

Neither Grainger nor Mom really knew what Mack felt or wanted, or—and here was the big one—if he meant to die that night. No one had said that aloud, but Will wondered if maybe that's what happened. What if it wasn't an accident? Could his mother have been so wonderful that Mack would kill himself over her? Or had Grainger's betrayal driven Mack to a desperate gesture? Had he gone overboard on purpose out of self-lessness or self-pity? It all came down to Mack, the only one who wasn't there to put his own spin on the story.

He needed a schematic, a line like those he'd had to draw in history class. This happened, then this, then that, and the result was Mack being dead, Grainger run off, and his mother pregnant.

Will sucked in a great lungful of salt air to clear the suffocating pressure within his chest, then went back into the house, found the out-of-date phone book, and looked up MacKenzie.

Just visible behind and to the side of the MacKenzies' house on Linden Street was a small guesthouse. The slow sunset cast interior shadows, and lights came on in both houses. Will sat in the idling car, watching, waiting for the moment of divine courage when he could do what he came to do. In the main house he could see an older woman moving briskly from one side of the room to the other, her hands lifting and disappearing into cupboards as she talked and went about making dinner. In the front room of the guesthouse Will could see Conor MacKenzie, slim and balding, buttoning a white shirt and knotting a tie.

Will got out of the car, his pounding heart nearly audible. Not even going up to Grainger's boathouse that first morning had made him this nervous. Repeating the Nike mantra under his breath, Will opened the gate in the picket fence. "Just do it." The gate scraped the cement of the walkway with a loud grinding—no backing out now. Will pushed the doorbell.

A man opened the door. Will instantly thought that he looked like Pop—bent over, white-haired, crepey skin loose around the jaw. The man was smiling with an expression of expecting to answer a question; he probably thought Will was lost, looking for an address. He was a doctor; doctors always anticipated questions.

"Can I help you, son?"

"Umm." Every rehearsed word fled from him. He swallowed. "I just wanted to come by to, ummm, to meet you. You and Mrs. MacKenzie. I'm Will Harris."

Dr. MacKenzie's friendly blue eyes grew shaded. "Come in, then. Doro!"

Mrs. MacKenzie came into the front room, wiping her hands on a half-apron tied around her ample waist. She seemed a lot younger than the doctor, maybe only in her mid-sixties. "Hello. Who have we here?"

"Will Harris." Dr. MacKenzie had one hand on Will's shoulder.

Mrs. MacKenzie didn't react to the name, just kept wiping her hands and looking at him.

Will awkwardly put out a hand to Mrs. MacKenzie. "Kiley Harris's son." He felt the reaction of his words in the sudden weakness of the hand clasping his.

Mrs. MacKenzie held on to his hand, pulling him fractionally closer as if to examine him. Then those soft white hands flew to her mouth, stroking parallel lines down her age-softened cheeks. Tears sprang in her eyes, and one hand slipped back to cover her mouth.

"We should have known." Dr. MacKenzie let go of Will's shoulder, stalking into the kitchen.

"Don't mind him. Come, let me give you something to eat and you can tell us all about you."

"No, thank you, no." Will began to back away. He had seen all the hurt and disbelief, the hope and expectation that his mother had avoided, rise up to meet him, and he didn't know how to deal with it. "I shouldn't have come."

"Don't say that. William." As Doro said the name, Will knew she believed he'd been named for Mack. Just like Grainger had.

"Actually, it's Merriwell William, like my grandfather. But that wasn't a great name for a little boy to go to school with, so they call me Will."

The assumptions weren't to be deprived. "It's close

enough." Mrs. MacKenzie reached out and touched Will's freshly shaven cheek. "Please don't leave."

"I can only stay for a minute." Will heard the back door open and men's voices.

"That will be Conor. Please come and meet him." Mrs. MacKenzie led the way into the cluttered kitchen.

A typical 1950s style Cape Cod kitchen, square, a maple table dead center, microwave on a crowded counter, heavy cupboards aligned above. A used, comfortable kitchen. Sort of like his at home in Southton.

Conor MacKenzie wasn't smiling, or looking at Will with any expectation, disappointment, or hope. He was looking with suspicion. "Whose decision was it that had you just show up?" Conor remained standing after the other three sat at the kitchen table.

"Mine. Mom doesn't know. I'm leaving tomorrow, and I just felt as if I hadn't, well, heard everyone's side of the story. I came to Hawke's Cove knowing nothing. Now I know something, and I just had this stupid idea that if I got to meet you all, I might be able to figure it out."

"Figure what out?" Conor challenged him.

"Who my father was." There, it was said.

Mack's name hovered unspoken. No one had said it, no one seemed likely to. A ghost, he filled the room with an invisible, unspeakable presence.

"I mean, Grainger or Mack."

Conor came across the linoleum, and placed his hands on the table. "We know who you mean."

Will stood up, sliding the wooden kitchen chair roughly against the linoleum. "I'm sorry. I shouldn't have come."

"Enough, Conor. The boy is just curious." Mrs. MacKenzie elbowed herself up from the table and held out a hand to Will. "Come see his room."

Conor and the doctor looked at each other with dismay. No doubt her family had made every effort to keep her out of the past and in the present. They probably avoided every reference to Mack, as if, by speaking his name, they would remind her of the thing she lived with every moment of every day. Now here he was, dragging the past back into their world.

"Mom." Conor's voice was edgy, warning.

"Conor, there's no harm."

Will followed Mrs. MacKenzie up the stairs to a small bedroom on the left of the central staircase. Eaves overhung the twin beds; anyone sleeping there would have to be careful about sitting up in bed too quickly. On the walls were posters, the sort any kid might have of favored rock musicians; on the dustless bureau a trophy, almost exactly like the one he'd gotten as captain of the team for the baseball championship last year. Stuck in the lower edge of the mirror frame were pictures similar to Kiley's collection, featuring the same three faces. Two small high school portraits were placed on either side of the frame at eye level. Will stood in front of the mirror and stared at his face reflected there between the faces of Grainger and Mack, exactly as old as he was now.

Grainger looked so different. Mack would never change. Will realized that he'd been conjuring up an image of Mack as an adult. Even as his mother and Grainger told him the story, he pictured them as they were now, not as kids. In the same way, he'd been picturing Mack as a grown man.

He wasn't. He never would be. Mack was a boy his own age, who had acted with a self-destructive arrogance. Had he thought, *I'll show them—they'll miss me when I'm gone,* before risking his life in that boat? Had he meant it to happen the way it did?

Mrs. MacKenzie said nothing as Will surveyed the small stuffy room, watching as he examined the photos. Only as Will studied himself in the mirror did she speak. "Conor was in college, and had moved out of this room by the time the boys were in high school. Mack and Grainger shared this room, as close as brothers."

Will was painfully aware of the catch in her voice. "Yes. I've been told."

"They both loved her. It was so obvious, and I knew that it could only end badly. Of course, I never imagined how badly. You have to know, I had no idea that you existed. If I had, she could never have kept me out of your life."

"I know. My mother kept me from Hawke's Cove, from knowing about anything. I guess I never thought that other people might be kept in the dark too."

"I blame your grandparents. They knew and they should have told us. Even if, even if you aren't . . ."—tears clogged her voice into a thin rasp—"a MacKenzie, we would have treated you like one."

"Ma'am, they *didn't* know. I mean, Mom never told them who . . ." Will couldn't think what else to say, and fumbled a little. "I have to go." Tentatively, he patted her soft rounded shoulder.

Doro MacKenzie dabbed at her eyes with the corner of her apron. "Will you come back?"

"I can't. We're leaving tomorrow." Will hated the disappointment in her eyes. "But I'll keep in touch. Do you have e-mail?"

Mrs. MacKenzie bit back a smile. "No, dear. But letters are good too."

As they came down the steps, Conor and Dr. MacKenzie stood like sentinels at the foot.

"Are you all right, Doro?" Her husband reached out to take her arm.

"Yes. Fine." Mrs. MacKenzie shrugged his hand off.

"I'll walk out with you." Conor grasped one of Will's elbows as if he was forcing him out of the house.

"You've opened up an old wound, Will." But even as he said it, Conor's expression of annoyance faded. "But it's done. Please don't do anything more to upset her."

"You mean like ask for a DNA test?"

"Yes. What good would it do?"

It was clear that Conor was afraid it would do more damage to take away her faint hope that Mack *had* lived on—in him.

"Don't worry, I won't ask for it. At least not yet."

"I don't want her hopes raised."

"I think she'd be okay either way." Didn't Conor understand that his mother had loved Grainger too?

"Look kid, tonight I'll be prescribing Valium for her. Don't tell me she'll be okay. You have no idea what she's been through."

"Aren't you a little curious yourself?"

"No." He walked back to the house.

Will pulled away from the curb, upset but not unhappy. Although he didn't have any answers, he at least had all the questions in order.

It was still quite light when Will picked Catherine up in front of the store. Light enough to show her the boat before they went to dinner. He drove them back into Hawke's Cove to Egan's Boat Works.

Grainger's truck was gone, and the only response to

his knocking was Pilot's bark. "That's weird. Grainger never goes anywhere without that dog."

"So, show me the boat anyway. I'm hungry."

Will led Catherine through the yard to the pier. The boat looked pretty unimpressive from this distance, bucking on her tether, her bow pointed straight at them. Not the effect he had hoped for.

"Nice. So, where are you taking me for dinner?"

"How about if I row us out to her, first? Then you can get a feel for all the work we've done."

"What's the big deal? It's just a boat."

"No. I was going to surprise you. Grainger gave her to me. She's not just a boat. She's *my* boat."

"Awesome. So, okay, let's go look at her up close."

Will and Catherine climbed into the wooden dinghy tied up to the pier. Its little two-cycle engine started up on the first pull, and the pair sped over the chop to *Blithe Spirit*.

Thirty-two

As they drove to the Yacht Club, Tony talked nonstop about the Lexus and all its attributes. Kiley couldn't decide if he meant to impress her, or was truly in love with this car. She nodded and made the same sorts of responses one might about a new baby. Nice, but not hers.

A string quartet played Mozart and voices burst through the open windows, a steady mutter punctuated by laughter. Kiley closed her eyes for a moment and imagined that she would be walking into a room full of kids, the Mozart an aberration. The taste of ginger ale came to her. Then Toby's voice opened her eyes and she took his arm.

Inside, clots of people filled the floor. Some sat on the bamboo and floral-cushioned settees—new fabric, same old furniture—others leaned against the window frames, large adult bodies taking up the view. The beach-stone fireplace was, as always, cold, and two tall men leaned elbows on the mantel, facing each other like conspirators or adversaries. Did she know them; were those familiar faces embedded in heaviness? This was going to be worse than a high school reunion. At least there, people had uniformly been out of touch and wore name tags. These folk had continuity. They had always been here; they didn't see the changes in each other. About half the group were dressed like Toby, in spiffy insouciance. The other half wore black tie, their dinner jackets shiny with age, no doubt hung under plastic bags from the dry cleaners, hauled out once a year for a summer event like this one and made to fit with moved buttons or held-in potbellies. No one looked comfortable.

The women all looked alike: dressed in linen suits, hot pink the color of choice this year, prevalent among green, yellow, and blue; streaked blond hair and tanned faces with white raccoon rings where sunglasses kept the sunlight away from tender, tightened skin. They all seemed much older than she was. Truly middle-aged, not quite her mother's age, certainly more than her own. They all held their martinis with practiced grace, props for the evening. Kiley looked around in near panic for someone she knew. As if on cue, Emily and Missy appeared and headed in her direction.

"Thank God. I thought I was going to be the youngest person here."

"Nonsense, all our set show up for these things. We're just glad you made it."

Had Emily really used the word "set"? Kiley imagined herself in an Edith Wharton novel. It was easy now to tell the twins apart. Emily had matured, Missy had expanded. The two men who had been holding down the mantel came over at Missy's signal, and introductions were made. Ralph Fitzgibbons belonged to Emily, Fred Detweiler to Missy. They seemed pleasant enough, clearly on familiar terms with Toby, who arrived to hand

Kiley a glass of indifferent white wine and earn her the sideways glances of the twins. *Take that,* Kiley thought, knowing they had expected her to show up solo—not that this was a date.

It was a pleasant enough few minutes until Fred Detweiler got wound up about a business project he was involved in. Kiley felt her eyes glaze over with the effort to look politely interested, and she looked around the room for someone she could excuse herself to greet. No one recognizable appeared, and it seemed as though her mother had at last proved her argument that hanging around with "those boys" would stunt Kiley's social life.

Finally, there was a call to start the auction. Kiley had no intention of adding to the stuff she already had to bring home, and it seemed like a good time to make her excuses.

"Toby, I have to finish packing, so I'll walk home. You stay and bid."

"No, no. The night is early yet. I was going to take you out to dinner after the golf weekend goes up for bid."

"I really can't." She wasn't going to let him make this a more intimate evening.

"Well, you certainly can't walk home in those shoes."

"I'm fine."

"Kiley, come on, just hang on a little while, then I'll take you home."

It was a reasonable suggestion, and the truth was, her feet were already sore. "Okay. But not for long."

After a few items were auctioned off and the golf weekend seemed no closer than it had been, Kiley excused herself. "I'm going to the head." She edged out of the crowded room into the quiet hallway.

The ladies' room was empty, the scarred wooden stall doors exactly the same as she remembered them, carved with initials she recognized from her youth. "A.S. 'hearts' S.P. '79" and "Gina loves Roy Truluv 4-evr '81." The place still smelled damp, like a bilge. All the money that belonged to this place, and they couldn't improve the lavatories? The only improvement was the condom machine bolted next to the tampon dispenser. Kids were so much smarter now—which made her think of Will. She knew how intense last nights could be, and she fervently hoped that he and Catherine were being smart. She shook off the unwelcome thought as she shook her hands under the weak dryer.

She lingered in the ladies' room, putting on new lipstick and fussing a little with her hair, loose and swinging on her bare shoulders. She should have brought a wrap, but didn't have one. The July night was warm, but Kiley knew that the breeze would begin to dampen and cool as the evening went on. There was weather predicted for tomorrow—another good reason to have everything ready to go. If it started to rain, they'd be trying to jam the little car full instead of working it through like a puzzle. At least she hadn't decided to bring home any furniture, and she'd put all the artwork back on the walls. The imaginary lighthouse would stay.

Kiley could hear the auctioneer's voice wheedling another five bucks out of the audience. Maybe she should have donated some of the stuff to sell here tonight. The lighthouse picture might have raised a couple of dollars, and the seaglass-filled lamp.

According to the program, they were getting close to the golf weekend. Almost time to put an end to this troubling evening. She folded the program neatly and stuck it in her purse, then pulled open the heavy door.

"Kiley."

Conor MacKenzie was coming down the hall. She smiled in greeting, then noticed that Conor was not.

"Do you know what your son did tonight?" Conor drew close, putting himself between her and the ladies' room door.

A familiar shot of maternal dread tensed Kiley for battle. "What?"

"He showed up at my parents' house. Did you put him up to that?"

"No. Certainly not. In fact, I told him he shouldn't . . ."

Conor cut her off. "One of two things should have happened. One, you told us about him from the beginning, or two, you never brought him here. What were you thinking?" Conor's blue eyes, no longer similar to Mack's, were dark with anger.

"I'm thinking that it's really none of your business. It never was, and it never will be."

"It most certainly is, now that your kid has foisted himself on my mother. If we're lucky, she'll just pretend he's her grandson; if we're not, she'll go back into a depression. I hold you responsible."

"He's eighteen years old. He can do what he wants." Kiley was furious. Even though Conor MacKenzie had no right to upbraid her, Will had no right to inflict himself on the MacKenzies. It wasn't bad enough he'd disobeyed her; if Conor's anger was any indication, he'd opened up the wounds she'd hoped had healed over. "Look, I'm sorry, but there's nothing I can do to change it. What's done is done."

"Is that how you felt about Mack's dying over love of

you?" Conor was very close to her, making her step back against the wall. She could smell the metallic odor of gin and fruit on his breath.

The emergency exit door to the back drive opened, and through it walked Grainger Egan.

Conor moved away from Kiley. "Egan."

Grainger stood a moment, assessing the scene. "Conor." His voice was a warning.

Kiley pushed away from the wall, toward Grainger.

Conor squared himself. "What do you know about her kid?"

"Will? Everything you do, I suppose."

"Do you think he's yours, or Mack's?"

"I think it doesn't matter."

"I think it matters very much." He looked at Kiley. "Keep him the fuck away from my parents." Conor walked back into the crowd.

Kiley remained where she was, aware of Grainger, aware of the distance between them.

Then Grainger came to her, gently resting one hand on her shoulder. "Are you all right?"

"I think so. Except I've probably lost my job reference."

Grainger lifted his hand from her shoulder to stroke her hair, as if to calm her racing heart.

How handsome he was. Clean-shaven for the first time since she'd seen him again, his shaggy hair now expertly trimmed, Grainger stood tall, straight-backed and lean, in a well-fitted dinner jacket. His gray-blue eyes studied her as if he was no longer looking at her through the stained glass of memory, but through the clear glass of the present. They were no longer the teenagers they had been; they were adults, matured by their experiences, independent and unrelated to the overwrought beings of their youth. For the first time, Grainger and Kiley looked at each other purely as man and woman.

"I didn't know you would be here," they said simultaneously, then smiled and laughed softly.

"I suppose we should link little fingers and say, 'Jinx, you owe me a Coke,' like we used to."

They stood in the narrow hallway, the sounds from the main hall clouding the silence between them so that it didn't feel like silence.

"Kiley, you look beautiful."

"So do you. I mean, handsome. Wonderful."

"I clean up pretty good." Grainger flashed her a smile. She saw the hidden dimples, rarely exposed until he was happy, dip into the tender flesh beside his lips.

They had been so careful to keep their new acquaintance within the bounds of his boat works, so diligent in keeping to the rules they had tacitly agreed on: the present, not history. Standing here, in their old place, it was too hard not to get pulled back into the past.

Kiley grasped at the first thing she could, to save them from plunging. "They've already gotten more than halfway through the auction. I hope you weren't planning on bidding on something at the beginning."

"No. I only came because I donated an afternoon's charter on my big boat and they gave me a ticket in thanks. I don't usually come to these things."

"Still?" It came out like an inside joke.

"I suppose. I've done work on most of their boats, and half the time some member comes up to me to see if he can wheedle me into hurrying up, or into giving him a deal. I don't think this crowd really cares if I come to their fund-raisers or not; they just like to keep me happy so that I give them preference."

"So why did you come?"

Grainger's dimple showed again. "Just to show the flag, support the kids' sailing program. What about you?"

Kiley felt a desire to reach out with one finger and press it into that small, hidden indentation. "I have no idea. Toby Reynolds strong-armed me. I think that I was in such shock at the offer he'd brought that I was speechless, and he took it as a yes."

"Are you really selling it, Kiley? You've accepted the offer?"

"Yes."

"But you could change your mind?" Grainger was close enough that she could smell his shaving cream— something vaguely limey, pleasant, not overpowering like cologne.

"It's too late. I've signed."

Grainger took Kiley's elbow with a tentative touch, as if afraid she might pull away from him. "Can we go outside?"

She nodded and let Grainger lead her out to the boardwalk.

The lights coming through the windows illuminated their path, bright enough to cast their shadows before them; alternate people, doppelgängers. Kiley paused to remove her shoes, Grainger still holding her elbow for balance.

"Are you cold?"

She must have shivered. "No. Well, maybe a little." Not cold, but excited.

Grainger slid his jacket off, his white shirt glowing in the muted moonlight, and draped it around her shoulders. They walked in silence to the pier and went out to the very end, to lean against the pilings, facing each other in the growing darkness. They stood exactly where they had stood on the last night of their youth. As it was on that night, the water slapped at the thick, tarred pilings, and halyards clinked against aluminum masts, chiming the rising of the wind.

"Don't sell the house."

"I have to. My parents have made it clear it's necessary to pay for Will's college."

"I'll pay for his education."

Kiley felt a lump rise in her throat. How easy it would be to say yes. And how impossible. "No. Thank you, but no. You can't do that. I won't let you."

"Kiley, I have the resources. I don't want to see you lose the house."

"Grainger, it's not your problem." The lump in her throat grew heavier. What was he saying? "Why are you making such an offer? You have no obligation to him. To us."

"Kiley, until three weeks ago, I had no idea of his existence. And, now, having begun to know him . . ." Grainger's husky voice softened and his sentence drifted off. "I don't have anyone else, Kiley. I want to treat him as Mack would have wanted."

"How can you know what Mack would have wanted? How can either of us make that claim?" Kiley turned away from Grainger, away from the look on his face, half hope, half grief. She dropped the jacket on the damp boards of the pier and walked away from him. She couldn't stand there another minute. Grainger's adult face mirrored the face she'd run away from all those years ago, before she knew Mack would die, before she knew she carried a child. Angry, upset, grieving, jealous. It frightened her, drawing her into the emotions so long held away.

Suddenly Grainger's hand was on her, yanking her around to face him. He gripped her arms in his hands, then rested his forehead on hers, as if trying to understand her thoughts through physical connection. Then he kissed her. Gently testing her to see if she would struggle. Kiley did not. Her mouth was as eager as his, and it was with an overpowering sense that they were on familiar territory that they renewed the acquaintance of their loving selves. Both knew it was time to put that night to rest; both trembled at the magnitude of the effort. If they didn't put it to rest, their lives would continue on in their muted, tarnished fashion, without hope and without love. They needed to release each other.

For the first time ever, it was only Grainger and her. Just the two of them, reigniting a stunted passion.

"I have never forgotten you. I have never had a day when I didn't regret how I'd behaved." He pressed his cold cheek against hers, his words spoken to the darkness beyond the shore.

"Grainger." Kiley stroked his face, trying to reconcile this strong man's face with the youthful cheek that once lay against her girl's hand. "You have nothing to regret. I was the one who damaged everything."

"We were children, behaving with the ignorance of children who don't know that feelings and lives are fragile. We need to let ourselves heal."

"I wish . . ."

"No wishing. No more looking backwards. Please don't." Grainger silenced her with his mouth on hers, his tongue inciting warm, moist feelings Kiley had rarely known before. "Promise me that you and I can get to know each other as adults? Rip up that offer; stay here. Give us back the time we've lost."

Now it was her turn to silence him with kisses. She didn't feel the damp night air until she shivered, unsure of its genesis, the breeze off the water, or Grainger's penetrating kisses.

He was slow to touch her body, focusing on her face and lips, tongue and ears. Then his mouth grazed her neck, lingering with soft brushes at her throat. After a tortured wait, his hands found her breasts, thumbing her erect nipples straining against the thin fabric of her dress. She stood with her back against the piling, arched against him, feeling his desire against her own.

Loud voices coming out of the Yacht Club brought the moment to a halt as a group of people tumbled out the doors and onto the boardwalk.

"That's Benny Altman, dragging a flock of half-in-the-bag sailors down to look at his new Soling. She's right over there, so I think we'd better pull ourselves together."

Even Grainger's whisper in her ear sent a thrill down her spine. She snagged his hand, pressing it in her warm one. "Come home with me." She was afraid to let too much time pass, to lose the momentum.

"What about Will?"

"He's out with Catherine, and he won't come home until the last nanosecond before his curfew."

Grainger bent to retrieve his jacket, placing it over her shoulders again. He kissed the back of her neck, sending pleasant chills through her. "I'd like that very much."

The crowd passed them, halloos of greeting as if seeing Grainger Egan with his arms around a woman at the end of a pier was the most natural sight in the world. Tomorrow, they both knew, the delayed reactions would get the gossip going. Kiley felt Grainger's arm around her waist, holding her as if he would never, ever, let her go again.

Just as they reached the parking lot, Toby Reynolds hollered at them. "Hey, Kiley, I thought you'd disappeared or walked home. I've been looking all over for you." Toby loped to where they stood beside Grainger's truck. "Oh, hi, Grainger. Didn't see you inside. The charter went for three fifty, not bad. Thanks for donating it. The winners will give you a call." Toby seemed oblivious to Kiley and Grainger's unusually close stance, or her wearing Grainger's jacket like a cape. "So, Kiley, how about a nightcap?"

"Can you give me a raincheck? I've got a headache." Kiley smiled at him, hoping that he'd just take the hint gracefully.

"Sure." He shrugged. "Get in the car and I'll take you home."

"No, that's okay. Grainger's taking me."

"Why do I feel like I'm in high school and I've just been dumped?"

She smiled. "Thanks for bringing me, Toby. Call me when you know about the closing."

"Right, the closing." Toby toed the gravel beneath his feet. "When do you leave?"

"Noonish."

"I'll come by around eight. To help you pack up the car."

"You don't have to." Kiley linked her fingers wtih Grainger's.

Toby shrugged again. His tie was undone and he looked as if he might have had one too many cocktails. But to his credit, he was a consummate salesman and knew when a deal was off. And his hoped-for deal with Kiley tonight was clearly off, beat out by another salesman. "Okay. Got it. Have a pleasant evening." He looked at Grainger. "See you at the coffee shop." Both niceties bore an edge, but not enough to turn Kiley off his handling the house sale. He knew when to cut his losses.

"Good night, Toby." Grainger helped Kiley into his truck, neither of them saying a word until Kiley giggled.

"He's right, he did get dumped. He's not a bad guy. Just not the guy I want."

Grainger scooped her hand off the bench. "And who is?" He kissed her knuckles.

"It has always been you." Kiley pulled their clasped hands to her lips. "When you and I had that afternoon together, I realized that Mack could never fill my heart the way you did. And I thought that he would understand."

Grainger pulled the truck into her driveway and turned off the ignition. They sat without moving for a moment, the weight of her confession still between them. How had they missed Mack's devotion? Believing that they wouldn't break anything, that everything could be fixed because they were friends.

"I still miss him." Grainger's admission barely above a whisper.

Kiley wiped a tear from the edge of her eyelid with one fingertip. "I missed you both."

"At least you had Will. At least you had something."

"I know. There has never been a moment when I wasn't glad of it. Sometimes I believed that he was the child of both of you. And some days I thought that by some accident of parthenogenesis, I had created him alone. That he was neither yours nor Mack's, only mine.

I didn't want him to be one or the other's. Where I once loved you and Mack equally, in the end I didn't. I loved you more. Yet I loved Mack with all my heart, just in a different way. If I knew that Will was yours, or Mack's, it would seem like my body had made a choice I was incapable of. It seemed more fair to keep him equally both."

Grainger covered his eyes with his hand, but not before Kiley saw the relief glitter in them. "Do you suppose I'll ever get over being jealous of a dead man?"

"You don't have to be, Grainger. Never again."

"I do if Will *is* his son. Did you know that Will asked me to take a DNA test?"

"No, but I'm not surprised. He's lived his whole life without a clue as to who he is, and now he's close. He just doesn't understand that knowing won't change things."

"But it will. Not the loving part—I would love him as a son either way. What would change is the way Will views me. Right now, I'm the guy who might be his father. If he finds out otherwise, I'll be the guy who slept with his mother."

"Will you do it?"

"I told him if he still wants to know in December, we'll do it. I told him I was worried that we'd both end up disappointed."

"It might just be a temporary disappointment. You'd both get over it."

"But the truth would always be there."

They sat in silence, the crickets outside the truck the only sound.

"Let's go inside, Grainger."

"Do you know that in all the time I knew you, I've never been upstairs in this house?"

"I never thought about it, but that doesn't surprise me. My mother has always been one for propriety. It doesn't seem likely she'd have let me have boys upstairs, although I don't remember even considering it. My room was always such a mess."

Kiley held Grainger's hand in hers, leading the way up the back staircase. They hadn't spoken their intent. In this soft, blessed calm there was no need to say that they meant to take their reunion to its ultimate end. Briefly embarrassed by the unmade bed and strewn towels, Kiley brought Grainger into her bedroom, once her parents' room. The oversoft double bed on the old-fashioned springs took their weight with squeaking complaint. They alternated between urgency and leisure, enjoying each moment, celebrating the small steps toward the final act.

Like a seductress, Kiley untied his bow tie and played with it, holding the ends in both hands and bringing his face to hers. Grainger slid the straps of her persimmon red dress down, drawing the top of the stretchy fabric lower and lower until her breasts were exposed. He lingered there until he'd consumed every taste they offered him. Urgency overtook them and they stripped each other of the remainder of their clothes, mindless of how they threw them on the floor. Then they paused, assessing in the yellow lamplight the changes time had wrought to their youthful bodies.

"You are so beautiful." Grainger let his eyes drift along Kiley's body, still trim despite the years and childbirth, still firm, high-breasted, and curved. Her skin, newly tanned by her three weeks at the beach,

glowed in the lamplight. He rolled her over to reac-
quaint himself with this body he had only once pos-
sessed. He kissed the dent above her buttocks, let his
tongue trail a shivery trace along her spine until he
reached her neck, when, tormented, she rolled back
over and began her own exploration of him.

The long lanky youth had been replaced by a solid,
muscular man. Everything about him seemed bigger,
stronger, more virile. She touched the hardened disks
of his nipples, then let her hand drift downward until
she found him, cupped him, admired the weight of
him, and teased him into an extraordinary hardness.

They entered into the dance of coupling, their passion not to be corralled any longer. A mere touch and
she came in endless waves of surreal sensation until she
felt lost, spinning out of control, never to reach the bottom. A moment later Grainger joined her, their voices
singing their exquisite joy. Afterward they lay panting,
entwined, his head on her heart. Silent except for the
sound of their breaths.

They might have lain like that for an hour, lightly
dozing, waking to feel their conjoined parts, renewing
the moment with kisses and touches until, without having fully separated, they brought each other again to
climax.

Sated at last, they dozed again, spooned together,
Grainger's breath tickling her neck. Later they were
wide awake and talkative, full of questions. Kiley whispered little things she thought he might want to know
about her, about Will and how he had lifted her so
many times from the despond of old misery. Then she
asked him, "What about you? Tell me about your life.
Have you been married? Have you been all right?"

Grainger stroked his thumb against her hand and

told her how he'd twice come close to marriage, and how he'd come back home. "I was able to make a new life here, after all. Like you, I was afraid I'd be consumed by the memories. You just have to set about making new ones." As if to illustrate his point, Grainger gently kissed her again, this time with simple affection.

The clock in the living room chimed, and he raised his head. "It's midnight. What time is Will coming home?"

Kiley untangled a foot from the tossed sheets. "His curfew is at one."

"Isn't that kind of late?" Grainger pushed himself over Kiley, leaned back down for a last bedded kiss, then extricated himself from the covers to pick up his shorts.

"Not at his age. Once they get to be eighteen, it's pretty hard to demand a curfew."

"What can he be doing in Hawke's Cove at this hour?"

"My God, you sound like a parent." Kiley sat beside Grainger, looking at their bare legs aligned side by side on the edge of the bed. She cleared her throat with a stagey cough. "He and Catherine are making the most of their last night together."

"Oh." Grainger pulled on his trousers, drew on the crumpled white shirt, and pulled his suspenders up over his shoulders.

Kiley sat naked on the edge of the bed and watched him. "You are incredibly sexy in that outfit. I'd make you wear it all the time."

"It would get pretty nasty after a while. Marine varnish is very hard on dinner jackets."

"You love what you do, don't you?"

"Yes, and I'm very good at it, which is why I can afford to send Will to Cornell."

The act of slipping on shorts and a sweatshirt covered her mixed emotions. It was too late; there was no recalling the forward motion of the house sale. Again Kiley felt the wash of regret that she hadn't come back, had waited all this time to renew her claim to this place. Now it was too late.

"It's not my decision to sell the place. It's my parents', and they aren't going to change their minds, despite your offer."

Grainger slowly buttoned the white shirt, studying each button as he pushed it through its buttonhole. "So, I'm still not good enough for them."

"No, that's not it. That was never it." Kiley stood against his back, her arms around him, feeling the hard muscle of his belly, her cheek pressed into the soft fabric of his shirt.

"Then why not let me help out? You'll come back, now that there's no reason for you to stay away anymore. Or am I wrong about that?" He had her back in his arms now.

"Grainger, it would be asking too much of you to take on this responsibility. To compromise your own financial well-being for a kid you've only known three weeks."

"I'm not going to lose interest in Will, like some impulsive hobby. You really can't expect that I'm going to back away, out of his life. Or yours."

"No. I won't let you. But I can't let you . . ."

"Pretend for a little while that he's mine? Act the role of surrogate father? Take some responsibility for an act nineteen years old?" Grainger's voice was rising and his arms around her were almost too tight, as if he was afraid she was going to pull away from him. "I'm being selfish. I want you to stay in my life; I can't bear the idea of—"

"Sssh. I won't disappear. Never again. I ran once, and kept you out of a part of your own life you should have had access to. I made big mistakes."

Grainger rested his cheek on the top of her head, rocking her slightly, as if they stood on the deck of a becalmed ship. "Do you think we can ever move ahead?"

Kiley reached up and pulled his mouth down on hers. "I think we've already begun very nicely."

As the clock in the living room chimed again, Grainger checked his watch. "It's one in the morning. Where is he?"

"Malingering at the girl's house."

"You're awfully calm."

"I'm relishing my uninterrupted time with you."

"What will Will think if we spring it on him like this: me here, in the middle of the night, lipstick all over my collar?"

"I was careful about that." Kiley pretended to examine his shirt. "I really don't know what he'll think. Or expect of us. Or if he'll even know what he wants."

Grainger took her hands in his. "What do you want, Kiley?"

Kiley smiled at Grainger. "To get to know you. As an adult, who you are now. To try and see if we have more than a shared childhood and a shared tragedy." She bent to kiss the hands grasping hers. "And we'll need to give Will the time to adjust to the idea."

"In that case, I'll go home now. It's best I'm not here when Will comes in. But I'll be back at eight."

"I'd be horribly disappointed if you weren't."

"A mere seven hours." He smiled around the words, but they seemed unduly heavy.

They rose and held one another as if afraid they would each vanish from sight once the screen door slammed. As if in the morning, they would wake to know the night had only been a dream.

Thirty-three

〰️

Blithe Spirit danced on her mooring with little up-and-down motions, like an excited dog. They climbed into the sailboat, taking care to tie the dinghy to the mooring. They were only going to be out here for a minute.

"Is she a lot of fun to sail?" Catherine ran a hand along the smooth coamings.

"I guess so. Grainger . . ." Will was going to say "hasn't let me," but the words seemed so weak. ". . . has me working nonstop on my grandfather's boat."

"But you're leaving tomorrow. When are you ever going to get to sail her?"

Ah, the looming question. If Will didn't take Catherine out now, when would he? What was the point of having the boat, if he was never going to sail her? It wasn't even like they were ever coming back to Hawke's Cove. The house was sold, and soon Pop's boat would be too. There would never be a reason to come back.

"Take me for a moonlight sail?"

"Now?"

"Sure. Why not? Just ten minutes around the cove."

Will shrugged, then smiled. "Great." Why not? After everything Grainger and his mother had put him through this summer, didn't he deserve ten minutes of pleasure? As he moved to the bow to release *Blithe Spirit,* he paused to kiss Catherine, happy to please her.

Maiden Cove, roughly U-shaped, funneled out between two low headlands through a narrow deepwater channel guarded by buoys. Grainger had told him that the outgoing tide was strong there, deceptive. Will wasn't sure which way the tide was running, but it really didn't matter—he had no intention of leaving the cove. Besides, he knew all the danger points of Maiden Cove already. Grainger always insisted that he cruise around the cove before heading out into open waters, and that's what he'd do now. Nothing fancy, just tack a couple times to show off, then back to the mooring and on to dinner.

The western sky was purple dark; the cloud-veiled moon offered a thin light. Along the curve of the cove, pinpricks of house lights began to show. Enough to steer by.

Will handed Catherine a life jacket from under the forepeak and fastened his own. Then he removed the boom crutch, slipped in the centerboard, and hoisted the sail. He was pleased with himself as he made fast the throat and peak halyard lines, then stepped to the stern with the practiced balance of an old salt. Within seconds the breeze caught the sail, making the mainsheet in Will's hand feel like a live thing.

"Why do they call her *Blithe Spirit?*"

"After some poem." Will tucked the tiller beneath his arm and reached over for Catherine's hand. The boat dipped unexpectedly, and spray lashed up to hit them in the face, much to their delight.

Under the cover of gentle darkness, Will thought he might tell Catherine what he'd done: how he'd impulsively visited the MacKenzies, only to find out life wasn't a Disney movie. If he could speak out loud the confusion he was feeling in having so disturbed their comfort, he might begin to squeeze his guilty conscience back into its box. He might be able to convince her, and himself, that he was justified in springing his existence on them. She was so solid, so pragmatic that she might put it into perspective for him, reduce the size of his error and thus the weight of his remorse.

But he said nothing as the wind bullied the sail, making the sheet in his hand feel like a live thing trying to get away from him. Suddenly, the line jerked away from his grip, and the boom swung out until the sail was perpendicular with the boat. He yanked the mainsheet hard and fast, wishing that he wasn't so wet. The line was slippery in his hand, making it more difficult to regain control of the wind-filled sail. A furtive whimsy touched Will. Was this unanticipated rise in the wind Mack's ghost?

He shook off the notion. This was a stupid idea. He needed to take them back in. "I'm going to jibe, so be prepared to shift to the other side. And remember to duck."

Mentally Will ticked off the elements of the procedure, Grainger's voice echoing in his inner ear. He let go of the sheet, careful to maintain a grip on it. The sail sagged, the boom swung, Catherine ducked and came up safely on the other side of the boat. Will moved the tiller to change direction, then hauled on the sheet to draw the wind back into the sail. Instead, the sail continued loose in the breeze, ineffective.

Will yanked harder on the line, then understood

what had happened. The old sail had split in half. The wind passed impotently through the tear. "Shit."

"What happened?"

"The sail's ripped."

"I'm guessing there's no motor."

"You'd be guessing correctly." Will made his way forward to release the lines and lower the sail to just above the tear, leaving a small triangle of fabric just above the boom. Immediately the wind gusted, ripping the worn canvas higher. The chop bounced the boat around. *Blithe Spirit* turned her nose back toward the outlet, and the outgoing tide pushed her closer to the mouth of Maiden Cove.

"We should have kept the dinghy."

Will tried hard not to show his annoyance at her for stating the obvious. "We'll be fine."

"So what are we going to do?" Catherine didn't seem frightened; she trusted him to get them out of this situation. "I don't suppose you have a cell phone."

"No, but I bet Mom will think again about not getting me one after this." Will looked at the shoreline, wondering if they might get pushed into it. At the very least they could swim, if they got close enough; at the very worst, they could end up on the rocks. "If the tide was coming in, we could just let her drift home, guided by the tiller, but I think we're headed out."

"What we really need is a paddle."

"We might as well wish for oars." Will knew he sounded angry at her, but he was very angry with himself. He wished that he could tell Catherine this was an adventure, but the truth was, he was too scared. He'd only had a handful of lessons, and hadn't been given permission to take *Blithe Spirit* out in the first place. He glanced at the lighted dial of his watch. It was only nine. His mother wouldn't start worrying about him until one-thirty. First she'd be mad; then she'd be panicky. Then, who knew? Would anyone think to look for them out here?

The tide was stronger as they neared the mouth of the cove, and the nearer they were to being out of the lee of the cove, the stronger the wind was, and the waves were no longer loose chop, but outbound rollers. Will felt the friction of the wet, rough line burn through the heel of his hand, but he ignored it, intent on getting the small boat turned around with the bit of sail left.

Blithe Spirit fell into a trough, pitching her on her side and dousing the pair in cold water. Catherine cried out, and Will knew that she realized what danger they were in.

"It's going to be all right; just don't panic." Will worked the tiller back and forth, and managed to finish the turn into the waves and away from the outlet. "It'll be all right." Yet against his every effort, Will felt the inexorable pull of the tide taking them nearer the tight channel where they might crash on the rocks, or get pushed, sailless, out into an unseen sea.

All the time he struggled, his prayers childishly alternated between hoping that Catherine would forgive him for his stupidity, and that his mother would never find out what he had done. His third petition, as the moon's weak light began to fade, was that they would simply survive. In broad daylight, this scene wouldn't have been as terrifying. It was the inability to judge the waves, to see where they were going, that was so frightening. They weren't even especially big waves, but frequent, erratic, and bullying.

Blithe Spirit was seaworthy; she'd already proven

that with one or two dips in the troughs. She wasn't going to capsize. They could just sit tight and wait for rescue. Surely it must nearly be dawn. Will managed a look at his watch and was amazed to find that it was less than two hours since he and Catherine had climbed aboard. In that two hours the waves had built and the moon's orb had shrunk, pulling the tide with it.

During his first sailing lesson, Grainger had told Will that things happened rapidly upon the sea and that no sailor left port without a weather report and a tide chart. He'd been so certain that he was capable of giving Catherine a pokey little sail around a safe cove he'd never given those things a moment's thought.

"I'm sorry, Catherine."

"I talked you into it."

"If I hadn't been so pissed off at Grainger." The first heavy drops of rain began to pelt down, splatting against the canvas-covered bow. "He told me not to take her out alone. I thought he was just being pig-headed about me asking him for a DNA test."

"He won't do it?"

"I can't go into it now, but no. Maybe in December, he says."

The moon was gone, obscured by the thickened clouds; the comforting pinpricks of house lights gone too, as the rain began to sheet down in earnest. They huddled in the cockpit, all bearings lost; top and bottom, inland and seaward, lost.

"If we survive this, I swear I'll never . . . ."

"Will—we will survive this. Don't start with the rash promises no one ever keeps."

"You don't know what else I did tonight."

"You went to the MacKenzies' house."

"How did you guess?"

"It's what I would have done."

The boat seemed to be spinning, but without any reference point they couldn't tell if it spun clockwise or counter, or if it was just an illusion of spinning, as the small vessel rocked side to side and up and down in no reliable order. Will felt the nausea rise up and he leaned over the tilting gunwale to vomit.

He wiped his mouth with the back of his hand. "Mrs. MacKenzie seemed really happy to see me."

"That's good then, isn't it?"

"Dr. MacKenzie and the old guy weren't. Dr. MacKenzie warned me about getting her upset."

"That's natural, don't you think?"

"Mack died in this boat. Her son."

"You're not Mack."

"No, but I'm doing exactly what he did." Is this what Mack felt in his last moments? The despair of knowing you've caused your own death? That an impulsive action would end so badly? There was no doubt in Will's mind: Mack had never intended to die.

Catherine pressed herself closer to him as they huddled on the floor of the cockpit against the biting rain and impenetrable darkness. "We're going to survive."

Will longed to believe her.

Thirty-four

❧

Half drowsy with physical and emotional satiety, Grainger was barely aware of the drive home. His headlights shining down the drive reflected against the taillights of a car, and for a confused moment, Grainger thought Kiley had somehow beaten him here. Pilot was barking and he could hear the dog's nails against the heavy wooden door. He let him out and flipped on the yard lights. The rain glittered in the spotlights, sparkling like snow. Beyond them he could see nothing.

"Will?"

Grainger opened the door of the car, half hoping to find the boy inside, but there was nothing except a girl's purse. Dread clamped down as Grainger grabbed his big lantern. He ran to the pier, calling Will's name over and over while Pilot barked merrily, happy to be a part of the game.

Once or twice in his life, Grainger had felt fear—real, bowel-watering fear. The southwest wind blew damp against his skin, chilling him despite its warmth. The halyards clanked against the aluminum masts of the boats tied to his moorings, loud and frequent as the boats rocked energetically. Where *Blithe Spirit* should have been, the dinghy faced him. As boats tethered in bad weather do, its bow pointed into the wind.

The moon was long gone and Grainger could see nothing beyond the limits of his lantern light as he swept it left and right.

"Kiley? Is Will home?"

"What? I don't know. I was asleep." Kiley's voice was on full maternal alert, her antenna up and active on the first ring of the phone.

"Go see." Grainger knew, and knowing, had already called the authorities. If Will was asleep in bed, the car mysteriously left in the boatyard, *Blithe Spirit* simply having slipped her mooring, he'd call them off. But knowing, he also knew that every second counted when someone was lost on the water.

"He's not here." The thin sound of alarm. "How did you know?"

"I'm coming for you."

Grainger sped to Kiley's house, his mouth so dry he knew that he would never be able to offer hope to her that everything would be all right. He drove the five miles to Overlook Bluff Road like a madman, Pilot's chin in his lap. When he got there, he could see her pacing in the front parlor in the light of the seaglass lamps, one hand pressed against her forehead, the other against her stomach. Feverish and sick, that's what she looked like, like someone in anguish—and she still didn't know what he knew.

Grainger ran up the front steps.

Kiley did not run into his embrace. "How did you know he wasn't here?" Grainger reached out to take her in his arms, but she pushed herself away, waiting for him to explain.

"Kiley, I know where they are."

"Where is he? They?"

"Will and Catherine have taken a boat." He couldn't say which boat.

"Jesus."

She knew. Of course she would know.

As they drove back to the boat works, Grainger told her he'd already alerted the authorities—surely they'd arrive to find them brought home, scared and chastened. Even if Will was foolish enough to go out at night, he was a pretty good sailor for a beginner. Grainger didn't speak of the gusting wind and strong moon tide, but Kiley well knew the dangers threatening even experienced sailors. The undeniable knowledge lay silent between them, and he pressed the accelerator harder.

As they pulled into the boatyard, they could hear the *whup whup* of a helicopter and see the beam of its searchlight as it circled the cove. But they couldn't still be in the cove. The very lateness of the hour spoke disaster. Will wasn't ready for this kind of sailing, at night and in a ten-to-fifteen-knot southwesterly wind. They couldn't know how long he'd been out, but surely much too long to still be in the cove. Unless he was on the rocks, or victim of some fluke accident. Overboard. They needed to enlarge the search area. Grainger nearly bent over with the emotional pain.

Kiley walked away from him, moving to the water's edge, then onto the pier. He followed. The sweeping circles of the helicopter's beam held their attention, the sound of the rotors loud in the night air. Pilot barked as two police cars pulled into the yard, followed by the town's Search & Rescue vehicle.

"I'll talk to them," Granger said.

Kiley made no response, but kept her eyes on the circling helicopter.

Grainger knew both of the cops in the first car. They'd been in high school together. They'd played football; he'd played baseball. Adults now, they met most often at Linda's Coffee Shop.

"We'll keep on the radio with the Coast Guard. That the mother?"

"Yes. The boy's mother."

"We'll send someone to talk to the girl's parents." The one behind the wheel shifted, easing his heavy gun belt. He gestured with his chin toward Kiley. "Why don't you try and get her inside? No sense her standing on the end of the pier all night."

He left them sitting in the cruiser, Kiley illuminated in their headlights, her back to him, her hands flat on the white-painted top of a piling. Pilot stood behind her, his nose against the back of her bare knee. Grainger walked to the end of the pier, and was cast into sudden darkness as the cruiser turned around.

Instinctively, he reached to touch Kiley. Her back was hard, resistant to comfort. "Kiley, they'll find them."

"What were you thinking, giving him that boat?" There was a long pause, and she stood very still as if afraid any movement would break her in half. "How could you bring that boat into his life? How could you compromise his life?"

"I wasn't compromising his life; I was trying to give him life skills."

"How could you let him take that boat?" Her voice rose as she turned to face him. The light coming from the boathouse illuminated the anger in her eyes.

"I didn't *let* him. I forbade him. I was with you."

Kiley lowered her voice to a rage-hoarse whisper. "You should have stopped him. You should have gone after him."

"How could I? I didn't know he was—" Then Grainger realized she wasn't talking about Will at all. It was Mack, and his failure to go after him, to stop him from sailing away. Meeting her whisper with his, he answered, "I know. And don't think there hasn't been a day of my life since that I haven't regretted it."

"Get away from me."

"Kiley, no, don't shut me out. We can go try to find them. We can take my Zodiac. Come on."

"What makes you think you can save Will? You couldn't save Mack." Kiley's voice was shrill and anguished. "You didn't even try." She struck both fists hard against his chest. Grainger let her hit him, over and over until she tired, and at last let out the bottled-up grief, laying her wet cheek against his bruised chest. He held her sobbing against him. Despite the sweetness of their reunion, she hadn't truly forgiven him. Now, if anything happened to Will . . . Grainger held her close, scalded by the burn of worry.

Eventually he was able to move her from the pier into the boathouse, and he gently wrapped a blanket around Kiley's shoulders, and left her nestled in his big easy chair. Grainger pulled on his rain gear, picked up his box of emergency equipment—flashlights, flares, and first aid kit—and went back out. He bailed the standing water out of the bottom of his inflatable boat, checked the gas tank, and loaded in his emergency kit.

"Hey!" One of the Search & Rescue volunteers waved a hand. "Where are you going?"

"Out." Grainger clipped on his life jacket. "I'm going to go look for them."

"Don't. We don't need to be looking for anyone else tonight."

It would be torture to be ordered on land by the authorities, to remain a nonparticipant in this thing. By daylight, if they found nothing, then the search would be expanded. People with boats would join in, women would begin to bring food to the firehouse, where the command center would be established. The people of Hawke's Cove knew how to go about these things. It would be enacted exactly as he imagined it had been for Mack. Except then the food was brought to the MacKenzies: the empty boat had been found, and they were funeral meats, not sustenance for the searchers still optimistic in the dawn.

"You won't have to look for me." Grainger turned his back on the man and shoved the Zodiac into the water. The outboard engine drowned out any further objections, and Grainger sped out toward the mouth of the cove, one hand on the tiller, the other sweeping the area in front of him with his wide-beam lantern; arcs of yellow light illuminating a narrow band of sea.

They were wasting time looking in the cove. If Will hadn't deliberately done so in the first place, the wind and tide would have taken them out to sea. It was almost two o'clock. The tide was slack at half after midnight, incoming by one. If they were adrift, the rising tide was going to bring them southwest, but the wind, diminished but active, would drive them northeast. It was random chance, which side of Hawke's Cove's peninsula they would end up on, the north or the south—if they weren't already out beyond sight of land. As Grainger motored through the mouth of the cove, he cut the engine and raised his face to feel the wind. If he chose wrong, his efforts would be useless. The rubber boat drifted to starboard and Grainger made his decision. He gunned the engine and began to explore the south side of the peninsula. Inlet by inlet, cove by cove, he would use up all of his battery power, all of his gas—but he would not go home until he had found them.

Thirty-five

Grainger had left his dog in the house, and it barked and scratched at the door until Kiley roused herself enough to holler at it. "Shut up!" Pilot looked back at her with a cocked head and immediately she felt bad. "Come over here." The gray dog did, sitting on her feet, keeping her in place when she would have been outside in the drizzle, pacing up and down the short pier. What if she lost Will in the same way she'd lost Mack? If anything happened to Will, she'd die. But first she'd kill Grainger. But she knew that neither of those things were true—death would be too easy.

All the time they were reveling in each other's bodies, Will was out in the wind and rain and darkness. It would be too tempting to see the ironic comparisons between the first time she slept with Grainger and this. Kiley shook her head. No. This time they'd find *Blithe Spirit* before it was too late. She wouldn't imagine the worst, not here, not alone except for this dog. Kiley slid her feet out from under the dog's rump, got up, and opened the door for him. "Get out of here."

"Ma'am, do you want me to take you home?" A very

young police officer in a long rain slicker was just outside the door.

"No. I'm fine. I'm waiting here."

"Just let me know. It could be a while." He seemed
awfully young to be so confident, betraying no discomfort at the sight of her tear-streaked face, no fear that
she might launch off into hysterics.

Kiley shut the door. She wasn't going to succumb to
hysterics, or wallow in inertia. She found the harbor
master's channel on Grainger's radio and a navigational
chart, beside it an Eldridge's Tide Chart. She'd follow
the progress of the search with a felt-tip marker.

Grainger had gone out to look for them. Maybe she
should have gone with him. They had come so close to
renewing the purity of their old love. But as the night
wore on, Kiley knew that whatever the outcome, that
renewal was tainted.

As she heard the crackle of static punctuated by a
voice reading off a location, she marked a red dot at the
spot. She needed to be here in case the Coast Guard or
the harbor master, or someone else found them, and
not Grainger. How awful would that be, for Will and
Catherine to be rescued and her not be here? What if
she'd gone with Grainger and then *they* were lost?

Kiley's mind sketched a million variations of lost
and found as she followed the slow progress of the
search.

Bell's Cove, Bird's, Morrel's, all empty. Was that good
news or bad? As long as there was no flotsam, no empty
life jackets or broken spars, there was hope.

Grainger fought the desire to close his eyes for a
minute. The wind had died, and the rain had diminished to a mere drizzle. Dawn was coming, less a

brightening than a lessening of dark. Gray, soupy dawn, a single gull bright white against the murk. French's Cove was next, smaller than the others, but more familiar. The Sunderland house, where he'd once lived, crouched on the headland. Its white-and-black chimney stood sentinel over the cove below, the rising sun striking fire in the eastern windows.

Below the headland, riding her anchor, he saw *Blithe Spirit*.

At the sound of his motor, two heads popped up from the cockpit. Two sets of arms waved madly. Grainger wiped the spray from his face, mingled with tears of relief and joy. He fired his flare gun into the new dawn.

Thirty-six

Kiley shivered, but not with the fresh air touching her moist skin. The weight of worry that had been holding her down, once released, levitated her limbs into a St. Vitus' dance of relief.

When the thin, raspy voice on the radio dispassionately announced the boat had been sighted in French's Cove, all hands aboard, Kiley fled past the young officer and into the dawn. She ran to the end of the pier, where she scanned the distance for the lights of the Coast Guard's search-and-rescue boat. After what felt like hours, the boat finally chugged into the cove. Two figures were clear, standing on the deck beneath the windows of the pilothouse. She waved, and they waved back. Just as the vessel pulled alongside the dock, Kiley spotted Grainger's Zodiac coming into the cove, *Blithe Spirit* towed along behind.

Suddenly a man and a woman were with her on the pier: Catherine's parents. She knew she should introduce herself as the mother of the villain in this piece, but she was so caught between relief and anger herself that she was incapable of civility. The three said nothing until the boat was made fast and the kids jumped onto the pier. After a slight hesitation, a swift kiss good-bye, the pair separated to go to their respective parents.

Will was quick to hug her and offer assurances. "Mom, we're all right. I'm so sorry."

"We'll talk about it at home."

Will knew better than to argue. Kiley kept her hand on his arm as if he would try to escape.

Catherine had run to her parents, taking their relieved hugs, soothing them away from their anger. "We're all right. We just got pushed out of the channel; the sail ripped."

Kiley heard her say, "It wasn't Will's fault," and knew that the relationship between Will and Catherine was about to come under siege.

It felt almost like that night she'd gone to the police station to collect Will. Disappointment that he would take such a chance; anger that he would endanger himself and someone else. The utter foolishness appalled her and reminded her viscerally of the helplessness of a parent—or a friend—to prevent such mistakes. The only thing she wanted now was to get him away, away from Grainger, away from Hawke's Cove. That she had ever believed they would find peace in Hawke's Cove, that it would help repair the damage to her trust in him, was laughable.

Grainger was securing *Blithe Spirit* back on her mooring. Done, he gunned the outboard to run up to the pier. Kiley pushed Will toward the car.

"Get in the car."

"But I want to talk to Grainger, to thank him."

"Get in the car, Will."

As they drove home through the village, up Seaview Avenue and along the bluff, it was already full daylight. The damp night air was warming toward the day's heat. Tonight the breeze would rise again with the moon, but tonight Will would be safely away from Hawke's Cove.

The human heart couldn't take too many blows, and hers had suffered two too many. Will had too closely reenacted the other accident. Kiley could barely remind herself that, as if in some cosmic consolation, this time it had ended happily, everyone chastened but safe. All she knew was that Grainger, by introducing her son to *Blithe Spirit,* had nearly cost her Will.

They went in by the kitchen door, and Kiley looked with weary eyes at the collection of boxes that needed to be packed into the small car.

"Can I thank Grainger later?"

"No."

"He found us, Mom."

"He should never have given you that boat."

"It wasn't his fault; it was mine."

"I know that. It *was* yours."

"So why are you mad at Grainger?"

"Go take a shower and get some sleep. We leave at noon."

"What about all the stuff? We need to get a roof rack."

"I'm going to leave it. All of it."

"No. You can't be serious."

"I am. It's time to go." Kiley kicked a box into a corner, then opened it, pulling out the bunched newspaper and dropping it onto the floor.

"Mom. Stop. What are you doing? Leaving it all behind won't help."

"Help *what*?" Kiley spun to face her son. The grittiness in her eyes had passed, fresh tears cleansing them.

"It won't help to make you forget. You can't take this place and Grainger out of your life, any more than you could forget about me. They're part of who you are. You can deny it, hide from it, pretend otherwise, but I've seen it in you all of my life. From the time I was a little kid, any mention of this place made you smile, whether you wanted to or not. It killed you not to be here.

"Don't do this to yourself. Why can't you just understand that even if you never took back a single object from this house, it, and everything it represents, still lives inside you? As long as you have me, you have a connection here. To Grainger."

"Or Mack."

"And Mack."

"Mack died. You could have died!" she hollered.

"Neither of which is Grainger's fault."

They stood in appalled silence until Will walked out of the room.

Suddenly Kiley felt done in. She had been thinking about how to punish Will; instead, he had stood in front of her, not as a child needing her reprimand, but as an adult in full comprehension of things she'd long kept hidden, reprimanding *her.*

He was all grown up. For the first time Kiley faced having to accept his adulthood. Her little boy was gone and she no longer held sway over him. She pressed her forehead against the cool wood of the doorjamb. Her job was over. What would she do for the rest of her life?

Kiley lay down on the old divan in the parlor. She was helpless suddenly against the need to sleep, as if sleep would protect her against the roiling emotion and confusion. She lay with her arms folded against her stomach, her legs drawn up, wondering if it was possible to die of memory. Everything was all mixed up: images of Mack's angry departure blended with Will's safe return, until, in half sleep, she imagined that Mack had been the one to come off that Coast Guard boat. The thought startled her awake; then she plunged into an exhausted sleep. Dreamless, for a while Kiley found a refuge.

She didn't know how long she'd been asleep. Her mouth felt metallic and her eyes heavy. She half opened them to see Grainger sitting in the armchair opposite, simply looking at her. He looked haggard, unshaven, slightly gray with his own long night of pain. She half expected that he was a ghost, that the real Grainger was gone. Then he spoke and his husky voice was thick with the fear that it wasn't he, but she, who was the ghost.

"Do you remember the letter you brought me? The day we made love, the last day we were together? Do you remember that the postmark on that letter was Boston, and the return address was blacked out? That letter was from my mother, Kiley. I managed to decipher some of the return address when I held it up to a light. I could just make out 'McLean Hospital.' "

"The psychiatric hospital?"

"Yes."

"Was she a patient?"

"That's what I feared, but no. She was working there as an aide."

Kiley was upright, sitting with her hands clasped, attentive, but distant. "How was she, your mother?"

"Surprised to see me. She didn't know me at first, as if she'd put me so far out of her mind I didn't exist. Then she cried and told me that she'd had to leave, she was afraid for her life. One time, Rollie found her packing us up, and he not only knocked her around, but he told her that unless she went alone, he'd hunt her down wherever she went. If she left me behind, she was free. I was the price of her freedom."

"I can't believe she'd do that. I can't believe she'd put herself first."

Kiley was ill with the thought of this woman leaving a small boy in the charge of a drunken, violent man. What kind of mother did that? Grainger's sad young face came to her then, his pale and pensive expression, smiling only when the three of them were alone together.

"She told me she honestly believed he'd treat me all right. She had no idea that he never imagined she'd actually do it. He was calling her bluff."

"Did you tell her how he treated you?"

There was a long silence. Grainger's breath seemed a little labored, his eyes turned from her, the imagery of his childhood nightmare before them. "No."

"Why not?"

"What good would it do to make her suffer any more than she had?"

"You forgave her?"

"Not in so many words, but I suppose so."

"I'm glad for you, Grainger." Kiley heard Will's footsteps above. "Why are you telling me this now?"

"Because I want you to know that I wasn't running away from you, and I didn't think that Mack was in any danger. I wanted you to go to him, because I believed he was the one you really loved. That you two were right for each other and I never would be. If I stayed, it would just spoil any chance you two would have together."

"You never believed me when I said it was you I loved."

"No. You were so anguished over Mack's hurt that I knew you were mistaken."

"Feeling sorry about hurting someone's feelings is a different thing."

"Do you hold me responsible for Will's actions?"

Kiley stood up, amazed at how wobbly she felt. "If anything had happened to Will last night, I would have done more than hold you responsible."

"You wouldn't have had to. I would, and do, hold myself responsible. For all of it." Grainger was on his feet. "If I had known what was going to happen, Kiley, I would have stopped him. I loved him."

"Who, Will or Mack?"

"Both of them."

Will was coming down the back stairs.

"I came to ask you to come with me. I have something I want us to do together."

"What?"

"I'd rather show you. It's something I need you to help me do."

"No. We're on our way in a few minutes."

"Please, Kiley. Come with me."

Kiley felt strength return. "No, Grainger. And I would prefer it if you left now, without seeing Will."

"I won't do that." His voice was low and even, uncompromising. "I won't let you keep him from me. He could be mine. And even if he isn't—"

"Get out of here." Her emotional bank account was overdrawn, the horror of thinking she might have lost

Will was the last check. She couldn't take any more drama or demands on her heart. "I won't have it."

"Won't have what?" Will was in the room with them, holding up his hands in a referee's gesture.

"Will, go put the suitcases in the car. Grainger was just leaving."

"I want your mother to come with me for a few minutes."

"Go with him. I'll finish packing," Will said.

"No. Get out of here, Grainger. Don't you get it yet? I want nothing to do with you."

"That wasn't how it was last night."

Kiley stepped across the room, her outstretched hand ready to slap Grainger, but he caught it in mid-strike. "I've had enough of your hitting me. It isn't physical pain you commit, it's emotional—and I'm a past master at receiving emotional pain. You're only hurting yourself. Maybe you still blame me for Mack's death, but I think you blame yourself too."

"Stop it!" Will shouted. "Grow up, the pair of you, and deal with it! Neither of you killed Mack. You aren't responsible for his death. *He* is. Mack chose to act stupidly, to make a dramatic point. Neither of you could have stopped him, any more than taking me away from D.C. and Mike would have stopped my smoking dope if that's what I wanted to do. Any more than taking me away from Catherine will stop us from being together. It was my decision to go out last night. Mom, if you chose Mack and then changed your mind well, you were kids, for god's sake. That's what kids do. Lori changed hers. I changed mine." Will's ocean blue eyes were wide with emotion as he looked from one to the other. "It doesn't mean anyone is responsible.

You've built a whole life regretting someone else's mistake. Isn't it time to move on?"

Kiley's wrist was still gripped in Grainger's hand as they stared at Will. Tall and blond and fiery in the sun streaming in through the big windows, his face a little shadowed, for an uncanny instant, he looked like Mack.

Grainger let his grip relax and slid his hand to take hers in a gentle touch. And as she took his fingers in hers, Kiley felt the slow dissolving away of years of pain.

The sultry morning had given way to a threatening afternoon. The eastern sky was nearly purple as they climbed into Grainger's Zodiac. Kiley fastened her life jacket with a trembling hand. Without discussing what they were doing, they began to act in tandem, little conversation needed, allowing the solemn activity to progress in respectful silence. There was nothing else to say.

Behind them, *Blithe Spirit* willingly came along. Her fresh white paint was bright in the eerie sky, her varnish like sweet maple syrup. At the top of her mast, her blue pennant fluttered. Kiley and Grainger reached the middle of Maiden Cove, just above the point he knew to be the deepest.

They climbed from the boat into *Blithe Spirit,* carrying two cans of gasoline. Grainger tossed her anchor over, careful that its line slid between the bitt and into the chock, then executed a figure-eight maneuver around a cleat to hold the anchor line tense enough, short enough, that there would be very little swing.

With a graceful sweeping motion, Kiley and Grainger

drained the two gasoline cans all over the deck, cockpit, and sole of the little vessel. The slow action reminded Grainger a little of the ritual blessing of the fleet, holy water cast at the bows of the fishing boats.

He handed Kiley back into the Zodiac and followed. Then he motored away just far enough that he thought his old pitching arm would still reach. Grainger lit a flare and stood up, and Kiley put one hand on his belt to balance him. He pitched and the flare landed in *Blithe Spirit*'s cockpit. In an instant the boat was on fire, flames spreading like liquid up the sides and to the mast, where the varnish bubbled and the fire crawled upward as a sailor climbs.

He remembered climbing the mainmast of the schooner he'd been first mate on, remembered the feel of the swaying beneath his feet in the footropes, his safety dependent on his sense of balance. Now Kiley held him, and he was balanced. He sat down beside her and they wept, clutched together, feeling the heat from the fire on their wet faces, and knowing that they both were free.

The smoke began to rise in the still, purple-colored air. In a few minutes it would begin to rain; lightning was already streaking the eastern sky. Thunder, its voice unrestricted by the open ocean beyond Maiden Cove, rumbled on and on, like a baritone singing plainsong.

Their pyre rose higher and higher, and in the smoke and flames they imagined that they saw Mack's spirit rise. He, too, at last was free.

Epilogue

It was just past four o'clock, and the living room was winter dark as Will came through the front door. Before he even shrugged off his coat, Will plugged in the Christmas tree lights, then stood back to admire the big spruce cluttered with packages under its widely spread lower branches. On Christmas Eve there would be even more, when Nana and Pop got there and added their gifts to the pile. And, in a silly adherence to implausible belief, on Christmas morning there would be three or four for him signed by Santa.

In his left hand, Will carried the mail. Mixed in with the bills addressed to his mother and the Christmas cards addressed to them both was an envelope with just his name on it—one he'd been waiting for ever since finishing his last class of the semester. One that, in some sense, he'd been waiting for forever.

Mom would be home from her new job at the hospital in a few minutes, so if he wanted to read it in privacy, he should open it now. Yet with deliberate slowness, Will sorted the day's mail into three piles. Holiday cards, bills, junk. He kept the envelope marked "GenSearch" in his hand.

Twice his mom and Grainger had come up to Ithaca to see him at school. The first time, on Parent's Weekend in October, they had told him they were moving the wedding date up. It seemed that they'd gotten a head start on a sibling for him.

"Too much information," he'd protested, but the truth was that he was very excited about having a little sister or brother, even if he was nearly grown and would pretty much be outside of the family unit. He pictured himself coming to visit, the look of adoring delight on a toddler's face as he brought a present guaranteed to please, making sand castles on the beach.

Will took the envelope into the living room, setting it unopened on the couch as he laid a fire in the fireplace. Next year, the Santa gifts would be innumerable. Never very far below the surface was the question: Would the child be fully his brother or sister, or genetically half? Despite the unwelcome persistence of the thought, Will knew that he'd never consider the baby anything less than his full sibling.

He sat in front of the fire, teasing the flame into catching, then building, throwing its warmth on his cold face. The old Sunderland house was still a work in progress, but Grainger and his mother had made great inroads on rehabbing the place. This fireplace was one of the first completed projects, and the best feature of the eighteenth-century house.

Will played with the edge of the envelope, running it between his thumb and forefinger, turning it over and staring at the address. In his grasp lay the answer to his lifelong question. He half hoped the envelope would open itself, a magical act that would absolve him of having asked the question. Grainger had lived up to his promise and allowed a swab of cheek cells to be sent to GenSearch. That was the second time he and Kiley had come together to visit, just before finals. Grainger had taken them out to dinner afterward, Catherine with them. While they told stories of life on campus to entertain the adults, Will could see Grainger looking at him, amusement or fondness in his eyes. It didn't matter to Grainger if their blood was the same or not. He loved him as a son; whether his own or Mack's, it didn't matter. It was Will's question, his search. And he knew that once his paternity was known, there would be no unknowing it.

Will heard the back door open and his mother call to see if he was home. He still held the envelope in his hand—the one that would forever define his life and his relationship to his sibling, and to his father, whoever he turned out to be.

"I'm in here, Mom."

Will stood up, and dropped the envelope into the flames.

A dark wisp of smoke rose up as the thin paper caught, rising skyward toward the night.